WHAT LIES BETWEEN THE LAKES

A Burgers Brothers Story

By

CLAYTON TUNE

WHAT LIES BETWEEN THE LAKES

This is a work of fiction. Murray, KY, and all surrounding towns and parks mentioned are real places. Those familiar with Murray and Land Between the Lakes may recognize historical landmarks, certain structures, events, or geographical layouts mentioned. However, the characters and incidents involving them are a product of the author's imagination and are used fictitiously. Any resemblance to actual persons, living or dead, is entirely coincidental.

Copyright © 2021 by Clayton Tune

All rights reserved. This book or any portion thereof may not be reproduced or used in any manner whatsoever without the express written permission of the publisher except for the use of brief quotations in a book review.

Printed in the United States of America
First Printing, 2021

Cover design by Lynn Andreozzi
Interior illustrations by Stephanie Woods
Interior Design by JW Manus

ISBN 978-1-7340987-3-0

www.claytontune.com

For Matt.
Where it all started; late nights discussing the craziness of the Funeral Brothers over coffee.

So much coffee.

AUTHOR'S NOTE

In 1960, when Alfred Hitchcock released *Psycho*, the story goes that he implemented a policy with theatre owners that anyone who arrived late would not be seated. Signs of Hitchcock himself, pointing at his watch, were placed outside the theatre, warning patrons that if they didn't see it from the beginning, they wouldn't see it at all.

What Lies Between the Lakes is the second half to the Burgers Brothers story, picking up right where the first half left off. I don't have the money or influence of Hitchcock to hang posters of myself outside bookstores, but I had an extra page so in lieu of fancy marketing, here is my request: if you've not read *The Burgers Brothers' Family Funeral Home*, please **STOP** here and do so. The objective of this is to help you enjoy the story more, and of course not be completely lost.

If you *have* read the first part of the story, thank you ...

And welcome back.

PART I

THE CURIOUS GRAVE OF COREY GRASSMAN

Tell me Miss; what is it you think you know?
Now leave it alone.
—Richard Morgan, *The Ring*

MURRAY, KENTUCKY
SUMMER 2017

SATURDAY
1

Frank Burgers stared at the dead woman's sweater.

It was still sitting in the narrow Amazon box it arrived in, now open on his desk. The package had been mysteriously left near the front door earlier that afternoon. A bubble of sickness blossomed in Frank's stomach the moment he pulled back the top flaps. Inside, neatly folded, was a tattered pink cardigan covered in dirt. The same pink cardigan that Sarah Piddleton was wearing when he accidentally dug her up the week before. The same one he'd thrown back into her grave when it fell off her corpse.

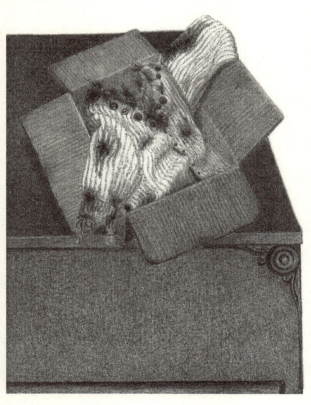

Cleverly displayed on top, tacked onto the sweater, were two pictures, and a handwritten message on a strip of paper: *There is a working pay-phone at the RacerFan gas station across from the arena. I will call it at 11pm tonight. Answer it.* Frank could suddenly hear his own heartbeat. He took a seat in his office chair and began nervously swiveling to the left and to the right, watching the box as if it were going to leap off his desk and dart into the hallway. He muttered to himself to think—even though he wasn't sure what he should be thinking about—and asking himself what he should do. He abruptly reached for his phone to text Cliff Samson, who was also in one of the two pictures.

Frank hit send and sank back into his chair, groaning and repeating to himself to "stay calm" and "think." His daze was so deep that he didn't hear his older brother Donnie knock on the door and announce he was leaving for Nashville.

"Hey," Donnie repeated.

"What?" Frank asked, sitting up, startled. "What's up?" He leaned toward the desk and closed the box.

"You alright?"

"Yeah," Frank lied. "You need something?"

"I just said I was leaving; gonna go meet Lexie for dinner. Sure you don't wanna go?"

"Yeah, I'm good. You have fun. Three's a crowd."

"Why are you out of breath?" Donnie asked. "And sweating?"

Frank hesitated. "I just did some pushups," he replied, noticing the dampness underneath his arms.

"Good times," Donnie said. "See ya tonight." He turned to leave and then cut back around. "That's her sweater, right?"

Frank's eyes widened. He sat with his mouth open, trying to come up with an excuse—anything—to assure Donnie that it wasn't what he thought. All he could muster was, "What?"

"I said what's the weather like? Any idea? Is it supposed to rain today?"

"Oh." Frank resumed breathing. "Yeah." He paused. "No. Sorry. No rain. Just hot. And humid."

Donnie grinned. "You sure you're good?"

"Yeah," Frank replied. "I think I'm still a little fried from everything that happened with the Kochs and with Officer Stutters this morning."

Donnie agreed and closed the door to leave. Frank immediately buried the box underneath a stack of papers. But not before removing one of the pictures and sliding it into his desk.

2

Frank reread the message and checked his watch for the dozenth time in ten minutes. This was agony. He needed something to keep the dread in his mind at bay until eleven p.m. and the minutes were passing like hours. *Working* through the anxiety was out; there were no scheduled appointments. So, with no clients to prepare or funerals to plan he figured leaving the house might be the best distraction.

He walked the streets of the downtown square and strolled through the long aisles at the town's indoor flea market, forcing himself to glance at every item in each seller's booth. He then grabbed a bite to eat and drove to the city park where he strolled through the wooded trails of the eighteen-hole frisbee golf course. The falling sun and sudden appearance of mosquitoes forced Frank back to his home where he paced around the main floor like a zombie while his parents watched *Blue Bloods* in the family room.

At just after ten, he heard the front door of the house open and close, then a tap on his office door. "Donnie?" Frank said.

Cliff Samson poked his head in, "Yo yo!" Cliff was a former intern at the home who now owned and operated the boutique gym next door, out of what was once the Burgers' detached garage.

"Hey," Frank said. He closed his laptop, silencing an episode of *Parks and Rec*. "You get my text?"

"Yeah, sorry man. I've had clients all day." He walked over to Frank's mini-refrigerator and pulled out a water. "Then I had to update member files, and log in some notes. Everything alright?" He took a seat on the couch across from Frank's desk.

Frank got up and closed the door. "We got a problem," he said quietly, nodding over to his desk.

Cliff got up and walked over to the desk. Resting on top was a crumpled funeral coupon someone had used the week before. A picture of a skeleton playing chess with the caption *You've Found a Killer Deal.*

Cliff chuckled to himself, shaking his head. "Might wanna move this so Donnie doesn't see it," he said, opening the flaps on the box. "Is that a sweater?"

Frank didn't answer—just stood with his back to the door, watching.

Chips of dirt sprinkled onto the hardwood floor when Cliff lifted the cardigan from the box. "What the . . . ?" He glanced at the floor and then up at Frank. "Sorry, was I supposed to leave it in the box?"

"You recognize that?" Frank asked.

"No. Why is there dirt all over it?"

Frank gave him a few more moments to see if recognition would come. Cliff appeared to be fixated on the sweater's eclectic makeup of pins: cartoon characters and educational pins like Hooked on Phonics and DARE lined the bottom while others—*I Saw E.T.*, *The Empire Strikes Back*, and *Top Gun*—were displayed just below the neckline.

"Did you look at all these?" Cliff asked.

"Not really."

"Wait," Cliff lowered the sweater. "I'm not holding a dead person's sweater, am I? Did you dig this up?"

Frank moved closer to the box. "Actually, *we* dug it up."

"What?"

"You don't recognize that picture?" Frank pointed inside.

Cliff lifted the black-and-white photo out of the box. "No."

"That's Sarah Piddleton," Frank replied, walking to the other side of his desk. "And that's the sweater she was buried in."

"Agh!" Cliff exclaimed, dropping it to the floor. Pieces of dirt scattered in the burst of wind. "The lady we dug up and put back last week? *That* Sarah Piddleton? Why'd you keep her sweater?"

"I didn't. That box was outside the front door this morning after Suthers left."

"From who?" Cliff asked. Frank shrugged, throwing up his hands. "Hold up," Cliff continued, studying the photo. "How did they know to send it to *you*? Did you tell someone about this?"

"Hell no!" Frank fired back. He opened his desk drawer and pulled out another photo. "Someone saw us." He laid it on the box.

Cliff surveyed the picture. It had been taken with a night-vision filter. The two of them were standing beside a grave that clearly said Sarah Piddleton. Frank was holding a shovel and looking away from the hole, while Cliff was crouched next to a large bag, his back to the camera. He cursed, then stood quiet several seconds before cursing again. "What do they want?"

"Apparently for now they just wanna talk." Frank pulled out the slip of paper and handed it to Cliff, taking a seat in his recliner.

Cliff read the note to himself and then looked at Frank. "Shit. Eleven tonight?"

"Yup."

"What are you gonna do?" Cliff asked.

"I don't have a choice. Whoever it is knows we were the ones who dug up that grave."

"Your brother know about this?"

"Nooo," Frank replied. "No, no, no. Definitely not. We agreed this morning that I'd stop messing with all this. Told me he'd stick around and help out with the home as long as I stopped hiding stuff from him."

"So, naturally you hide this from him."

Frank thought about that, clamping his bottom lip under his teeth. "Touché." He rubbed his temples with the palms of his hands. "What do I supposed to do? I need to at least figure out what the guy wants."

"Where's Donnie at?"

"Nashville. He went to see that Lexie Porter girl he ran into last week." Frank checked the time: it was nearly eleven.

"You want me to go with you?" Cliff asked.

"Nah, I'll be alright." Frank got to his feet and gave a long exhale.

"Hey," Cliff said, "there was nothing in that box about *me* was there? I mean, *I* know that's me in the picture but only because I was there. It's just my back in the shot."

"How many other large Filipinos do you know in town?"

"You can't tell I'm Filipino here," Cliff replied.

"True," Frank said, "but you're wearing a shirt with your name on it. Not a lot of muscular guys with the name Samson."

Cliff leaned in closer. On the back of the shirt was the large S logo that appeared on all his promotional material, including the large banner on his gym. Underneath in script were the words *Samson Elite*. Cliff cursed, shaking his head.

3

Monty Suthers had been sitting in a booth at Sally's Diner for over an hour before Sophia Stills arrived for work. He hadn't seen her since the night she rushed out of the restaurant in a panic, alleging something about her husband running over the dog. Monty's gut told him their dog was fine. Her eyes connected with his immediately, almost as if she were looking for him. She smiled and waved. Monty did the same, trying not to show his disappointment with her over what Donnie Burgers had revealed to him earlier that day.

Monty had been visiting Sally's for years and had grown close to Sophia—maybe too close in his own mind. In his defense, he was mindful of his behavior around her and even more careful not to disclose or even hint at his feelings toward her to anyone. She was quite a bit younger, and more important, married. Donnie had humiliated him that morning at the Burgers' home. He called Monty's behavior around her inappropriate and unprofessional. To make matters worse, he said that *Sophia* was the one who brought it up; that she laughed at him. *Was he making it up? Does she really laugh about me?*

Monty occupied the same booth most every night, next to the service station. The other server sparked a conversation with Sophia when she walked by. She turned to Monty and whispered "hey," still giving an attentive ear to the guy wiping down the bar. Monty lifted his Kindle to commence reading, but only continued to stare at the same paragraph he'd already read five times. He could see her out of the corner of his eye tying her apron around her waist. She punched in a series of clicks on the computer screen and mumbled something. Monty's mind was swimming in how or if to engage her over what Donnie had said. He kept hearing her voice, thinking she was still talking to the server.

A straw wrapper blew across his vision, startling him. He sat back and looked at Sophia, who was holding a straw between her teeth. "You must really like that picture." She smiled and pointed at the Kindle which now displayed a black-and-white portrait of Mark Twain. The device had timed out.

"Wow," Monty said. "Sorry." He pushed out a short, friendly laugh. "I thought you were talking to someone else."

"I just asked if you ate yet."

"Yeah. I had a chicken salad a while ago," Monty replied.

"That's boring."

"It was. How are you?" Monty asked. Then, "H-how's your d-dog?"

The brief glimpse of confusion as her eyes shifted from Monty over to the half-full coffee mug on the table and back to him was all he needed to confirm his suspicion. "Oh. He's fine. False alarm," she said. "Nick *thought* he had hit him with the car. It was a tree limb."

"Good to hear," Monty said.

"And thank you for . . . you know . . . offering to help. I'm sure I looked a wreck—sorry if I was rude or anything to you. I didn't mean to be."

"Oh no," he replied. "It's no p-p-problem at all. I'm j-just happy everything's okay."

She poured a refill of his decaf and began making the rounds to the tables while the other server clocked out beside him. Monty tried to read again and made it almost two sentences in before his mind started to wander.

"You have any leads?" Sophia asked, coming back over to put in an order and prepare drinks. She looked around and lowered her voice, "On the grave robbing stuff?"

"I do. I did—I don't know." Monty sighed. "Ran into a bit of a problem today."

"Oh no. What happened?"

Monty started to say that he couldn't tell her yet, but she cut him off and told him to "hold that thought." She finished filling glasses of ice with Pepsi and dropped them off to a couple of college students. When she returned, she slid in across from Monty and leaned forward. "Okay, all ears. What'd you find out?" She looked so giddy, a far cry from the frightened girl he encountered the other night.

"I c-can't r-really say."

"Come on! Who'm I gonna tell?" She asked. "Please?"

"It's not that—I just have to do some m-more work b-before I can be sure."

"Maybe I can help. Who do you suspect? I know most everyone in this town—I'll tell you if they're a likely grave robber or not."

Monty gave an amused smile, dropping his eyes to the table. *Just ask her.*

"You okay?"

"I want to ask you something."

"Okay, shoot," she said.

"Something serious, and I n-need you to b-be honest with me, okay?" Monty heard the uneasiness of his tone slip out, and saw it wipe away a little of the playfulness on Sophia's face.

"Okay..."

"How well do you know Donnie Burgers?" he asked.

She didn't flinch. "Donnie? Pretty well. Why?"

"G-g-good friends?"

"I guess so. We were close a while back before he moved. We still chat through text sometimes, or we'll catch up when he's home. Why? Is he your guy?" She was all smiles again at the thought of insider information.

"D-do you tell your husband that I come here a lot? Or that y-you and I talk?"

Her face sunk. "I don't know what you mean."

"I m-m-mean just what I asked." He caught the authority in his voice and dialed it back. "D-do you tell N-Nick that I come in here all the time? That I t-talk with you?"

"I... I'm sure I've mentioned to Nick that you come here. I don't think I talk about you as if we were best friends, but I probably mention that I enjoy having you here. You're fun to talk with. He knows that." In a blink, her face flashed something reminiscent of discovery—surprise. "Did Nick say something to you?"

"No. B-but D-Donnie did."

After a pause, "Monty, what are you talking about?"

"I w-went to see him t-today, over at his family's f-f-funeral home. He s-sa-said th-that I w-w-wa-wa—" and then he stopped. "Dammit," he whispered, wiping the sweat from his forehead with the side of his hand. He drew in a long breath and looked away from her, toward the other side of the diner.

"Hey," she said softly, and reached forward to take his hand. "It's okay. What happened?"

Monty's hand flinched when she touched it. He stared at her hand—at her ring—and pulled it away. "I'm s-s-sorry. I ca-can't do that."

"Do what? What is going on?" She asked.

He glanced around the restaurant, then finally began to explain what happened earlier. He didn't want to, but he *needed* to. He needed to because it was affecting him, and it shouldn't be. If things were really okay, he would have no problem telling her about the things that Donnie said to him. They could laugh about it and continue with their night. If there was no issue, he wouldn't have brooded over it all afternoon and into the evening. If there was no issue, he wouldn't have felt his stomach drop when she touched his hand. But there was an issue. And he needed to set his mind straight.

"He t-t-t-told me that I n-n-ne-needed to s-stop t-talking to y-y-you. He s-sa-s-said th-th-that—"

"Hey," Sophia cut in. She leaned forward, resting her arms on the table and lowered her voice. "Hey. Look at me. It's okay. We talk all the time without that stutter. Just breathe."

He took another moment and looked out the adjacent window into the parking lot. The diner's well-lit interior clashed with the darkness outside, revealing a clear reflection of Monty in the window, sitting across from Sophia. Cutting into her image were the radiant lights of the RacerFan gas station in the distance where he noticed a car pulling in. "D-Donnie said that y-you told him I was h-hi-hitt-hitting on you." He turned to meet her eyes. "He made it s-se-seem like you w-were m-m-making f-f-fun of me."

Monty had not expected the face he saw on Sophia. He'd anticipated one of confusion, or surprise, or maybe even nothing. But the face he saw instead was one of great pain—as if he'd slapped her. He may as well have told her that *he'd* run over her dog on the way over. It was heartbreaking to look at, and he now felt regret for even bringing it up.

"I told Donnie that you . . ." she stopped and turned toward the service counter, but not before Monty could see water welling up in her eyes. "I told Donnie you're probably the only good thing about working in this place. My words were that talking with you is the highlight of my shift most nights." She met his eyes. "I could never make fun of you," she whispered. "Look at me. I would *never* do that. I don't know what Donnie's trying to get at—or if maybe he talked to Nick, and Nick thinks there's something going on that he hasn't accused me of ye—" she caught herself and stopped. After a breath. "I promise you, Donnie didn't get that from me."

Monty didn't take his eyes off of her, neither did she avert her own from his. He wanted to trust what she was saying.

"Do you believe me? I would never . . ."

Monty didn't know what to believe but given a choice between her word and Donnie's . . . "I'm sorry," he said. "I b-be-believe you. It just . . . it got to me p-pre-pretty bad."

"Why?" Sophia asked.

Monty had a couple of options here: in the movies, this is the scene where *his* character reveals how he truly feels about the other, age and marriage be damned. But he also knew that the responsible thing would be to *not* say anything about his feelings and simply say how it felt to be the punchline of a joke.

"It's a little embarrassing to say. I d-don-t have a lot of f-fr-friends here." He swirled the coffee around in his mug. "As you can probably imagine."

"Because you're a cop?"

"Well, that and . . ." Monty paused for a moment, staring at the coffee. "I don't know. I m-moved to M-Murray late in my life, didn't know hardly anyone. I p-probably get a little too held up on my s-st-s-st-st—" He pointed to his mouth. "This."

"Oh."

"I try to avoid t-talking to people." He wasn't sure how to say this next part responsibly. "But d-d-despite my interest to just be l-left alone, there's something about you that I . . . find calming." He paused. "I'm sorry. That's . . . you're a very nice girl. That's w-w-what I'm t-trying to say. And, I was hurt when D-D-Donnie said all of that b-b-because . . . well . . . despite my attempts to avoid conversation with p-people, you're someone I l-look f-forward to b-b-being arou—I mean, t-to t-talking to." He took another breath. "What am I doing? I'm so sorry. This was . . ." Monty grabbed for his wallet, now fully embarrassed. "I d-did n-not m-m-mean to say all of . . ." His voice trailed off, but he caught a glimmer of a smile on Sophia's face just before she looked down at her lap. She then turned her head toward the other side of the restaurant, scanning the tables, trying to bite the smile between her teeth. She was blushing.

"I don't know what to say," she said.

"Sophia, I'm not good w-w-with t-t-talking sometimes, and I say the w-wrong thing—"

She cut him off by reaching across the table to grab his hand. Monty flinched and it was Sophia this time who drew back. "Sorry," she whispered.

Monty didn't make a sound.

She leaned her head forward as if about to deliver a secret. While she spoke, Monty noticed that she would not look at him. Her attention was toward the unused napkin under the fork and knife. "I know it's totally inappropriate to say this, but I um," she stopped. "Never mind. *Never mind.*" She sat back. "I don't need to say it. I'm sorry."

"What is it?" Monty asked.

"It's nothing. Really. I don't want to be inappropriate. Or awkward. So, I guess I'll just say that I like your company too. That's okay to say, right?"

"Sure," Monty said, nodding. "I think I better go." He reached for his wallet again, but Sophia put her hand out.

"Don't worry about it. It's on me tonight."

Monty dug out two bills and laid them on the counter. "Well, maybe you can give this tip to the other waiter then. If he didn't already leave."

"I'll give it to him," she said. "Or probably just keep it for myself." She winked.

"It's your conscience," Monty said back. He gave her a half smile and got to his feet.

"Hey," she said, sliding out of the booth. She turned her back to the other tables and softened her voice. "I know you say you don't have a lot of friends, and I don't know why anyone would ever move to Murray who isn't from here," Monty started to say something, but she continued, "but I'm kinda glad you did. And I'm a little glad you don't have a lot of friends." She began looking at the ground. "Because if you did, well, you wouldn't be here. With me. And . . . I like when you're here." She stopped and looked up at him. "You're not the only one going through a rough time." The blush in her cheeks was running down her neck now. "Gosh, it's hot in here." She laughed. "I'm sorry. I shouldn't have said that." There was an awkward moment where Monty wasn't sure what he was supposed to do. For a split-second he thought she was going to go in for a hug but instead she held out her hand and said, "Good talk." He shook her hand and agreed.

"I'll see ya soon," he said. Before he got to the door, he heard her say his name, and turned to see her approaching.

"Why were you going to see Donnie? Can I ask?"

"Just had some questions, that's all."

Sophia smirked. "He's a suspect, isn't he?"

"I didn't say that," Monty replied firmly. Then, "Are *you* saying that?"

"No. But it's funny you mention him. He and I spoke yesterday or the day before—just briefly. He was stressed about stuff at home. I asked what was wrong and he wouldn't say. But when I asked how long he was gonna stay in town, he said he wasn't sure, and that it depended on whether or not his brother could get himself and the funeral home out of a mess."

"What does that mean?" Monty asked.

"Don't know. He changed the topic and I haven't thought about it until just now. I don't know his brother, but I know Donnie. There's no way *he's* robbing graves."

Monty could feel the corners of his mouth upturn slightly. "I bet you're right," he said.

4

It had to be the only working pay phone in town. The RacerFan gas station was located across the street from Murray State University's basketball arena, which sat at the intersection of Kentucky 121 and Highway 641. There were several businesses nearby: Walmart, a salon, Lowe's, and the only twenty-four-hour diner in town, Sally's.

Despite the substantial illumination from the facility, it took Frank a little while to find the phone. It was located away from the storefront's well-lit windows, against the building's side. Frank glanced around to make sure no one was watching before getting out of the truck—not that it mattered. *What's suspicious about using a pay phone in the middle of the night?*

The message from the morning's letter replayed in his mind while he stood by the box: *There is a pay phone... I'll call... answer it.* "There's no way that thing still works," he muttered. He picked up the receiver—dial tone. "Never mind." He placed his finger back over the cradle. A metallic *clang* rang out around the corner, signaling that someone had arrived at the pump. Frank leaned out and watched a young man in shorts and a tanktop walk toward the entrance. The guy flicked a cigarette away from him and suddenly the phone rang loud, long, and shrill, causing Frank to jump. The man paid no attention and continued walking.

Frank picked up the receiver. "Hello?" No one on the other end, just silence. Frank spoke into the receiver a couple more times but heard nothing. After another moment of silence, he hung up. Frank went still, watching the phone as if it was suddenly going to start speaking to him. It rang again and he snatched it off the cradle.

"Hello?" Frank asked again. "Who is this?"

The voice on the other end was low, but clear, no doubt using a distortion device. "Is this Mr. Frank Burgers?"

"Yes sir... or ma'am." Frank replied. "Is this the person who sent me a note?"

"I am," the voice replied. "You did some work for a friend of mine. Tom Middleton." A pause. Perhaps waiting for Frank to admit it. Then, "Did you finish the job?"

"I don't know what you're talking about," Frank replied.

The line was quiet and then it clicked dead.

"Hello?" Frank asked. The dial tone sounded. "The hell?" As soon as he replaced it, the phone rang out again. Frank picked it up.

"Mr. Burgers, lying is a waste of our time. Please be honest with your answers. I'd like to keep this short to avoid attention from the officer down the street."

A wave of dread turned in his stomach. "What?" He looked out toward the arena but there was nothing to see. *What officer?* "What are you talking about?"

"I anticipate my package conveyed the seriousness of this situation."

"Definitely," Frank said. "How did you get those pictures?"

"I have a job I'd like to you to do. Are you interested?"

"What kind of job?"

"You did some specific work for Tom recently, correct?"

Frank sighed. "Fine, yes, I did. And it's done."

"What did you do?"

"Who is this?" Frank asked.

"Did you dig up Tom's wife?" the voice asked.

Frank paused. "Yes."

"Were you paid?" The voice asked.

"That's none of your business."

"How much?"

"I'm not telling you that."

There was silence on the other end.

"You can give me the silent treatment all you want but I'm not te—" The line went dead again. "Are you serious?" Frank whispered. He slammed the phone back onto the cradle. It rang out again.

"Mr. Burgers, I don't *need* what it is I'm asking you to do. But I want it enough to offer you money, and from what I understand—given some recent events—you're in need of that money." Another pause. Frank took a breath. "How much did he pay you?"

"Over five grand."

"I'd like to offer you more."

"What type of work are we talking about?"

"Same as Tom's. My understanding is that you find particular items that are, let's say, hidden—gone, if you will?"

"You'd like me to get something for you," Frank said. "What is it?"

"Yes. Something *unique*."

"Jewelry?" Frank asked.

"No. A book."

Frank's eyes narrowed. "A *book*? Like, a regular book?"

"Sure."

"Where is it?"

"Will you do the job?"

Frank paused. "Does anyone else know about this? About you and me talking?"

"No one else."

"Will anyone be upset if I found this book?" Frank asked.

"You're digging up a grave. Of course, someone will be upset."

Good point. "I just wanted to make sure I won't have anyone *especially* dangerous on my ass should I find it."

"If you do it right, you'll have no more danger than you do right now."

"How much are you offering?" Frank asked.

"Twenty thousand."

Frank paused. "*Twenty* thousand? Like, with a T?"

"*Twenty with a TW*," the voice rasped back.

"You're gonna pay me twenty thous—" he stopped himself and looked around, mindful of his increasing volume. "You're gonna give me that much for a book?"

"Do we have a deal?"

Frank deliberated: on the one hand he promised Donnie he was done. Taking the job would put him at risk of Donnie leaving again. On the other he could make the price of four funerals in two days. *I'll figure it out.* "Sure. Let's do it. What do I do?"

"Look at the letter I sent. The last word is the title of a book. Go into the library tomorrow before ten a.m. and look on the shelf with this book. You'll find the details you need. Do not try to contact me. I will contact you." The voice paused.

"So, wait. This letter is *in* the book *at* the library?" Frank asked.

"Correct. If you do not have the letter by ten a.m., I will assume you are no longer interested and terminate the deal," the voice replied.

"I got it. But what do I do when I have it?"

"I'll find you."

"That's unsettling," Frank said back.

"Mr. Burgers. If you try to contact Tom Middleton, those pictures will be sent to the Murray Police, and the *Murray Ledger*. Do you understand?"

Damn. "Yeah. I got it."

SUNDAY

5

The stranger's directions and the note led Frank to several copies of Stephen King's *IT*. Two copies were showcased on the front "Popular Reads" table. He lifted each copy and scanned through them as innocently as possible—nothing. Then he walked back to the fiction section where he found more copies on the top shelf.

He first made sure no one was around and then began pulling every copy of *IT* and flipping through the pages. Nothing out of the ordinary. With a handful of copies stacked at his feet, he ran his hand along the inner top and sides of the shelf. Finally, he grabbed a footstool and felt along the top of the shelf where a manila envelope was taped down. "Bingo," he whispered. For good measure, he checked out a copy of the book.

Donnie was sitting at the kitchen table eating breakfast and reading the *Murray Ledger* when Frank walked in through the back door.

"Where've you been?" Donnie asked.

"Went to the library," Frank replied, walking past him toward his office, waving the book. "What time did you come in last night?" Frank threw the envelope on his desk and closed the office door.

"Little before two," Donnie called out. "I forgot how miserable that drive from Nashville is, especially going through LBL—hardly any streetlights the whole way through. Did you say the library?"

"Yeah. The movie comes out in a couple of months, I wanted to read the book. How was Lexie?" Frank asked, attempting once again to change the subject.

"She's good. She had something come up last minute, so I ended up meeting another friend for dinner, and then dropped by her store afterward for a drink."

"You guys drank in her bookstore?" Frank asked.

"Yeah, it's got a full bar. And a full coffee shop. It's pretty snazzy."

Donnie stood up and yawned. "Two people called while you were out. A guy wants to meet and schedule a funeral for his dad, or his uncle—can't remember which one. And then another guy called and asked if he could make a 'reservation' for five-thirty." Donnie held up air quotes as he spoke. "He didn't give me any details other than that."

"Who was it?"

"Didn't say," Donnie replied.

"Just said he'd be here at five thirty? Did he ask for me?"

"Nope," Donnie said, folding the newspaper back up. "Asked if we had any openings at five thirty, and that he and his girlfriend would be here then."

"Oh." Frank smirked. He poured himself a mug of coffee. "That's probably a mix up. You want to each take one or you wantin' to double-team them both?"

"Nah, I can take the weird guy. It's probably best though if we refrain from telling clients that we're gonna *double-team* them, FYI."

Frank winked at his brother and walked back to his office.

💀

"Yo yo yo," Cliff said, tapping on the door. "You free?"

Frank checked his watch. "Yeah, I got someone coming at two. Check this out."

"So, what happened last night? You good?" Cliff asked, closing the door.

"Yeah. Guy told me to go to the library and get this." Frank held up a copy of *IT* with the folder inside.

"He wants you to read a book?"

"No. It's this." Frank slid the paper out from the envelope.

"Oh. What's it say?"

"I don't know. I was waitin' on you." Frank laid out a single typed page on his desk for Cliff to come around and see. He began reading out loud, but Frank hushed him, noting that Donnie had previously listened in on their conversation last week about the Joe Jackson shoes. "He's a snoop."

The letter disclosed the story of Corey Grassman, a student from Calloway County High School who died in 1997.

"Corey Grassman. That name ring a bell?" Frank asked.

"Nah," Cliff replied. "I didn't know *anyone* from Calloway. Turn it over."

The letter made mention that many believed Corey's death to be a suicide, but some people—including his immediate family—thought he was murdered. "Damn," Frank mumbled.

Cliff kept reading. "Check it out." He pointed at a paragraph and began whispering, "'At Corey's funeral, a book was made available to sign by all who attended—a guest book, if you will. Attendees were encouraged to write a note to Corey. This book was then placed in the coffin at Corey's burial.'"

"That's what the guy wants," Frank said.

"No way I'm touching that," Cliff said. He set the letter down on the desk where Frank took it and continued reading to himself. Cliff spoke softly, "Why the hell would you have people sign a book to someone who died? And who would pay twenty grand for something like that?"

"Maybe he thinks the killer was at the funeral?" Frank suggested.

"I thought it said that Corey killed himself."

"It says he might've," Frank replied. He kept reading.

"So, the guy wants the book to see if the killer wrote a note to Corey?" Cliff asked.

"I don't know." Frank glanced back through the paragraphs and turned the note over to its front, then looked back inside the envelope. "That's it. He doesn't explain anything, just says he wants to see the book. He also says not to read through the notes."

The phone on Frank's desk began to buzz and he answered it. Cliff scanned through the page once more. "Yeah, something ain't right about this," he mumbled.

"Sounds good," Frank said." I'll see you shortly." He hung up. "My appointment is almost here. What do you think? You in?"

"I don't know, man. It's not the same as diggin' up that other lady. This is a kid."

"But what if it really *was* a murder?" Frank asked.

"So, what if it was? You wanna mess around with that? It ain't like we gettin' credit for discovering anything. It's illegal," Cliff said.

"Yeah, but we'll *know*."

"Know *what*? What do we care? We don't know this kid," Cliff said. "Besides, we aren't allowed to read the book so, we *won't* know."

Frank clicked his tongue. "Good point. But we'll be twenty grand richer. I know you've been wanting a couple of new machines for the gym. And some more Funko Pop dolls."

"Yeah." Cliff sighed. "Guess it could be for a good cause." He paused. "He's not buried in LBL is he?"

Frank looked down at the paper. "It's not in LBL. I think I know where it is . . ." He walked back over to his laptop and clicked it on. "Wait for it," he mumbled. Finally, he turned his laptop around. "Yeah. It's right here in Murray. Old Salem Cemetery."

"Never heard of it." Cliff leaned in to look at the pictures on the screen. "Great. Creepy-looking." He groaned.

"It's not far. You want to go scout it out tonight? Do a quick drive-by?"

"I'd prefer to go before it gets dark," Cliff said.

Frank weighed that option in his mind and checked the time. "I can do that." A knock sounded in the foyer, startling Cliff. Frank chuckled to himself, assuring Cliff that it was the door.

"Why did I say yes to this?" Cliff exhaled.

6

Frank opened the door and could feel his face flash a moment of confusion when he saw the young man standing on the porch—he had not expected someone Asian. He caught himself and smiled. "Ben Flores?"

"Yes sir. Frank Burgers? Or Donnie?"

"I'm Frank. Nice to meet you, come on in."

Frank led Ben into his office and offered him a seat. He sat at his desk and reached for the yellow pad he kept for taking notes. He flipped to the first blank page and paused. "Well, shoot," he whispered. Normally Frank did research on the deceased as well as the individual meeting for an appointment, but this meeting had been scheduled last minute and his mind was drowning in theories about Corey Grassman and the mystery note. He knew nothing about the guy in front of him or even more important, *who* he was here for. Frank apologized and quickly stepped across the hall to privately ask Donnie what information Ben had left over the phone. Donnie only had a name and an appointment time.

Frank returned and took a seat at his desk, reaching for his notepad again. "How can we help you today? I know you spoke with my brother earlier. Were you wanting this to simply be an informational meeting to help with future preparations or were you wanting to go ahead and begin setting up a date and memorial event?"

"Unfortunately, I need to go ahead and set up a memorial event. It's for my father-in-law—or ex-father-in-law, I guess."

"Oh." Frank looked up from his notepad. "I'm sorry for your loss."

"Thanks. My wife and I divorced a while ago, but he and I stayed pretty close."

Frank started typing on his laptop.

"The whole thing sort of caught everyone off guard—him dying, I mean. He wasn't the healthiest, so maybe it was to be expected."

"Will you be the main contact person on this? Any other family?" Frank asked.

"I will be, yeah. His parents passed away several years ago. He has a couple brothers and a sister out in Wisconsin, but they've uh . . ." Ben paused and shrugged. "They told me this morning that they're not coming. Too far to travel apparently." He shook his hands with sarcasm.

"What about his daughter? Your ex-wife? Is there a good relationship there between her and her father?"

"No. But even if there was, she passed away too."

"Oh my gosh," Frank said. "Man. I'm so sorry."

"It's alright. She was a bit of a succubus so, it wasn't a huge let down."

An unexpected burst of laughter escaped Frank's mouth. "I don't mean to laugh. I've never heard anyone be called a succubus before."

"Well, she was pretty terrible," Ben sighed. "Anyway, I figure with most of the family being out of the picture, I'll take care of the guy. I've lost most of *my* immediate family as well, so I'm probably the best guy to handle all this anyways."

"I assume that your wife was from here as well?" Frank asked.

"She was, yeah. That was the last time I was here actually was for her funeral. Not *here*, here. But, somewhere in Murray. I can't remember the name of it."

"How'd you hear about us? Can I ask?"

"Word of mouth. I got in yesterday afternoon and went to that restaurant over next to the campus—Vitello's, I think?"

"Yeah," Frank confirmed.

"The bartender said you and your brother were good guys."

"That's awesome," Frank said. He reached into his desk and pulled out a business card. "In that case, you get five percent off the funeral charge."

"What?" Ben asked.

"A few of us business owners in the area like to promote one another. Word of mouth referrals give you a five percent discount."

"Hey, I'll take all the discounts I can get."

"You like donuts or beer more?"

"Beer, I guess." Ben replied.

Frank took hold of one of three small brass stamps near his computer. He pressed it into a pad of ink and then carefully rolled it onto the card. A blue circle with an overflowing mug of beer inside was now stamped over the funeral home's address. He handed it to Ben. "Take this over to Vitello's and give it to Evan. He's the guy you talked to last night—he owns it. It's good for a free draft, or wine if you're classy. It's only if you order food, though. And you have to give it to Evan."

Ben gave it a once over.

"We normally save these for our in-town clients, but you seem like a cool guy. It's just incentive for doing business with us."

"And people say funerals are depressing," Ben joked.

"No one here says that," Frank beamed, then began typing as he spoke again, "Alright, let's talk about your father-in-law and how you'd like to present his memorial." Frank slid over an iPad with a colorful collection of columns on the screen. Frank had designed a tier system that offered different packages of funeral services to help individuals plan more efficiently. Very few people would plan more than one funeral in their life, and most of them weren't in the right state of mind to think clearly about the day or what needed to be done. Frank explained each package and price to Ben but was cut off shortly after he started talking.

"What's the *If You Build It, They Will Come* package at the bottom?" Ben asked.

"That's à la carte. You make it exactly how you want: people speaking, PowerPoint, music, food, etcetera. We even included some specialty services to give people ideas. Those can be added on to any package." There was a pause as Ben continued reading.

"Cake Face?" Ben asked.

"Yeah, that's a popular one. Mrs. Boswell is an artist with cakes. She'll make one in the shape of the client's face, even a full body cake—not life size, of course."

"Of course," Ben said. He scanned more of the list. "Ice sculptures?"

"Yeah, we've only done that once. Only in the winter, unfortunately." Frank let Ben continue reading.

"Do people actually do these?" Ben finally replied.

"Oh yeah. Lots of cakes. The magician gets booked a lot—he's pretty awesome. Don Ross wrote and directed a little ten-minute play about a client's life once. We staged that here. We've had violinists, full bands. Had a lady come and do watercolor art for the guests. Jamie is our graphic design girl. She can make just about anything you think of. She's reworked movie posters and had the client on the poster. Those are a big hit. Usually we put them on a display near where people walk in, instead of the boring old head shot from thirty years ago that no one recognizes."

"I mean, as cool as putting Tom's body on the *Braveheart* poster would be, let's stick with the traditional service. The second package seems fine."

"The *Goonies Never Say Die* package? You want to keep everything as is?"

"Yeah, that's fine. And no viewing if that's okay. Just the service." Ben said. Frank gave a thumbs up and continued writing. "I'll take the eulogy so you can go ahead and put me down for that."

"Perfect." Frank plugged the information into his laptop. "Anything else? Otherwise, we'll take care of music, programs, and the readings—unless some of the family wishes to participate. And there won't be a PowerPoint."

"Nah. Like I said, I'm pretty sure they won't make it," Ben said.

He and Frank continued talking about the service and developing plans. After Frank took him through coffin models in the virtual showroom, he explained what he needed in order to dress the deceased and requested a picture of him for makeup and preparation.

"Oh." Ben clicked his tongue off the roof of his mouth. "Your brother told me to bring one—I completely forgot. Can I email it to you?"

"That's fine." Frank wrote a few more notes down and then started scanning over it. "Oh my gosh." He looked up at his computer screen and then flipped back a page in his pad. "Sorry Ben, I forgot to ask. What's your father-in-law's name?"

"Oh, no worries. Tom Middleton," Ben replied. "You need his middle name?"

Frank froze. He held his gaze on the surface of his desk for a long moment and then finally asked, "Did you say Tom *Piddleton*, or Middleton?"

"Middleton. With an M."

"Huh," Frank muttered. "Okay." He was speaking but his brain was on autopilot. Fragmented reflections began surfacing but they wouldn't sustain long enough to become full thoughts. He looked at Ben, and then back down at his notepad. He heard himself say Tom's name again.

"Did you know him?" Ben asked.

Frank, in a daze, nodded his head slowly and muttered, "No." He saw Ben narrow his eyes and cock his head. "I mean, sorry. Yes and no. I know his name, but I didn't know him personally."

"Oh," Ben said.

"His name was in the newspaper a few days ago." *Shit. Was it his name or his ex-wife's name?*

"Yeah. I heard about that. The grave robbery?"

Snap out of it! "When did he die?"

"Yesterday. I got a call from his neighbor after breakfast. Tom's door was standing wide open. Neighbor walked over, found him dead in his bedroom."

"Do they know what happened?" Frank asked.

"Nope. Not yet. He wasn't in the best of health, so wouldn't be surprised if his heart just stopped."

"Man. I'm really sorry," Frank said sincerely. Ben shrugged and opened his palms as if to say, *what are you gonna do?* "Rough week for the Middleton family." Frank sighed. He wrote a few more notes down on his notepad and printed out an invoice for Ben. Ben asked about payment, confessing that he would need to speak with Tom's relatives about the cost before deciding to take it all himself.

"That's not a problem. We do normally request ten percent down..." Frank looked past Ben into Donnie's office to see if his brother was paying attention, then lowered his voice and leaned in closer. "But if money is tight..." Frank paused, noticing the Zelda Triforce logo on Ben's polo shirt. Frank moved his eyes down to Ben's chest and then back up to his face. "We can probably work something out."

Ben cocked an eyebrow at Frank, looking a tad cautious. "What do you mean *work something out?* Like, I have to *do* something?"

"What?" Frank asked, now aware of how that comment may have come across. "No. Sorry. I meant we can do a lower percentage down or work out some sort of payment plan if you need it. I just need something to lock in your date and assure us that we have your business." He laughed. "Sorry. Didn't realize that came out a little awkward. Awesome shirt, by the way."

"Oh, thanks. Big Zelda fan. Ten percent is fine." Ben brought out his wallet. "I'll likely end up covering the whole thing but it's probably good to check with everyone else, so I don't step on people's toes."

"I understand," Frank said. He ran Ben's card and passed him a receipt to sign. "You're all set. We have you down for a memorial service on Tuesday at ten a.m. And you're sure you want to skip the viewing?"

"Yeah. I talked with his sister this morning. Even if they do make it down here, they aren't interested in a viewing. She said if people wanted to view the body they could come to the funeral."

"Fair enough. I'll send you an email with all the details, and what to send family about arrival times and such. We recommend somebody stop by before the memorial to make sure Tom looks his best. Is that gonna be you?"

"Yeah, probably. And if it's okay with you, I'll just pay the rest when I come check him out."

"That's perfect," Frank said. The two of them shook hands and Frank walked him outside onto the porch, wondering how to phrase the question running through his mind. "Hey, this is gonna sound weird, but we like to ask just in case special accommodations need to be made. Is your father-in-law gonna be buried with anything of considerable size, or worth?"

Ben walked down the steps of the porch and put on his sunglasses before turning back to Frank. "I guess with those recent robberies, it's good to ask," Ben said. "I don't think so."

"Exactly. If there was anything expensive like jewelry or heirlooms or something, we would try to make sure it stayed out of view until the burial. That way, no one would know it was in there."

"I'm glad you said something. He doesn't have anything that's expensive, but he called me last week about a necklace he found—family heirloom. We thought my ex-wife had it, and then we thought *Tom's* ex-wife had it. Turns out he had it the whole time." Ben chuckled. "I'm sure he'd want to keep that with him, and I don't know what else to do with it. I'll bring it by later. He can just wear it underneath his shirt if that's okay."

7

Donnie Burgers had spent his afternoon on the front porch compiling a list of churches and contacts in the immediate area. Murray was often referred to as the "Bible belt" which meant that there was a church on every corner—and often one in between. As far as he knew, it had been years since the funeral home had reconnected with the churches to let them know of their services, and their existence. It was time to rebuild those relationships.

He heard his brother and Cliff walking up the driveway. When he looked up, he saw Frank jump off the ground, toward Cliff, and lift his leg—probably letting out a fart. Frank had barely landed before Cliff swatted at him with the fanny pack he was holding, and Frank raced toward the car. Donnie yelled out, "Where you guys goin'?"

"Out to eat," Frank yelled back, still warding off Cliff's attacks.

Donnie closed his laptop. "I'll go. Let me get my wallet." He heard Frank yell "what?" but ignored him and went inside.

The two of them were standing outside the car when he walked back out. "You're going to eat with us?" Frank asked.

"Yeah. That alright?"

Frank shot the briefest look of hesitation. "Yeah. I guess. Mom or Dad home to answer the phone?"

"Nah, they left. I got it routed to me," Donnie replied, holding up his phone. "If you guys want a man-date I can hang back."

"Nah, it's cool," Frank said. "You always eat in, so I didn't think you'd want to come."

"Don't feel like cooking tonight. Where you guys goin' to eat?"

"Tacos. That place on the square," Frank said.

"Perfect," Donnie said, crawling into the back of the car. He began reading through an email when Cliff abruptly slammed on the breaks, throwing him forward into the back of Frank's seat. The beginnings of an accusatory and curse filled question began to flow out of Donnie's mouth when he saw Cliff had turned around and was staring out behind them. Donnie gazed out the back window at the police cruiser parked at the end of their driveway, blocking them in.

"Is that Stutters?" Frank asked.

"Looks like it," Cliff replied. Monty got out of the car. "Are we supposed to get out too?"

"No," Donnie said. "Stay in the car." He glared at Frank.

"What? I've been home all day," Frank said.

Monty walked up to Cliff's window as it was going down. Donnie put his down as well. "Hey, Mr. Suthers. How are you?" He asked.

Monty leaned down and looked into the car, first at Donnie and then at Frank. "You m-mind if I chat with you for a moment?"

"Sure. Go ahead," Frank replied.

"Y-you mind stepping out of the car?" Monty said. "I don't feel like crouching the whole time."

"Um . . . sure. Am I in trouble?"

Monty didn't answer. He straightened and walked to the front of the car to wait. Frank looked at Cliff and then back at Donnie. "Dude, I swear. I don't know what this is about," he said. He unclicked his belt and exited the car, closing the door.

"I find that hard to believe," Donnie whispered to himself. He opened his own door and stepped out; Monty didn't stop him.

"You doin' alright?" Monty asked.

"I was," Frank replied. "Not sure now. What's goin' on?"

"Tom Middleton died last night," Monty said. "That name mean anything to you?"

Donnie stood motionless against the car, listening.

"Yeah. I mean, yessir." Frank folded his arms and looked down for a moment. "I heard. His son-in-law came by earlier this afternoon. We're having the funeral here."

"You know who Tom is?" Monty asked.

"I know he's the husband of the woman whose grave got messed with last week. Other than that, no."

"You n-never m-met him before?"

"No sir."

"You ever talk with him on the phone?"

"Nope," Frank replied.

"D-did you know he d-died before B-Ben came to see you?" Monty asked.

"No sir," Frank answered.

"So, wh-why do you think B-Ben came to see you? Wh-Why not go to Life Memorial?" Monty asked.

Donnie caught the annoyed eye roll when Frank looked away. "Maybe he heard we were better?"

"Is that what he said?"

"No. He told me that Evan Vitello recommended us last night at the bar," Frank answered. "Do you know something I don't?"

"I think you know more about Tom that you're letting on—or maybe he knew you."

"Well, I told you I didn't know him, so . . ." Frank shrugged. "That's all I got."

"W-why then do you think Tom had your n-name on a card at his house?" Monty asked.

Frank let out an emotionless chuckle. "Really? That's what brought you out here?" Donnie said his brother's name; a warning that Frank was getting a touch disrespectful. Frank shook his head. "I don't know. Probably because I've printed like ten thousand of those things and I give them out everywhere—no telling where he got it. Maybe I *did* meet him at one point, I don't know. You know how many *events* I go to each year? I gave out nearly a thousand of those things at the Paris Fish Fry a couple months back."

"I'm n-not talking about your business card, Frank. I'm talking about a n-note card with your name on it. Frank. Burgers."

Frank let his mouth hang open, likely unsure of what to say. "I don't know," he finally said. "Is there something wrong with him having my name on a card?"

"Your n-number was also written on the card," Monty said. "Your cell number."

Frank stood still.

"You sure you n-never spoke with Tom before?" Monty asked.

"Pretty sure," Frank lied. "Wish I could be more help."

Monty looked back at Donnie. "Y-you ever t-talk to Tom?"

Donnie shook his head slowly. "No sir."

"Okay," Monty said, rubbing the back of his neck. "Just seemed a little strange that a card with your n-name and n-number was lying on top of his desk. Thought maybe you could help clear some things up. Death seems a little sudden."

"Ben said this morning that he wasn't in the best health so, maybe it wasn't that sudden. Wish I could be more help," Frank tried to sound sympathetic.

Monty gently nodded and extended his hand for Frank to shake. Frank did.

"If I hear anything suspicious, I'll let you know," Frank said as Monty walked back toward his cruiser.

Monty peered at him from the other side of his car. "I bet you will," he called back.

8

Rather than follow behind Monty toward the main road, Cliff turned down a side street. They drove in silence. Frank could feel Donnie's gaze burning a hole into the back of his head. "I know what you're thinking," Frank finally said. "Why did I give away a thousand cards at the Paris Fish Fry."

"Did you have anything to do with Tom's death?"

"Dude. Are you serious?" Frank turned around in his seat. "Why would you ask that?" Donnie arched his eyebrows and tilted his head to the side as if to say *really?* And waited for Frank to answer his own question. "I dug up graves, I didn't kill anyone."

"Yeah, and you just happened to dig up a grave for *this* guy," Donnie said. "Seems a little convenient that not more than a week later, he winds up dead."

"It's not convenient for Tom," Cliff joked. He looked at Donnie through the rearview and stifled a laugh when he saw Donnie wasn't smiling. He began whistling instead.

"I don't understand why you're pinning this on me. You honestly think I would kill someone?" Frank asked, turning back around.

"It's not the killing I'm worried about. What else is he gonna find in that house?" Donnie asked.

"He's not gonna find anything. Tom and I only communicated by phone—never through text or email," Frank replied.

"So, if Monty looks at his call history, he'll see your name," Donnie said. "Great."

"Tom only had a house phone. If Stutters wants to run phone records to a landline, yeah, he'll find out that he called my cell." Donnie cursed in the back seat. "Nothing I can do about that now—didn't realize the guy was gonna keel over a week later."

"What about the necklace?" Donnie asked. "What if they find that?"

"So what if they do? Who would know that it came out of his ex-wife's grave?" Donnie didn't answer. Frank sat quiet for a moment staring ahead. "Besides, Ben has it. He's supposed to bring it by later so we can put it around Tom's neck."

"No. Absolutely not!" Donnie exclaimed. "We're not taking that thing back."

"What am I supposed to do? I already said we'd put it with the body. Relax, alright? Everyone who knows about that necklace being with Sarah Middleton's body is either in this car or dead."

"How sure are you of that?" Donnie asked.

Frank hesitated. "Ninety-two percent?"

Donnie mumbled something to himself. They rode in silence for the rest of the way to the court square. Cliff stretched his neck forward to look out at the sky above. The clouds had merged into a menacing, erratic sea of black and deep blue ripples. "Yo," Cliff whispered. "Made it just in time."

"I'm not complaining," Donnie said, staring out his window. "We need the rain." The car came to a stop in one of many vacant spots along the square.

"Storm's comin'," Cliff growled in his best Christian Bale Batman voice.

"Let's go!" Frank yelled, opening his door, and taking off in a sprint into the wind, toward the restaurant.

Light flashed across the sky with a thunderous explosion. Ginny Burgers shrieked in the passenger seat, startling her husband Dave to nearly swerve into the funeral home mailbox as he turned in. His mind cycled through several distressing scenarios: a terrorist attack; an explosion; maybe the Lord's return—all in the span of a few milliseconds. A deafening growl rumbled overhead, at once followed by machine gun fire-rain began blanketing the car's roof and windshield.

"Lord, have mercy!" Ginny cried. "That scared me to death." She began laughing in relief. "I think the worry on your face scared me more than the thunder," she bellowed, peering up at the sky.

"You almost made me hit the mailbox, Gin." Dave sighed, backing up and pulling into the driveway.

Ginny looked up at the black sky. "Would you look at that! I hope everyone made it home before it started."

"I can't see a thing," Dave said. "You have an umbrella in here?"

Ginny pulled it out from underneath her seat as Dave clicked on the radio. "Just want to make sure there's no tornado activity," he said.

"It's just a storm with high winds," Ginny said.

"That's what a tornado is," he said. "You want me to pull up onto the grass and let you out onto the porch?"

"I'm not gonna melt, you old fart, I'll be fine. We'll make a run for it."

"Well hang on. Maybe we can wait it out. I'd rather not get my suit wet." He continued listening intently to the announcer's voice on the radio when he heard Ginny's door open. "Where are you goin'!"

"Coming around to get you." The umbrella popped open. She slammed the door shut and galloped around to his side. Dave could hear her screaming over the water slamming onto the car. When she opened the door, Dave cursed and stepped into the torrential downpour. The umbrella didn't seem to make a difference. His face was pelted with small, stinging raindrops while his suit shimmered from the water blowing in from all directions. The two of them locked arms and huddled close underneath, walking up the driveway as if they were playing hopscotch.

"Couldn't just wait in the car?" he yelled. Ginny then went still, yanking Dave back toward her. "What are you doing?" he yelled.

"I want you to kiss me," she yelled back.

"Kiss you? I'm soaked. Come on!" He tried to keep walking and gave an extra tug on her interlocked arm, but she stood firm.

"Kiss me!" she said again.

He went in for a peck on the lips, but she shook her head when he pulled away. "Nope. Real kiss. Right here in the rain." She did her best to smile against the wind-blown water pummeling her face, but all she could manage was a scrunched face and one barely open eyelid. Dave finally gave in and leaned in to kiss her wet mouth. She breathed in when he did and wrapped one of her arms over his shoulder, leaving the other still up and holding the umbrella. After a moment, Ginny opened her eyes and dropped her arm with the umbrella. Dave's eyes shot open as his body tensed from the cold water now pouring down behind his shirt collar and onto his neck. He could see—and now feel—her starting to laugh. She held his kiss for a few more seconds as she convulsed out several short breaths through her nose and then finally drew back, still laughing at herself. He pulled her closer for one more kiss.

Dave carefully stepped up the porch steps and turned to extend his hand to Ginny, making sure she didn't slip on the way up. They shook out their arms, and Ginny wrung out her hair. Her face was joyous. "Always wanted to do that," she said.

"Give me a heads up next time, I won't wear a suit." Dave unlocked the front door and growled with relief upon entering the foyer. They both kicked off their shoes and stood dripping on the hardwood floor. Ginny scampered up the stairs to go look for towels. Dave peeled off his suit coat and an let out an audible shiver. He was about to start unbuttoning his shirt when he heard Ginny scream from the upstairs hallway.

9

The owner of My Uncle's Basement brought out a round of drinks for the table and caught up with Frank and Cliff. Donnie returned to the table from the bathroom and Frank stood up to let him in the booth. Donnie's phone chirped but he ignored it. "Donnie, this is Marco Cruz—he runs the place. Mark, you haven't met my brother, have you?" Frank asked.

"Not officially." Mark extended his hand for Donnie to shake. "I remember you from high school but you were a few grades above me. Nice to finally meet you. This guy never shuts up about you." He motioned to Frank.

"Marco Cruz," Donnie said to himself. "Oh. You were on *Top Chef*."

"That's me." Marco smiled.

"Yeah, Frank told me all about it. Congrats, man."

"Hey, thanks brother. It was a fun ride. Even better with these two cabrons hyping it up around town for me." Marco smiled and elbowed Cliff's shoulder. "So, what's the news? Frank says you're coming back to open up a restaurant here in town."

Donnie's shoulders slumped as he turned to give Frank a deflated expression. "Oh, he did, huh?" Donnie asked. Frank innocently smiled. "I think his hearing is selective. I'm looking at some spots but nothing nearby."

"You in town for a while?"

"At least for a few months, yeah. Doin' some stuff at the home; may head back up to New York after the new year, we'll see."

"Don't listen to him," Frank cut in. "He'll be here for a while. Especially once I tell him about my bed and breakfast idea." A waiter scooted in and brought waters for the group.

"So, how you guys been? Haven't seen you in a while," Marco said.

"We're here nearly every Sunday. Where've you been?" Cliff replied.

"Ah, que bueno. Sunday's my day at the lake. Usually out there with my cousin. You guys should come out with us."

"Definitely," Frank said.

"As long as it's not at night, I'm down," Cliff said.

"What's on Sunday nights?" Frank asked.

"Nothing. I'm just not goin' to LBL at night."

"Yeah, my cousin and me, we don't mess around that place at night. We outta there before sundown."

"They still got that curfew up? From that girl who drowned last year?" Frank asked.

"Nah, that was two years ago," Cliff answered. "The Maddox girl. They lifted it last summer."

"Oh. Wait, hold up." Frank shot a look of surprise to Marco. "This isn't because of that Bethel cemetery stuff is it?"

"Yeah brother," Marco replied. "My mom *messed* me up with those stories."

"Yo, my dad's got pictures of that place," Cliff said.

About the same time as Marco asked Cliff if he was serious, Frank dropped his head in exasperation onto the table. "You've gotta be kidding me," he muttered to himself.

The conversation eventually shifted from local ghost lore back to Donnie when Mark asked about his next spot. Donnie felt his phone go off again and slipped it out of his pocket onto the table. He caught a glimpse of the name and slid it over to Frank, who stepped away and answered it.

It wasn't even two minutes before Frank rushed back over to the table. "Mark, I'm sorry to cut you off," Frank said quickly, handing the phone back to Donnie, "but we gotta go. Family emergency back at the house."

"What happened?" Donnie asked.

"Everything okay?" Mark asked.

"Not really," Frank said, pulling keys from his pocket. "Our roof just caved in."

●

The rain fell heavy for nearly an hour before it let up into a light drizzle. The roof had given in just over Dave and Ginny's bedroom, soaking the floor and surrounding furniture. The water covered most of the carpet in the bedroom, extending into and through the upstairs hallway. Frank was the first one in the house, bounding up the stairs and letting out a curse when he saw the damage. He ran back down as Donnie and Cliff were coming up.

"Where you goin'?" Donnie asked.

Frank jumped off the steps and rounded the corner without answering. Dave was moving things out of his room into the hall.

"You guys okay?" Donnie asked.

"We're fine—stuff isn't. Water's all over the furniture. Carpet is soaked."

"What can I do?"

"Well, your mother's in there picking up the debris that had fallen through. I'd say just grab what you can out of there and move it somewhere else," Dave said, inching past him. "Cliff, you might want to go check your gym—make sure there isn't a leak."

"Should be all good, Mr. B. That roof is brand new," Cliff replied.

"Never know," Dave yelled from Frank's room. "I'd go check in case you need to move equipment."

Frank came up the steps. "Parlor two is soaked. Looks like water was coming in from y'all's room," Frank said, looking to his dad.

"Any other damage? You check parlor one? And the offices?" Dave asked.

"Yeah. The floor in one is wet, not as bad as two, but noticeable enough. No clue where it's coming in from. I'll need help getting the podium and stuff out of there."

"Dammit," Dave whispered as Ginny reentered carrying a black trash bag. "Water's comin' in downstairs too, hun."

"Great." Ginny exhaled. "Dave, I need to run to the shop; the phones are out. There might be damage there too."

"Can you bring back one of the Shop-Vacs?" Dave asked.

"They're both here," Ginny replied.

"Oh, good. We're probably gonna need a couple more." Dave turned to Frank and Donnie. "One of you boys mind going to Lowe's and grabbing two?"

"Yeah, I got it," Frank replied.

"May want to go quick before they run out."

"I'll go now," Frank said before Donnie could answer. "Cliff, you wanna go?"

"Nah, I'm gonna hang back. I'll go make sure nothing's getting in over at the Chamber and then I'll go check my house. I'll come back in a bit and help you guys out if I can."

"Thanks, Cliff," Dave said. "Alright, let's get to it."

Frank beat the rush and grabbed three Shop-Vacs, but before he returned home, he made one more stop. He pulled into the church parking lot across the street from Old Salem Cemetery, and drove around to the back of the building, out of view from anyone passing by.

The only things out this way were a few houses and the church he was parked at. Frank couldn't imagine there being much traffic. It was probably less than three miles from the funeral home, yet he'd never once buried a client here. To his recollection, he wasn't sure if he'd even been in the cemetery before.

Frank left the engine running as he stepped out of the truck and checked the straps holding the three Shop-Vacs in the bed. He glanced toward the cemetery and jogged across the street toward the stone steps of its entrance. To the left of the entryway was a large wooden sign; the

bottom portion had either been lost to age or vandals. Frank stopped and read it aloud to himself: "All you good people, as you pass by, as you are now, so once was I. As I am now, so you shall be."

"That's morbid," Frank whispered. He checked once again to make sure no headlights were coming down the road and then proceeded to move through the plot, checking the headstones. "Alright, where are you, Corey?" He started in the middle and worked his way back to the left, scanning quickly as he went—nothing. He moved back toward the other end. Dozens of trees stood throughout, shrouding the names from the little bit of light that remained. Finally, he saw it. At the far por-

tion of the lot was a lone white memorial of two figures—a man and a woman—sitting and leaning back against a traditional headstone. The man's head laid on the bosom of the woman as she wrapped her arm around him. Her head was resting back onto the stone. Written to the left of the man was the name GRASSMAN. Frank stepped closer to see the words inscribed underneath: 1979-1997. TO OUR COREY, TAKEN TOO SOON. WE WILL NEVER FORGET YOU.

"Damn," Frank whispered. He surveyed the grave and glanced around, analyzing visibility from the road. It was situated toward the back of the lot, and the trees provided him a little cover. The slight elevation should help him and Cliff stay hidden. The tricky part would be the first two feet. If someone drove by, hiding would be nearly impossible except behind the trees.

Once he was back in the truck, Frank eyed the cemetery from the side of the road once more. At this angle, the two of them could likely squat down—especially if they were even a little way into the hole—and be out of view. "Unless of course someone decides to come walking through late at night," he said to himself.

MONDAY
10

Frank opened his eyes and sat up. He turned to look out the window, through the blinds. Outside, where the road should be, were trees and a familiar collection of small, slanting gravestones. Frank pulled back and peered around his bedroom, which looked normal, except for the window which was now larger and without blinds. Outside, the forest had become more dense, almost enveloping Frank's house. He stared out at the small gravestones feeling a sense of familiarity. Something shifted beside one of the markers. A tall black tree had taken on a different shape; now it wasn't a tree. Now it was a figure—a person—standing bent to the side.

The wind picked up, a low hum. He'd been here before. Whatever was out there came closer—yanking itself forward with each step. Then it dissipated into the trees. The floor of his room had become dirt, blooming with overgrowth and leaves. Now he was outside, surrounded by trees. The sun was going down. His body tingled at the thought of needing to leave before dark. He spun around to see a free-standing door—his closet door—nestled in the woods. Perhaps a way out. He reached for the handle as the door started to creak open on its own. Something was standing on the other side, glaring at Frank through the crack. The humming no longer seemed to be around him, but rather escaping from the figure's mouth as the door opened more—at once Frank's eyes shot open. He sat up, gasping for breath.

He was home, now drenched in sweat, and panting as if coming out of the water for air. It took his mind a moment to register his surroundings. He was in the family room, on the couch. Sunlight was coming through the window, and the low, buzzing whirr of the industrial fans could be heard running in multiple rooms of the house. His heart began to settle and he fell back onto the couch, trying to recall what it was that woke him up. His mind couldn't recollect all the details other than that he was alone in the woods next to a cemetery, and that something had been with him, and its presence had made him extremely unnerved. He took one final breath. "Screw that," he whispered.

Footsteps sounded. Frank sat back up to give the impression he was getting up. Dave walked past the couch where Frank was lying and looked at his watch. "Hey. What time is it?" Frank asked.

"Seven-twenty," Dave replied. "Just because the house is flooded doesn't mean you can sleep in." Dave winked at him. The Burgers family had spent the evening before cutting carpet out of the affected rooms and drying up as much of the water as they could in the house.

"Wouldn't dream of it." He stood up and refolded the blanket before going into the kitchen where his mother was on the phone and Cliff was making breakfast at the stove. "Donnie up yet?" he asked.

"Yeah, he's outside with the contractor looking at the roof," Cliff said.

"This early?"

"Early?" Cliff asked. "They were already up at six forty-five when I got here." Cliff tried to tap Frank lightly on his nuts with the spatula, but Frank recoiled and blocked it with his arm.

He took a seat at the table with his mug of coffee across from his mother. "Man. I just had the craziest dream. I was back in LBL, in that same cemetery as before, and it felt like someone was there—"

"Whoa, whoa, whoa!" Cliff cut in. "Don't be telling me this." He dumped the eggs into a bowl. "I ain't tryin' to have nightmares tonight."

Frank swatted at Cliff's comments as if they were nonsense. Just then, his mom pulled the phone away from her ear and clicked it off. "Second appraiser will be here in thirty minutes. I need to go into work, will you be here?" Ginny asked Frank.

"Yeah, I'll be here. Nothing going on. Do we have any idea of how long it'll take to fix?"

"The guy outside seemed to think a few days," Dave said, entering the kitchen. "Donnie's already been on the phone with Todd for our insurance. Hopefully, we can get it started by tomorrow."

"Wait, we have the Middleton funeral tomorrow," Frank said. "I was gonna try to get parlor two to look presentable today."

Dave sighed and slumped against the counter. "Son, I don't know how you're gonna get that room ready. We ripped half the carpet up last night. Even if you could, you don't want to have people here with a roof being put on. Guests can see up the stairs as soon as they walk in, the place is a wreck."

"We can just tell them there was a flood—they'll understand."

Dave's eyes moved up from the floor, looking at Ginny, then Frank. "I'm not your boss, so, you make your own decision here, but I would strongly recommend *not* having the funeral here with the house looking like this. It's going to smell awful. We'll have fans running. It's not the kind of atmosphere someone wants for their loved one to be remembered in."

Frank took a sip of his coffee. "What am I supposed to tell Ben? He wanted *us* to do it and I don't want to miss out on the money."

"I know," Dave replied. "But there's not much we can do. Again, it's your call, but I would strongly advise against it—it's not professional. If you want, I can call Randy or Vince and see if they'd be willing to step in."

"Yeah," Frank cut in. "That's a winning idea." He revved his tongue against his bottom lip, making a long fart noise while shooting his dad a dramatic thumbs down. "I'd rather take the risk of hosting it here than giving those two queefs our business."

"What are queefs?" Ginny asked.

"Slang for—" Frank cut himself off. "Just, slang term for morons."

"Isn't that a food?" Ginny asked.

"No, that's *quiche*," Cliff cut in. "You don't wanna know." He turned to Frank and shook his head in disapproval.

A loud thud came from the ceiling. Out of the corner of Frank's eye he saw something fall past the window. He got up to look when another black object dropped down onto the grass outside—roof tiles. Frank scanned over the backyard. And then it hit him. "Hey! I got it! What about hosting the funeral outside?"

Ginny looked at Dave. "That's a possibility."

"Yeah, I've been looking for a reason to do this—it's perfect." He walked back over to the table and typed something into his phone. "Weather's supposed to be cloudy tomorrow. We bump up the time a little bit; we could do it in the morning while it's still cool."

"How are you going to get the casket down there? That cart won't roll on the grass. And where will you get the chairs?"

"Pallbearers. That's what they're for. They can carry the casket down the aisle to the front, then I'll pull the hearse up, they can carry it back and load it up. Easy."

"That's a long way for them to walk, son. If one person trips or steps in a hole, the whole group goes down. Plus, someone could get hurt holding up something that heavy."

"I can rent the chairs from the banquet center. We only need probably twenty—twenty-five?"

"Gin, what do you think?" Dave asked.

"I think it could work. I agree with Franklin, I would rather not lose out on the business. If Donald's on board, I'd say let's do an outside funeral."

Frank clapped his hands. "There she is! We're gonna do this! I'll get a hold of Ben and explain what's going on. Hopefully, he doesn't shoot it down." Frank was dialing the numbers into his phone when he heard the outside door open, followed by the screen door. Donnie walked into the kitchen, and over to the sink to wash his hands. "Hey, so what's the damage? When can they get it fixed?"

Donnie fixed a cold glare on Frank, lathering his arms and hands with soap.

"Whoa. You alright? What happened?"

Donnie yanked off a paper towel from the spindle. "When's the last time you checked that roof?"

"*Checked* it? What do you mean? Like, went up there?"

"Sure," Donnie said. He opened the trash can lid and threw the soiled napkin inside forcefully. "Last time you went up there."

"I don't know. Maybe five years ago? Six? When did we take over?" Frank looked to his dad. "Six years ago, right? We got it replaced around the same time. Why? What happened?"

"Insurance isn't going to cover the roof," Donnie shot back. "Can anyone guess why?" Silence.

"What?" Frank asked. "Why not?"

Donnie turned to face his brother. "I want you to think real hard about this." His brother narrowed his eyes and shrugged. "You say that roof got replaced six years ago?"

"Yeah. Maybe five. I know it's not older than six."

"You're sure?" Donnie asked.

"Dude. Yes! I'm sure. You and I even talked about it. You told me to hire that really hairy guy from high school—Eddie—to do all the work."

"I know Frank." Donnie held up his phone. "I still have the email string."

"So there! We got this all taken care of. Did they not do a good job or something? I'm sure we're under warranty."

"I'm sure we're *not* under warranty because the roof was never replaced, dumb ass," Donnie shot back.

"Hey!" Ginny spoke up. "Language."

"What are you talking about?" Frank asked, becoming agitated. "We. Replaced. The roof!"

"No. *You* didn't," Donnie replied. "And you know how I know that?" He reached into his pocket and pulled something out. He held it up for a moment, not saying anything to give Frank a chance to register what was in his hand. "What is this?"

It was a blue Power Ranger flip-head action figure. "Holy crap! Where'd you find that?" Frank asked.

"On the roof," Donnie said pointedly. "Do you know whose it is?"

"No."

"It's mine. Do you know why it's up there?" Frank's eyebrows furrowed and his lips pursed. Donnie continued, "Twenty years ago—probably ninety-six or ninety-seven—when the show came out, you walked outside, grabbed this guy out of my hand and threw it up on the roof."

Frank looked at the floor, trying to recall the event. "Oh! Ye—wait! That's not what happened!"

"Then how did it get up there?" Donnie asked.

"I threw it up there. But don't make it sound like you didn't deserve it. You golf clubbed an ant hill into my face!"

"I what?"

"We were outside, and I was minding my own business, you yelled my name and when I turned around you swung dad's golf club into an ant mound right into my face."

"I remember that!" Ginny exclaimed. "Why would you do that?"

"Are we forgetting the problem here?" Donnie yelled.

"Who knocks an ant hill onto someone? I literally had ants in my pants. You got what you deserved," Frank replied.

"Forget about the ants! The point is that our roof hasn't been touched in at least twenty years! It's a mess up there."

"Wait a minute, wait a minute," Frank replied. "We took care of all this."

"Obviously, you didn't." He pulled out his phone and began swiping his finger across the screen. "We discussed insurance. Contractors. But nothing ever got done." Donnie flipped his phone around. "It's all right here. I even wrote in an email, 'I wonder if my Power Ranger toy is still up there.'"

"Yeah. I remember all that," Frank said, taking Donnie's phone and scanning through the emails. "I took pictures. We got estimates. Dad and I even cleared some of the lawn stuff out of the backyard to adjust for funerals." Frank looked at his father who was standing next to the sink, arms crossed, with a fist pushed onto his mouth and a grave look over his face. "You remember all this, right? I'm pretty sure we even got an insurance check." For a moment Dave didn't say anything. He just stood motionless, staring back. "Dad?"

Dave's eyes checked in with everyone in the room. "Frank's right," Dave said. "Oh my God." He shook his head. "It was me."

"What do you mean?" Ginny asked.

After another moment of quiet Dave began to speak, astonished. "Frank's right. He did everything. We did, we sat right there and talked about the arrangements. You got the check, and I had you put it in the bank." A pause. "Oh my gosh. I can't believe it." He raised his head toward Frank. "You had to leave town for a CE course, and then you were scheduled to go to California immediately after that to visit someone, so I was going to make the arrangements for the roofers to come out."

"That's right! I forgot about that," Frank exclaimed. "I knew we took care of this. Obviously, the roofers screwed something up—"

"No. No they didn't. I did," Dave cut in. "Because a day or so after you left," Dave looked over to Ginny. "*You* went into the hospital."

"Oh, man, don't tell me," Donnie said.

"And I ended up coming home early from my trip," Frank said softly.

"Yup. And after you went in, I forgot all about making the arrangements—your brother and I were so focused on keeping our appointments and being with your mom. We were in and out of that hospital the rest of the year and I forgot all about the roof." Dave sighed. "I can't believe it."

After a momentary pause, Ginny spoke up. "Way to put the blame on me." Dave looked up and saw she was smiling.

"I kept thinking about it," Dave said, "or thinking to remind Frank about it, but it just . . . it slipped my mind. Before long it was winter, and then after that, out of my mind completely."

"Awesome. So now, we have two *big* holes in our roof, and barely any money to fix it," Donnie said.

"It'll be fine," Ginny said to her son sharply. "We'll take care of it.

We've had setbacks before. I'll talk with Todd and see what insurance can do at this point and see what money we have set aside. I'm positive everything will work out."

"Well, no offense Mom, but a positive attitude isn't an accepted currency to a lot of—"

"I'm gonna stop you right there," Ginny cut in, "before you say something that gets you slapped in the face." Though her voice was calm, her eyes were piercing. Donny saw his dad's eyebrows go up in surprise. "I want you to really think if what you're about to say is a smart and helpful response to this situation."

Donnie held his tongue.

"Now, your father made a mistake—a big mistake. A very stupid, large, and idiotic mistake."

"Thanks, honey."

"Well, you did. But he and I have been running businesses longer than you've been alive. So, when I say that things will be okay, and that we'll figure it out, and that I'm positive about it, I believe I know what I'm talking about. I'm more than happy to listen to an idea or an encouraging word, but if all you have is a smartass comment, I'd prefer you to keep it to yourself."

"Daammmn," Frank said in a high-pitched voice from behind his hand.

"Shut up," Donnie whispered back. "Sorry, Mom." He slumped in embarrassment.

"We have another company coming soon for a second estimate. Let's all go and cool off. There's nothing we can do until we know a cost. Once we have our numbers, we'll talk about what to do next."

"I'll look at the accounts and see how much money we have. I'm sure we have more than you think, Donnie." Frank eyed his brother, moving his eyebrows happily.

11

Frank didn't need to look at the account to know that the new roof would likely wipe out the home's available funds—twice. It was a different story if they used the money made from his most recent and illegal side gig. Donnie rapped on the door frame, startling Frank's attention away the computer screen.

"Got the quote," Donnie said. "It's not good."

"The roof's not good or the quote's not good?"

"Both. Almost twenty grand." Donnie exhaled then put the slip of paper on Frank's desk and took a seat on the couch across from it.

"Was that the first guy or the second guy?"

"That's the second guy—he's the cheaper of the two."

"Jeez." Frank's gaze shifted back to the screen of his laptop before closing it. "I mean, it's not *that* bad."

Donnie raised his eyes toward his brother. "I'm glad twenty grand is *not bad* to you."

"No, I mean that's a lot of money, but it's not like we don't have some emergency funds, if you know what I mean."

Donnie shook his head and exhaled a long breath. "How are we supposed to account for that? Dad was there when the guy was giving the estimate; he knows how much it's going to cost. You don't think he's gonna ask questions when we just throw down twenty grand in cash?"

"We don't have to pay it off at once. We can tell Dad that we're setting up something with the bank and then we'll just pay it off privately ourselves in cash. He'll never know."

"I'm sure he'll know when our spending account numbers don't change," Donnie replied.

"He never checks those things." Frank paused. "And Mom only writes a check. I don't even think she's on the account anymore."

Donnie leaned forward to rest his arms on his knees and scanned his eyes around the room. "The roof is gonna kick us in the ass. Never mind the interior." He cursed. "As much as I didn't want to use *your* money, I was kind of glad we had it. I was going to pump a lot of that into finishing the main floor and redoing parlor one and two—maybe sprucing up three. Strengthening our Google placement. But now there's no way. Especially with one funeral a week."

"I mean . . ." Frank stood and came around to close his office door. "We don't have to do funerals to make money." He gave an overly animated smile. Earlier in the summer, Frank had begun a venture with an employer named Living Pieces, a private company based out of Morehead, Kentucky. They specialized in transforming human remains into high-end collectible items, most recently chess sets. The point of contact declined to provide any other information and only communicated when body parts were needed, and to give instructions on delivery. Though he promised Donnie he wouldn't take any more jobs, Frank felt it was now a good opportunity to test the water. "Few body parts here and there, make some quick money."

"I'm not doin' that," Donnie said, rubbing the bridge of his nose.

"Just throwing it out there."

"Well, I'm throwing it back."

"Look. I get that the body parts into chess pieces thing is weird—"

"It's illegal," Donnie cut in.

"Sure. But, unless you have another idea, we're right back where I was earlier this year—worse, actually. We need updates to get more clients, and we can't update until we get more clients." He paused and spoke quietly in an Irish accent, "It's a vicious cycle." Then, "Look, we're gonna need outside funds." Donnie remained quiet. "I really think you need to reconsider popping off a femur or a few fingers here and there."

Donnie leaned back onto the couch and rested his head against it. There was silence for several moments before he finally took a deep breath and started to speak. "If, *if,* I decided to say yes, how much do you think we could make? And how long would it take you to make it?"

Frank's phone dinged. "Ugh. Sorry. Hang on." He typed in a message.

"What happened with the funeral tomorrow? Did you ever ask the guy about doing it outside?"

Frank looked up from his phone. "Yeah. Kind of. I left him a voicemail. Asked him to call me back." He finished the message on his phone and laid it on his desk. "Okay. Hear me out. I've thought a lot about this." Donnie groaned and Frank shushed him. "I don't think it would take long to get the amount we need. The letter we got says there are several preorders for those chess sets already. We can probably put together fifty grand by Christmas." Frank let his words sink in. "That would take care of a lot of updates—problem solved."

Donnie looked at his watch. "Yeah. There's gotta be another way. I'll think of something."

"Don't think too long. I'm sure Ben won't mind Tom's funeral being outside, but you know as well as I do that we're gonna need a miracle. This place needs a tummy tuck." Frank's ring tone went off. "Speaking of the Tom Middleton..." He answered, lifting a finger to Donnie.

"Ben? Hey how are ya?... You got my voicemail?... Yeah, it did a ton of damage to our roof. We're getting it fixed right now but I figured it would be—... No, we could still cater to the same number if that's your concern... What if we bring out fans?... No, I understand... Would you like me to call the Kochs and have them pick up Tom?... Okay. I'll wait for you to call back... Sorry again for the mix up... Yup, you too... bye."

Frank threw the phone on his desk and reclined back. "Great."

"He doesn't want to do it outside?"

"Nope. Said it'll be too hot, and he doesn't think we can cater to that many people," Frank replied.

"Our backyard is huge!"

"It's also four hundred degrees outside. If it was the fall, we could make it work, but unfortunately we may have to go a couple of weeks without a funeral." The two of them sat quietly. Finally, Donnie mumbled something to himself.

"What?" Frank asked.

His head fell back onto the couch again and he stared up to the ceiling. "I said okay. Let's do it."

Frank went still. He waited, though he wasn't sure what for. Then, "You serious, Clark?"

"Get in touch with the guy; tell him you'll do it."

"Wait, are we talking about Ben or the bone stuff?" Frank asked.

"The bone guy. Tell him we'll take the deal." He paused. "You're right. We can't afford to close our doors for two weeks. So . . . do whatever you gotta do."

Frank got up from his desk and came around to the couch. He sat down, not taking his eyes off Donnie, who wouldn't return the glance. "You better not be playin'."

Donnie let out a long breath and brought his gaze down. "At this point I can't th—" He didn't get to finish the sentence because Frank had grasped his head in both hands and pulled him closer to press a kiss on the top of his hair. He then embraced him tight. "I love you, man."

"Hey, get off me!"

"I love you!"

"Frank!" Donnie's tone was sharp. "Stop!" He shoved off his brother, who held up his hands in surrender. "Calm down, psycho."

"We're back, baby!" Frank clapped his hands and rubbed them as if he were cold.

"Now, hang on. Look. I want details on how *all* of this is going to work. I want to know *everything* you're doing and every limb you take. You pull off a fingernail, I want to know about it, okay? If someone has a fake arm or leg or head—"

"We don't do heads."

"Whatever. I don't want to be caught off guard. And I'm serious, do not get us in trouble. Get us to fifty grand, then we're done. Okay? Deal?"

"You got it." A knock came at Frank's door. He leapt off the couch and opened it. Cliff was standing on the other side. "Hey, man."

"Yo Yo! What's goin on?" Cliff asked.

"Just talkin," Frank replied.

Donnie got up off the couch. "I'm gonna go empty out the dehumidifiers. Then get back to calling the rest of the churches nearby—maybe I can get another outdoor funeral or two while all this is going on."

"Hey, what if we offer food for Tom's funeral? Would you cook?" Frank asked.

"Yeah. Didn't you already offer that?"

"Not yet. We can make it an early funeral, with a cookout afterward."

"We can't afford to do it for free, you know that, right?"

"I know. Maybe do it a little above cost. I'll run some numbers and see. The Cock Brothers won't cater unless it's from that BBQ joint."

"Bad Bobs?"

"No. They're not good enough for Bad Bobs," Frank said.

"If he'll do it here, then yeah, I'll cook up something. No problem. You want me to call him?"

"Nah, I got it. I'll do it now, hopefully before he calls those twats about coming to pick up the body."

"Let me know." Donnie left the room and walked down the hall into the kitchen.

Cliff leaned out the door to watch him, then turned to Frank. "Was that what you wanted?" he asked. "Did he think I was Ben?"

Frank mouthed for Cliff to close the door.

"What happened?"

"I needed him to think the funeral was being canceled tomorrow," Frank said.

Cliff shook his head slowly. "You're ridiculous." His tone was not playful—more irritated.

"What am I supposed to do? We're in a jam. It wasn't like it was a *full* lie. That same conversation happened thirty minutes ago between me and Ben. I just needed Donnie to hear it. He started talking about wanting to look at other options to make all that money for our roof and for remodeling—we don't have any time! Everything I told him was true. Ben called me to say he wanted to do it with the Kochs. Thought their place looked nicer."

"They talked to him?" Cliff asked.

"I don't know. Tried throwing in deals but he wasn't interested. Mentioned doing the funeral outside, he shot that down too. Finally, I asked if he'd reconsider if I had Donnie cook up something for the family and he said yes."

"Didn't he pay you a deposit? Just let him go and keep the deposit."

"No way. We need the business. And the Kochs offer to cover the lost deposit if someone switches over. This has happened once before," Frank said. "I figured if I could have Donnie watch all that play out, maybe it would give him enough sense of urgency to let me do the chess thing. And it worked; he's on board." He stood up and went back over to his desk.

"I mean, he has put together a handful of restaurants in his time, and I'm sure he's pretty decent at getting funds to do it. You didn't wanna just trust that he'd figure out a way to raise the money without having to make bones into bishops?"

Frank considered this. "First off, Bones to Bishops is an awesome name. Second, doing it this way seems easier. Albeit, not the most moral—I may have some trouble sleeping." He paused. "Look, you're probably right, but if someone is offering us an opportunity to make the money *now*, then it seems foolish not to take it. We're the last family-run funeral home in town, and when our competition looks like the love child of Paul Walker, Dwayne Johnson, and Channing Tatum, we have to up our game—make our own love child."

"I lost interest in this conversation at the all-male three-way," Cliff said.

"What I'm trying to say is that I'm all for Donnie helping us secure some extra money, but as long as our parlors and foyer stay looking like they do, customers will almost always choose *them* over us. And like I told him, this isn't forever. I'm only doing enough to get us back on our feet. Should be hardly any risk."

"As long as you don't bury left over parts in Asbury again."

"Touché," Frank replied. Cliff opened the door to leave. "You got clients right now?"

"Nah. Mondays are admin days for me. I only see two or three clients in the morning. What's up?"

"You want to go get a burger for lunch?" Frank asked.

"Where at?" Frank grinned and left Cliff hanging in suspense. Cliff's face came alive with excitement, lifting his eyebrows and rounding his mouth, making an "ooo" sound. "Hell yeah! Those milkshakes! Does Donnie wanna go?"

"Nah. He doesn't care for that place." Frank swiped his keys off the desk.

"What!" Cliff clicked his tongue off the roof of his mouth and shook his head. "His palate isn't sophisticated enough for Belew's."

12

Frank had been coming to Belew's Dairy Bar for thin burgers and peanut butter milkshakes since he was a kid. Despite the fact that it was tucked away on a tiny two-lane road in a little lake town fifteen miles outside of Murray, its presence was anything but hidden from locals or travelers. He could never understand how with no advertising—or even a website for that matter—the place had grown into such a summertime culinary treasure for so many. Frank was hopeful that he could find the perfect way to outsmart the rush by arriving at odd times: early lunches, early dinners, during severe thunderstorms, peak heat hours, weekdays during work hours. Nothing seemed to affect the crowd.

Today was no different; the parking lot was crammed full. His truck came to a stop as both he and Cliff let out a sigh that gave way to a guttural growl. The temperature was slated to be well above 105, but even this did little to deter the crowds standing at the windows and sitting at the picnic tables, taking their sweet time.

"Don't these people have jobs?" Frank asked.

"Right there!" Cliff pointed at an open space in the adjacent lot of the gas station and bait shop. "Can we park there?"

"If someone comes out, I'll go move it."

No one ever came to check on Frank's truck though he did see two teenage girls take a picture next to the skeleton decal on the side.

"It's never anyone attractive who takes a picture with that thing," Frank said, reaching for a collection of crinkle fries that had fallen onto the silver tray.

"Nah man, that girl from a couple weeks back was pretty hot." Cliff wiped his mouth with a napkin and threw it in his fry box.

"Yeah," Frank said. "She *was* hot. She was also standing beside her husband in the photo so . . ."

"He was pretty hot too."

Frank agreed. He offered Cliff the remaining fries, who waved them off. "You mind if I make a stop before we head back?"

Cliff face drooped. "You son of a bitch. Tell me we're not going to LBL. Or to go bury something."

Frank laughed. "It's just across the bridge. I want to run by the Visitor Center. See if they have any books on the cemeteries in LBL."

Cliff sighed.

"I need a new spot to bury what Living Pieces doesn't buy and I figured a book of cemeteries would help me hide the stuff better."

"You can't just bury the stuff in Murray? Or dump it into a coffin underneath the body?"

"I could do that. But I don't always have a funeral following a trade, and I don't want to keep the bones in the house in case Stutters gets curious and brings a warrant. You know once we dig up Corey's grave, he's gonna come looking for me—can't have any loose ends."

"Alright. But only to the Visitor Center. Don't be draggin' me to some decrepit spot in the woods."

Frank shoved the last of his burger into his mouth and gathered the remnants of lettuce and bread sprinkled across the table onto his tray. "You can't be this scared of ghosts." Frank chuckled.

"Bro. *Scooby-Doo* makes me nervous." They both got up and began walking to the truck. "Know what else makes me nervous? Being on that rickety old bridge."

"I know. Why do you think I brought you? Driving over that thing scares the shit out of me."

The Visitor Center was a short drive from Belew's, across the uncomfortably narrow two-lane Eggners Ferry Bridge. The beauty of the lake below was overshadowed by Frank and Cliff's fear of colliding with an oncoming car, or simply dropping to their death should the old, rusted out bridge suddenly decide to give way. Their eyes stayed glued on the road; Cliff was sitting noticeably tense in his seat as Frank drove slowly over, their hands digging into whatever they happen to be resting on. An audible breath escaped both their lips as they crossed to the other side.

When they pulled into the nearly empty parking lot, Frank reached into the glove box and pulled out a map. He noticed how worn it had become along the edges and down the center crease. "I could probably use a new map too."

Cliff noticed the markings Frank had made on it. "What are the different shapes?"

"Helps me know which cemeteries I'm interested in. The squares are the good spots I've seen. The triangles are ones I need to check out. The Xs are the ones that don't work; they're either still being used or they're by the road." He patted Cliff's arm with the back of his hand and pointed over to a sign by the door as they walked up the sidewalk.

Land Between the Lakes
Cemetery Clean-Up Day
Saturday 10, Sunday 18

"That's not good. You think they'll notice anything in the places you were at last week?" Cliff asked.

"I don't know. Should probably see which ones they're going to be cleaning, though."

Once inside, their attention was drawn to the walls depicting historic life in the area: murals, photos, artifacts, and taxidermied animals.

"Are you here for our reptile rodeo?" A robust man in overalls asked from behind the information desk.

"Excuse me?" Cliff asked, startled.

The jolly man pointed at a poster of a lizard on the wall. "We got a special presentation in about thirty minutes just out back there. Reptiles, snakes, spiders."

"Did you say rodeo?" Cliff asked.

"That's just the name," the man replied. "It's really just a chance for kids to see and touch stuff. But we get a lotta adults. Anything I can help you with? Need a map?"

"Yeah, a map would be great," Frank replied. He walked over to the desk. "Do you know anything about the cemetery clean-up?"

"Yessir. I'm one of the fellas putting it together. You interested in helpin'?" He replied.

"Maybe. Are you cleaning up *all* the cemeteries?"

"Oh, good Lord, no. We try to do as many as we can, but a lot of that depends on who shows up, what kind of day it is, how bad the places are, etcetera."

"Do you know which ones you're working on?" Frank asked.

"Got a list right here." The man bent down and began rummaging underneath the counter. "Well, thought I had one." He pulled up a chair and sat down at the computer, drawing up the glasses tied around his neck, and scanning the screen. "You boys in a hurry?" he asked.

"No. Not at all," Frank replied.

The man talked to himself and hummed as he searched through files. He pulled it up and printed off a copy. "Here we go," he slid it toward Frank.

"Can I keep this?"

"For three dollars."

Frank looked up at him and turned his head. "Three dollars?"

The man laughed. "Hell, I'm kiddin'. You can take it. As long as you're willin' to come volunteer." The man's face went serious for an awkward moment, and then he laughed again. "I'm kiddin' about that too." And then he went back to serious. "Unless you want to come help."

Frank chuckled. "Yeah, maybe."

"Y'all from around here?"

"We're out in Murray. I own a funeral home out there and he runs the gym next door."

"You own a gym next to his funeral home?"

"Yeah. Been open for about two years," Cliff replied.

"Hmm. Never heard a'that," the man said. "Business alright?"

"Seems to be," Cliff replied. "We do some client sharing. People who attend funerals always ask about the gym, and when I have really overweight clients or clients with heart conditions, I let these guys know to keep an eye out."

The man's smile faded. "You serious?"

"No." Cliff grinned. "That was a joke."

A raucous laugh erupted from the man. "That's a funny joke."

Frank studied the sheet. He recognized many of the names from his research and knew some of them were close together.

"That's my number up top. Just gimme a call if you decide to come with us, that way we don't leave without ya. A lot of the places are hard to find on your own."

"How 'bout a map?" Frank asked.

"Almost forgot." He crouched down and began shuffling items around. "You got family buried out here?"

"Nah, just like looking at old cemeteries," Frank replied.

"Lord alive! I swear Im'mo slap somebody. Who keeps moving the maps—oh! Here we are." The man straightened up and dropped a nicely folded square pamphlet onto the counter. "Now that actually is three dollars."

When he realized the man wasn't joking, Frank pulled out three dollars from his pocket and paid.

The map folded out to a large, colorful, two-sided illustration of the area. It was more detailed than the one Frank had in his car, and he noticed some differences immediately. Historic landmarks were added, trails were colored in more clearly, as were rivers. What caught his attention was that there were fewer cemeteries than in the one he had. He heard the man say something about the map being updated recently.

Frank leaned down onto the counter tracing trails with his finger and trying to mentally compare the copy to the one in his glove box. He scanned the north side for an isolated cemetery he intended to visit soon but to his surprise it wasn't there, at least not where he remembered. "Are there cemeteries missing on this map?" Frank asked.

"It's possible," the man replied.

Frank shifted the map on the counter for the man to examine and pointed his finger at where he remembered a cross marker to be; there was now only open space.

"I don't know for sure," the man said, "but if you remember there being a cemetery there, it's possible that it's been taken over. The map before this was done almost thirty years ago, so there's a good chance some things have changed. We have a book that details all the official burial spots—whether they're still here or not." The man pointed to the bookshelf and then continued to inspect the map. He turned it over to the south side illustration. "I'm a part of the committee that goes and scouts these things. For many of them, if we can't get to it—and we try—then chances are that cemetery is lost to nature." He ran his finger along the coastline. "We've lost a few of them over the years to the water."

"Does that book you were talking about have pictures?" Frank asked. "Of the layout or what they look like now?"

"Kinda sorta. There's some basic illustrations of how the plots are situated. The neat thing is that it includes every cemetery that's ever been on this peninsula that we know of—even ones not on the map. That one's forty."

"Jeez. Forty dollars?" Frank whistled. "Okay, well, I was kinda wanting something with pictures. I'll take the map for now and if I need the book, I'll come back." Frank thanked the man and turned around to notice Cliff standing over by the door looking up.

"You ready?" Frank asked.

"Yo, check it out. You see this?" Cliff pointed up. Hanging above the door was a large map. Frank recognized it immediately. It was Land Between the Lakes. This map was much older than anything Frank had seen in person or online. He yelled back to the man in the gift shop, "S'cuse me, sir?"

"Yessir," the man replied.

"How old is this map?"

The man's sigh sounded like a motorboat. He thought for a moment and then blurted out, "Not too sure. Nineteen forties? Maybe a little earlier?"

"You have a smaller copy I can have?"

"Nah, that's the only copy we got. It was donated to us years ago."

"You know who gave it to you?" Frank asked.

"Not a clue. It's been here a while," the man replied.

Frank took out his phone and took a photo of it.

13

The sight of a police cruiser in the driveway made Frank's insides shift. After he dropped Cliff back at the gym for Monty's appointment, he drove back into town to get the food Donnie needed for the funeral. Monty's car was still there when he returned. He tried calling Donnie to come out and help him carry in groceries but there was no answer. Frank saddled on all ten bags to his arms and waddled up the front steps into the house. He could hear Justin Bieber playing from the speakers in the kitchen and found Donnie standing at the counter over a roast, seasoning and stirring something in a pan.

"That smells awesome."

"Whoa," Donnie exclaimed when he saw Frank struggling with the bags. "Why didn't you call me to come help?"

Frank noticed the phone standing up next to the stove playing music. "I did call you, dingus. Turn your ringer on." Frank dropped the bags and went back to lock his car and close the door. "Is that dinner?"

"Yeah, should be ready in a couple hours. I didn't realize Suthers was working out with Cliff now. Freaked me out for a second when I was sweeping the porch."

"He say anything to you?" Frank asked.

"Nah. Cliff was moving a tire onto the driveway when he pulled in, so I think that distracted him. He waved, I waved." Donnie moved over to the bags and started picking through them. "Hey, Ben Flores called while you were gone." Frank froze. "Said he wanted to meet us at the cemetery to look at the plot and go over a couple of things."

"Did he say what he wanted to go over?" Frank asked.

"No. Said he has to leave pretty quick after the service tomorrow—just wants to discuss last-minute details."

"Oh. I've got something tonight that I need to be at—"

"I told him I'd take care of it. I didn't know when you were free and said I'd meet him after dinner." Donnie began taking things out of the bags. "We're planning for about ten or twelve guests, right? For food?"

"Yeah," Frank replied, "no more than twelve."

"Did you get everything at the store?" Donnie asked.

"Yup. They didn't have andouille, so I just got chorizo."

"Perfect. You talk to that other guy about the . . . *stuff*?" Donnie looked back toward the door, checking to see if anyone was around.

"Earlier, yeah. All set. He asked if I could come up with a few bones by Wednesday, shouldn't be a problem."

"Okay," Donnie said. He took a moment, processing the idea of sawing off parts of Tom Middleton's body, and then picked up his phone from the counter.

"But um . . ." Frank trailed off and leaned out the door into the foyer and looked around. "While we're on the subject, there's something I haven't told you." Donnie looked up. "A job. It's a bit of a weird one. But the pay is pretty nice."

"What kind of job?"

"You remember when Suthers was here on Saturday?" Donnie nodded. "After he left, I found a box outside by the door. Found it actually just before you left to go see Lexie. I didn't show you because I wasn't sure what it was." Frank waited for Donnie to say something—yell at him, even—but Donnie remained quiet. "There was something in it." Another pause. "Something from one of the graves." Frank could see Donnie's mouth beginning to open as if he were going to interject. "You remember that woman I had in your closet?"

"Piddleton, yeah," Donnie whispered. "What was in the box?"

"A sweater." Frank paused. "And a couple of pictures of me and Cliff at the spot. There was a note too."

Donnie rolled his eyes and sighed. "Son of a bitch," he said to himself.

Frank explained everything he knew: the anonymous letter, the phone call at the gas station, the letter about Corey Grassman's death, and what the caller wanted.

After a lengthy spell of quiet Donnie spoke while looking down at the floor. "What did you do with that sweater?"

"I've still got it. It's in my office." Donnie's hands shot up in frustration. "I'm getting rid of it—don't worry."

"Why does this guy want a book?" Donnie asked.

"Didn't say. I sorta think the kid was murdered. Maybe he's looking for the killer and suspects he wrote a note in the book."

"What's the kid's name, again?" Donnie asked.

"Corey Grassman. Ring a bell?"

Donnie thought for a moment. "No. When did he die?"

"Ninety-seven, I think. According to the letter there's some debate about whether he's actually dead."

Donnie said the name a couple more times to himself and shook his head. "He went to Calloway?"

"Yeah."

"You ask Dad about him?" Donnie asked.

"Hell no. In two days that name will be all over town. I don't want Dad tracing a grave robbery back to me."

"Wait . . . you're taking the job? We didn't agree on this. I said the other thing was fine—you never said anything about digging someone up."

"What do you want me to do? The guy has pictures of me and Cliff." Frank didn't give his brother a chance to fire back a response or ream him out. Instead, he went to his office and grabbed the note from his desk drawer. "He's buried in Old Salem Cemetery."

"Is that supposed to make this better?"

"No. I'm just trying to give you as much detail on this as I can, and keep the conversation going so you don't kick me in the nuts. It's close by. With me and Cliff doing it, I don't think it'll be too risky."

"That's over past the railroad tracks, right?" Donnie asked. Frank nodded and Donnie leaned against the counter, folding his arms, and biting his lip. "Why didn't you say something before now?"

"What would I have said? You told me to drop everything illegal. I didn't have a choice in this one."

"Still would have liked to know."

"I'm telling you now," Frank said, removing stuff from the bags on the floor. "Cliff and I are going tonight."

"Why do you keep dragging him into this?"

"Cause he's my boy." Frank shoved packs of deli meat into the refrigerator. "That, and I can't dig a grave by myself. With two of us there it's done in half the time. We could go faster if there were three—even less risky." Frank raised his eyebrows and pointed a finger at Donnie.

"Absolutely not," Donnie replied. He took a long pause, tapping his fingers against his chest. "This isn't good. The bones are one thing, but this . . ." He trailed off. "We don't even know who this guy is. Could be a trap. Could be nothing in there. Or it could be like last time and you screw up by digging around in the wrong cemetery."

"Like I said, I don't have much of a choice."

Another deep breath. "Guess not." Donnie straightened up and paced around the kitchen. He opened the pantry and stared inside for a few seconds, then shut the door. "What the hell are we doing?" He mumbled to himself in a whisper, rubbing his temples.

"Look at it like this: in a twisted way, it keeps us out of trouble. And it gets us money."

"Yeah, because thinking of it that way lessens the jail time. Perfect."

"You want to ride along with me and be my lookout?" Frank asked.

Donnie handed the paper back to his brother. "Let me know when we get the twenty grand and try not to get yourself arrested."

"I'll see what I can do." Frank felt his back pocket for the LBL maps but noticed they weren't there. He searched the bags on the floor. *Did I get them from the car?* He hadn't. The front seat and glove box were empty when he went out to check. Cliff must have taken them when he went in. *Dammit.*

Monty was inside throwing a medicine ball against the concrete wall and catching it while Cliff counted out loud. When Cliff noticed Frank standing there, he turned the music down.

"Wuddup?!" he yelled at Frank.

"Nothing," Frank replied. "Did you by chance take the papers from my car? Hey Mr. Suthers."

Monty was too out of breath to answer. He waved and continued throwing the ball. Frank walked in a few steps toward Cliff's desk and noticed that his map was lying on a stack of papers.

"The LBL map?" Cliff asked. Monty caught a glimpse of the abrupt expression on Frank's face as if Cliff had said something wrong. "Oh. Yeah. *The papers*." Monty averted his eyes when he noticed Cliff turn toward him. "They're on my desk."

Monty watched Frank pick up what looked like a brochure. *Land Between the Lakes?*

"Got it. Thanks, man."

Cliff finally called "fifteen" and Monty fell to his knees and gasped for air.

"Alright, I'll let you guys get back to it. Bye, Mr. Suthers." Frank waved.

Monty nodded his head, unable to respond with words. Instead, he gave a thumbs up and went back to catching his breath. *What's in Land Between the Lakes?*

14

Frank parked his truck in the same space as before near the side of the church. The soaking humidity left over from the previous night's storm was still in the air, prompting Cliff to heave a sound of disgust when he opened his door. The two sprayed themselves with bug repellant and put on gloves. There were no streetlights in this part of the town. It was a thick darkness with no moon above to illuminate their troublesome activity.

Frank pulled out a small ladder, and threw several bottles of water into his backpack, along with a handful of fruit snacks and peanut bags to munch on. He heard the shovels grind against the bed of the truck and peeked out to see Cliff holding them both. "You good?" Frank asked.

"Let's do it," Cliff replied. "No flashlights, right?"

"Definitely not." Frank led the way, creeping across the street, and up the rock steps into the cemetery.

"Whoa, whoa, whoa. What is this?" Cliff whispered to Frank, who had already begun to make his way over the grounds. Cliff was standing in front of the cemetery sign.

"As I am, so you will be . . . ? Hell nah!"

"It's a poem, man. Come on!" Frank replied.

"Man . . ." Cliff clicked his tongue and peered around. "This some bullshit."

Cliff's nerves started to ease up once the digging started. Frank knew to try and keep the conversation going to take Cliff's mind off the possibility of there being a ghost or ancient spirit to torment him. But as the digging got more strenuous, casual conversation faded. At one point, while Cliff was dumping the rest of a peanut bag into his mouth, he let out a choked, panicked noise and motioned for Frank to get down into the hole and out of view.

After an awkward quiet Frank whispered, "What did you see?"

"Shh!" Cliff shot back. Then, "I don't know. I thought I saw a light."

Frank peeked over the edge of earth and looked around, then raised his head a little more. There was nothing: no lights, no movement—nothing. "There hasn't been a car for nearly two hours. I'm sure we're fine. Come on." The two of them stood cautiously.

"Hey, you checked the grave, right? We're in the right one?" Cliff asked.

"Shup up," Frank whispered.

They continued digging off and on for nearly half an hour until Cliff's shovel made a harsh thud when it stabbed the dirt. Frank muttered a thanks to God and threw his shovel up onto the grass before getting onto his knees to clear dirt. Cliff started to go up the ladder. "Where you goin'?"

"I ain't lookin at what's in there! I haven't unseen the last two dead bodies you dragged me to." Cliff climbed out and retrieved a water from the backpack. Frank could hear him drinking and panting. He called for him to throw down the large Ziploc bag as he used Cliff's shovel to dig around the latches.

Frank worked his fingers around the earth and metal enough to get a grip and pulled so hard that when the coffin finally did crack open, he fell over onto his butt, knocking his head against the dirt. He cursed sharply, favoring his head, and peeked into the now open top half of the coffin.

At first glance he couldn't believe what he was seeing and thought the whole thing to be a joke. He expected to find Corey resting peacefully, wearing a black suit or maybe a sports jersey of some kind. Perhaps even a pair of jeans and his favorite t-shirt. He expected the body to show signs of decay, or be half decomposed—perhaps something even a little scary. What he didn't expect to see was *no* body in the coffin.

Donnie had gotten so sidetracked on the phone with Lexie that he left the house thirty minutes early for his meeting with Ben Flores at the Murray Cemetery. He didn't notice until he commented that Ben was late, and Lexie reminded him that it was only six thirty-five. A frustrated breath rattled out of his mouth as he put the car in park and cut the engine.

Donnie walked along the cemetery's paved pathways and continued chatting on the phone. It eventually buzzed in his ear with a text from Ben that he was close. Before he could text back, he saw Ben's car come through the main gate. Since he'd arrived, a handful of cars were now in the cemetery. The humidity had faded with the setting sun and given way to a pleasant evening.

Donnie said goodbye to Lexie and made his way through the fresh-cut grass over toward Tom Middleton's now open plot when he heard a voice at one of the graves nearby—a familiar voice—speaking softly. And then a *stutter*. He stopped and glanced around a headstone to see Monty Suthers, still in his uniform. Monty was sitting on a small stool, staring at the front of a sizable memorial stone. "Pfannerstill," Donnie whispered to himself. It wasn't a name he recognized. Two names were inscribed below it, but he couldn't make them out. A horn honked in the distance, startling both him and Monty. Donnie jerked himself away, back toward the road.

When he got out of his car, Ben confessed that he got lost coming in from Paducah, which Donnie waved off. "No worries. The plot is over here." He and Ben walked down the path toward the awning. "What can I help with?" Donnie could hear Ben talking, but he became distracted by Monty, who was now moving toward them, stool collapsed and in tow. Donnie told himself to look away as Monty was now only a few steps from them, but it was too late. Monty had made eye contact. "Hey Mr. Suthers," he said. Ben quit talking and looked up.

"Evenin'," Monty sighed. He stopped and looked at the two of them with a curious expression.

Donnie, uncomfortable with the silence, blurted out, "We're just going over some last-minute details before a funeral tomorrow. He had some questions about the graveside—" He was about to introduce Monty to Ben when he was cut off.

"Hey Ben. Good to see ya," Monty said, more genuinely than he had greeted Donnie. He extended his hand. "We m-m-met the other day at Tom's house." Monty then asked what time the service was. He told Ben that he and Tom went to the same church and that he might try to stop by if he could. There was an awkward moment of quiet, and once again Donnie felt he had to break it. "So, what brings you out here? More grave robberies?" *Why did I say that?*

Monty's eyebrows scrunched. "No. N-no grave robberies. Hope those are long done with." He surveyed a crowd gathering at the opposite end. "Just here visiting some . . ." He directed a thumb over his shoulder but looked as if he lost his train of thought. Finally, "Just f-f-figured it was a n-nice night, I guess. W-w-wanted to go for a walk."

"You have any relatives here?" Donnie said back.

Monty's eyes were looking past him and Ben toward the gate as if in a trance. His head gave the slightest of shakes before he spoke softly. "No. No relatives here. Just enjoying the evening." He reached to shake Ben's hand. "You guys have a g-good night." He turned to Donnie, placing his hand back in his pocket. "Donnie," he said, tipping his head.

Ben apparently didn't notice the obvious avoidance of hand shaking at the end. He immediately went back to what he was saying earlier. Ben explained to Donnie that he wouldn't be able to make it to the graveside as he was being called to work. He went over details with Donnie and asked if there was anything he needed to know before the service, or anything he needed to do before he left. The two of them discussed Tom's memorial, and how it would flow, as well as the order of events for the graveside.

"Also, a fair warning," Ben said, "there are a couple of people who are going to take pictures with Tom."

Donnie laughed. "No warning needed. Happens nearly every funeral. There's always someone who snaps a photo."

"No, no," Ben replied. "I mean, like, selfies with the body. Or group shots. I'm talkin' like ... set up the tripod and tell everyone to say cheese with Tom in the photo."

"Yeah," Donnie said, "perfectly normal. I mean, not *normal*, but ... normal."

"I didn't realize that was a thing," Ben said. "Glad I'm not the only one who grew up taking family photos with dead aunt Sylvia."

Donnie nodded. "I had to step in once after a funeral. A couple of distant cousins were taking selfies with the deceased, but they were dressing him up. They had put a hat on him, and a pair of sunglasses. Thankfully, I caught it before the wife or siblings saw it. I don't think they were trying to be disrespectful. But it was *completely* disrespectful."

"Glad to know you won't be judging the family tomorrow, then," Ben said.

"Now, if they sit the body up and pose with their arms around him like a scene from *Weekend at Bernie's*, I may have to say something." They shared a laugh. "Anything else I can do?"

"Nope," Ben said. "I think that's it. Thanks for meeting me here for this. Probably could have just chatted on the phone but I wanted to see the plot before I left. You guys have been great."

"It's not a problem," Donnie said. "Happy to do it. I'll see you all tomorrow morning. Call me if you have any other questions."

15

Frank attempted to process what his eyes were telling his brain. "What?" he whispered. His mind raced through all sorts of scenarios: *Was this a trap? Was he being Punk'd? Was he in the wrong grave?* Panic was rising in his throat. "Cliff," Frank yelled in a whisper. There was no answer.

"Cliff." Again, no answer. "Cliff!" Frank's voice was getting louder. *Maybe it was a trap.* "Shit." He paused and looked back at the casket. "Cli—"

"Dude, I hear you."

"Why didn't you answer?" Frank asked.

"I did. I didn't want to yell."

"Get me a flashlight, will ya?" Frank asked.

"You told me not to bring any." Silence. "Yo, I ain't walking back to the truck by myself." Another moment of quiet. "What's wrong?"

"I don't know yet! But I need a flashlight!"

"Dammit," Cliff sighed.

"You come down here and make sense of this and I'll go get the flashlight, then," Frank called back.

"I ain't goin' down there with that!" Cliff shot back. "I'll be back."

"Hurry up."

He suddenly remembered the flashlight on his phone and pulled it out of his pocket to scan the casket. "What the hell is that?" The casket was filled with what Frank would have estimated to be over a hundred different objects: shirts, jerseys, books, CDs, VHS tapes, papers, toys, pictures. He got down and sifted through the mess as Cliff came running back.

"Here's the—are you kidding me! I thought you didn't have a light! Whoa." Cliff paused, taking in the sight. "What is that?"

"See for yourself," Frank moved away and shined the light toward the full coffin.

"The hell is all that?" Cliff exclaimed in a whisper.

"Exactly."

"They buried him with all of that?"

"I don't think they buried him," Frank replied.

"Move some of the stuff around and see if he's underneath," Cliff said.

Frank held the light to his face, giving Cliff a tight-lipped expression. "You think they just dumped this stuff on top of him?" He moved the phone to his pocket and began pulling stuff out of the coffin.

"Man, I don't know! What are you doing?" Cliff asked.

Frank was on his knees, frantically removing items and tossing them aside.

"Yo, what are you doing?!"

Frank suddenly stopped and sat up. "Trying to find the . . ." He trailed off. "Shit, I can't see. Can you shine that light?" He called up. Cliff looked around for any onlookers and kneeled down to hopefully suppress any unwanted illumination. "Move over here and shine it down so I can see inside the bottom." Frank was on his knees, with his head peering into the bottom portion of the casket. "I think I got something." He reached his hand in and began feeling around. After a couple of maneuvers, he pulled his arm out, holding a large red book.

"Is that it?" Cliff asked.

"I guess." He flipped through the pages with his fingertips to reveal signs of handwriting. "Yeah. This is it. Here." Frank put the leather book into the plastic bag and tossed it up to Cliff. He remained in the hole, staring at the disarray for a little while longer. Cliff said something, but it was drowned out by the hundreds of questions racing through Frank's mind.

"Frank!" Cliff whisper yelled. "Let's go!"

Frank took a picture of the casket and the items on the ground before throwing them all back inside. He stood on the lid to mash it closed and crawled out of the hole. After pulling the ladder out, the two of them erratically shoveled the dirt back into the hole and made their way back to the truck. Frank was down the cemetery steps and halfway across the road when he stopped and turned around, looking back toward the grave.

"What's up?" Cliff asked.

"I wonder if he's watching us?"

"Who?" Cliff asked.

"The guy. Or the girl." Frank held up the book "Whoever wants this. Hold up. I need to go back and just make sure we didn't leave anything out." The two of them had done an exceptional job cleaning up. Cliff had even patted down the dirt to keep the fresh mound nearly out of view from the road.

Cliff was sitting in the truck looking through pictures of the casket when Frank returned. "You think that guy was messing with you?"

"Who?" Frank asked.

"The guy who set this up. The pay phone guy."

"Doesn't seem like it. The book was there, we got what he wanted."

"But the Corey kid *wasn't* in there. How would he know that a book was in there but no body?" Cliff said.

"Maybe he did and didn't want to tell us."

"Seems like a pretty important detail," Cliff said, staring ahead. Then, "Who did the funeral?"

"No clue," Frank said. "It wasn't us. Definitely wasn't the Kochs—the coffin was still in good shape. Maybe Shanahan or King."

"Is that normal for people to fill a coffin like that?"

"Sure, but usually there's a body. If he's missing, then why buy a coffin? I've never had someone do that—especially one as nice as that. Usually there's just a memorial. No casket, no burial."

"Could you call the funeral home and ask what happened? Do they keep records like that?"

"Any home around in ninety-seven—except for us and Life—is out of business. Most all those records are with the Kochs now. Guess I can talk to Dad."

"Or maybe talk to someone who was at the funeral," Cliff suggested.

"How would I know who went to his—" Frank looked over to see Cliff was holding the book.

"If he died in ninety-seven, we're bound to know somebody in here," Cliff suggested.

TUESDAY
16

Despite the late night and strenuous labor, Frank willed himself out of bed before dawn. He crept down into the preparation room to finish preparing and removing parts of Tom's corpse. Even with only running on a few hours of sleep, adrenaline over an outdoor funeral—and keeping Tom's fake body parts hidden—was keeping him alert. By the time he was finished, Donnie was finishing up breakfast in the kitchen and getting ready to move tables and chairs outside.

Ben Flores arrived a little before nine, along with who Frank assumed to be his girlfriend. She was wearing white capris and a bubble gum pink blouse. Frank thought to go and introduce himself but she began talking to herself and raised a finger up to her ear to adjust what he guessed was an earpiece before going to sit by herself. Frank instead waved at Ben and walked over to the family room.

Ben stood over his former father-in-law's body looking somber. Frank decided to give Ben some time to himself and began putting water bottles in a cooler, trying to make it seem as if he was doing something useful, all the while watching Ben's body language. Tom's arm and hand had been switched with silicone replacements and hidden under a folded Nashville Predators jersey. Should Ben make any move to touch or look, Frank would have to distract. The moment passed with nothing but a simple head nod. Ben turned around and walked back toward Frank, giving a thumbs up.

By nine-thirty, people had begun to arrive. Two friends of Tom assisted Frank and Donnie with moving the casket outside, to the front of the seating area. Ginny and Dave welcomed guests in the parking lot and ushered them around the side of the house, to the back yard.

Frank asked Ben to join him in his office to go over the details of the morning. He handed Ben a copy of the program. "I have the song you recommended set to play before you give the eulogy but it's an easy switch if you'd rather hold it off until the end."

"Actually, I meant to tell Donnie last night, but you mind if Tom's cousin shares a memory before I get up? Something short?"

"Yeah, no problem." Frank made a note in his binder. "I'll skip the song and play it at the end. When Addy gets here, I'll introduce you to him. At about five minutes till, I'm going to call you along with the pallbearers back into the kitchen—just right through the back door—and give a quick overview of the service so we're all on the same page." Frank took a sip of his coffee and set the mug on the desk.

"What about payment? Are we all settled?" Ben asked.

"Yeah, I think we're good. Don't sweat it; this is a family day. I'll double check your invoice tonight and give you a call tomorrow if I need to."

"Just charge whatever else to the card I gave you. I'm not worried about it," Ben said.

Frank checked his watch. "All set? Any questions?"

"Nope. I'm good."

Frank now checked his phone for a text or call from Addy who was late. "Hang on, sorry." He typed out a text and hit send, taking another sip of his coffee.

Ben stifled a laugh when he noticed the writing on Frank's mug. "Tell me you have more of those mugs," he said.

"Oh definitely. This is the twenty-seventeen mug. I've got plenty. Sell them for ten apiece. You want one?"

Ben fished out twenty dollars from his wallet. "I want two."

"Sweet," Frank said. He walked over to a cabinet at the far end of his office and pulled out two small, black boxes. Inscribed on the box's side was the red Burgers Brothers logo: two Bs back-to-back, with a subtle image of a casket in the middle where the lines meet. Ben opened the package and pulled out a white mug. On it was a cartoon skeleton wearing a tuxedo, sitting in a large armchair with its legs crossed. In one hand was a brandy snifter and beneath the picture were the words, *For Your*

Viewing Pleasure. Beneath it, *Burgers Brothers 2017.* "These are awesome," Ben said. "You do one every year?"

"The last seven, yeah. Usually around Christmas. Twenty-ten was my favorite. I only made about twenty and broke mine last year. Keep hoping one surfaces at a flea market around here so I can get another one."

A knock rapped behind him at the door where the girl in the bubble gum blouse stood. "Oh, hey babe. Check these out. Frank, this is my fiancée, Shannon. Shannon, this is Frank. He runs the home."

Shannon stepped in, smiling, and stuck out her hand to shake. "Nice to meet you." Her laugh was genuine when she saw the mugs. "These are hysterical."

Donnie peeked his head in with a knock. "Hey, you seen Addy?"

Frank checked his phone again, no response. "No. I'll try calling him."

"You got a backup?" Donnie asked.

"Me," Frank said. "He sent me his notes last night. I'm sure he'll be here."

Ben noticed Donnie's eyes connect with Shannon. "Oh. Hey, Donnie." He pointed over to his right. "Sorry, this is my fiancée, Shannon. Babe, this is Donnie Burgers."

"Hey," Donnie replied, stepping into the room to shake her hand. "Nice to meet you."

She shook his hand with a curious grin. "We've actually met before."

"Oh." The comment caught Donnie off guard. "Are you from Murray?"

"No." She laughed. "I live in Lexington. It was in Puerto Rico—The Lure, right?"

Donnie held out "What!" for a brief moment. "You ate there?"

"I was there with a friend. She was a food critic. You came out and talked with us; sent us out a bunch of apps to try." She chuckled. "I think she gave you her number before we left."

Donnie's head turned down toward the floor, and then sprang back up, "Oh my God! Yeah! Shannon...um..." Donnie snapped his fingers.

"I remember you guys. She wrote for an online food blog . . . Jane . . . Jamie . . . uh . . . Jersey. Jersey James!"

"That's her."

"I'm pretty sure Jersey James is *not* the name of a food critic," Frank said softly.

"Shannon . . . Pennington!" Donnie exclaimed.

Her eyebrows shot up in surprise. "Wow. Color me impressed," she said back.

Donnie smiled. "I'm good with names." He glanced at his watch. "Shoot. I gotta get back to work. So great to meet you guys—or, I guess, nice to see you again. Small world."

Shannon held up the mug and asked about coffee so Frank took them to the refreshment stand he had set up outside and poured them a cup. He noted the time and instructed Ben that he would pull him and the family to the back shortly.

"Actually, it's just us," Ben said, sipping his mug.

"No family at all? Nobody showed up?" Frank asked, surprised.

"I mean, two of his cousins and a nephew are here. Some close friends—they're all the ones staying for lunch. But his siblings . . ." Ben turned to look at Shannon, and then shrugged. "They're weird. I don't know what the deal is. Thought they'd show up last minute but, guess not."

"Wow," Frank said. "I'm really sorry. Is there anything I can do? To help?"

"Nah, I think we're good. Their loss, right?"

"Hey, so, what's up with Land Between the Lakes?" Shannon asked.

"What do you mean? Like, how do you get there?"

"No, I mean. What's the story behind it? That's why no one wants to come, right?" Shannon asked Ben. She turned to Frank when Ben shook his head and smiled nervously. "Apparently there's something to do with—"

"Babe," Ben cut in. He turned and tapped her on the arm lightly with his hand. "Can we not? It's stupid and it's their deal; if they wanna be a bunch of whack-a-doos and not come to their brother's funeral, none of my business."

"That was their reason?" Frank asked. "Land Between the Lakes?"

Ben bit his lower lip, and let out a soft laugh, throwing up his hands. "I don't know. I got a text yesterday that they were all of a sudden deciding to fly in last minute. Then his brother called me this morning and said they weren't; said it was something to do with having to drive through Land Between the Lakes. I tried to understand the reasoning, but I've learned that's probably asking too much with those guys. And, you know what? I don't care at this point. The less drama, the better." He tipped his mug up as if to say *cheers*.

An alert buzzed on Frank's phone signaling it was almost time. He excused himself to go and call Addy but there was no answer. Frank went into the kitchen to check with Donnie who hadn't heard from him either. "Man, this is the second time he's done this in a week. What is his deal?" Frank said.

"You tried calling?"

"Yeah. He doesn't answer," Frank replied. "Hey, nice moves with the memory, by the way. How'd you remember that girl's name?"

Donnie grinned. "She had the same name as my friend from middle school—Pennington. Not a lot of people with that name. Always stuck out to me."

"Smooth, brudda," Frank said back in an exaggerated Jamaican accent. He looked at his watch and sighed a curse. He was going to have to do the service himself. He went back to his office to print off Addy's notes. The printer began to whir as Frank looked out through the blinds and noticed Monty's cruiser now sitting on the side of the road. Monty himself was walking up the driveway. "Oh, come on!" Frank exclaimed.

17

"We got a problem," Frank said as he walked into the kitchen. "Stutters is here."

Donnie was standing over the stove, licking sauce off his finger. "I know. Ben invited him yesterday. He was at the cemetery too."

"What? Why was Suthers at the cemetery?"

"I don't know," Donnie replied, adding salt to another dish. "When Ben and I got there, he was already there looking at a grave nearby—"

"Which grave?" Frank interrupted.

"Someone over by Tom's."

"Who was it?"

"I can't remember—I didn't recognize the name."

"What was the name?"

"Dude!" Donnie exclaimed. "I don't know! Jeez!"

"Sorry," Frank replied. "Why did he invite him? They know each other?"

"Nah, Monty said he knew Tom from church." Donnie quickly checked the dishes inside the oven.

Frank walked over to the back door. "Great. He's standing by the body, talking to Ben."

"What are you freaking out over? It's a funeral. He knew the guy. Relax."

"I'm freaking out because Tom doesn't have an arm. Or a leg. All Deputy Dewey has to do is touch Tom's hand and he'll know something's wrong."

"I'm sure he's not gonna touch his hand. That's more of an emotional gesture."

"It's got nothing to do with emotion, he's looking for something suspicious. Anything to pin me with," Frank said.

"Frank. He accused you of grave robbing, not harvesting body parts.

Just don't act weird." Donnie dipped his finger back in the saucepan, and then into his mouth. There was a tight, wet *click* when he pulled it out.

"Didn't feel like washing the saliva off before you stuck your finger back in there?" Frank asked.

"It's a chef's secret. Adds flavor," Donnie said dryly, not taking his eye off the pan.

"Gross," Frank said. He checked his phone; still nothing from Addy.

Frank walked down the middle aisle toward Ben and Shannon—and Monty. They were standing at the casket. He reached out his hand and gently touched just behind Ben's elbow to get his attention, "Hey, it's time to come on back. You wanna grab the other pallbearers?" He motioned toward the house. Frank was about to distract Monty away from the Predators Jersey when a hand suddenly landed on his shoulder, startling him.

"Good morning, Frank," the voice said. Frank jumped, turning to see Eugene Atlas, his formal high school principal standing behind him. "Did I scare you?"

"Hey, Mr. Atlas, good morning. No." Frank chuckled. "Thought I was bumping into someone. It's good to see ya. You knew Tom?"

"I did. Of course, livin' here all my life, can't say there's many I don't know. Old golfin' buddy of mine," he said with a bob of his head.

"How are ya?" Frank asked.

"Feelin pretty good this morning. Knees are little achy but I'll manage. I'm gonna see if I can pay my respects up here before we start, if that's okay." He grasped Frank's hand in an awkward gesture and shook it as he stepped away.

"Yes, sir. Let me know if I can get you anything."

Eugene and Monty stood beside Tom's body for a moment. They exchanged words that Frank couldn't hear before Eugene patted Monty on the arm and hobbled over to his seat, near the front. Frank waited, motionless, unsure of whether to pull Monty away or not. "Mr. Suthers, we're gonna start, if you'd like to find a seat," Frank said.

Monty turned and eyed him suspiciously, then shifted his gaze to the jersey. "You guys did good," he said, placing a fist over the Predators logo and patting it. He looked to Frank and gave a single nod, then inched past, and down the aisle.

Frank let out the breath he'd been holding after Monty stepped past and cursed quietly to himself. He checked the body again, then started back up the aisle toward the house.

●●

After the prayer by a nephew, Frank delivered Addy's words on the human spirit and Tom's belief in God. Ben, without shedding a tear, offered the eulogy, recounting two stories about Tom that encouraged a hearty laugh from the audience. Frank had left the coffin open during the service and at the close of his final announcement walked over to it and put his hand on the lid. He looked down and caught a glimmer of the necklace he'd only a week before dug up and removed from Tom's ex-wife. The chain came down around Tom's collar and fed underneath the light blue button-up. Frank couldn't help but chuckle a little to himself as he closed the lid. As the requested song played over the speaker, he backed the hearse onto the grass and the pallbearers carried Tom's coffin down the middle aisle and placed him inside.

While Frank was waiting in the hearse for the escort to arrive, he scrolled through listings of different yard games on Amazon. A figure approached his window and rapped on the glass making him jump and swear. It was Monty. Frank brought down his window. "You scared the crap out of me," he breathed.

"Wh-Wh-What happened to the p-p-preacher?"

"Addy? We have no idea. He didn't show up this morning."

Monty grunted and continued on his way.

"Headin' back to work?" Frank asked, leaning his head out.

"Technically, I'm w-workin' now," Monty replied, turning to address him.

"Yeah," Frank said. At a loss for what to say next, and caught in an uncomfortable stare, he patted the side of the hearse and said, "Me too." The "me" was held out for an awkwardly long time. An uncomfortable silence between them followed.

Monty's raised his eyebrows and nodded. "Okay then. I'll see you at the g-g-graveside." He turned and started toward his cruiser.

Frank put the window up and spoke to himself in the rearview mirror. "Smooth, Frank. Real smooth."

18

Monty closed the door of his cruiser and pumped the AC to full blast. He put the windows down, and let the car idle on the side of the street while he waited for the escort. Dispatch was on the radio about something, but he'd tuned it out, trying to analyze Frank's behavior. He seemed nervous, but why? Monty's gut told him that something wasn't right with this funeral. But maybe he was overthinking; maybe he *wanted* something to be off.

Two policemen arrived on motor bikes and motioned for Frank follow. Monty fell in behind the line of cars making their way leisurely toward Murray City Cemetery. A sharper tone on the radio cut through the cloudy mental chatter of Monty's brain and snapped his mind back to reality. He identified himself and requested dispatch to repeat the report. A domestic disturbance in Coldwater. A woman called the police claiming that her husband had been physically assaulted by a third party.

"I'm on my way to a graveside. Tanner's on duty, check with him and let me know."

"They specifically asked for you. Call came in just a bit ago."

Who do I know in Coldwater? "You got an address?"

Dispatch gave him the address. "The house is registered under Sophia and Nick Stills. She's the one who called it in."

A wave of pressure bubbled up from Monty's stomach into his chest. "I got it. I'm right there."

"I thought you were at a funeral," dispatch came back.

"I'm getting ready to turn on 121 South. Be there soon." Monty flipped on the cruiser's lights and siren on as he pulled around the caravan, speeding past Frank and the escort.

☠

When Monty arrived at Sophia's house, she was sitting outside on a swing that hung down from the giant silver maple tree in her front yard.

She stood up when she saw that it was him and walked over, giving him a hug when he got out of the cruiser. "I was hoping it would be you."

"I got a c-c-call that there was a d-domestic d-disturbance," Monty said. "Where's your husband?"

"He left about ten minutes ago."

"You okay? What happened?"

She explained that her husband had lost his job that morning and that when he called to deliver the news, she could tell that he had already been drinking.

"He drinks this early?"

Sophia made a sound of disgust. "You don't know Nick. Depending on the day, this is late to him." She explained that anger and alcohol didn't mix well for her husband and thought she better call for someone to help get him calmed down before he hurt himself. More than likely he was going to come home, have more to drink, and then get back out. So, she had called Addy Michaels.

"The preacher?" he asked.

"Yes," she replied.

"He was sup-p-posed to be at a f-fu-funeral this morning."

"Oh. I didn't know."

"You suspected your husband to be drunk and you c-called a p-preacher?"

"The three of us have been friends since we were kids. It seemed like a good idea at the time." She shrugged and took a seat back on the swing, exhaling out a long breath. "I don't know what I expected him to do. I really just wanted someone to be here when he got hom." She explained that when Nick arrived, she and Addy were talking on the steps of the house. Nick became belligerent; started calling her names and accusing her and Addy of having an affair.

"When Nick said that, Addy got up and walked over to him. It seemed like he was trying to keep his cool, but Nick just kept going. I couldn't hear what Addy was saying to him, but I saw him approach

Nick's car and then . . ." She paused again. "Out of nowhere, Nick pushed him—like, hard. Addy's back hit the car, but he didn't do anything—at first. They talked for maybe five seconds more and then . . . that was it. Before I knew it, Addy had Nick by the throat, and just started punching him. I yelled for him to stop. He looked back at me, and when he did, Nick shoved him off and picked up a rock to hit him with. Addy ducked out of the way and then slammed Nick's head into the car door—the window, actually." She pointed over toward the driveway where Monty could make out the shimmer of glass shards on the rocks.

He ran both hands over his mouth, stretching his face down as he let out a frustrated sigh.

"That's when I ran inside and called the police. I came out and Addy was kneeling on the ground, trying to talk with Nick but he was out cold. Addy asked if he could wait inside—for Nick to wake up, but I told him that he needed to go. He really didn't want to leave him that way, he thought waiting would be best. But when I told him I called the police, he left."

Monty looked around. The car in question was gone. "Where's Nick?"

"Left as soon as he came to."

"How l-long was he unconscious?" Monty asked.

"Not long. Couple minutes, maybe. When Addy left, I sat with Nick until he woke up. He pushed me off and . . ." Sophia stopped and took in a deep breath. "He called me all sorts'a names. Then he drove off."

"He say where he was going?" Monty asked.

"No. But if I had to guess I'd say he went to Vitello's Bar."

"Vitello's b-bar is open at eleven in the m-morning?"

"Ten, actually."

"I know you said you c-called Addy because he knows you and Nick. Is that the only reason?"

Sophia didn't answer.

"W-w-were you afraid s-something would happen?"

She redirected her gaze from Monty to the ground. "I figured if Addy was here, maybe Nick wouldn't try anything." She swallowed and tightened her lips.

"Sophia. D-does your h-h-husband h-hit you?"

She continued staring at the ground and finally looked over at him, meeting his eyes. The corners of her mouth slowly drew upward, a soft smile. "I hope you don't think this is mean. I had a stutter when I was younger. Had it all the way through high school. Did I ever tell you that?"

Monty didn't know what to say. "No. You didn't."

"I hated how people looked at me when I was a kid—especially while I was talking to them. Made me sick to think about having to speak to someone—most times I never would. You wouldn't believe it now with as much as I go on and on about things." She looked over toward her house. "You're a lot braver than I am."

"D-does Nick h-hu-hurt you?"

She turned her head back toward him—pain and fatigue in her eyes, and, Monty thought, a hint of confidence. She seemed to slump in surrender. "Sometimes. Yeah. If it's a bad day at work. Thankfully, he doesn't get too many of those. His parents can be a trigger, too. He's not an angry drunk, but if he's angry, he will become drunk, and then . . . yeah."

"Okay," he said.

"What are you going to do to him?"

"Probably not much of anything today." He got to his feet. "Sophia, if he's h-hurting you, I advise you to get some h-h-help. Okay? And I'm not just saying this as a p-police officer. Don't wait on this. If there's a p-problem with abuse, get help now. Okay?"

"Okay," she replied.

Monty's demeanor noticeably changed in front of her. "I mean it," he said.

"I will. We will."

"Where did Addy go? Any idea?" he asked.

"He didn't say, why?"

"'Cause he's the one I have to go after now."

"Why him?"

"Did you see Nick attack Addy?"

"He pushed him and tried to hit him with that rock."

"So, if I'm understanding you right, N-N-Nick called you about his job, y-y-you called Addy, afraid that Nick would be upset and take it out on you—w-which you were right to think—but instead Addy attacked your husband?"

Sophia thought about Monty's explanation. "But he was protecting me."

"But Nick hadn't done anything yet," Monty replied.

"I mean, he pushed him—technically, he started it."

"I kn-kn-know. And I b-b-believe you. But going after your husband for p-pushing someone is hard to justify w-w-when he's w-wearing Addy's bruises."

Sophia didn't make eye contact. She just nodded her head and whispered, "Okay."

"Okay. Are y-you sure y-your husband had b-been drinkin' when he got home?" Monty asked.

"No . . ."

"I'll run to Vitello's to see if he's there and try t-to get a statement about what happened. If he c-c-comes back home, c-c-call me." He pulled out his card and began writing his number but she stopped him saying she already had one. "I'll go check on Addy, then."

"You're not going to arrest him, are you?" she asked.

Monty sighed. "We'll see."

19

When Addy heard the knock at the door, his heart sank. "Dammit," he whispered. Officer Suthers was standing on the other side.

"Hey preacher," Monty said. "I come in?"

Addy didn't hesitate. He stood back and away from the door. "Yes sir. Come in." Addy replied. "What's up?"

Monty turned around and looked at him as if he just asked if the world was flat. "W-w-what do you mean *w-what's up*? You were supposed to be at Tom's funeral this morning—where were you?"

Oh, Addy thought. *Maybe he doesn't know.* "I got sick last night—called Frank just a little bit ago. I take it you went. Everything go okay?"

Monty pushed a breath out through his mouth sounding to Addy like the beginning of a laugh. "Wow," Monty muttered. "I'm disappointed. Y-y-you're the last p-p-person I expected to lie to me."

He knows.

"W-what happened at Sophia's?" Monty asked. Addy didn't flinch and held his gaze. "I've already talked w-with her. Come on."

"Shit," Addy breathed out. He sat down on the couch and switched the TV off. "What did she tell you?"

"Assume she t-t-told me everything. I w-want to hear it from you."

Addy gave in and began to explain the situation: the call from Sophia, the relationship he had with her, what he knew of Nick, and the experiences he had with Nick in the past.

"I d-d-didn't realize she and that asshole w-w-went to our church," Monty confessed.

"You might notice them if you stayed through the entire service."

"W-why did you hit him?"

"You said it yourself: the guy's an asshole. He needed to be hit," Addy replied, coldly.

"P-p-probably true," Monty sat down on the couch, "but you said you've known him for a w-while. I get the f-f-feel-feeling that he's always been a prick. Is there anything b-b-be-be—" Monty paused, and internally reminded himself to slow down. "Something going on between you and Sophia?" He immediately regretted asking the question.

Addy looked appalled. "What? No! Absolutely not, she's married. Why would you even ask that?"

Monty's head fell to the side, eyeing Addy suspiciously.

"Yeah, okay, fine. I get that I may have hit someone, and I just lied to your face, but what kind of person do you think I am to go after a married woman?"

"I've seen crazier," Monty replied. "So, w-why'd you hit him?"

"He said something."

"No kiddin'," Monty replied, sarcastically.

"It was something personal."

"Like what?"

Addy sat on this one for a while. He was embarrassed about the entire situation now and wished that he could just take everything back. As much as Nick deserved what he got, it didn't need to come at the price of his job and that's exactly what Addy put on the line when he drove Nick's head into that car window. Addy then spoke slowly, "He asked why I was there. I told him that I was visiting someone in the neighborhood, and I was just dropping by to say hey. Then he made some accusation about Sophia cheating on him with me and I told him I wouldn't do that. And then he brought up what happened at my last job and I tried—"

Monty cut him off. "Y-y-you were let go, right?"

"I was. It wasn't for messin' with someone's wife, though. Just so we're clear."

"So, what were you doin'?"

Addy kept quiet. No matter how remorseful you might be about your past, it always affected how people perceived you. The board that hired Addy felt his situation warranted forgiveness and believed it was *not* something the board needed to share with members of the congregation. They were comfortable saying that he was released from his previous employment over an ethical disagreement and encouraged him to keep the details of termination to himself to avoid unnecessary gossip. It was no one's business; it was in the past. "I'd rather not say," he finally said. Monty's head fell. "Look, I know I screwed this up. What happened at my last job—all due respect—I'd like to keep between me and the guys that hired me."

Monty sat back, rubbing at the back of his neck. "Addy, I'm gonna have to—"

"Mr. Suthers," Addy cut in, nervously chuckling. "I can't tell you how bad this will be for me if it gets out. There won't be a chance to explain; I'll just be fired."

"Addy y-y-you drove a guy's head through a w-window," Monty replied. "W-what am I supposed to do?"

"He wasn't in a good space when he got home. He was gonna do something."

"Y-y-you can prove that?"

Addy looked away, and shook his head in defeat. "No . . ."

Monty sighed. "Yeah." The two of them sat quiet. "How long have you known about them?" Monty asked.

"Suspected it for a while. She had a bruise on her forearm at church one time. She'd reached over and grabbed my hand as she was walking out the door and when I looked down, I saw something peeking from under her sleeve. So, I turned her arm, and slid her shirt sleeve up; there was a dark set of bruising—like someone had been holding her wrist. I'm sure my look was concerning because when I asked what happened, she laughed and told me there was nothing to worry about. I made some passing comment about Nick and I distinctly remember her being uneasy. I told her to let me know if I could do anything—I could tell she knew what I meant but a second later she waved it off, and said she was fine.

"That's p-p-pr-probably why she called today," Monty said.

"Yeah. I guess she thought I would help deescalate the situation. I don't think either of us thought he'd react like that. I tried to keep him calm, but he made a comment that the reason I lost my last job was because I stuck my nose where it didn't belong. And that he would make sure it happened again. That's what did it. So, I punched him. And when he picked up that rock, his head went through the window."

"You're n-n-not making my job easy. Sophia t-t-told dispatch w-what happened. A report has already started. W-w-wha-what am I supposed to do? Just say everything is f-fine?" Monty asked.

"I don't know," Addy replied. "Anything but arrest me."

Monty got off the couch and walked over to the door. He breathed out a curse and finally spoke, "Okay. I'll t-t-take care of it—say that everything was a misunderstanding. The husband fell, and when Sophia walked outside, she thought you w-we-were attacking him. I don't know, I'll figure it out."

"You serious?" Addy asked.

"Yeah. But y-you listen to me," Monty said sternly. "You of all people know how sensitive y-your p-position is. W-what if someone else had seen you go over there today? Or seen you hit her husband? If I were you, I'd b-be a b-bit more careful with your p-public image. I know you're t-t-trying to h-he-help but m-m-maybe you should think about ge-get-getting your own temper under control."

Addy sat there quietly, nodding to himself.

"Next time this happens, you need to call me. I got a similar feeling about that scum bag earlier and as glad as I am to see him get his, y-y-*you* can't b-b-be the one to do it. Y-y-you understand me? I'm not sticking up for you again."

Addy nodded. "Yes sir." There was another pause. "I owe ya."

"Yeah, you do." Monty opened the door and paused.

"What are you gonna do about Nick?"

"Not sure. I don't think he knows that she called the police. Just have to hope he doesn't press charges."

"I mean in regard to her. I can't let him keep doing that."

"You're gonna have to," Monty said. "Don't you go near him, again. Maybe you should take your own Sunday advice and p-pray for yourself; ask for a little self-control."

"Not a bad idea."

⦿

Monty left Addy's apartment and headed back into town. He turned onto Old Salem Road and cut off the radio, going over the situation in his head and talking to himself about how he could handle reporting what had happened. Given Sophia's assessment of her husband, it was more than likely that Nick would be drunk—or heavily buzzed—by now. *Was Nick going to be defensive? How would he respond after finding out that she called the police? Was there a way to talk with him and get him to open up—*

Monty slammed on the brakes—a cat leapt onto the road and quickly cut back before deciding to continue its original path. Monty yelled as the cruiser came to a stop. He watched the cat dart to the other side, and into the field. Monty's eyes followed its path into the Old Salem Cemetery on the right.

He let out a breath and checked his mirror to make sure no one was behind him. "Stupid cat." It had slowed down to a walk, moving gracefully through grass as if its near brush with death was no big deal. And that's when Monty saw it. He had driven right by it earlier, but his mind had been so preoccupied with Sophia and the preacher that he wasn't paying attention. In a field of green, one grave stood out. The grass just below the headstone had been upturned into a mound of dirt. Normally Monty wouldn't think twice about something so trivial, but given the recent events, something about this was unsettling.

He flicked his light bar on to get the attention of oncoming drivers to slow down and he stepped out. Monty had never been in this cemetery. He looked around the grounds to see if there was anything suspicious—tire tracks, footprints, or something where it should not be. Everything looked normal except a large patch of fresh dirt at a headstone. "Corey Grassman," Monty whispered. "Nineteen seventy-nine to nineteen ninety-seven."

Monty kicked at some of the dirt and determined that the disturbance was related to tampering rather than upkeep—the grave was twenty years old and nothing else in the cemetery was touched. He then reasoned that if digging were done, it likely would have been after the rainstorm, given the neatness and texture of the dirt pile. "Corey Grassman," Monty said again. The name sounded familiar. He would run a search back at the office, but first thing was first; notifying the cemetery's owner, and the family.

20

Frank was sitting at his desk when Cliff rapped on the door with the rim of his water bottle. He took a drink and moved directly over to the couch, letting out a tired groan as he flopped down onto it. "So hot outside!"

Frank looked up. "You're not sweaty, are you?"

Cliff shot up his middle finger and rubbed the bridge of his nose under his glasses with the other hand. "Whatcha workin on?" Cliff asked.

Frank was squinting at his laptop screen. "Trying to find more on this Corey kid." He leaned back in his chair and rocked, throwing his hands behind his head. "It's crazy there's nothing on him! Except his obit in the *Ledger*."

"Just open the book and look for someone who knew him," Cliff said.

"Nah. I'm not trying to mess up my payday. The guy said don't open it, I won't open it," Frank said.

"Did he get back to you?" Cliff asked.

Frank looked up on the top of his bookshelf where he could see the plastic wrapped red book sticking out over the ledge. "Not yet. And I have no idea how to get a hold of him."

Cliff noticed the Amazon box in the corner of the office, beside the closet door. "You don't still have that lady's raggedy old sweater, do you?"

"Yeah. I'm gonna bury it when I go back out to LBL. I'm meeting up with the bone guy. Hopefully before Suthers gets another hunch and decides to search the house. May have to burn it."

"Let me know when you start conducting business outside of LBL again," Cliff said. "Might start helping."

"I seriously don't understand your brain. You have no problem mouthing off to four dudes in a bar but the slightest mention of an old woman in the woods and you freak out."

"Yeah, four dudes in a bar is real—I can handle that." He got up and crossed over to look at the map on Frank's desk and tapped his finger on it. "But this place at night? Bethel Cemetery? Screw that."

"Well, if it means getting to bury stuff where no one will find it, I'll take my chances with a made up witch. Check it out. I think I've found a couple of spots that look good." He pointed at the map of Land Between the Lakes that was laid out across his desk, inscribed with several notes and symbols. Next to it was a book from the library that Frank had checked out earlier—the same one for sale at the Visitor Center. It was exactly as the jolly man described. Every cemetery in Land Between the Lakes was accounted for, along with drawings to depict the layout of each one.

"This one looks like it's the most secluded," Frank said, tapping a spot on the map with his index finger. "The problem is whether or not we can get to it."

"Again, no *we* on this one," Cliff said, wincing. "I gotta sit. Back's killin' me." He took a seat beside Frank and leaned forward. It was hard to see the full thing from his chair. "Where's that other map you had? The old one."

"Threw it away," Frank replied. "Why don't you just use this one?"

"Because you're taking up all the room, and you keep breathing on me."

"Oh wait." Frank clicked on his phone and pulled up his photos. "Here's the one I took of the old map at the Visitor Center." He looked at it for a second and zoomed in. "Yeah, it has cemetery markers." He located the area he was considering and handed the phone to Cliff. "Alright, if we take this road toward the water—"

"No *we*. You. If *you* take this road . . ." Cliff interrupted.

"Fine. Take this road and then move down a little bit, that's Champ cemetery. Do you see the cross?"

"Yeah."

"Okay. There's another place on the north side, near Tharpe Road. If you zoom out and follow that back up to—"

"What about this one in the middle of all the shaded area?" Cliff asked. "All this area is trees, right?"

"What do you mean?"

Cliff sat forward and pointed to a large area of green on Frank's copy. "We're looking here?"

"Yeah."

Cliff studied the phone. "Okay. Well, there's a cemetery right in the middle. Seems pretty secluded." Then, he started talking softer, as if to himself. "Actually, it may be too hard to get to."

Frank lifted the map closer to his face. "What are you talking about?"

Cliff laid the phone on the desk with a groan. "Right here. It's hard to see but look, here's Champ Cemetery—I think. Tharpe Road. And if you go up into this area right here, which I guess are trees." Cliff zoomed in more on the image. "There it is. Right in the middle. See the cross?"

Frank took the phone and stared at the screen. He then meticulously scanned over the map on his desk. "Um . . ." Frank trailed off. He abruptly began flipping through pages in the book and came to a stop on a page with a hand-drawn map. "That's weird."

"You find it?" Cliff asked.

"No." Frank stared at the map inside the book then back at the one on his desk. "It's not on here."

"Oh. Well, didn't that guy say that some of the cemeteries probably got left off? It's a new map," Cliff said.

"Yes," Frank replied. He pointed in the book to the spot of land that Cliff referred to. "But this map was made in 1971. If there's a cemetery in that clearing, it should at least show up on here."

Cliff looked at the phone photo again. "Maybe it's not a cemetery. Could just be a smudge."

"It's definitely not a smudge, look." Frank zoomed in on the photo. The shape was most certainly a cross. He shifted the image up. "There's the same symbol here—at Champ. That's a cemetery. So why is it not in this book?"

"You went back and bought that thing?"

"No, they had it at the library. It's supposed to have every known cemetery on that peninsula." Frank turned to another page in the book and showed Cliff an example of a cemetery that had been flooded along with a list of those who had been buried there, and a rendering of the layout. "This place isn't even there, and she included it."

"How old is that map you took a picture of on your phone?" Cliff asked.

"Didn't he say the forties?" Frank picked up the phone and dialed the Visitor Center for the LBL. The same jolly man answered and confirmed a date in the forties but confessed he was not certain. Frank asked about the author of the book. The man knew the name—Mary Ellen Rhodes. She was a local historian who occasionally taught courses at Murray State, but other than that, he didn't know much about her. He believed she lived in Mayfield, a small town close to Murray. Frank hung up the phone and began searching on Google.

"What are you doing?" Cliff asked.

"Trying to find this woman," Frank replied, tapping the book. "Maybe she can tell me what this cemetery is."

"What does it matter? Just pick a different one. That one's probably too far gone anyways."

Frank looked up at him. "It doesn't. I'm just curious."

Cliff gave an unsmiling glare. "So, you're hoping you'll get lucky and discover Bethel Cemetery?"

"Can't discover what's not real." Frank winked at Cliff. "If it's accessible, then it's obviously the best spot to bury what Bones to Bishops doesn't use."

"That is a catchy name," Cliff said, looking at his watch. "I gotta get back down to the gym. You know, there could be a reason it's not on her list," Cliff said as he stood up to leave. He yelled from the hallway, "Maybe you're not supposed to go out there."

"Sure you don't wanna go with me?"

Frank took the sound of the front door closing as a no.

21

Monty scooted into his regular booth and gave a thumbs up when one of the workers asked if he wanted his usual. After the waiter brought over a mug of decaf coffee, Monty pulled up Addy's number and called him. Addy picked up after one ring. "Preacher?"

"Who is this?"

Shit. There was something about being on the phone that made Monty stutter more—especially on his first name. He curled his lips in to make the M sound but knew nothing would come out without forcing it.

"Mr. Suthers?"

Thank God. "Yup," Monty replied. He exhaled away from the receiver through pursed lips.

"Nobody else calls me preacher. How are ya?"

"I'm okay. You got a minute?"

"Sure. Everything all right?" Addy asked.

Monty explained that he went to Vitello's Bar looking for Nick, but he wasn't there. Never even showed up, according to the other patrons. "I'll handle m-my end but if I get w-wind that Nick is going to press charges, I'll call you and go to Nick myself."

Addy breathed into the phone, then said something inaudible. "Okay."

"You g-g-gonna be alright?" Monty asked.

"Yeah. I mean, I don't know how far I can stay from the two of them. We got church Sunday. What am I supposed to do? Ignore them?" Monty tried to interject but Addy continued. "I also don't want him making a scene if this thing doesn't get resolved."

"D-d-don't sweat it. I should know something b-b-by tomorrow or Thursday. And I'll be there Sunday if he decides to show up." Monty saw Sophia walk into the diner wearing her apron and spoke a little quieter into the phone. "M-my m-m-money says that Nick isn't gonna show up on Sunday. Sophia might." Monty nodded when she caught his eye and waved. "B-b-but I think Nick is as concerned as you are. The l-last thing he needs is a fight."

"Yeah. You're probably right."

"While I have ya," Monty said. "You're about what? Thirty-five?"

Addy chuckled. "Sure."

"Where'd you go to high school?"

"Murray High." There was a pause on the other end. "Why do you ask?"

"Did you ever get around any kids from Calloway?" Monty asked.

"I knew a few. Most of my friends were at Murray, obviously. Donnie and Frank Burgers, couple other guys. I knew maybe a handful of people from Calloway. Why?"

"The name Corey G-G-Grassman ring a bell to you? A few years older than you, I believe."

"Corey Grassman," Addy repeated. "He went to Calloway?" Monty gave an audible approval. "No, doesn't sound familiar."

Monty leaned his forehead onto his hand and began scrunching and pulling the skin across his brow. "Thanks, preacher. I'll see you Sunday."

"This have something to do with Nick?" Addy asked.

This question caught Monty off guard. "No. W-why would Nick be involved?"

"Because he and Sophia went to Calloway High School."

☠

About the time Frank's stick hit the cue ball was when his cell phone started to ring. The number was out of state; he didn't recognize it. "This is Frank," he said into the phone.

"Yes, hi. This is Jessica Lear. My mother is Mary Ellen Rhodes." There was a pause as if she was waiting for Frank to say something. He didn't. "She received a voicemail this afternoon from a Frank Burgers. Is this him?"

"Oh. Hey. Yes! This is Frank. Thanks for calling back. Did I not have the right number?"

"No, you did. But my mother doesn't live in Kentucky anymore. She's . . ." Jessica lowered her voice. "She's had some health issues and we had to move her out to Tennessee with my husband and me."

"I'm sorry to hear that."

"Thank you. I usually check her voicemails once a week back at the house—today was the day. I hope I'm not calling too late."

"No, no. Not a problem. I just had a question for your mom about her book, *The Cemeteries of Land Between the Lakes*. Would there be a good time tomorrow or this week for me to call and chat with her?"

"I mean, she's here with me now if you're able to talk. I just wanted to make sure it was something legitimate. Hang on just one moment."

"Sure. That's fine." There was a light sound of scuffling on the other end and some mumbled conversation, and finally a soft, airy voice spoke into the receiver.

"Hello, Mr. Burgers."

"Ms. Rhodes. How are you?"

"I'm alive. Not a bad way to end the day. We'll see what happens tomorrow. How may I help you?"

"Well, I've been doing some research on LBL and came across your book."

"Oh, you're the one."

Frank laughed. "I had a question about it—or a question about your research, I guess."

"I don't know how much help I'm going to be. I put that book out ages ago and don't even think I've seen a copy of it since I left Kentucky. But we'll see what I can do."

"Great. Um . . ." Frank put down the pool cue and jogged back across the wooden floor to his office where the book was still open on his desk. "How long did it take you to write the book? I mean, you have a ton of material in there: names, pictures . . ."

"Heavens. To actually write the book and put it together? Maybe two years. But from start to finish, between all the traveling through LBL, the interviews, and sifting through death certificates—nearly eighteen years. The representation drawings took the longest to create."

"Goodness. That's a long time."

"It's a lot of research," she replied.

"I have a question about a cemetery I located. I can't find anything on it in your book."

There was an audible grunt on the other end. "It's probably under a different name. Unfortunately, some of the names have been lost or changed—they aren't always searchable by the cemetery name. Even when I compiled the information, I had to catalog a few of them as *unknown*. You have to consider that this research is over thirty years old. It may even be that a member of the family changed the name of their property after I put all that together."

Frank hesitated. "I mean this in the kindest way possible. How do you know that you got all of them? Is it possible that you missed a couple of places?"

There was a sigh on the other end. "I guess you can say I just know. Lots of research. Lots, and lots, and *lots* of research. That project began as my dissertation—looking at particular cemeteries and the connection to families of prominent members of the towns in Land Between the Lakes. Someone finally said, 'You should do this for every cemetery.' I dug through a ton of material and walked a lot of miles—practically lived at Pogue Library at the university campus for several years going through names, dates, and maps. I guess to answer your question of how do I know I got them all? Because when I was done researching there was nothing left to research." There was a long pause. Frank could hear another voice on the other end. Finally, the older woman spoke, "This isn't about that old haunted cemetery is it? Bethel."

"No ma'am." Frank chuckled. "Why? Is it real?"

The hesitation was minimal—barely noticeable—but long enough for Frank to sense that something got her attention. "No, Mr. Burgers. It is *not* real. I'm sure the cemetery you've found has just been renamed. If that's the case, you won't find it searching alphabetically. There should be a collection of maps in the back, with each cemetery numbered. Try to match the place you found with its number on the map, then trace it with the name index in the back."

"Well . . ." Frank hesitated. He didn't want to keep pushing. "I tried that. The place I saw doesn't seem to be anywhere in your book—not even on the maps. You see, when I was in the Visitor Center at LBL, they had this really old map on the wall. It showed a lot of the cemeteries, and there was one in particular in the middle of a clearing but—"

"What is it you want, Mr. Burgers?" The woman's voice was cold. "I have now told you twice that I did not miss any locations in Land Between the Lakes, but you keep telling me that I'm wrong." He could hear the other voice talking in the background.

"I just . . . I'm sorry . . . I just wanted to know if you knew anything about it."

"As I've already said, everything I know is in that book. Now, I don't know what you think you're seeing in that clearing, but it is most certainly not a cemetery. Please do not waste your time venturing out there for a better look." Her voice had gone soft, almost begging.

"Do you think it might be a misprint on the—" Before he could finish, the line went dead. "Hello?" Frank looked at his phone screen. The call was ended. "Jeez." He contemplated calling back but about the moment he decided against it, the phone buzzed in his hand. It was the woman's number. He swiped to answer. "Hey. Sorry about that, I think I lost—"

"Hi. It's Jessica again. Sorry to . . . keep calling. I just wanted to apologize. I'm really sorry. My mother isn't normally like that but as I told you, she's been having a rough time lately: being here, getting adjusted, and what not."

"Oh. It's okay," Frank replied. "Sorry that I got her upset."

"It's not you. It's . . ." Her voice went almost to a whisper. "Discussing her book can be a mixed bag. Sometimes she's fine, but other times something in the conversation will trigger an emotion and she . . . overreacts. Dad says it was a stressful time for her when she was writing that."

"I'm sure it didn't help that I was saying she might have missed some stuff," Frank said.

"No, probably not," Jessica replied light heartedly. She started to say something else but was cut off by another voice in the room. Jessica responded to it—Frank heard his last name—and then the voice got louder. He could hear it getting closer to the phone when the earpiece erupted into a series of static noises and *thumps* before finally the line went dead again.

Frank looked at the phone screen. Call ended. He mouthed *okay* to himself and put the phone down. "That was bizarre." He looked down at the map. "And completely unhelpful."

22

Monty ended the call and set the phone down on the table. He took a sip of his coffee while he glanced around the diner. Sophia was standing a few tables over taking an order and then moved over to refill Monty's water.

"Hey you," she said.

"Hey. Doin' alright?"

"Yeah," Sophia replied. "Not too bad." She looked at her watch nestled between what looked to be half a dozen skinny bracelets. "You been here long? Little early for you, huh?"

"N-no, n-n-not too long," Monty replied. "Since t-t-ten." He took a breath, acknowledging his frustration over the nerve-induced stutter.

Sophia smiled. "Wow, a lot going through that brain tonight huh?"

"Yeah, w-w-weird day. How's Nick?"

"Ugh, I can't even deal with that right now."

"Everything okay?" Monty asked.

"It's fine," she replied. "He came home still pissed about Addy being there, and about me thinking what I did . . . about him . . . you know . . ."

"That h-he-he'd hurt you?" Monty finished.

"Yeah." Sophia poured more coffee into Monty's cup and noticed another patron waving at her. She went to put an order in at the computer before returning to sit in the booth and continue talking, though it wasn't about anything particular: work the night before, a conversation with her mom, a book she was reading. Occasionally, she would get up to run food or give refills to other customers but always returned to sit across from him and continue the conversation.

Monty had never seen her this talkative, or even experienced her being this open about her life. She told him about her and Nick's relationship: how they met, why they were still together, and even moments that Monty deemed to be abusive despite Sophia's insistence of the opposite. He wanted to offer advice but knew that he shouldn't. A prior relationship had taught him that more often than not, most people just wanted to talk without being advised. So, he listened. He smiled, nodded, and threw in some "yeahs," "wows," and "you're kiddings" when necessary. The more he listened, the more she talked. And he loved it.

"What about you?" she asked. "I've been talking nonstop—I'm sorry. How was your week?"

"It's been okay. Little odd at times," he replied, swirling the coffee in his mug. "Actually, I wanted to ask you if you knew someone—"

"Ooo. Sorry. Hold that thought." She grabbed the coffee pot and held up a finger. Monty exhaled the rest of his thought as she walked away, toward the counter, and then over to another table. He watched her for a while, and then clicked on his phone to begin scrolling through Facebook.

Several minutes later, she returned. "Sorry about that. Seems like one of those tables where you can't get anything right. All clear now." She looked back at the table. "Maybe. Wouldn't be surprised if they all ended up sending their food back and changing their order. Anyways, where were we? Oh, I meant to ask you, what happened with those grave robberies last week? Did you ever find out anything else about them?"

How much should I say? "Eh," Monty said. "I thought I did. Still causing me some grief though. Think I m-m-may have stumbled across a new one earlier today."

A group of college kids walked in and yelled "Aye Oh!" startling Sophia. She turned back toward Monty and rolled her eyes. "*Another* one? Are you sure?"

"Do you need to get them?" he asked.

She turned around toward them. "You guys grab a seat, I'll be over in a bit."

"Gracias mi cisne negro!" one of them yelled back.

"Idiots. Anyways, so, there was *another* grave robbery?" she asked, her eyes brightened.

"I don't know. It's only a hunch right now. I was driving this m-morning after leaving the preach—I mean, Addy's house, and I saw a grave that had been . . ." Monty didn't know the right word. "D-d-disturbed, maybe? Covered in d-dirt, n-not grass like the others. And it w-wasn't a r-recent b-burial." Monty sighed. "Goodness," he muttered and then smiled. "Having a hard time tonight I guess."

"What'd they take?" She asked.

Monty paused. He had learned earlier that evening after speaking with the owner of the cemetery that there was no scheduled maintenance for Corey's grave. It should *not* look like it does. He also learned after some supplementary research that Corey's corpse was never found and therefore never buried. He was still a little perplexed as to why that was, but more so as to why someone would start to dig in a grave that *wasn't* occupied. Unless the diggers didn't know. He hesitated to tell Sophia this detail. "We don't know yet," he said. "Stuff like this has to be approved before we can dig it back up to look."

"But the person was already dug up," she replied. "Wouldn't that be cause for you all to see what was stolen? Probable cause, right?"

"It d-doesn't quite w-work like that." He smiled. "The family m-may not want him dug up."

"So, it's a he?" she said, getting up. There was a devious grin on her face, and she lowered her voice. "Can you tell me who it is?"

"I ca—"

He started to reply but she cut him off. "Don't answer yet. I'm going to go take their order. Think it over and when I get back, I want you to tell me who it was. I'll give you free coffee for a year."

She wasn't gone long. When she came back, she slid back in across from him and folded her hands. "Okay. I'm ready. Wait! What about the other graves? The ones last week. Was anything stolen from *them*?"

Monty tightened his lips. He opened his mouth to speak and then sipped his coffee. The paper only reported that graves were vandalized. There was still no mention of robbery, let alone that robbers stole a corpse.

"Come on! Who am I going to tell?" she whispered.

"If you t-tell, it'll get back to me," he replied.

"How?"

He looked at her. "I don't know." And then he laughed.

"See. Come on, tell me. What'd they take? It's been over a week, it's practically ancient news."

"O-o-one of the robberies was minor. We never identified what was stolen—if anything. But the other one was p-p-pretty big. They took the wh-whole b-b-body." He lowered his voice to a whisper, "Two women, one elderly and one about m-m-middle aged. Sarah M-M-Middleton, and Sarah P-Pi-Piddleton." *Damn this stutter.* "Sorry."

"Hey. That is nothing to be ashamed of. I love it." She smiled.

Monty could not make sense of Sophia's actions. *Was this flirting?*

"They took the whole body? Like, it was just gone?"

"Most of it," Monty replied.

"Whose body"

"Sarah Piddleton," he replied hesitantly.

Sophia sat back. "Damn. Why would someone take an entire body? How long ago did she die?"

"A while ago. Practically b-b-bones by now."

"Weird," she whispered. A bell went off in the kitchen and Sophia got up to retrieve the plates. Monty turned on his phone and scrolled through an email until she returned. "Okay. Now that we've broken you down, what about the new one you found. Who was it?"

"I can't tell you that yet—there may not even be anything really wrong. As of this evening, w-we were still waiting to hear back from family. It's not public at the m-m-moment."

"Well, isn't it though? I mean, if I walk into the cemetery and I notice a grave with fresh dirt that has an old headstone, a disturbance is pretty noticeable right? Seems public to me."

Monty's guard could not withstand her smile. He gave a hum and shrugged, then sipped another mouthful of his coffee. He tried changing the subject, but Sophia brought the conversation right back. Monty was not getting out of this one unless he could convincingly declare that he would not share information.

"Come on, Monty..." She'd never called him by his first name. Usually it was *Officer Suthers*, or just *hey you*. "I promise, I'm not going to tell anyone," she whispered, placing her hand on his. He fought the urge to look down at it—*that would be too intimate.*

Monty sighed. As soon as he asked about Corey, she'd know that his grave was the one in question, and likely push him for more details if she did in fact know him. She had never told Monty when she graduated or given any hint of her age, but Monty guessed her to be around the same age as Corey—probably a little older. He shook his head and looked around as if someone would be listening. No one was. "Old Salem Cemetery," he mumbled, making eye contact. "That's where it is."

"Okay. So, who is it? I don't even know where Old Salem Cemetery is. Is that nearby?"

"Other side of town, just past a set of railroad tracks," he replied.

"I think I would remember going to a cemetery called Old Salem. I definitely don't know anyone out there. Come on."

"I think you might, actually," he muttered under his breath. Her eyes narrowed. Monty took one more swig of coffee and pressed out a slow breath from the side of his lips. "Corey Grassman." He watched the expression on her face slowly shift: her eyebrows furrowed, and her head tilted slightly. Nothing about her face gave away any recognition of the name. She seemed to be thinking. Sophia broke eye contact and leaned back in her booth. She repeated the name to herself a couple of times as if trying to conjure up a memory. "You know him?" Monty asked.

"Haven't heard that name in years. He died in, what, late nineties?"

"Ninety-seven," Monty replied. "Y-you know him?"

"No. Definitely didn't know him—we did go to the same school, though." Her eyes shifted down toward the table. It was the longest she'd been quiet since Monty arrived.

"What's wrong?" Monty asked. "You know something?"

"No. If it's who I think it is... you said you haven't dug in there yet?" She asked.

"No. N-not yet," Monty replied.

"He died well after I graduated—he was a freshman, I think, when I was a senior. I don't remember any details, but I know it was something weird. Didn't they say he committed suicide, or he was killed? There was some kind of conspiracy, right?"

"That's him," Monty said.

"Yeah. Seems an odd choice for a grave robbing," she commented.

"W-why's that?" Monty asked.

"Because there's nobody in there. That was the weird part; there was never a body."

She knows. "Yeah," Monty replied. "That had me a little baffled too."

"I thought you said you didn't dig anything up yet," she smirked.

"We didn't. W-when I looked him up, that's what I found—no body."

Sophia laughed and got back up with her coffee pot. "I don't know why you were being so secretive about the whole thing. If there's no body, then what's the big deal?"

"B-b-because we d-don't know w-why they went down there—the diggers."

"You think there was something in there?" She asked.

"Hell if I know." Monty laughed. "Family hasn't called us back." He stopped and threw his hands to indicate surrender. "M-m-maybe I'll know more tomorrow." The order bell dinged from the kitchen counter and she slid out of the booth. She started to walk away when Monty called her back over. "You don't by chance know anyone w-who w-w-went to the funeral, do you?"

"I'm sure I do. I didn't go. I knew his old girlfriend; used to babysit her when she was a kid. I'm sure we're friends on Facebook."

"Girlfriend?" Monty asked, pulling out a pen.

"Yeah, I knew *her* more than him. Connie Lancaster. Or Lassater. I think it's Lancaster. Connie Lancaster. See if you can get a hold of her, she may know something. But other than that, no, I don't think the friends I had would have gone to it. Plus, I don't talk to many people from Calloway anymore so, I wouldn't be much help there."

"H-how did you know about the b-body?" Monty asked.

"Everybody knew about that," she replied. "Murdered kid with a missing body. It was like our own episode of *CSI*."

When she returned from filling coffee and running food, she sat back down and told Monty, "Don't funeral homes keep a record of who comes to the funerals?"

"No," he replied. "That's a gues-g-guestbook. That goes to the family."

"Hmm. Well, now I'm interested to know what was in that coffin. What are you doing tomorrow night?"

Monty looked up at her, unsure of how to respond. "I d-don't know. Why?"

"Can you come by here again?" she asked. "I want to hear more."

Monty realized he was awkwardly smiling and stopped. He cleared his throat and replied, "If I hear anything, I'll stop by."

"What happens if they don't want you to dig it up?"

Monty laughed. "Then I guess we'll never know." He finished his cup of coffee. He didn't want to, but he said, "I think I'm g-gonna head home. I'm beat. I'm serious though, try to keep all this to yourself."

Sophia placed his check on the table. "I will. And hey, if you want—off the record—I've got some shovels in my truck. If the family doesn't want to exhume the body . . ." She winked at him, turned, and walked toward the kitchen.

WEDNESDAY
23

The Land Between the Lakes beach where Frank was scheduled to meet the Living Pieces buyer was full of people enjoying the cool water's escape from the sweltering humidity and blistering sun. Frank met two individuals this time instead of four. *Probably a sign they trust me.* The transaction was similar to the one a week prior: neither man appeared to be in a pleasant mood, hardly any words were exchanged, and their inspection of each piece was meticulous, choosing only four of the six, leaving Frank with two limbs to now go and bury. At least they let him keep the cooler this time.

Frank was relieved he hadn't turned his car off. He closed the driver's side door and leaned his face into the air conditioning's icy breeze. His radio said 2:32. "Ugh."

He could already feel sweat in his shirt beginning to stick to his back and for a moment he reconsidered trekking out into the woods—or anywhere outside—to hide the bones. "Now or never," he whispered, laying his cemetery map across the steering wheel. He'd placed an X where the mysterious cemetery should hopefully be, in the middle of a green clearing.

One of the differences with the updated map was the addition of trails, and their vehicle accessibility. Frank didn't have much to go on other than the fact that the cemetery was situated somewhere in the woods. If he followed the trails indicated on the map, surely, he would run into it. Accuracy of those trails aside, what worried him was whether he could get out before dark, and if he truly had the courage to go by himself.

The campground where he made the exchange wasn't far from where he estimated would be a good starting point. After ten minutes of driving, he located the entrance trail indicated on the map and turned onto it. The dirt path began to thin out and Frank pulled as far to the side as he could before turning his truck off.

The humidity hit him in the face like a hot towel when he opened the door. He let out an exasperated grunt as he tucked his pant legs into his socks. He sprayed himself with bug spray and slipped the two remaining bones—now wrapped tightly in Sarah Piddleton's pink cardigan—into his backpack along with bottled water, protein bars, and a box of cheese crackers. Armed with a shovel for assistance through the overgrowth—and possible protection—he made his way into the woods.

Frank checked his cell service: none. Without trails or directions, there was no way to know how long it would take to find the cemetery. He was confident, however, that getting out would be next to impossible without some help, especially once it got dark. Frank crumbled cheese crackers onto the ground to mark his path.

He proceeded forward, keeping an eye out for any indicators that he was on the right track. He came to a creek that was indicated on the map, though he was surprised to realize he hadn't walked as far as he thought. Eventually he came upon a small family cemetery—also marked on the map—though he had somehow veered off to the right and was now going away from his destination.

Frank retraced his way back toward the creek—a fifteen-minute walk—and then altered his direction. This time, he came upon an organized collection of rocks. It was the foundation to an old building, as noted by the map, and once again he was going the wrong direction. "Son of a bitch," Frank whispered. He reoriented himself and followed his cracker trail back, dusting it away as to not come this way again. Then he noticed it; a wooden sign nailed to a tree. The lettering on the sign had nearly faded away but Frank could make out enough to understand he was near Wild Dog Hollow. On the map, a trail by the same name made its way toward Frank's estimated destination, though it would eventually veer off away from it. "Finally," Frank whispered. With no indications of a foot path around the sign, he tried to go as close to south and east as he could, moving the weeds and shrubbery as he went, still crumbling orange crackers along the way.

He walked through several hundred yards of knee-high overgrowth—stepping over decomposing tree limbs, dead leaves, and rocks—to what looked like a creek on the map, except this one was dried. If it was the same riverbed, then he was going in the right direction, and best of all it would route him to the vicinity where he believed the cemetery to be. He checked his watch. It had already been over an hour. He leaned against a tree and took a water bottle from his backpack. No telling how close he was, but even if he knew where he was going, getting to this location was taking way too long. He couldn't afford to eat up this much time every time he needed to come and bury something, no matter how perfect of a spot. *Already this far in, may as well finish it.*

Frank followed the dried-up river bed until it came to a fork. He breathed a sigh of relief. It was the same creek on the map, and he knew he needed to follow it to the left. The bad news was that it would soon veer off course, leaving him in empty space: no path, no creeks, no direction. Frank cursed. It had been an hour and forty-five minutes and to make matters worse, his stomach was starting to hurt. He took out a protein bar from his bag and nibbled on it as he continued walking.

When his watch showed two hours, he felt he now understood why this spot was not listed on any map. No cemetery clean-up volunteers were coming out here, and even if they would, they couldn't imagine dragging yard tools out this far to help clear the area. After a while, nausea settled into his stomach—a feeling Frank was familiar with when he got too hot. *Shit.* He continued moving but drew out the other bar from his bag and his third bottle of water. He shifted his focus from the map to the ground: map to ground, map to ground—all to keep his mind off the heat and the gurgling in his stomach. Keep moving, he told himself. He had become so distracted with his stomach, and the map, that had there not been a sudden sting on his calf he would have walked all the way through the now *open* clearing without even noticing. At the sensation of being stung he slapped his calf and knelt to readjust his pant leg and sock. He set down his backpack and looked to place the shovel against a tree. That's when he realized the dense forest that had been around him for over two hours had disappeared. He never even noticed he'd walked *out* of the woods. "That's odd." He was now kneeling in a large field overrun with tall grass and weeds, encircled with woods like a barrier.

Frank stabbed his shovel into the ground and looked at his map. The solid green area was no more than a collection of dots to indicate trees. There was nothing to suggest a clearing of this size. Then again, why would there be? There was nothing here. He refolded his map and started moving forward when his foot hooked on something hard, landing him flat on the ground.

24

"Seriously!?" Frank said to himself, lying on his side.

He shifted and moved the grass around with his hand to uncover a thin slab of rock lying flat on the ground. It looked like a gravestone, but it was blank, even on the other side. Often, gravestones wore away with time and ceased to display the engravings. This one looked as if it had never even been carved. "Jackpot," Frank whispered.

He scanned the area around him. It appeared that the ground just south of the headstone was sunken in. Frank stood and took a couple of steps back when his heel clipped something hard, causing him to stumble. "Dammit!" Another stone was lying on its back, cracked into two pieces. Overgrowth had practically wrapped itself around both slabs to conceal its location, and like the other, it was blank.

He sidestepped away from the two graves and heard a crunch. He knelt down and noticed several shards of what looked to be a seashell. "Odd place for a shell." Something dark caught his eye just to the left; it was a gravestone, barely standing and completely overwhelmed with vines. Just beside it, a similar stone lying face down.

Once his mind registered that stones were hidden beneath the weeds,

they became easier to spot. If it was a cemetery, it was completely plausible that one could walk right by and not see anything—if they were lucky enough to not trip. It looked like they were all laid flat; none of them even appeared to be engraved. *Maybe it's a depository for headstones?*

The large city cemetery back home in Murray had a section designated for broken or faded headstones. It was not a heavily trafficked section. The stones were piled near the south end of the cemetery where plots had not yet been purchased. You wouldn't see it unless you were looking at it. *Why would—how would—someone bring headstones all the way out here?* The stones were obviously grave markers, but even if they were the oldest stones in Kentucky, signs of engraving should be visible.

Smaller family cemeteries were often laid in such a way to display the head of the family and then the children. These graves—if they were graves—were ordered haphazardly. Moving a little farther into the clearing, he spotted a mound of rocks, overtaken by weeds and plant life. Another headstone rested at the head of the pile, broken into sections, also blank. "This is crazy," he mumbled. He counted them. "Twelve . . . thirteen . . . fourteen. Is that it? Fourteen?"

He moved around the field to see if maybe there were straggler stones elsewhere, but he found nothing. "Fourteen graves . . . no names . . . no dates." Something caught his eye at the very edge of the clearing, on the opposite side of where he entered. A battered-looking tree loomed in the distance. It surprised him that he didn't notice it sooner. It was the only thing—besides himself—standing in the field. The tree was no doubt dead, its limbs thick and twisted together. Many of the lower ones were beginning to hang down toward the ground. Frank took out his phone and snapped a picture of it then took several of the clearing and the graves themselves, making sure to capture the absence of names or dates.

Suddenly there was another wave of nausea and Frank's mouth went dry. He took a few deep breaths and bent over, resting his hands on his knees. "Do not throw up." After a few gulps of his water and some deep breathing, the feeling passed.

He carried the Piddleton sweater and two limbs back toward the first sunken plot he found and placed the items on the ground. "Let's do this and get out of here," he said, sliding his shovel into the sunken earth. The queasiness from his stomach surfaced once again but he pushed it from his mind.

Frank was careful to set the dirt close by as to quickly be able to knock it back in once the job was done. His mouth stayed dry. *Probably all the cheese crackers. Did I check the date on those?* Now the thought of cheese crackers was making him feel sick. He grumbled and continued. There were still several minutes of digging and at least an hour hike back to the car, assuming an animal didn't eat the crackers.

Eventually, Frank sensed an ache in his head and reasoned that his allergies were to blame. Likely, also the cause of the uneasy feeling that had taken over his stomach. When he was looking at a hole that he guessed was a little over two feet deep, he decided it was enough and retrieved the sweater. He lowered himself slowly onto his knees to lay the wrapping in the ground when he noticed something white sticking of the dirt.

He reached and touched the object with his finger, thinking that it was possibly a stick or a rock, and pulled it from the dirt. What came up set off a ripple of panic through his body. "Holy shit," he exclaimed, promptly letting go and pulling his hand back. Frank instinctively looked around to see if anyone was watching. "There's no way," he whispered. He scooted the sweater aside and began clawing the dirt with his hands. Finally, he reached for his shovel, and continued shifting dirt around inside the hole. It didn't take long for Frank to be convinced of what he was digging up.

He peeked around again then peered back into the hole. "How is that even . . ." Before he could finish, vomit came ripping up through his throat, and out of his mouth. He turned his head at the last minute to avoid getting it in the hole and sucked in a deep breath when it finally ended. He groaned, sitting still on all fours until he was sure nothing else was coming out. "Protein bars and vomit don't mix," he said to himself, spitting and wiping around his mouth with the bottom of his shirt. He took a swig of water, sloshed it around in his mouth, and spit it onto the ground.

His stomach felt much better, but his head now felt as if it would split right between his eyes. He turned back toward the hole and attempted to raise himself up to his feet when his hand slipped into the loose dirt and brushed something hard. Frank paused and lifted the object out of the earth. "What the . . ." he muttered, spitting again. He got himself to stand—slowly—and rubbed the dirt off onto his jeans before reaching for his phone to take a picture. "Ho. Lee. Crap."

The headache was not easing up. Frank closed his eyes and ran water down the back of his neck, cursing himself for not doubling up on his allergy meds before coming out here. There was also the chance he might actually be sick with something—he needed to get home in case he got nauseated again. Frank shifted the bone-filled cardigan toward the lowest spot of the hole, then proceeded to fill it back in.

When he finished, he patted his pockets to make sure he wasn't leaving his phone, wallet, or keys behind. No way in hell was he coming back out here. He started to hurry back in the direction he entered from when he heard another crunch under his foot. Right as he was about to cross over the threshold back into the woods, he saw hundreds—maybe thousands—of seashells resting at the edge of the clearing along the tree line. He was too distracted to notice when he walked in. As far as Frank could tell, they encircled the entire field. He snapped another photo, now having to squint his eyes from the migraine, and started back toward the truck.

The cheese cracker trail was essential to his navigation, cutting the exit time to almost half. When the truck came into view, he ripped off his shirt and dumped the rest of his water all over his body to cool him down. He sat inside on a towel, basking in the freezing cold breeze pumping from his air conditioner. The nausea and shaky equilibrium had leveled out as he got closer to the car, but the unseen vice grip on his skull seemed to be holding strong as he backed out down the trail and made his way home.

⚫

The road took him back by the Visitor Center. It was well after closing but Frank saw two cars in the parking lot with their lights on. He turned in and pulled up next to one of the running vehicles.

"Excuse me," he said after rolling down his window.

The gentleman rolled down his window. It was the jolly man who sold Frank the map. "Can I help you?"

"Hey, I was up here a few days back, you sold me a map."

"Yessir?" the man replied.

"I had a question about cemeteries," Frank said.

"Well, we open tomorrow at nine a.m. If you'd like to come back, someone can help you then. The park area is closed, and it's not really recommended that people visit our cemeteries after dark."

"No, I wasn't planning on visiting any, I just had a question about burial practices," Frank replied.

"I don't know how much help I'll be with that one. Come on by tomorrow, the lady here will be able to help you with any historical questions. I gotta turn it in for the night."

"Is she pretty knowledgeable about how people are buried here?" Frank asked.

The guy sighed. "You're asking about the pipes in the ground, aren't you? Yeah, she'll know about those. They're not all that odd for the period—you'll see them quite a bit. It usually catches people off guard at first."

"Pipes?" Frank asked. "No, I'm talking about the seashells."

The man looked at him for a second. "You say seashells?"

"Yeah. Like . . . what you find on a beach. Seashells."

"I don't understand your question, son. Are you asking about seashells being used in burials? Like burying someone under seashells?"

"No. Not in the burial. I'm talking about seashells in a cemetery—like, *around* a cemetery. Is there any significance to that?"

"I ain't never heard'a that. Did you see that somewhere around here?"

Frank hesitated to answer this question. "No," he lied. "Buddy of mine told me he ran across a cemetery with seashells around it."

"We don't have anything *like that* around here," the man replied.

Frank noticed something peculiar about the way he said it. "What do you mean 'like that'? What do the shells mean?"

He sighed, obviously exhausted. "I don't know, son, it's an old wives' tale. Some people think seashells ward off evil spirits. When you see them on a grave, people want whatever is in there to *stay* in there." Something prickled up Frank's spine and crawled over into the flesh of his arms. "If you're looking for stuff like that around here, you'll just be spinning your wheels." He waved his finger around the landscape. "These are mostly church cemeteries or family cemeteries."

"You've been out to all of them?" Frank asked.

"Yes sir. Every one. I can personally assure you that I have never seen a seashell in this part of Kentucky except for on the back of our toilet, thanks to my wife." He laughed.

"But, if there was a cemetery with shells around it, you're saying that would probably not be a good thing, right?" Frank asked.

"Son, I don't know. Like I said, I ain't ever seen 'em but I imagine if you stumbled on something like that it's probably because of some crazy old kook or kids playing a prank."

"Interesting..." Frank mumbled.

"If you want to come back tomorrow afternoon, I'll be here but Debbie might be someone you should talk to. There's some interesting stuff in these parts but unfortunately not too much in the way of ghost stories or hauntings, know what I mean?"

Frank tapped the side of his door a couple times. "Okay. Thanks. Maybe I'll do that."

"Drive safe. And don't forget we don't recommend exploring in the dark. We don't have any police who patrol out here."

"No worries. I'm heading home. Good night."

The man held Frank's gaze. "I mean it. It's really not safe exploring this place in the dark."

Frank paused. The man didn't break eye contact. "Thanks for the tip. Good night."

"Night," the man replied.

Frank didn't wait around for the man to drive off and leave him alone in the parking lot. He pulled back onto the main road back to Murray—and into cell service—as quickly as he could.

25

By the time Frank got home, the family had already eaten dinner. Ginny and Dave were in the family room yelling questions at *Jeopardy*, Donnie was at the kitchen table typing, and Cliff was at the sink doing dishes. He said *hey* to everyone and took a fast shower before coming back downstairs and into the kitchen.

"Cliff, you don't have to do the dishes every time, man. We'll get it," Frank said.

"Nah, I gotchu. Your mom cooked me dinner. She put a plate for you in the microwave."

Frank walked over to Donnie and stared down at the screen. "What are you doin'?" He stuck a finger in his mouth before wiggling it around and inside Donnie's ear.

Donnie jerked his shoulder up, knocking Frank away from his ear. "Hey! Seriously?" He wiped the spit from his ear. "What is wrong with you? And why's it so wet?"

Frank laughed and went to the microwave.

"I'm working on our website."

"What's wrong with our website?" Frank asked.

"For starters, the not one but two live hyperlinks to funeral coupons that I asked you to take down," Donnie replied, clicking the mouse. Underneath the words, *You've Found a Killer Deal* was an image of a skeleton sitting in the driver's seat of a semi-truck giving a thumbs up and wearing a hat with *Large Marge* stenciled across the front of it. Underneath, in bold letters, it said, *Tell 'em I Sent Ya!* followed by a notice for ten percent off.

"Oh, my bad."

"Mmm hmm," Donnie muttered. "So, taking off all your hyperlinks, updating and adding pictures, and changing some of the layout to make it less busy. Where were you today?"

"Dropping off those things for that guy," Frank replied.

"All good?" Donnie asked.

"Yeah," Frank said. The microwave beeped and he pulled the plate out and sat down at the table. "I put the money in my office."

"FYI, I'm giving you a heads up now so you don't freak out when she gets here and embarrass me. Lexie is coming over tonight."

Frank said "what!" but it came out as nothing more than a muffled noise with the food in his mouth.

"She'll be here in a bit," Donnie said.

Frank replied in his best Kool-Aid man voice. "Oh Yeah!"

Donnie stared blankly at him over the laptop screen, shaking his head and then went back to typing. The two of them continued to chat off and on until Cliff finished up at the sink. "You guys wanna hear something weird?" Cliff asked. "I talked to my dad about Bethel Cemetery today; asked if he could send me the pictures he had."

"And he told you those pictures didn't exist?" Frank smiled.

"No." Cliff took a seat. "Turns out, they weren't *his* pictures. They were Lolo's—my grandfather's. Now, I talk to Lolo probably twice a week, always pretty chill. Today I call him, we chat for a bit and then I asked him about the pictures. Yo, you would have thought I insulted my grandmother. He was a whole different person. I mean, at first, you could tell something was off in the way he tried to redirect the conversation. He said he didn't know what I was talking about, and I told him I'd seen them before. It was like a switch went off. He started getting real short with me. Said he didn't want to talk about Bethel. Said it wasn't real and that I shouldn't ask about it."

"Damn," Frank said.

"Yeah. I made the mistake of asking again and he hung up on me. He has *never* done that before."

"He did say he didn't want to talk about it," Donnie said, not looking up from his screen.

"Still. Lolo has never hung up on me. I tried to call him back. He just sent me a text back that said he was in the middle of something, which was also weird because he doesn't text."

Frank thought about Cliff's story for a moment and then spoke up. "Same thing happened to me last night. With that author," Frank said.

"What author?" Donnie asked, now giving his attention.

He told Donnie about the cemetery book of LBL and the map he found at the Visitor Center. He recounted to Cliff and Donnie the strange conversation with Mary Ellen Rhodes and the abrupt, irritated end to the call.

"And you wonder why I don't like going to LBL. Something's off about that place," Cliff said as the house phone on the wall began to ring, startling him. Donnie stood up and made his way over to the phone.

"You know who you should ask?" Cliff said. "Principal Atlas. He had all those stories about that place in high school. He had to have gotten them from somewhere."

"Probably made 'em up," Donnie added. He picked up the receiver. "Burgers Family Funeral, this is Donnie. How can I help you?"

"That's a good idea," Frank said.

"Oh, I forgot! Speaking of high school," Cliff exclaimed, "I got something to show you! Be right back." Cliff scooted his chair back and hurried out the back door.

Frank reached for his cell phone and groaned when he realized he left it upstairs. He scooted away from the table to go retrieve it and returned in time to hear Donnie say, "We'll be by tomorrow to pick him up." Frank mouthed *who is that?* but his brother ignored him. Donnie hung up the phone.

"We have a funeral?" Frank said.

"Yup. Tomorrow morning."

"What? You just said you were picking up the body tomorrow morning," Frank said.

"Yeah, there was a mix up. You know anyone named Cal McLaughlin?" Donnie asked.

"I don't think so. Why?"

"That was his sister, Gail. Cal passed away a couple days ago and they planned on having the funeral with the Kochs. Come to find out that much of his remaining family knows Mom and Dad really well. They assumed the funeral was with us, but the wife had ended up booking with Life Memorial. Long story short, family got pissed and demanded they change venues."

"Jeez. Didn't the *Ledger* already run the obituary and details?"

"Yup. Gail said it didn't matter. Plus, apparently, one of the brothers has an issue with Vince. Looks like we're having an impromptu funeral."

"Alright! Suck it, Vince!" Frank said, crossing his arms over his crotch and thrusting his hips forward.

"That wasn't necessary," Donnie commented dryly, walking back over to the table.

"Oh! Wait. You told her we have construction going on, right? The place is a wreck."

"I told her. She said it was fine. We'll just have to make do."

"What am I supposed to do about a eulogy? And brochures?"

"Nothing. All taken care of. We're just the venue. The minister from their church is doing the funeral, they have a CD of songs they want played, and the Kochs did the handouts. It's just a venue change," Donnie said.

"How many?" Frank asked.

"Maybe twenty people. Ten a.m."

"Easiest funeral ever," Frank said, nodding. "We'll just need to clean the foyer and reset the chairs outside."

"Yeah, shouldn't take too long," Donnie said. "I'll run and grab the body first thing tomorrow from the Kochs and we'll get it all set up."

Frank finished his plate and put it in the dishwasher. He filled a mug with coffee and walked over to Donnie, stopping to analyze the picture up on the screen. He started to say something but was cut off when the back of Donnie's hand swatted Frank in the genitals. "It's not done yet, get back," Donnie said.

Frank turned and instinctively shielded himself, avoiding a *direct* hit. "Well, use a better picture. That one's old."

"It's the most recent one we have."

"No, it's not. We took a family picture like six months ago."

Donnie stopped and glanced up from the screen, thinking. "That was for Christmas. And we're all wearing elf ears."

"At least we were all smiling. Dad's not even looking at the camera here. Plus, our Christmas one is eye catching," Frank replied.

"Yeah, and so is a picture of all of us at the beach with our shirts off, but neither is appropriate for a funeral home's website."

The back door reopened, and Cliff entered holding his duffel bag. "Check this out," Cliff said, dropping it onto the chair beside Donnie. He snapped his head to Frank, "Wait, he knows about the book and stuff, right?"

"Yeah. He's good."

Donnie eyed the object in Cliff's hand. "Is that a yearbook?"

"Yup," Cliff replied.

"From Calloway High School?"

"I think I found some people to help us track down what happened to Corey's body." Frank wanted to cut Cliff off, but Donnie beat him to it.

"Wait, what? Whose body?"

Cliff looked back to Frank and then to Donnie. And then back to Frank, "You just said you told him about Corey," Cliff said.

Frank pursed his lips out and widened his eyes. "I mean, I told him we were digging up someone's grave whose name was Corey. Didn't think he'd care to hear about the rest."

"I thought I told you to keep me in the loop with this stuff," Donnie said.

"Look, I'm still trying to make sense of everything that happened.

To be honest, you don't wanna be in the loop on this one. *I* don't even wanna be in the loop."

"Corey's the guy with the book, right?" Donnie asked.

"Yeah," Cliff said. He turned the open yearbook toward Donnie to a page with the word JUNIORS across the top, and a single individual circled in red—Corey Grassman. "You recognize him?"

"I don't think so. Should I know him?"

Cliff shrugged.

Donnie pulled the book toward him. "He graduated six years ahead of me. I definitely wouldn't know him. I didn't hang out with anybody older, especially at Calloway."

"He didn't graduate. He died the next year," Cliff said, taking the book back and flipping to a new page. "Supposedly. They're not really sure what happened."

Donnie thought about it for a moment and then closed the laptop. "Actually, you're right. This is just gonna stress me out." He picked up his computer and headed toward the foyer. "You guys have at it."

When he left, Cliff brought out a yellow pad with several lines written on it. "You hear anything back from the guy yet? How you supposed to get that book to him?"

"I'm supposed to drop it off tomorrow over at the consignment shop on the other side of town," Frank replied. "He wants me to leave it on a bookshelf in one of the booths."

"You need me to come along?" Cliff asked. Frank assured him he would be fine. Cliff poked at the notepad with a pen. "I went through some of my contacts and found a couple of people who graduated around the same time as Corey at Calloway." Cliff pointed to two names on his paper. Next to each name were a few lines of script that Frank couldn't read.

"What'd you say to them?" Frank asked.

"Casually made up some story about a girl I dated mentioning his name."

"Casually, huh?" Frank asked.

"Good news is that they remembered going to the funeral and seeing people put stuff in his coffin: CDs, shirts, pictures, stuff like that. They said it was more of a memorial."

"They say why his body wasn't in there?" Frank asked.

"He wasn't in the coffin?" Donnie asked, walking back into the kitchen, crumpling a bag of chips.

"I thought you weren't interested," Frank said.

"Hard not to be with how loud you both talk." Donnie came and sat down. "There was no body in there?"

Cliff explained to Donnie what happened at Old Salem Cemetery. "Once we got home, I Googled Corey and looked through some old papers on the library's database. The obits didn't list a cause of death and there was never a definitive reason given for his disappearance. Some people think he overdosed, some think he got killed. The only consistent thing is that he straight up vanished."

"Maybe he ran away," Donnie said.

"I thought the same thing, but it seems that got ruled out. If he did run away, he took hardly anything, not even his wallet or cash—both of which were still in his room."

"Weird," Frank said. "So, no one has any idea what could have happened to him?"

"Nope," Cliff replied.

"Ugh, I never liked these pages," Donnie said, scanning the yearbook.

"What pages?" Cliff careened his head over to look.

He turned the book around so Cliff could see the page. It was an ad memoriam page at the back. "Yearbooks are supposed to be fun and encapsulate the year with good memories, and then, this. *Womp Womp*. Always a downer."

"I always thought they were nice," Cliff replied. "He slid the book over to himself. "Helps me remember what happened that year."

"Did Corey have one of those?" Donnie asked.

"Don't know. Honestly, didn't think about it. I'll go pick up the next year and check," Cliff replied.

There was a knock at the front door. "Did they know anything about that book?" Frank asked.

"Oh yeah. They even described it to me!"

"This is the one that guy wanted you to get, right?" Donnie asked.

"Yeah. They said that everyone at the funeral wrote notes to Corey in it. They thought it was a little weird, but they all did it. Apparently, the mom announced that the notes would not be read, and that they'd be placed in the coffin before burial."

"So, if he was killed, you think the guy who killed him went to the funeral?" Frank asked.

"I think that's what your guy wants to find out," Cliff replied. "Crazy right? I kind of want to read it now to see what everyone wrote."

Frank pulled out his phone. "Since we're talking about crazy, check this out." He laid his phone on the table and began to cycle through his photo gallery. "I went to go bury those parts in that cemetery we found..."

"Hold up. You took pictures of that?" Donnie asked. Frank stared back blankly as Cliff took the phone. "And you still have them on your phone—Frank, come on, man! Are you serious?"

"Oh shit," Cliff said. His eyes widened as he pulled the phone closer.

"What?" Frank asked.

It took him a moment to answer. He looked from Donnie to Frank. "You found it. This is it!"

"This is what? What are you talking about?" Frank asked.

"The pictures my Lolo has. This is Bethel Cemetery."

26

"What?" Donnie asked, reaching for the phone. "Lemme see that."

"I promise you, man, this is it," Cliff exclaimed. "It looks exactly like my Lolo's pictures."

"Guys, there's no *Bethel* Cemetery," Donnie said, looking closely at the camera.

"See," Cliff said, smacking Frank in the arm. "I told you it wasn't just one grave."

"Where'd you find this?" Donnie asked.

"Oddly enough, I sort of stumbled on it," Frank said. "There's no path out to it. None of the graves are marked, either. The stones are traditional, old gravestones but they're all blank. No dates—nothing. They don't even look like they were stabilized. They're just lying on the ground."

Donnie was now scrolling through and zooming in on the photos. "How do you know they were graves and not just a spot for old headstones?" Donnie asked.

"Because the plots were sunken in." Frank replied. "There was something else too. That whole clearing is surrounded by seashells."

"Seashells? Like, real seashells?" Donnie asked.

Frank squinted his eyes toward his brother and tilted his head. "As opposed to fake ones? Yes, real seashells."

"Any idea why?" Cliff asked.

"The park ranger didn't know, but he said that in some places seashells represent a barrier. A way to keep what's inside from getting out, or maybe something out from getting in. I don't remember now."

"Mmm mmm," Cliff hummed, shaking his head. He got up and walked over to the refrigerator. "If you're going to be burying things out there, you're going to have to do that al—"

"Hey," Donnie said, holding up the phone for Frank to see. "What is this?"

The unsettling tone of Donnie's voice got Cliff's attention. He closed the refrigerator door and peered over Donnie's shoulder. "Yeah, what is that?"

"That," Frank said, "is a human body."

"Shut up," Donnie said back.

Frank took the phone from Donnie. "I'm being serious." Frank held it out for Cliff to see. "Ready for the weird part? I was maybe two feet down when I saw that."

"Did you move it at all? It's . . ." Donnie's voice trailed off as he examined the picture at different angles.

Frank finished Donnie's sentence, "On its side? No, I didn't touch it. I'm sure whoever it is wasn't buried alive, but I definitely don't think that's the corpse that's supposed to be down there." Frank gave a few swipes over the screen before he finally handed it back over to Donnie and Cliff. "Now look at this one."

They stared at the image. "Is that a . . ." Cliff began.

"That's a pager." Donnie cut in.

"Yup," Frank confirmed.

"You found that in the ground?" Cliff asked.

"Yup," Frank said again.

"Screw off," Donnie said. He took a seat in the chair and zoomed in closer, examining the item in question. "That's not real."

"You're right. I had that photoshopped. This is all just a big joke." Frank shot back derisively.

"I don't mean the pager isn't real. I mean it probably doesn't mean what you think it means."

"Oh, yeah? Then give me some rational explanation for why there would be a pager up in the middle of nowhere buried beside that," Frank said. Donnie continued staring at the phone until Cliff asked if he could see it.

"Something is definitely not right about that plot," Frank continued. "I think someone is buried on top of whoever is really down there."

"A pager was what? Nineteen nineties? Early two thousands?" Cliff asked.

"Nineties," Donnie replied. He sat, staring ahead in a daze. "There's no way. Someone had to have dropped their pager years back."

"And it magically sank down two feet and stopped right next to a corpse that *should* have been buried six feet down? Come on, man. I think we should go back out there."

"Absolutely not," Donnie replied.

"Hell. To. The. Naw," Cliff said. "I ain't goin' out there." A series of knocks sounded from the front door, startling Cliff, who cursed and hastily stood up.

"Calm down, killer," Donnie said, getting up from the table. "It was the front door."

"See? I can't even deal when someone knocks at the door," Cliff said. Dave Burgers yelled from the family room that he would get it.

Frank continued, "I have a theory: what if it *is* someone else? What if someone went missing in the nineties—"

"Oh, don't play that bullshit! You're already tied up in enough schemes. Plus, if it is a missing person, how are you going to explain *how* you found the body?"

"He's got you there, bro," Cliff replied.

"Now wait, hear me out" Frank said. "What if it's *Corey Grassman*?"

"Donnie!" Dave called from the family room.

"I promise you, we're not that lucky," Donnie said back, going to leave.

"But what if we were?"

"If it is, you're not going to know it." Donnie turned to face his brother. "Did you see an ID? Was it wearing a name tag? You're gonna dig up the pager and go through its recent contacts?"

"Cliff, come on," Frank said. "We can go in the morning—nothing scary happens in the morning."

"Yo, I interned at a hospital during early morning shift. *Lots* of freaky shit happens early in the morning. I'm not going out there," Cliff replied.

"If you're that concerned, go to the cops," Donnie said.

Frank sat, staring at Cliff, who was still going through the pictures. "You really won't go out there?"

"Bro. I'm not setting foot in that place. That's Bethel." He passed the phone back to Frank.

Frank crossed his arms and leaned back in the chair. "Fine. Maybe it's not Corey. But what if it *is* a missing person? And we found it? I'm not trying to sound shallow here—"

"Too late," Donnie interrupted.

"But if it is a missing person there might be a reward," Frank finished.

"That's you *not* sounding shallow?" Donnie asked, chuckling. "What if it's just someone who got buried two feet down?" Donnie replied.

There was a knock on the door frame leading into the kitchen. Lexie Porter was standing just inside the kitchen holding her purse. "Jeez, are you guys deaf?" The three of them looked up at her in surprise. "Must be a great conversation to not hear me knocking. Or your dad hollering," she said with a laugh. "Thank for answering your phone, cheese ball."

Donnie patted his pants and groaned. "Oh man! I'm sorry. It's in my office." He gave her a hug. "You been out there long?"

"No. Your dad opened the door. He yelled for you a couple of times but then we chatted for a bit."

"Sorry. You ready to go?" Donnie asked.

"Whoa, whoa, whoa there, cowboy," Frank said, getting up out of his chair. "You're not gonna offer her something to drink first or introduce her to your friends?"

"You told me you already met her at the Markham funeral last week.

And we're going out to eat, why would—never mind. You want something to drink? Water? Coffee?"

Lexie laughed. "I'm good, thanks."

"Hey Lexie," Frank said, extending his hand out in a wave. "Good to see you again."

"Hey, Frank," she replied. "How you been?"

"Good. Staying busy."

Lexie's head turned curiously as she eyed him. Her eyes floated up toward his hair. "You used to have long hair, didn't you?"

"Yeah!" Frank exclaimed excitedly. "You remember that?"

"Not really," she said with a shy smile. "I sorta looked you guys up in my elementary school yearbook after Mitch's funeral last week."

"Oh man, I loved that hair. Rocked that well into my junior year. Ended up cutting it for my senior pictures, though. Thought it made me look fat," Frank said, running a hand through his hair.

"I'm pretty sure it was the fat that made you look fat," Donnie said.

"Shut up," Frank said, reaching over to twist Donnie's nipple. He was blocked and pushed away. Donnie then excused himself to go get his wallet.

Lexie looked over at Cliff and waved. "Hi," she said.

"Oh, sorry," Frank said. "Cliff, this is Lexie. Lexie, this is Cliff. We call him Cliff *the Stiff*."

Cliff walked over to her. "Hey. Nice to meet ya." He reached out his hand. "They've never called me that, by the way."

She smiled. "We've actually met a couple of times, but you were a lot younger. We were at the same chess tournaments—long time ago."

"Whaaaat?" Cliff exclaimed. "No way. You still play?"

"Eh. Not as much as I'd like."

"Drop by the gym if you get some time. I'm always down for a match."

"What? You always say you're busy when I ask." Frank exclaimed.

"Because you consistently call the pieces by their wrong names and you yell *king me* when you take one," Cliff replied.

Lexie giggled and Donnie returned. "You ready?"

"Yeah." Lexie pulled out her phone and looked at the time. "What were you guys talking about? I heard *missing person*. Anything to do with the Murray High curse?"

The three of them each fixed their gaze on Lexie in an uncomfortable pause. "*The Murray High curse?*" Donnie asked. "What is that?" He looked at Frank or Cliff for an explanation, but their faces were noticeably just as confused.

"Are y'all serious? You all went to Murray High, right?" Lexie asked.

"Yeah," they said in slow unison.

"And you never heard about all the kids who went missing?"

"Oh," Frank and Donnie said. Frank continued, "Yeah, *that* we heard about."

"Never knew there was an official name for it," Donnie added. "I didn't get the sense anyone took it seriously—*I* never thought it was real."

"Did anyone go missing while you guys were there?" Lexie asked.

They all looked down in contemplation. "No," Donnie and Cliff said together. Frank, however, said, "Yes."

Donnie turned to his brother. "Who?"

"Seriously?" Frank said. "Your best friend from middle school? Pennington."

Donnie's brow furrowed. "Brian? He didn't go missing. He moved."

"You sure?" Frank asked.

Donnie looked like he was rolling the idea around in his head. "No. Addy would know though. He and Brian were pretty close in high school—lot closer than I was."

"How did you all miss this?" Lexie asked.

"Yo, I never heard of anything about a curse at Murray High," Cliff said. "Pretty sure I would have moved if I did."

"I'm surprised. I heard about it when I was a kid. It's been happening ever since my—" she stopped abruptly. Something about her face made it seem as if she knew how she wanted to finish that sentence but was afraid to say it. "For a long time."

"Oh!" Donnie snapped. He looked over and nodded to Frank, "Hey, you staying in tonight?"

"Yeah, why?"

"You might wanna go ahead and get the chairs ready for tomorrow. That way we don't have to do it all in the morning."

"Alright. I'll take care of it," Frank said, sitting back down.

"You ready?" Donnie asked Lexie.

"Sure," she replied, then waving a finger between Cliff and Frank, "Look into the Murray High thing if you don't believe me."

Cliff said, "No thanks," as Frank said, "Definitely."

THURSDAY
27

Monty spent the morning at the office running a search history of Corey, his parents, and the whereabouts of Connie Lancaster per Sophia's instructions. He didn't know what he hoped to find by locating Connie. Nor was he sure what he would ask if he *did* find her. The disturbance of Corey's grave was not yet public knowledge. Monty wasn't even sure if it *was* fully disturbed, but he couldn't shake the question of why anyone would want to look into a coffin that wasn't occupied. Unless something was put in there of considerable value. That's where Corey's parents came in, but they were little to no help. His father had passed away less than a year after Corey's disappearance. His mother confirmed that several things were placed inside, mostly by students, and that she herself put in two or three items: a shirt or two, and maybe a watch. But in regard to things of value, she was clueless.

Monty vaguely remembered the case from when he first moved to Murray, but the conspiracy of murder or suicide was new to him. He asked Corey's mother about what happened in the case, but she gave him only what he'd already read in the newspapers: one night Corey was in his bed, the next day he never came home. Both parents left for work early in the morning, and it was common for them not to see Corey before school. She wanted to believe at first that Corey ran away—and tried hard to hold to that belief. But she knew the situation showed no signs of such a decision and after a while, any hope of Corey's return was extinguished when even his closest friends heard nothing from him.

The search for Connie Lancaster didn't take long. She passed away in 2014 from leukemia. He attempted to contact her family but only her mom was still living, and she had no recollection of who Corey Grassman was other than a familiar name from Connie's past. The ex-husband, Connie's dad, had died just after Connie graduated high school in 1999.

At around eight a.m. Monty hit a dead end. He leaned back in his desk chair and crossed his arms, letting out a slow breath. He reasoned that there may be there was nothing to this case. No signs of abduction. Where would he go? Where would he vanish to in a small town without someone knowing? *Maybe Corey did run away? He was practically of age, kids do it all the time.* His intuition—that strange gut sensation—kept nagging at him to believe otherwise. Likely because this situation reminded him too much of someone else.

Of *her*.

The thud of someone on the roof startled Frank awake. The clock on his bedside table read 7:16. He sat up with a jolt and cursed, flinging his sheets back—he'd slept through his alarm! Heavy steps were walking up the creaky, wooden stairs outside his door. Finally, a violent pounding at his door.

"Get up, turd sack," Donnie yelled from the other side. "Need your help getting the coffin out."

"I'm already up," Frank replied. He heard his brother reply "hurry up" and continue walking down the hall.

Frank slipped into some running shorts and a t-shirt and walked downstairs. He yelled for Donnie and then saw him outside through the window, straightening chairs in the backyard.

"Sorry, man. Slept through my alarm, somehow," Frank called, walking onto the back porch.

"No worries. I couldn't sleep. We stayed up too late and overdid it on coffee and bourbon. I was already up at six thirty, so I just went over and got him. Vince helped me load him in. I'd say let's just roll him into the foyer for now until we get started, it's already so hot out here."

The two of them removed the dark-stained oak coffin from the hearse and rolled it inside. Frank knocked on the wood and made a questioning comment about the coffin's integrity.

Donnie laughed. "They both assured me that this model was exactly as advertised," he said running his hand along the smooth, rounded finish of the coffin's lid.

They finished organizing the area designated for the coffin and those who would be speaking. Donnie placed hand fans on the chairs, each marked with a white Burgers Brothers logo. He noticed one of them had a sticker underneath with Frank's skeleton icon giving a thumbs up. He held it up for his brother. "Yo, hand me another one. This one has your sticker on it."

"No, no. Leave it there, it's supposed to. I do that sometimes. Whoever has it gets a ten percent off card over at Mom's donut shop. At the end of the service, I'll announce that there's a sticker on one of the fans. People love it."

Donnie's face was expressionless. He and Frank stared at each other for a long moment until Donnie casually ripped the fan in two. "Wind must have ripped this one. Get me another fan, will ya?"

"You're such a child." Frank went inside and pulled a new fan from the box in his office closet and stuck another skeleton decal on the back.

The first guest car arrived a little after 9 a.m. Frank realized he was still wearing his running shorts and rocking his bed head. He bounded upstairs and into the shower and emerged in what he felt to be record time fully dressed, shaved, and smelling delicious. When he came downstairs, it was nine twenty and there was a handful of teenagers in the living room, sitting on the couches on their phones. Frank said "hey," but they ignored him.

He walked around the house looking for the other guests but there were none to be seen. He found his brother outside in the front yard sweeping off the front porch. "Where is everyone?"

"Hopefully in the living room where I left them," Donnie replied.

Frank paused and glanced inside the house, and then back at Donnie. "The Garbage Pail Kids are the only ones here?"

"Ugh. Yeah. They got dropped off by one of the parents. Some of the family wanted to meet in private before the funeral—there's some situation. They asked if they could just wait here for a bit while they went somewhere to talk—didn't want the kids around in case things got too heated."

"Where'd they go to talk?"

"I didn't ask. They said they'd be back by nine-thirty, though."

"Wow. Okay. That's a first," Frank said. "What else do we need to do?"

"It's all done. I'm gonna finish sweeping the porch if you want to make sure the bathroom is clean. I ran the vacuum, programs are in the kitchen, we're ready to go. We'll just need to wheel the coffin around, and pull the water bottles up from the fridge once people start arriving."

"I took care of the bathroom last night. You want some breakfast?" Frank asked.

Donnie looked at his watch. "Dude, don't start making breakfast. People are gonna be here in ten minutes."

"Pop-Tarts, man. I was just gonna throw a couple in the toaster."

"Oh. Nah, I'm good."

Frank went inside and peeked into the living room. No one had moved, and no one was talking. They looked like statues. He pulled out his phone and snapped a picture—no one noticed—and sent it with a message to his mom. Afterwards, he went into the kitchen and sat at the table eating a pack of blueberry Pop-tarts with a cup of coffee.

At 9:45, Dave came through the back door carrying two plastic bags with a white box in each. He commented that there were no cars in the driveway and asked about what was going on. Frank explained the situation with the kids. "Not sure where the parents are though. They said they'd be back by nine-thirty."

"I'm sure they'll be here," Dave said. "Need anything else?"

"No, we're all set. You goin' back up there?"

"Yeah, one of the girls is out. Your mom needs help taking orders. I'll see ya this afternoon. Good luck." Dave closed the door behind him, and Frank walked the sacks over to the family room. "Hey guys," he said.

"How's it goin?" No one looked up or spoke. Frank stood in front of them. "Cool. Cool-cool-cool-cool-cool..." His voice trailed off.

He placed the sacks on the coffee table in front of where they were sitting. Dead air. "You all live in Murray or you from out of town?" He pulled out the boxes and placed them on the table. "Oh yeah?" he said, after another awkward moment of silence. "I've been there a few times. It's pretty nice." Finally, one of the girls sitting in the armchair looked up with a scrunched face, practically scowling at Frank. She had a colorful floral wreath around her blond hair. "How 'bout you, flower patch? Where you from?"

One of the boys looked up at Frank and then over to the girl in the chair. He chuckled. "Yo, he just called you flower patch."

"My name's Frank," he replied and pointed to the girl's hair. "Your wreath is actually really pretty. You make it yourself?"

She nodded, hesitantly.

"That's bad ass," Frank said.

She gave the slightest of smiles. "Thanks."

"Anyone else do anything interesting? Make anything? Do impressions? Beat box?" Dead air. "Contact juggle?" Nothing. "Tough crowd," he mumbled to himself. "Alright well, I brought you guys some donuts." That got their attention. "Oh, that woke you up, huh? These are the best donuts in Kentucky, bunch of different flavors. Help yourself."

"Are our parents here yet?" another girl asked.

"Nah, not yet." Frank replied. "Where'd they go?"

"Family drama," one of them muttered, in a low, drawn out voice. A few of them chuckled at the response.

"Family drama at a funeral. Nothing new there," Frank said. "I'm sure they'll be back soon."

"Probably not," a boy said. He was squeezed in beside Flower Patch on the armchair, staring over at her phone. Then Flower spoke up. "There's always drama with our family, they're a hot mess." She clicked off her phone and sat forward, moving toward the donuts. The rest of them followed.

"Chocolate, blueberry, strawberry, cinnamon, and banana," Frank said, watching them pick through the boxes.

"These look really good," armchair boy said. The rest of them offered a thank you.

"Yeah, no worries." He pulled napkins from the bag, then scooted the paper plates forward for them to use. "And there's waters and sodas over in the cooler by the back door if y'all get thirsty. Let me know if you need anything else."

"You work here?" Flower asked.

"Yes, ma'am," Frank replied. "Own the place with my brother Donnie. He's outside somewhere."

"You live here, too?" A boy asked.

"Yup. All my life."

"You ever see ghosts in here?" Someone chimed in.

Frank looked around to give the impression he didn't want anyone to hear him. He spoke soft and slow, "All the time." They froze in wonder.

"You bein' for real?" Another of the boys asked. Frank nodded his head. "I couldn't do it. You actually leave that shit here overnight?"

"I assume when you say that *shit*, you're referring to the dead bodies?" There was a murmur of laughter from the others as the boy nodded. Frank continued, "Oh yeah. Have to. Usually have bodies here for one to three days, depending on how much work needs to be done and funeral planning," Frank said. He heard Donnie call him from the kitchen and yelled he was coming.

"Have you ever had someone who wasn't . . . like . . . dead wake up—or something—during a funeral?"

"Nah. If they're not dead when they get here, they're dead before they go in the box. Everybody gets embalmed before a funeral now days."

"What's embalmed?" Flower asked.

"It's where they take all your muscles out," armchair boy replied.

"Good guess, but not exactly." Frank winked at him. "You take all the *organs* out, then fill the body up with a fluid to keep it preserved," Frank said.

"Ew," Flower said quietly.

Frank started to walk out and turned to face them. "Haven't had anyone wake up, but we have had someone die during a funeral." There was a collection of shocked exclamations and curses. "Long time ago. This woman lost her husband and during the funeral she stepped out of the parlor to get some air and walk around a bit. Found her dead after the funeral." Frank started to leave again but stopped and motioned toward the couch where many of them were now sitting. "Right on that couch, actually." And then he walked out, smiling at the sound of frantic movement and sharp commotion as he entered the kitchen.

"What are you laughin' at?" Donnie asked.

"I told them about Carolyn Barnes," Frank replied. "Freaked 'em out."

"Was Dad here?"

"Yeah. I asked if he could bring them some donuts. Only way I could get them to say anything—or move for that matter. What's up?"

"First guest just pulled up. You wanna go ahead and get the body outside?" Donnie asked.

"Yeah. You check and make sure he still looks okay—not jostled from the drive or anything?" Frank asked.

"Nah, not yet," Donnie replied.

Frank started walking toward the foyer where the casket was resting on its cart. "Did he look okay when you picked him up?"

"Honestly, I was too out of it to even to look. I'm sure he's fine though. They said they were done with him and the funeral was scheduled for this morning."

Frank stopped and turned toward his brother. "You didn't look in the coffin when you picked it up?"

"No. They wheeled it out to me and helped me put it in the car," Donnie said. Frank's head fell back, and he groaned. "What? What's wrong?

You think he's gonna look bad or something?" Frank began unlatching the coffin. "What is your deal? They told me everything was all ready to go—" Gloria Gaynor's "I Will Survive" blared from the coffin's interior as soon as Frank lifted the lid. Wiring pulled up a stuffed doll made of what looked like potato sacks; its face bore a beaming smile and its arms were brilliantly engineered to come forward, revealing two hands in the shape of a finger gun, pointing at the two of them."

"What the *fuck* is that?" Donnie exclaimed.

"That's Higgins," Frank sighed. "I meant to tell you before you went over there to make sure you look in the coffin before you take it. They use this as a joke when they're showing coffins. Tried to give it to me once but thankfully I noticed before I put it in the car. Dammit!" Frank rubbed the sides of his head with his palms. "I really didn't think they'd do this after what happened last week."

"Call them. Tell 'em to bring the body, now!" Donnie said coldly.

"Oh yeah. I'm sure they'll drop everything and speed right over here. I'll ask them to bring over some champagne too." He grabbed his keys. "Any embarrassing attention we get is a win for them. I'll go grab him. You stay here and start meeting the guests."

"Wait, hold up! We gotta start soon, what am I supposed to say?"

"Just tell them there was a problem at the Kochs," Frank said. "No one is here yet. They don't know that we came back with the wrong body. Tell them the Kochs are being assholes and holding us up. Really sell it, ya know? Maybe they'll leave them a bad review." Frank shoved Higgins' extendable arms down as he lowered the lid.

Donnie cursed again under his breath. "Fine. Just, hurry and get back before people start showing up."

Frank started toward the door as Donnie went to push the coffin toward him. "What are you doin'?"

"Helping you put this back in the car," Donnie replied.

"Screw that! This is a nice coffin. Take it downstairs."

28

The funeral started fifteen minutes late, but no one seemed to mind. Donnie attributed it to the Koch brothers at Life Memorial for their unprofessionalism. He threw a couple of lines in there about them having to redo parts of the face because it looked so atrocious. People bought it and even joined in the criticism.

When Frank returned, Donnie helped him unload the coffin and wheel it around to the back. After the service began, Frank stayed nearby the house on the back deck to act as an usher for late guests and to observe. Donnie went around to the front to decompress and be alone. To his initial dismay, when he rounded the corner, there was someone sitting on the swing beside the front door: an elderly woman, staring out at the road. She didn't notice Donnie walk up beside her.

"Hey there," Donnie began.

"Oh," the woman jumped slightly and turned to see him. "My goodness. You scared me." She laughed. "Am I in the way?" She moved to get up, but Donnie held out his hand and stepped forward.

"No, no. You're fine. I was just walking around here to get some fresh air. Are you here for the funeral?"

"I am. Kinda sorta, I guess. I was a good friend of Calvin's for many years. He and I were sweethearts. A long time ago." She extended a hand toward him. "I'm Charlene Porch."

"Nice to meet you Ms. Porch." Donnie returned the gesture. "I'm Donnie Burgers, one of the owners. They just started. I can help you find a seat if you'd like, or set one up in the back—it was kind of full when I came around—"

"Oh, no. Don't you worry about me. I only came to see his sister Gail and maybe sneak a peek at Cal if I can." She leaned forward and spoke in a softer voice. "Don't get along too well with his wife. She kinda thinks he and I . . ." Then she winked at Donnie. "You know."

Donnie didn't know what to say so he just said, "Oh!"

"We didn't, in case you were wondering."

"Hey, I wasn't gonna ask."

She grinned. "Not while they were married anyways." It looked to Donnie like her eyebrows were struggling to hop up and down.

He decided to take a seat on the top step of the porch. "How long did y'all know each other?"

"Oh, goodness. Since grade school." She sighed. "Cal and I grew up around here. Actually, we met out in what used to be called Golden Pond, Kentucky in Land Between the Lakes."

"You grew up in LBL?" Donnie asked.

"Mmm hmm," she replied. "My family was in that area much of their life. My parents lived in a place called Birmingham, Kentucky. Ever heard of that?" Donnie shook his head. "Beautiful little town. It got flooded in the forties. To their misfortune, they moved to Golden Pond." She laughed. "They stayed as long as they could until they got forced out, and finally moved to Mayfield."

"You should talk to my brother. He's been doing a lot of research on LBL. He'd love to hear some of your stories."

"Well, I left after high school, and moved out east, but boy I could tell him some things about living there. What's your brother doing research on?"

"Bethel Cemetery," Donnie replied. He waited for a laugh or a sigh—or any indication of annoyance at the old legend—but it never came.

"Bethel Cemetery," she muttered with interest. "Haven't heard that name in a while. Let me guess, something to do with that woman?" She paused and looked down at the ground. "What was her name?"

"Avilla Bethel."

"Yes! Avilla. Always thought that was a pretty name," she said. "Can't say I know a lot about the *cemetery*, I'm afraid. I do remember, growing up, hearing about *her* from our minister. Just a horrific story, what happened to her."

Donnie's tilted his head in interest. "I grew up always hearing *ghost* stories about her, but never from a minister. What happened to her?"

She gave him a puzzled look. "I'm not familiar with any ghost stories," she replied, shaking her head. "My father was quite strict on my sister and me. Stories about ghosts were not allowed in our house. It was a terrible thing—just awful."

"You mean with her attacking all those kids?"

Charlene leaned her head in as if she hadn't heard what Donnie said. "Attacking kids? What in the world?"

"Isn't that the story? She lived in the woods and attacked children?"

"Lord, no. I hope that isn't the story," Charlene replied. She let out a soft laugh. "If it is, I didn't hear that version. Lord, have mercy! No wonder my father didn't want us talking about her. No, Mr. Burgers, she was sick."

Donnie paused. "Like, cancer sick?"

"It might have been. I'm not too sure. She was a schoolteacher, as I recall—and a Bible school teacher at her church. One month she got sick. *Really* sick. Practically bed ridden. She was unable to do anything for herself: couldn't feed herself, couldn't clean—couldn't even get up to go to the bathroom."

"Man," Donnie muttered.

"As sad as that may sound, the real tragedy is that no one came to visit her. She didn't have any family, even church friends wouldn't come to see her. Likely scared of catching whatever it is she may have had. Then one night her house caught fire, and she was trapped inside. Burned alive. No one even knew for days." Charlene was staring out at the road. "They found her in her bed, looking like she was trying to crawl off it and onto the floor." Donnie wasn't sure if she was finished.

"Wow," Donnie muttered. "That's horrible."

"Yes, it was. The preacher used her story every year to remind us to make sure we always check in on one another. No one deserves to die alone, no matter what the situation is."

"This is gonna sound a little insensitive, but if the house burned down, and no one knew about it for days, how do they know she was crawling out of the bed? I mean, wouldn't everything be ash?"

Charlene sighed through her nose and turned to give Donnie a look of disappointment. "Mr. Burgers, try not to let facts get in the way of a good illustration."

Donnie chuckled softly. "Fair enough. That is *definitely* not the story I heard."

"What did you hear?" Charlene asked.

"Something a lot darker," Donnie replied.

"Oh. Well, I don't know how much of it is true. Like I said, the point was to make sure everyone was looking after one another. Plus, it sticks with you."

"I'm not saying I don't believe it. I was just asking a question." He glanced at his watch; the funeral was at the 30-minute mark. "Shoot. I need to go around and help with the coffin." He quickly got to his feet. "Can I bring you anything? Coffee? Water?"

"No thank you. I may use your restroom if that's okay. When you get to be my age you don't want to miss an opportunity for that."

"Absolutely." Donnie assisted her off the swing. "And if you'd like, once the service is over, maybe I can get the family to come around front and give you some privacy with Cal. If you want."

"I'd like that," Charlene said.

Frank was the last one to leave the graveside. He leaned against the driver's side door of his car while a handful of guests exchanged final hugs and lunch plans. He waved goodbye as the two cars drove past him and then, finally, took off his coat and loosened his tie. He sighed with ecstasy as he stepped into the car's chilled interior and rested his forehead against the dashboard to get a face full of cold, crisp air.

He could see his cell phone in the lower vestibule blinking a yellow light to signal a missed call—and then it hit him! "Oh shit!" He exclaimed. "Shit, shit, shit!" He'd missed the appointment to deliver Corey's book to the mystery caller. There was nothing he could do. There was no way to contact them, and it was too risky to leave the item in the consignment shop now. Most unfortunate, he was still stuck with that horrid book.

●

Donnie was taking down folding chairs and carrying them over to a cart when Cliff walked out of the gym. "You seen Frank?" Cliff asked.

"He's finishing up a funeral. You need something?" Donnie asked.

Cliff pulled out his phone. "Not really. I asked a couple of friends about that Murray High curse; seems legit. I guess Lexie was right."

"How did we never hear about that?" Donnie asked. He lifted two padded folding chairs onto his arms and began walking toward the house. Cliff followed behind, staring at his phone.

"I know, right? Found something else too. You ever hear of anyone named Marcus Taylor?"

Donnie set the chairs down onto the cart. "Nope."

"Me neither. Apparently, he disappeared in the early nineties. The guy I talked to mentioned him, friend of his cousin I think."

"Cool," Donnie replied, dryly.

Cliff could read Donnie's disinterest. He put his phone away and scooped up seven folding chairs, walking with ease over to the cart. He asked how everything went with the funeral and Donnie explained the mix up with the Kochs. Cliff burst into laughter.

"They finally got him back," Cliff said.

"What's that mean?" Donnie asked.

"The same thing happened a year ago, except it was *you all* that had to give up a service. It was a last-minute change with the family, and Vince came to pick up the body for an afternoon funeral. Frank gave him all the material with the body, and then handed Vince a CD and said that it was a song list from the family of the guy's favorite songs. Frank instructed him that the family wanted the coffin wheeled in only after everyone sat down and that one of the songs on there was to be played as an accompaniment. There was of course no such instruction from the family. The song they wheeled him in to was cued up to the chorus of "Stayin' Alive"—the Bee Gees' song." Cliff couldn't keep the laughter in. "They played it for nearly a full minute before Randy ran back there and cut it off." Donnie sighed. "I think a lot of the family thought it was hysterical, but Vince was pissed."

"Now it makes sense why he was freaking out on me over not checking the body when I picked it up. I'm thinking to myself, why would I have to check the body?"

"Oh yeah, man. He's been watching his back ever since."

"What an idiot," Donnie said, shaking his head. He heard a car door. "Speak of the devil." Frank walked around to the back of the house and yelled something to them. "Just in time," Donnie said, folding two more chairs and carrying them toward the back porch.

"I figured you'd be done by now. I've been gone for forty minutes—what have you been doing?" Frank called over to them.

"Someone stuck around after you all left and talked to me for nearly half an hour."

"Was she the one that you were helping out at the end?"

"Yeah, she just wanted a moment alone with the guy. The wife wasn't too thrilled about her being here. I should have introduced you to her. She grew up in LBL."

"Did you get her number?" Frank asked.

Donnie gave his brother a quizzical look. "Why would I get her number?"

"I don't know," Frank replied with a shrug. "You didn't introduce me to her. Figured maybe you got an email or something."

"Oh. Yeah, sorry, man. Didn't even think about it," Donnie called back.

"Did anyone call the house while I was gone?" Frank yelled.

"Nope," Donnie replied.

"Shoot," Frank said. He turned to Cliff and picked up a single chair to load onto the cart. "I forgot to drop that book off this morning. Got completely sidetracked with all this."

"That's not good," Cliff said, grabbing another six chairs.

"Tell me about it. I'll have to wait for him to call again, I guess."

"Hey, so," Donnie yelled, positioning chairs on the cart. "Fun fact. That lady gave me a completely different version of the Bethel story."

"What do you mean?" Frank asked, hoisting the single chair over his head and walking toward the house.

Donnie explained what happened—according to Charlene Porch—to Avilla Bethel. He recapped her sickness, the fire, and the misunderstanding about her mythical killing of children.

"That's a lot different than that what Mr. Atlas used to tell us," Cliff said. He was standing by the cart watching Frank. "Dude, could you grab more than one chair at a time!"

"Shut up, Mom! I've been working all day!" Frank shot back.

Cliff kicked his leg out toward Frank, narrowly missing his butt.

Frank called back toward them, "This is why I don't buy these stories; there're too many versions. Though, that one's a little more believable than the ones we heard at school."

"Yeah. More sad than scary," Donnie said.

"But then where did all the ghost stories come from? And the stories about her eating kids and having her house burned down?" Cliff asked.

"I'm sure they just got adapted over time," Donnie said. "Sick old woman that no one wants to be around eventually becomes some hideous, sadistic old witch in the woods who will eat anyone who comes near. An accidental house fire gets turned into an angry mob's act of revenge. Easy." Donnie leaned the podium toward Frank and lifted his end. They walked back toward the house, leaving Cliff to contemplate the stories.

"Maybe. Doesn't make any sense why people would make such a big deal about her grave though," Cliff said, as he carried the remaining seven chairs over.

"You get 'em all?" Frank asked Cliff, carrying the podium up the porch steps. Cliff's forehead crinkled as if he'd been insulted. "What? I'm carrying the podium!"

"Bitch, of course you are. You work here!" Cliff exclaimed.

Frank and Donnie maneuvered up the steps to the back door where Frank set down his end of the podium and turned around to open the screen door. He jumped back and screamed, startling Donnie into almost dropping his side. There was a woman standing inside, staring back at him.

29

"I'm terribly sorry," the woman spoke out through the screen door. "I didn't mean to scare you."

"No, it's okay." Frank could feel his heart rate creeping up from the scare. "I just wasn't expecting someone to be standing there." He took a big breath and moved to open the door. "Can I help you?"

"I guess I should have called first. I came in around front and didn't see anyone in the offices. Then I heard talking out here. Is Frank Burgers here?" she asked.

"I'm Frank," he said. "What can I do for you?"

She stepped onto the porch and looked at Donnie and Cliff, then back to Frank. "I'm Jessica Lear. We spoke the other day. Mary Ellen Rhodes is my mother—the author."

"Oh my gosh! Yes. How are you?" He extended his hand to shake.

"I'm well, thank you." She shook his hand and glanced back toward the door. "Do you have a moment to talk? In private?"

"Um . . ." He looked at Donnie who waved him off, saying he would finish cleaning up. "Sure. Come inside. Can I get you something to drink? Coffee?"

"No, I'm fine. Thank you."

"Is your mom here too?" Frank asked.

"No, she's at home," she replied, walking back into the house behind Frank. "She doesn't actually know that I'm here."

"Everything alright?" They stepped into his office.

"I felt a little uncomfortable with how that conversation went the other night between you and her. I know how she can be sometimes and that . . ." She paused. "How do I say this? That book gave her a tough time." Frank was about to interject but she continued, "Not the book necessarily but several things while she was writing that book. So, I just wanted to make sure you didn't leave that conversation thinking she was . . ." Jessica stopped again and shifted her mouth to the side in search of the right word. "Crazy."

"I definitely didn't think she was crazy—not at all. I just figured it was late and she wasn't in a mood to talk." He smiled.

Jessica sighed. "There's more to it than that. That's why I came to see you." She slid her purse off her shoulder, onto the fold of her elbow, and reached inside. "You asked her about something she left out of her book. A cemetery." She pulled out a manila folder and looked at Frank. "My mom did a ton of research for that book: interviews, libraries, articles, cemetery visits. Many of those drawings she did by hand, you know. With so many visits and interviews, word got around about what she was doing."

Frank moved around to the other side of his desk and took a seat, which in turn prompted Jessica to finally sit down. "When I was older, my dad was the one who told me all this—told me more than my mom ever did, anyway. Apparently, she started getting letters in the mail from someone about that cemetery—Bethel—telling her to not include it in the book and to stop looking into it. At first, she was confused because she'd never heard anything about it. The stories, I mean."

"Is she not from around here?" Frank asked.

"She is, but according to my dad, before her research she knew nothing about it. She found that place on her own—stumbled into it, practically. So, when she started getting these letters, naturally her curiosity was piqued. Whose wouldn't be? She tracked the person down, met with them, and after that . . ." Jessica stood and reached out her hand with the manila folder toward Frank. "She took these out."

Frank hesitated but took the envelope. "Am I supposed to open this now?"

"Sure. It's the missing section of her book, that's all." Frank opened the envelope and pulled out three sheets of paper. On top was a hand-drawn image: a large circle with an arrangement of fourteen boxes inside, placed in a chaotic arrangement. Two of the boxes had something illegible scribbled underneath.

Frank recognized the layout immediately and his stomach leapt. "Is this what I think it is?" Frank asked. Jessica didn't respond. He turned to the next page, a handwritten list of numbers from one to fourteen. Next to one and two were the names Daniel Owen and Clifton Stone. Three through fourteen were blank.

"Does this correspond to the drawing?" Frank asked, reexamining the previous page.

"Supposedly," Jessica said back, softly.

Finally, Frank turned to the last page, a black-and-white photo of a dark-haired woman, probably in her late thirties, standing in an open field. The woman wasn't smiling, simply staring into the camera. "Is this your mom?"

Jessica nodded. "I don't know if someone took that photo. She probably did it herself."

Frank recognized this field. It was the very one he'd just been in; he recognized the ominous tree looming in the darkness of the background. Just above it was written one word in black marker: *Bethel*.

Frank cursed and looked at Jessica. "Is this for real?" He laid the papers out across his desk and stared at each of them. "Holy shit," Frank whispered. "Sorry." He traced his finger over the word *Bethel* scribbled at the top of the photo. "She thinks this is really Bethel Cemetery?"

"She seemed to believe it was. And, for whatever reason, that it didn't belong in her book."

Frank turned back to the first drawing and then flipped to the page with fourteen numbers on it. "What's the deal, here? Why are all these blank? Did she not figure out which one was Avilla's?"

"I don't think so. She found those two obviously, but, according to my dad, gave up before she found the rest—or that woman's," Jessica replied. "Like I said, she's never talked about any of it. She doesn't even know I have this or that I came to see you. She'd be furious. I've asked about this place a couple of times, and she reacts in a similar way that she did to you; like it's not real."

"I actually just stumbled on this place, too." Frank tapped the sheet of paper with his finger. "A friend of mine thought it might be Bethel, but I've never thought the place was real. That's why I wanted to talk to your mom." He nodded, examining the photo. "Doesn't look like it's changed. Can I keep these?"

She clicked her tongue. "Sorry, no. This is the only copy she has, and she would know if they were gone. But you can take a picture."

Frank pulled out his phone and snapped several photos of the papers. "Why did she not put this stuff in the book? Or at least finish the research on it?"

"All my dad knew was that one day she was writing about it, and then one afternoon she came back from an interview, and it was like a switch went off in her brain. She wanted to stop researching cemeteries—stop going into LBL. She didn't even want to finish the project. My dad finally talked her into completing it and told her to just leave that place out of it."

"Jeez. Where's your dad now? You think he'd talk to me about any of this?"

"He would've," Jessica replied. "If you'd have asked a year ago, that is."

"Oh. I'm sorry."

"No, he's not dead, technically. He was diagnosed with Alzheimer's in twenty fourteen. Until this past year he wasn't doing too bad. Now though it's just . . ." she trailed off and finally went quiet. "Yeah. It's been a lot."

"I'm sorry to hear that," Frank said. "I can't even imagine what it's like to lose a parent like that."

"I wish I couldn't either," Jessica said back. Frank put the papers back into the envelope and handed them over to Jessica. "I came out here to show you this, but I also wanted to tell you something—warn you, I guess."

"Warn me?" Frank said.

"I don't want to sound crazy. If you knew me, you would know it takes a lot to make me say what I'm about to say because I don't believe in stuff like this. But after watching my mom for the last several years and hearing the stories from my dad about what this was like for her," she indicated the envelope, "I think there's something . . . *disturbed* . . . out there. Something that's not right. My mother is the strongest person I've ever met. With so much controversy over this particular spot in LBL, she would have normally jumped at the chance to write about it. Strangely enough, she wanted no part of it." Jessica dug out a ring of keys from her purse and looked back up at Frank. "Take all this for what it's worth. Maybe it's nothing. But I wouldn't feel right with myself, knowing what I know about my mom, if I didn't come out here to warn you. My parents were convinced that something is troubling those woods and if I were you, I'd stay away from it."

A prickly chill began to crawl up Frank's back. "You wouldn't happen to know what this person said to your mom about the place would you? To make her want to stop?"

"I don't, but I had a feeling you'd ask." She pulled out a folded envelope from her pocket. "His name is Edward Hubbs. This is his last known address. I found it in a mix of papers she had. Again, she doesn't know I've done any of this." Frank took the envelope and wrote down the address before handing it back to her. "I don't know if he's still alive, but if you insist on going out there, maybe you'll reconsider after talking to *him*."

30

Frank spent some time that afternoon searching through his town database and funeral records for any information on Edward Hubbs. Obituaries and current living records all came up empty. He tried doing a Google search on the two names from Mary Ellen's list but as he expected, it got him nowhere.

Mary Ellen's research indicated that Avilla Bethel's grave was somewhere in the midst of those fourteen graves. But which one? How would he figure it out? And as interesting as *that* was, there was still the mystery of what he found buried there. There was a knock at his door. Donnie came in and asked if he wanted to shoot some pool.

"Starting to like that thing, aren't ya?" Frank asked, getting up.

"I never said I didn't like it. I said it was a dumb buy."

Donnie started racking the balls and asked about the woman who showed up earlier.

Frank recounted the exchange, telling him about Mary Ellen's experience with Bethel Cemetery, Edward Hubbs, and the warnings to stay away.

"That's unnerving," he said. "Who's the guy—Hobbs?"

"Hubbs. No clue. Couldn't find any records for him either. No funeral notices, at least for anywhere around here."

"You ask Dad?" Donnie asked, lining up his shot. "He knows everyone around here." His cue connected with the ball and a loud crack echoed through the living room as it sent the other balls scattering.

"No," Frank replied. "Hey, Dad!"

"He's out, whatcha need?" Ginny called back.

"Can you come here?"

"I didn't mean right now," Donnie muttered.

She appeared in the doorway, holding a magazine.

"You know anybody named Edward Hubbs?" Frank asked.

She appeared to be processing the name in her own mental database. "It sounds familiar. Hubbs. Is there a connection to a Shirley Hubbs?"

Frank's shot connected with the blue solid ball, but it ricocheted off the side, missing the pocket. "I don't know," Frank replied. "Never heard of him. Someone asked me to chat with him."

"The name sounds familiar. Let me think and I'll get back to you. Is this for a funeral?"

"It's about ghosts," Donnie said, squaring up his shot and then taking it.

"Shut up, man. No, just some historical stuff in LBL. Nothing major."

"Top secret, huh? I'll let you know."

"Maybe he's not in the area anymore," Donnie said, as his mom walked away.

They both heard the back door open. Cliff yelled out something.

"In here," Frank and Donnie yelled together. "It's possible." Frank leaned down to eye his next move.

"Guys, check this out," Cliff entered carrying a yellow pad and several sheets of paper and placed them on the pool table in front of Frank's white ball.

"Dude, come on," Frank said. "Right in my shot."

"*Dude*," Cliff said back. "You're gonna wanna see this." He splayed the sheets of paper out across the felt. They were copies of yearbook photos with names circled.

"Don't you work? Who's watching your gym?" Donnie asked.

"It's a *gym*, not a daycare." Cliff flipped through the first few pages in his yellow pad before he placed it on top of the printed pages. "I have an emergency button that goes to my phone in case something happens." On the notepad, amid what looked to be several lines of writing, Cliff had drawn a box around four names with dates beside them. "Frank was on to something when he said missing persons," Cliff said.

"This again?" Donnie groaned. "I thought you didn't want anything to do with the whole Bethel story."

"This isn't about Bethel. This is about that Murray High curse your girlfriend was talking about."

"Even better." Donnie rolled his eyes. "Can you at least move the pictures so Frank can miss this shot?"

"You might actually want to see this too," he said to Donnie. "This is some Nancy Drew stuff."

"I love Nancy Drew," Frank replied, pounding the end of the pool cue on the wood floor. "The shot can wait."

"Of course it can," Donnie said back with a cheap smile, and slid his stick into the rack on the wall. "Alright well, I'm gonna go finish up the work on our online ads. I mean, one of us should probably be doing something to bring in money to fix this place."

"Oh, give me a break. You were just playing pool. Calm down," Frank replied.

"Actually, there could be some money in *this*," Cliff said, indicating the sheets of paper on the table.

Donnie turned back toward him. "What does that mean?"

"It means that Frank may have actually found something up there," Cliff said. "I told you," talking to Donnie, "that I came across another name. Marcus Taylor." Cliff turned to Frank. "When I was asking around about the Murray High thing, one guy mentioned another disappearance back in the nineties. I went to the library and did some searches for Corey and this other guy—they've got all the *Murray Ledgers* on computer. For a while I wasn't getting anything different from what we already knew—Corey Grassman vanished." Cliff moved a printed page across the felt over to Frank. It was a yearbook page with Corey's face circled and the number *1997* written in black marker at the top. "But then I came across this." He placed a copy of a newspaper clipping on the table. "The guy was right, someone else did disappear—in nineteen-ninety. No explanation behind it." Cliff looked at Donnie. "And your dad did the funeral." The clipping was of an obituary. Marcus Taylor's face was circled, and the number *1990* written at the top.

"So what?" Donnie said. "Two kids went missing. No big deal."

"That's what I thought, too. Kids disappear all the time. So, I asked the librarian if she recognized the names. She had said she'd been in Murray all her life, I figured she might know something. Unfortunately, she didn't recognize *those* names, but she rattled off four other kids who died. One got sick, the others were accidents, but one of those struck me as a little odd, so, for shits and giggles, I checked it out." Cliff laid down another sheet of paper like it was a winning poker hand; a yearbook page with a boy's face circled in red. "Jermaine Warren. Ever heard of him?"

Donnie and Frank shook their head. Frank reached for the picture.

"She said Jermaine died in seventy-six. Drove his car into Kentucky Lake. Sounded a little sketchy to me so I go back to the *Ledger* and turns out, he did in fact drive the car into the lake but . . ." He flipped another printout of a newspaper clipping.

"*They didn't find the body*," Lexie finished, surprising everyone else in the room.

"Jeez!" Donnie exclaimed, as they all turned around. "You scared the shit out of me."

"I'm sorry. I tried calling. And knocking. I heard Cliff talking when I peeked in." Lexie looked at her phone. "You told me to be here at six. You still wanna go eat?"

"Yeah," Donnie said, looking at his phone. "I didn't realize it was already so late. We got caught up in something."

She looked at Cliff and the stack of papers in his hand. "I come at a bad time?"

No one said a word. Donnie looked at Cliff, who in turn looked to Frank. Frank looked back to Donnie.

"You looked up the Murray High curse, didn't you?" she asked.

"Maybe," Cliff said. "Do you know much about it?"

"I mean, only what I remember from exaggerated rumors in high school. There was something like five or six kids who just up and vanished."

"Vanished or died?" Frank asked.

"Who knows. Nobody ever seemed to have a clear idea what happened or where they went. As far as I know, it was only at our school though."

"You said five or six?" Cliff said. "Do you know names?"

"Oh, the names always changed. I couldn't tell you any of them. The stories usually involved someone's cousin, or some mom's best friend when she was at Murray High, or just some random guy or girl," Lexie replied. Cliff flipped up a sheet on his yellow pad.

"*Murray Ledger* says Jermaine was a suicide," Frank said, reading the paper Cliff had put down.

"Yeah, but as far as I know they didn't find a body," Cliff said.

Frank pointed at a white paper sticking out of Cliff's yellow pad. "What is that?"

Cliff slipped the final picture out and laid it on the pool table. Another yearbook printout, this time with a female's picture circled. "When I was looking into Jermaine, I found an article that made reference to a similar incident." At the top of the yearbook page, 1988 was scrawled in black marker. "Pamela Climber. In eighty-eight, she went missing before basketball practice. No one's seen her since."

The group scanned the photo of Pamela and the accompanying article beside it. After a moment of silence, Cliff continued, "I don't know if it means anything, but this definitely isn't rumor or some collection of exaggerated stories. Between nineteen seventy-six and nineteen ninety-seven, four students went missing in Murray. And none of them were ever found. On top of that, each of them went missing either in the late afternoon or evening." He pointed to portions of the article printouts that he'd highlighted.

Cliff fanned the pictures out on the pool table. "What's more bizarre is that for every one of these, somewhere in the writeups, a point is made that the person never told anyone where they were going—or that they *were* going. It's almost as if on their way home from school—or practice in Pam's case—they just *poof*. Vanished." Cliff made a popping sound with his lips.

"You said this was exclusive to Murray High, though," Donnie said to Lexie. Then to Cliff, "If that's the case, how does Corey fit in?"

"Yeah," Cliff sighed. "Still not sure about that one."

"Corey who? Corey Grassman?" Lexie asked.

The three of them turned to look at Lexie, practically stunned. "You knew Corey Grassman?" Cliff asked, slowly.

Lexie paused, darting her eyes to each of them. "I didn't *know him*, know him. I remember him—when he went missing. It was a big deal."

Donnie picked up the articles for a closer look as Frank pulled out his phone and started texting. "She said there were five or six, so there might be a couple more," Frank said.

"Oh, don't quote me on that," Lexie said. "It was just a number. A couple of my friends would always tell freshman about the five or six kids who went missing in the school. Like I said, most of the time they just made up names." She turned to Cliff. "The fact that you found these people and put some reality behind these stories is a little unsettling."

"This is all I could find in the hour or so that I was there," Cliff said.

"So, what's the point?" Frank asked. "We've got three people missing from Murray High. Is there a connection?"

"Seems like there was something going on," Cliff replied.

"Nobody ever talked about this stuff when you were in high school?" Lexie asked.

"Not while I was there," Cliff replied.

"I don't remember anybody dying, let alone disappearing, while we were there," Donnie said. "I know one girl died from the flu when we were freshmen."

Frank's phone buzzed on the pool table with a text message. "Ben Markham," he said to Donnie. "That name sound familiar to you?"

Cliff looked at his notes.

"Yeah, I know the Markhams," Lexie said.

As Frank typed another message on his phone, he said, "He was the son of that guy we had last week. The leaky anus guy."

Donnie's eyes rolled as Lexie's widened. "The leaky what?" She asked, on the verge of a laugh.

"Don't ask," Donnie cut in.

"I just texted Mimi Markham—that hot redhead that was here. She was his sister," Frank continued.

"Do you categorize all your female clients with sexual adjectives?" Lexie asked.

"No, I do it to the males too," Frank replied. "I'm not sexist."

"Holy crap! Yes!" Donnie exclaimed, "I remember the Markhams. What about 'em?"

"Yeah, when she and I were meeting, she told me her brother disappeared a long time ago. Said he ran away. I just texted her and asked if he really did run away or if something else happened."

"Let me guess, he went to Murray too?" Cliff asked.

"Don't know, just asked."

"Ben and Mimi went to Murray High," Lexie said. "Their dad was my chess coach."

There was an uncomfortable silence in the room as this new information settled.

"Can I ask what all of this is for? You have pictures from old Murray and Calloway yearbooks? You writing a book?" Lexie asked.

"Frank was up at LBL and found a skele—" Frank hit Cliff in the arm before he could finish. "What was that for?"

"Dude, she doesn't know," Frank said.

"Yeah, that's why I'm telling her. Frank was up in LBL walking around. He stumbled into Bethel Cemetery and found something buried on top of one of the graves—"

"Wait. *Bethel Cemetery*?" Lexie asked. Her eyes checked in with each of them before landing on Frank. "You *found* Bethel Cemetery?" Her tone was skeptical.

"I didn't—no, there's no Bethel. I found an old cemetery that was a little unusual. That's all."

"Were there fourteen graves?"

Frank's eyes narrowed at Lexie. "How did you know that?" he asked. Donnie looked up from the papers. She had his attention too.

"Everybody knows that."

Frank's phone buzzed again. "Am I the only one that heard the place has one grave?" He asked, looking at his phone.

"No, I heard that too. But I heard the fourteen graves version more often," she replied.

Frank read from his phone, paraphrasing the message from Mimi, "Mimi says that Ben disappeared in nineteen ninety-three. She likes to think he is still alive but after twenty years she doesn't hold out much hope. They still have no clue what happened." He clicked off his phone and laid it on the table. "And he went Murray High." Frank looked at the group. "What is that then? Four students from Murray High School in the last forty years that disappeared?" Frank looked at the pictures of the students again, then snapped his fingers and looked at his brother. "Maybe five. We still don't know what happened to your boy Pennington."

"Or what the Calloway connection is," Cliff added.

Donnie didn't say a word. He was leaning against the pool table, running his thumb and forefinger over the outline of his mouth. He appeared to be lost in a daze until he spoke in a soft, almost inaudible voice. "Is your computer on?"

"Yeah," Frank replied. "Why?"

"Hang on." Donnie walked over to Frank's office as Cliff wrote Ben Markham's name on the yellow pad.

31

"Did you see her grave?" Lexie asked Frank.

"I didn't find her grave." Frank replied.

"But you found something?"

"Yeah, I found something." He leaned his head closer and lowered his voice in case his parents were within ear shot. "But, as cheesy as this sounds, the less you know about what I'm doing, the better."

"Well, I already know you were grave robbing." She smiled.

Frank and Cliff stopped dead in their tracks and turned to look at her.

"What?" she asked. Her face quickly fell to one of dread. "What happened?"

"Why did you say that?" Frank asked. "What do you mean you know I was robbing a grave?"

"*He* just said that." Lexie pointed to Cliff. "He said you were up in LBL and you found something on top of a grave. I was just making a joke." There was a long pause where Cliff and Frank exchanged glances and then simultaneously looked back at Lexie. "What?"

"Sorry," Frank said. He let out a chuckle. "I was accused this past weekend of grave robbing. It was a whole thing. I thought maybe someone had told you."

"Oh. No. Just a joke. What does Bethel Cemetery have to do with Corey?" She abruptly took in a sharp breath of air, and her eyes widened—practically sparkling with excitement. "You found something up there! Oh my God, you found a body. Is that why you have the yearbooks? Did you find one of the kids who is missing?"

Frank shushed her, raising his hand to get her to lower her voice just as Donnie yelled from Frank's office, "Hey guys." There was something foreboding in his tone. He was sitting in Frank's chair, staring at the computer screen. Donnie looked up and connected eyes with Frank. "You remember someone named Nina Etheridge?"

Frank took a moment to think. "Yeah. That girl Mom and Dad used to scare us with?"

"Yup."

"Wait, what?" Cliff asked. "Who is Nina Etheridge?"

Donnie didn't answer. He looked to be examining something on the screen. Frank spoke up. "When we started driving, our parents told us this story from their high school days to scare us from being out too late. I was always sure it was made up though. On the night of their prom, there was an accident with a girl and her boyfriend. A group of students were driving to a party in Cadiz, and they went through LBL. Apparently, at some point along the way, Nina's car stopped following the group. Everybody thought maybe they stopped off somewhere. When they didn't show to the party, everyone just assumed they went home. Come to find out, they never made it home. Never made it anywhere. They were gone."

"What do you mean, *gone*?" Lexie asked, examining the shelves of books on Frank's office wall.

"We always heard they crashed into the lake. How they got there depended on the type of warning my parents wanted to give: either about us not staying out to late or us not drinking and driving."

"And if they wanted to scare Frank away from hookin' up with dudes in his car late night . . ." Donnie began.

Frank sneered at his brother with a fake, low mocking laugh.

"Let me guess," Cliff said. "It's a real story."

Donnie turned the laptop screen around to show the black-and-white face of a teenage, blond-haired girl holding a large first-place ribbon. "Looks like it." The group leaned in to look closer at the picture. "Mysteriously vanished. No trace of a car. No trace of them."

"Where did you find that?" Frank asked.

"Dad's records. Grandpa did the funeral for her. And look," Donnie said, pointing to the screen. "Nineteen sixty-six. The guy she was with; his name was Bruce Winfree."

Donnie's words, coupled with the girl's photo staring at them made Frank whisper a curse. "She *was* real."

"And she went to Murray High," Donnie said.

"What is that? Five people now?" Cliff asked.

"Six from Murray if you count Brian Pennington," Frank replied.

"Dude. I'm tellin' you, Brian moved," Donnie said.

"Cliff," Frank said, "you didn't come across those names? Bruce and Nina?"

"I didn't go back that far."

Frank looked down at Cliff's yellow pad and wrote down Nina's name under the others. "What are the numbers here? Next to the names?"

"Oh, yeah! I forgot, that's what I wanted to tell you. Two families are still offering reward money for information that leads to finding them or figuring out what happened to them."

"How much?" Frank asked.

"Does it matter?" Donnie asked.

"Like, nine thousand," Cliff replied.

Silence fell over the room until Frank cut it off, "*Nine* thousand dollars?"

"I know, right?" Cliff said. "And they're still active."

"How do you know that?" Donnie asked.

"I called," Cliff replied.

Both Donnie and Frank flashed a look of disapproval. "That seems a little insensitive, don't you think?"

"I didn't call the parents. I called the police. I said I was doing a report on missing persons in the local area and wanted to know how rewards worked. They explained and listed off some of the ones that are still active. There are quite a few, but I checked, and Jermaine and Pamela are on there." He took the pad from Frank and flipped the page. "Five thousand for Pamela, and I think four for Jermaine."

"Cliff those things are like, what? Twenty years old? Thirty? How do they know the family is still willing to pay that?" Donnie asked.

"That's what I thought. But the lady I spoke with told me that each year the police department calls anyone who has an active reward. And each year they've continued to say they will pay it if any information is found leading to the whereabouts of their son—or daughter."

"Nearly ten grand?! We gotta get that money!" Frank exclaimed.

Donnie put up his hands. "Can we please just focus on getting the home up to code? This is what you wanted me to stick around for. I don't want to be the only one actually doing stuff around here."

Frank shot his brother an exasperated look, "Why do you do that? You act like I'm not doing anything—"

"I didn't say that," Donnie interrupted. "I said I don't want to be the only one doing anything. Which will happen if you end up going off on another idiotic scheme for easy money."

"Alright, first off, this definitely wouldn't be easy money. Second, have you missed this entire conversation? I told you what I found up there. It's not like I'm leaving you high and dry. You don't want to at least see?"

"I'm not going up there," Donnie replied.

"Cliff just said this could be worth ten grand," Frank said. "Even after we split it three ways, it's more than we had before."

"You're assuming that the person you found—if you found a person—is one of those missing kids," Donnie said.

"I knew you found someone up there! Who is it?" Lexie asked.

"Tell her about the pager," Cliff replied.

"You found a pager?" Lexie asked.

"Could you guys quit talking?" Frank replied.

"I don't care if you found a wallet with Nina Etheridge's driver's license, those are real graves up there. I'm not gonna start digging on top of them over a hunch. How will you explain it to the police? You just happened to trip on the exact grave where a girl who disappeared forty years ago is buried with no reason as to why you were up there?"

Frank thought for a moment. "Yeah, that works."

"No. You just got a target on your back from Suthers. If you so much as kick dirt off someone's grave, you're done. And again, you don't know *who* it is up there, or even if there *is* someone up there—besides the normal occupant."

"What is that?" Lexie asked. She was looking up at the top shelf where a red book was sticking off over the edge. Two stickers with noticeable lettering were partially visible on the book's cover: UNDGARDEN on one and the other had RVANA written in yellow with what looked like a yellow tongued smiley face below. By the time Donnie looked up, Frank had jumped up to knock the book back against the wall and out of sight.

"That's nothing. Old journal of mine," Frank said.

"No, it's not," Lexie countered, confidently. "I know that book."

Frank stood motionless. "I'm serious, it's an old journal. I used to keep them when I was in high school."

"Then bet me," she replied, pulling Frank's office chair over to the shelf and holding it steady, as if she was about to stand on it. "Bet me your truck that it's *your* journal and not Corey Grassman's funeral book."

PART II

WHERE ALL THE KIDS GO TO REST

Eleanor Rigby died in the church and was buried along with her name.
Nobody came.
——Paul McCartney and John Lennon,
"Eleanor Rigby"

32

Nobody moved. Lexie's eyes were locked menacingly on Frank. "What is that book?" Lexie asked again.

Frank glanced at Donnie who threw up his hands and said, "Don't look at me."

"I'm not saying it's Corey's funeral book. But how do you know about that?" Frank asked.

"Because I was at the funeral and I rem—"

"You were at Corey's funeral?" Cliff interrupted.

"Yes. And I remember *that book*. It was a red book with stickers of his favorite bands on the outside cover. You want to tell me those weren't Soundgarden and Nirvana stickers?" Lexie began to stand on the chair, but Frank stepped over and touched her arm.

"Wait, wait, wait. Just, hold on," Frank said, "You still haven't proven that it's Corey—"

She rolled her eyes. "Just tell me. Why do you have that? I'm serious." And then she took in a quick breath, showing the faintest glimmer of surprise in her eyes. "Oh my God." Her head turned to Donnie. "Oh my God. Suthers. Monty Suthers. The cop? You just said that if he so much as kicks dirt from a grave *Suthers* would be all over him." Then, to Frank. "It was you wasn't it. Those grave robberies in town last week. Did you rob Corey's grave?"

"Shhh!" Frank threw up his hands to stop her and hurriedly went to the door to close it. "No! We didn't rob Corey's grave." He looked at Donnie again for guidance, and then at Cliff.

"You may as well tell her man, she knows that's his book," Cliff said.

"Fine. Just, don't be so loud." Frank motioned for her to take a seat in the chair at his desk. "You went to the funeral, huh?"

Lexie nodded.

"Okay, so, here's why we have the book. Do you remember the funeral home that did it?"

"No..."

"Didn't think so."

"I remember it was over in the town square," she replied.

"Yeah, well, about ten years back, my dad purchased that business. All of their records then shifted to us. *That* book," Frank said, pointing to the top shelf, "was part of those records. I pulled it out of the box when I heard that Corey's grave got robbed." He threw his hands up as if in surrender. "So there, see? I didn't rob Corey's grave and I didn't steal the book. But yes, that is Corey's funeral book."

Lexie sat quiet, watching Frank like he was prey. "Did you read it?"

"Definitely not. I looked in it but I was uncomfortable reading the notes. Did *you* write in it?"

"No way," she shot back. "I wouldn't even know what to say with something like that. Plus, I didn't know if his parents were going to read it..."

"So, you guys were friends?" Donnie asked.

Lexie whipped her head around to Donnie. "I knew who he was. He was older than me. We had some of the same friends. It wasn't like I knew him well." She turned her head back to Frank. "I know you're lying, by the way."

"What?" Frank replied.

"I said, I. Know. You're. Lying." Her voice was cold. She held his gaze for a long moment, perhaps waiting to see if Frank would speak but he never did. "I watched his mom put that book in the coffin before they lowered him down. Besides, even if she didn't, why would you have it? It wouldn't be part of the records. His mom would have kept it."

Frank had nothing left.

"A friend of mine told me yesterday that something might have happened to Corey's grave. It was you, wasn't it?" She asked.

Frank shrugged, turning his palms out. "I'm not admitting to anything."

She laughed. "You're not a very good liar."

"I'm actually a very good liar when I'm not put on the spot," he replied.

"Look! I'm not gonna turn you in, okay? I just want to know why? It wasn't like there was anything valuable in there—it was all personal items or pictures." Lexie followed Frank's eyes when they suddenly shifted over toward Cliff. "Wait. Did you not know he wasn't in there before you dug him—" She stopped when Frank's eyes bulged, and he held up a finger. "Sorry. When all the dirt magically blew off of the coffin and you peeked inside?"

"Exactly," Frank said.

"No. We had no idea," Cliff said.

"What were you looking for?"

Silence again and then finally, "That," Cliff finally said, pointing to the book.

"Dude!" Frank said.

"What? She knows now. She just said she won't turn you in. Relax," Cliff continued. "Someone called us—we don't know who—and asked if we would retrieve the book that was in his coffin."

"Who? Did they say what they wanted with it?"

"No clue. They just said they wanted the book," Cliff replied.

"I asked, but he or she wouldn't tell me. They were using a voice changer. Could have been anyone," Frank added.

"So why do you still have it?"

"Because I forgot to take it to them," Frank said. "We were supposed to meet up and I had something come up."

"Wow." Lexie shook her head slowly back and forth. "You really haven't read it yet?"

"I told you, no way," Frank said. "That thing gives me the creeps."

"I think the guy wants it to see if there's a clue to Corey's disappearance. I think it's his dad," Cliff added.

"Couldn't be his dad. He died the year after Corey did," Lexie said. "What about his mom?"

"Or maybe it was him," Donnie said. "Did you ever think of that? The guy disappeared, right? What if he came back to Murray twenty years later, heard about the book that was placed in his coffin, and called Frank to go and dig it up?"

"That's not a bad theory," Frank replied.

"No, he's dead," Lexie said, calmly.

The three of them turned to look at her, "Why do you say that?" Donnie asked.

Lexie's gaze shifted from Donnie and then to Frank, and she shrugged. "Because . . ." She looked to be searching for words. "He left behind a lot of important people. Especially his mom. There's no way he'd just abandon her like that. I didn't know him well, but I know he really cared for his mom, and he had a couple of friends that came in a close second. I don't think he would just up and leave without telling anyone, especially after his dad died."

"That too is a very good theory," Frank said, stroking his chin.

"I think we should just read it. Won't hurt. What do you think?" Cliff asked Donnie.

"Don't look at me. I'm not getting involved," Donnie replied. "Between the home and whatever the hell he's doing up in that LBL cemetery, that's enough stress for me."

"Let's just do it." Cliff turned to Frank.

"What if he finds out we read it?" Frank asked.

"How's he gonna find out? It's not booty trapped." Cliff jumped up and snatched the book off the top shelf.

"Booby trapped?" Frank asked.

"That's what I said. Booty trapped."

"Is anyone hungry? I wanted to have Mexican before I left town. Mexican and some beer," Lexie said abruptly.

"We have tons of beer. Gatsby over here keeps a bunch of different kinds stocked for after-parties," Donnie said, and could see Lexie was confused by that statement. "Sometimes, after funerals, families stick around for a while to chat and hang out. He'll bring up a cooler of beer." Donnie thumbed over to Frank who in turn gave a thumbs up.

"People don't find that weird? Hanging out at a funeral home?" Lexie asked.

"Why would they?" Frank said. "It's also a house. And it's *awesome*. Pool table, two hundred board games, basketball, cornhole, top grade karaoke system, Super and regular Nintendo." He raised his hand to hide his mouth from Donnie and whispered, "Might even have an arcade machine in the next month."

"We're not getting that," Donnie said.

"You don't even know what it is yet," Frank said.

"Well, if the nine-hundred-dollar *House of the Dead* arcade in my eBay cart is any indication, I think I've figured it out. We're not getting it."

Frank leaned back out of Donnie's view and mouthed, "We're gettin' it!"

"Damn," Cliff said. He was looking at the inside of the book. "This thing is full."

"Wait!" Lexie walked over and put a hand over the book's open pages. "Seriously, is anyone hungry? I want to look in it but maybe we can eat first?"

"Food sounds good," Frank agreed.

"Yo, how many people were at this funeral?" Cliff asked, pulling the book away and flipping through the pages. He sat down in Frank's office chair behind the desk.

Lexie stepped over beside him and looked over his shoulder. The pages were filled with one liners above signatures, and personal notes ranging from a quarter to half a page of memories and well wishes. Many apologies, and countless promises of prayer for both Corey and his family. "Oh wow!" Lexie exclaimed. "Can I see that?" Cliff handed her the book and asked what grabbed her attention.

"Hang on, let me see if this is who I think it is." She read quietly to herself, mumbling the words out loud.

Lexie whispered, "Listen to this:

> *Good for you. You fooled them all.*
> *All but me. I'm happy you're gone.*
> *They wish you well, I wish you to hell.*
> *You're a piece of shit,*
> *And the pain you gave, I hope you get.*
> *CL*

"Whoa," Donnie said. "Who is that?"

"CL. I think that's Connie Lancaster. The two of them dated. Rumor had it he raped her, but nothing was ever proven. She was a psycho."

Everyone again stared at Lexie, quiet over her newest observation.

"You seem to know a lot about this whole thing," Cliff said.

"I can't help it if I had a lot of friends in high school," Lexie said.

"Feisty," Frank whispered, walking over to Cliff. "What if *she* did it?" Frank looked over Lexie's shoulder at the book. "Maybe she killed him."

"It's possible," Lexie replied, turning the pages in the book. "To be honest, the more I heard about it, the more I thought it *could* be her."

"What's her name again?" Cliff asked.

"Connie Lancaster."

Cliff swiveled in the desk chair and began typing on Frank's computer while Lexie continued to look through the book. Frank stepped back against the wall in silence, still a little uncomfortable with flipping through it.

Cliff made an audible hum. "Connie Lancaster is dead."

"How do you know?" Lexie asked.

He turned the computer around to reveal her picture. "Obituary," Cliff said. "Three years ago. Guess there's no way to know now."

Frank leaned in to look: "Buzz, your girlfriend. Wuff!"

"Dude," Cliff said, swatting Frank's arm. "Come on."

"And that's actually a good picture of her," Lexie said. "Heroin took a toll on her last I heard."

"I'm tellin' ya, the guy could have just left," Donnie said. He was sitting on the couch now, leaning his head back against the wall, with his eyes closed and his arms folded. "Not uncommon for someone to want to be out of Murray."

"Let's get dinner, I'm starved," Lexie suggested, shutting the book. "There's too many of these to read on an empty stomach."

"I'm down. You wanna bring the book?" Cliff asked.

"No!" Lexie and Frank said together. Frank continued, "Leave that thing here. Already feel weird with it in my office. Let me get my wallet."

Everyone was in the car by the time Cliff locked up his studio and walked down the driveway.

"Shoot. You didn't grab my purse, did you?" Lexie asked, as Frank began backing out.

"No, did you bring a purse?" Donnie asked. "I can pay."

"No, I don't want you to have to do that," she replied.

"Believe me, he'd love to pay," Frank said.

"I don't mind you paying, but I need my ID. Are we drinking?"

"Yes," they all said in unison.

"Okay. Then I need my ID." She opened the car door. "Oh. You guys have any tequila in the house?"

There was a curious calm.

"I'm gonna need some shots if we're going through that book. Maybe we could make a drinking game out of it. Is that wrong?"

Donnie said "I like it" as Frank and Cliff said "yes." Donnie continued. "Could be fun. Let's do it."

"Because that's not morbid," Frank replied.

"Coming from the guy who dug up a grave," Donnie replied.

Frank turned to Lexie in the back seat. "He's only saying yes because he wants to make out with you later, FYI," Frank said. He faced forward, buckling his seat belt.

Lexie closed the car door and bent down to rest her arm on Frank's open window. "Maybe I want to make out with him too," she said, leaning in and giving Frank a tiny peck on the cheek. She turned and quickly jogged up the driveway, and into the house.

Frank took in a long breath. "I think she likes me, bro."

33

Frank volunteered to drive while the others split a pitcher of margaritas. The conversation centered mostly on questions from Frank and Cliff to Lexie and what she'd been doing over the last several years until *she* turned the conversation back to Frank and his future plans. He mentioned, after getting a pool, talking Donnie into opening a restaurant next door.

"Oh yeah, cause having a restaurant next door to a funeral home isn't awkward."

"That's what you thought about the gym and look what happened," Frank said.

"Yeah, look what happened. There's a gym next door. And it's awkward," Donnie said, and then looking to Cliff, "No offense."

"Screw off," Frank said. "People love the gym—it's unique," Frank said. "So is a restaurant next door. It doesn't have to be fancy. Haven't you been kicking around that concept for a small bar? That would be perfect. Clients could have their funeral and then go to you for lunch or dinner. It's a killer deal!"

Lexie snorted through her drink. "Please make that your logo." She laughed.

"That actually *is* his logo," Donnie said, shaking his head in irritation. "You haven't seen his merch line? Or his coupons?"

"Wait. What?" Lexie asked, wiping the droplets of margarita from her mouth and the table. "Coupons?"

"Funeral coupons," Donnie replied. "They're embedded on our site—well, they *were*. Took them down finally."

"I can't say I understand the coupons, but the merchandise line I can see," Lexie said. "Like what? Coffee mugs with your name on them?"

Donnie said in a deadpan voice, "Yeah, our name and a picture of a skeleton playing ping pong."

"Chess," Frank said.

"You're kidding," Lexie laughed.

"Coffee mugs, stress coffins, t-shirts, skeleton key chains, mouse pads, the works," Frank said, eating a chip from the basket.

"What's a stress coffin?" Lexie asked.

"Same as a stress ball, just coffin shaped," Frank replied. "People dig it."

"Not entirely true. Someone did complain that they were insensitive." Donnie finished his margarita.

Frank made an audible disagreement and waved his hand as he finished chewing. "That complaint was never substantiated. Pretty sure Mom made it up," Frank replied.

"Do people ever buy them?" Lexie asked.

Frank ate another chip. "I don't know. *Donnie*, what do you think? Do people ever *buy* items from my spectacular merch line?" He grinned.

Donnie bit his lip and let slip a soft laugh. Finally, he mumbled, "I sold four coffee mugs today." Frank made him say it a little louder for everyone at the table to hear, as the owner came by to drop off the check. The woman smiled and pointed at one of four small, round pins stuck on her breast pocket. It was a smiling skull with the letters BBFH underneath. Donnie sighed.

"Told ya," Frank said to Lexie. "People dig it."

It was after eight p.m. when they arrived back at the house. Cliff retrieved the book from Frank's office and brought it over to the pool table where Frank was standing, scrolling on his phone. They played a makeshift game of cutthroat, each one reading out loud from the book until it was their turn to shoot. Lexie wrote down a list of popular phrases on Frank's large, portable whiteboard. Whenever someone read a phrase containing lines like, *so sad, miss, words can't describe,* or *looking down,* the group—except for Frank—took a drink. If someone read *I'll never forget you* it was two drinks.

"You guys are gonna get trashed before nine, you know that right?" Frank asked, knocking in a stripe ball.

"Seems to be helping our game. You're still losing," Donnie replied, tapping the butt of Frank's stick with his own as Frank squared up another shot.

"Don't come to me when Corey's ghost is standing outside your window tonight," Frank replied, making another shot.

Cliff, who was reading through a page of short messages, suddenly stopped and muttered to himself, "That's weird."

"What's up?" Lexie asked.

"Check this out." Cliff opened the book flat and lifted it up to their eye level. He ran his finger over the inside of the spine. A torn strip along the binding was all that was left of the page. Donnie came closer to look. "Someone tore out a page."

"Who wrote on the page before it?" Lexie asked.

"Multiple people. But the last entry finished. See?" Cliff said. The page before had four paragraph-long entries from different attendees. The following page seemed to continue from the page removed. Cliff read the words aloud and then flipped the pages back and forth to verify that was all that was written. "Why would someone tear a page out?"

Frank's cell phone rang from the other room. Donnie grabbed the bottle of rum and poured Cliff another drink while Lexie flipped through the book to look for any other sections that were torn out.

A loud thud came from behind them. Frank was standing in the doorway waving his hand. He pointed at his cell phone and mouthed, *It's him.*

"Who?" Donnie asked.

Frank said something in the receiver and began pacing around the room in a frantic search for something. He finally pulled a pen out of his pocket and wrote on a napkin resting atop the bar. "The guy."

"What guy?" Donnie asked.

Frank's eyes bulged and he fiercely pointed to the book on the pool table. "The guy!" he exclaimed, voiceless. Frank brought the phone back up to his mouth. "Yeah, I'm here. Sorry, the reception is really bad on my cell phone. Can I call you from—" The line went dead. "Hello?" He looked at his screen and then tried to talk again. "He hung up."

"What did he want?" Lexie asked.

"Hopefully, he wants the book." The phone rang in the office. Frank gave the signal for everyone to be quiet and answered the phone on speaker. The person on the other end was still using a voice changer.

"Mr. Burgers," the voice said.

"Yessir, thanks for calling back. I'm sorry about the other day. We had a funeral come up last minute and I—"

"Do you still have my book?"

"I do. Actually, looking at it right now."

"You opened it?"

"No, no. I mean, I'm looking at it—at the cover. It's on my desk."

There was a lengthy silence on the other end. "Are you alone?"

"I am," Frank replied.

"Where's your brother?"

"He's out with a friend of ours, Cliff."

"Then whose car is that in the driveway?" The room became hauntingly still. Everyone's eyes shifted to the window.

He's outside, Cliff mouthed, moving his hand toward blinds to try and peek out. Frank waved him back.

"Be honest, Mr. Burgers."

Frank lowered the blinds and peeked out himself. The light in the room reflected off the glass making it impossible to see into the dark. "Are you outside my house?"

"Get in your car and drive to the pay phone we spoke at the other night." Frank began to ask what time, but he was cut off. "You have ten minutes. And don't bring your brother. Or the others." The line went dead again.

"Others? Can he see us?" Cliff asked.

"What are you gonna do?" Lexie asked.

"I'm gonna go to the pay phone. Donnie, get me the book, will ya?"

"What? No way," Lexie exclaimed. "We're not done looking at it yet. What if there really is a note in there from the killer?"

"Guys, I'm tellin' ya, there's no letter from the killer," Donnie answered.

Frank went and grabbed his keys from the kitchen.

"How 'bout this? We'll keep looking through it. I'm sure he's not going to want you to drop it off tonight," Lexie said.

"What if he does, though?" Frank asked.

"Then just tell him you thought he was going to give you instructions about where to drop it off," Lexie suggested.

Frank sighed. "Okay. But hurry. If he has me come back and get it, I won't have any other excuse."

"There has to be something in there that's making him want to read it," Cliff said.

"Anybody want to make a bet that this person is actually Corey?" Donnie laughed.

"I'll call Donnie if anything happens," Frank said.

Donnie patted his pockets. "I don't know where my phone is, call Cliff's."

It took Frank less than five minutes to drive from his house to the pay phone at the RacerFan station. The same nervous waves he experienced before commenced battering his insides when the phone box came into view. He exited his car and looked around. *He's obviously watching. But from where?* There were no cars at the tanks, no one driving down the road or stopped at the nearby lights. The only cars in view were his truck and one he guessed to belong to the night manager of the gas station.

There were businesses nearby, but the lots were empty. Apart from the soft glow of tall streetlights along Route 121 South, the surrounding landscape and structures were cloaked in black and devoid of any noticeable human existence. "No wonder he keeps choosing this spot," Frank whispered. He turned and looked out down the road, toward the main intersecting highway. A structure caught his eyes a few hundred yards away. Shimmering white and yellow light poured into the surrounding darkness: Sally's Diner.

34

Monty didn't notice the ringing of the diner phone until he realized it wasn't being answered. He looked up; nearly every booth was full. Sophia and another waiter were on the floor taking orders from customers. Finally, probably after ten rings, the shrill clanging stopped. Monty shrugged and went back to reading when he heard it ring again. He looked to Sophia.

"Will, can you get that?" Sophia asked. The other waiter who looked to be in the middle of taking an order.

"Yeah, hang on." Will said something to the group in the booth and then walked to Sophia and handed her a slip of paper. Monty watched her take an order from both tables.

"Hey you," Sophia said. She was at the drink station filling glasses with ice and soda. "I have a question; a personal question if you don't mind answering—you don't have to answer it if you don't want to. Completely up to you. Either way is fine." She scooped another clump of ice into the glass. "Actually, never mind. Don't worry about it. None of my business."

Monty laughed. "W-what is it? I'm sure it's fine."

"Okay. But, if it's too personal, just tell me. I'm not trying to pry."

Monty put his Kindle down and took off his reading glasses. "All ears."

"Are you married?" She stopped putting glasses onto the tray and looked at him. "I've made comments about a wife to you before and you don't say anything—so I'm guessing you're not . . . ?" Monty glanced down at the table. "I'm prying. I'm sorry. Just, pretend like I didn't ask." She picked up the tray of drinks before Monty could get a word out and walked away. He watched her drop them off and then scooted his coffee cup to the edge of the table as she came back toward the server station. She returned with an orange rimmed carafe and filled it up back up. "Really, I shouldn't have asked—"

"It's okay. It's not p-prying. It's just . . . it *is* a little hard to talk about." He pulled the mug back toward him. "I'm n-n-not m-married, no. But I *almost* had a fiancée. Her name was Jean." Sophia slid her notebook into her front pouch and leaned against the server station. "I w-w-was w-with her for a c-couple of years—this was a long time ago. I f-finally g-got the courage to p-p-pr—" Monty stopped, and sighed. "Stupid stutter. Ruinin' a good story."

She smiled. "It's okay. Didn't even notice." She looked behind her to the kitchen to make sure no plates were up and slid into the bench across from him.

"I got the courage to give her a ring, and uh . . ." Monty raised his head to meet Sophia's eyes as he sat back and shrugged. "Yeah."

"She said no," Sophia whispered.

"P-pretty much," Monty said. "Said she didn't know. She w-w-wanted to, but she w-wanted to think about it—about if it was the r-right time. There was something going on w-with her p-p-parents . . ." Monty paused and looked over toward the other waiter who was standing at a booth on the other end, then back to her. He started to speak but stopped himself, letting out a breath. "Things sorta get shaky from there."

"I'm sorry," Sophia replied, softly.

"It is what it is. Wasn't meant to be." Monty could feel Sophia's eyes on him for a long moment.

She sat forward. "Well, whoever it's meant to be with will have found someone really good." She tapped his hand with her finger. "I mean that."

"I don't know about that," Monty replied, not bothering to move his hand away.

"Well, I do. And I hope that whoever you end up with knows what I know about you."

Their eyes connected until he felt his stomach drop then averted his gaze. "What do you know about me?"

"I told you—you're good. Other guys got good qualities, but you. You're just good. That's all there is to it."

"You know that, huh?" Monty suppressed a laugh.

"I know it. And I think Trent Allen knows it too."

Monty's brows furrowed. "Trent Allen? H-how do you know about that?"

"He's in here all the time—was here just before you showed up," she replied. "Overheard him say what you did for him."

"That son of a bitch," Monty whispered with a grin. "I told him to keep his mouth shut. What'd he say?"

"Don't worry. It wasn't to me—I was eavesdropping. He was here with his brother. I wouldn't have noticed him except that he was practically crying. Overheard him say *you* took the fall for the missing collection money at church. Didn't say why though."

Monty sighed. "'Cause they thought he stole it and it'd've g-gotten him arrested. He was the one who took it to be deposited that morning."

"You sure he didn't do it?"

"I am," Monty replied. "Because I know who did."

"Who?" she asked. Monty looked around as if someone might be listening. "Who would I tell?"

"Sorry. I can't tell ya."

"How do you know?"

"D-doesn't matter. But I know it was her." Monty caught the slip too late and held up his hand to calm down Sophia's excitement at knowing it was a female. "I can't give ya a name. I t-told the leadership I offered to take the money to the bank and misplaced it somewhere along the way. Then I confronted who actually took it."

"Why didn't you tell anyone?"

Monty shifted his head back and forth. "Because it would have been embarrassing for them. Turns out they were in a bit of a bind."

"A bind worth stealing from the church?"

"Let's just say it was medical," Monty said, sipping his coffee. "Anyways, the money got 'returned.'" Monty flashed air quotes. "Trent wasn't accused of a crime, this person got the help they needed, and I worked out a deal where they could just pay me back in private."

Sophia sat back against the booth, with a warm smile on her face.

"After I heard what happened, I figured it b-best not to cause a scene."

"And that's how I know you're a good man," she whispered to him.

Something caught Monty's attention with Will, the other waiter standing nearby. "Well, being *good* put me six grand in the hole so I might need to reevaluate my behavior." Monty's focus suddenly shifted to what Will was saying to the people in the booth. His experience in law enforcement had given him an innate ability to *keep his brain open*, as he called it, at all times. Even when his mind was focused on something specific, like a one-on-one conversation, his brain would pick up on cues or happenings that interrupted normalcy. The diner had become a choice oasis for him after work because of its late-night predictability. He could read or talk with Sophia and hardly anything outside of a loud group at a table, or drunk student(s) stumbling over themselves when they walked in ever occurred. This might be why Monty became distracted when he noticed a sequence of sounds repeating in the same intonation and cadence.

Will was walking to each table, asking something to the customers. Monty saw them shake their heads or offer a "no" and then Will moved on to the next one. Monty couldn't make out the words Will was saying, only that it was the same question to each booth. Sophia waved her hand in front of his face, but he was too focused on trying to hear Will's question.

"You in there?" Sophia asked.

"What? Sorry." Monty looked up at her and then back at Will. "I w-w-was trying to see what he was saying."

"Who?"

"Hey Mr. Suthers," Will said, approaching. "Do you have a pair of binoculars on you?"

"Binoculars?" Monty asked.

"What are you talking about?" Sophia asked. She stood up out of the booth.

"Somebody on the phone over there asked if anyone had a pair of binoculars. I said I would ask around."

"Who is it? Did he say why he was asking?"

"Nope," Will replied. "Just apologized for askin' a random question and told me not to make a scene about it. Weird, huh?"

Monty agreed and turned his head to look out the window. He leaned close to the glass, cupping his hands around his face, and peering out to the parking lot. He looked past his cruiser, out at the road. There was nothing out there other than a radiant, white light in the distance from the RacerFan station.

"You have a caller ID on that phone?" Monty asked. "W-w-what's the number?"

Will moved back to the phone and covered the earpiece before speaking a series of numbers, beginning with 2-7-0. Monty ran a search in Google. It came back with an address just a couple hundred yards from where he sat.

•

Frank was assured by the guy at Sally's that no one was using binoculars. He hung up the phone and looked around the parking lot, still wondering if the caller could see him.

He was startled when his cell phone rang; it was Donnie. He ignored it. Finally, the pay phone let out a shrill ring. Frank answered it abruptly, "Hello."

"Has he called yet?"

"Who is this?"

"It's Cliff."

"How did you find this number?"

"Google. It's the only pay phone in town," Cliff replied.

"No, nothing yet," Frank said.

"Come back. Lexie found something."

"I'll call you back! You're tying the line up."

He hung up the phone. Almost as soon as it landed in the cradle, it rang out again. Frank answered it, "Hello?"

"Do you have the book?" the voice asked.

Frank cursed in his mind. "No sir. You didn't say to bring it. I thought you were just telling me where to go drop it off."

There was a sigh at the other end. "Tomorrow morning. Eight a.m. I assume you're familiar with the Murray Cemetery. At the end of the main road is a tree that has no place in that landscape. At its base you will find a sizeable hole—" Frank's concentration snapped when the blue lights flashed on from the corner of his eye. He turned and saw the cruiser sitting next to his truck. "Shit," Frank whispered. He hung up the phone.

"Evenin' Frank," Monty said, stepping out of his cruiser. "W-w-what are you doing out here?"

"Just . . . you know. Making a call."

"Oh yeah? On a p-p-pay phone?"

"Yeah," Frank said. "My battery's dead. Can I help you with something?"

"Guy over at Sally's says someone was c-c-calling over there, askin' if anyone had b-binoculars. Spooked some of the customers."

"Binoculars?"

"Who w-w-were y-you calling?"

"Oh. Just now? That was Cliff Samson." Frank was shielding the cruisers brights with his hand, trying to see Monty's face.

"That w-w-wasn't y-you that called the diner?"

"No sir. I just got here," Frank replied. The pay phone rang, startling Frank to jump back with a soft yet audible note of surprise. Monty's eyes moved toward the phone and then back over to Frank.

"That Cliff again?" Monty asked.

"I don't know," Frank replied.

"Answer it."

Frank stood there. Declining would be suspicious but answering it may be worse. He picked it up. The voice on the other end started to ask if Frank heard the instructions to deliver the book, but Frank played as if it was the wrong number. "Yeah, sorry, this isn't Luis." The voice paused. It tried to ask Frank what he was doing, but Frank didn't give it a chance to finish. "Yeah, you're calling a pay phone." Monty began to walk toward the phone. "That's okay. Bye." Frank hung up. "Wrong number."

"No kiddin'," Monty replied, stepping toward him. "You w-w-wer-were j-j-just up here callin' Cliff, huh?"

"Yes sir. Like I said, dead battery."

Monty sighed.

"Officer, with all due respect, I feel like you're going out of your way to try and pin something on me." Monty studied him. "Is there something illegal about using a pay phone?"

"Nope," Monty said, matter-of-factly.

"Okay, well. Like I said, I just got here. Tried to call Cliff to see if he wanted anything from inside. My battery was dead. That's it." Frank was still trying to shield his eyes, while Monty held his gaze, not saying a word. "Can I go?"

"You kn-kn-know I can run the number that j-j-ju-just called, right?"

"Yeah. Run it. 270-444-9980. Cliff Samson. I don't know what that other number was though. Like I said—wrong number."

"Okay," Monty breathed, extending his arm toward Frank's truck. "You're free to go then."

35

When Frank returned home, he took a walk around the house to make sure no one had followed him, or that someone wasn't hiding out. He walked over to his office window. Donnie, Lexie, and Cliff were standing around the desk talking. Frank stood at the window with his face pressed against the glass, and moaning, hoping they would turn and see him.

Lexie was in the middle of telling a story when Donnie held out his hand and said, "Shh." Everyone got quiet. "You guys hear that?"

"Your parents are watching TV I think," Cliff said.

"No, no. Like a . . . a moaning sound."

"Yo, quit playin', man," Cliff said, moving away from the other two. "Don't do that shit when I'm drinkin'."

Lexie screamed when she turned to the window and saw Frank's face. Donnie and Cliff jumped and cursed.

"Dammit, Frank!" Donnie yelled.

Frank was still laughing when he came inside. "A little jumpy, aren't we? Probably shouldn't have been messing around in that kid's book."

"Not cool," Lexie breathed. "No, I'm jumpy because I'm in a funeral home. This house gives me the creeps."

"So, what's up?" Frank asked. "What'd you find?"

Lexie handed the book over to Frank who refused to touch it and reiterated that he wouldn't be reading it. She instead read the selection on the opened page to him: "Mr. Grassman, Albeit callous to say, your time here was not well spent. Your end was the result of many a regretful decision. It is surprising—and rather disconcerting— that so many will mourn this result despite all that has transpired. However, I am confident that we are all now in a better place—even you. Learn from this life, son. WR."

"Holy shit," Frank replied. He walked around behind Lexie and read the selection again over her shoulder. The cursive on the page was flawless and could have easily passed for a computer font. "Who writes that at someone's funeral?"

"Right?" Cliff said.

"Who is WR?" Frank asked. "Do we know?"

"We do. You don't?" She replied.

"No," Frank replied. "WR... WR... WR." He read the words again. "Should I know this person?" Lexie gave him a look to say that he should. Frank looked at the page again. "It sounds like an adult. Disconcerting, disconcerting. Albeit? And son," he said. He began reasoning to himself, "Who says son? Besides a cop. Or a dad. An adult. Has to be an adult." He repeated WR to himself. "Sounds like a teach—" he stopped. "Oh my God. Mr. Rose?"

"Yup. Coach Rose," Cliff said.

"No way he would write this," Frank said. "The history teacher, right?"

"I had him as a softball coach," Lexie said. "But yes."

"Hold up. What are you saying?" Frank asked. "You think he's the one who killed him?"

"I don't know," she replied, shrugging. "Maybe." Frank held out his hands to inaudibly ask if he could see the book. He flipped through some of the other pages.

Donnie hit another ball with his cue. "Come on, you guys really think *Mr. Rose* killed a bunch of kids? How would he even do that? And still not be caught after all this time?"

"Coach Rose would have been what? In his seventies when we were there? Maybe late sixties?" Frank asked.

"Wait!" Cliff interrupted. He cursed and snapped his fingers. "Guys, it couldn't have been Mr. Rose. Corey went to Calloway. They wouldn't even know each other." A collective "oh" hummed through the room.

"No," Frank said in a sudden realization. "They would've. Academy class, remember? Murray and Calloway shared facilities and they bussed kids back and forth for special classes. Mr. Rose taught photography. When I took that class, most of the kids were from Calloway."

"Oh shit," Cliff blurted out in a whisper. A silence fell. "I just thought of this: what if Mr. Rose was at Murray High in the sixties?"

"What does that have to do with anything?" Donnie asked.

"The missing kids . . ." Cliff replied, arching his eyebrows.

Donnie shook his head and chuckled to himself. "Are y'all serious right now? You really think Mr. Rose had something to do with this?" Donnie asked, pointing to the stack of papers on Frank's desk.

"It could work," Lexie said. "Does it strike anyone else as a little odd that Mr. Rose would write something like that?"

"Guys. He didn't kill anybody." Donnie laughed. "The guy was a jerk, but he didn't murder anyone. We don't even know WR is Winston Rose."

"Where is he now?" Lexie asked.

"No clue," Cliff replied. "I ran a search on him a bit ago but couldn't find anything."

"He's bound to be in Murray still," Lexie said. "Unless he died."

"Well, if he died, it wasn't in Murray," Frank added. "I don't remember any funeral for him. I would have noticed it. I'll talk to Addy tomorrow."

"Does Addy keep up with him?" Donnie asked.

"No, but he knows everybody from high school and keeps up with preachers in the area. Surely someone has seen him or knows where he is."

The group sat quietly for a moment until Donnie asked if anyone wanted to play another round. Cliff declined in favor of heading to bed, and Frank agreed and put the book back on top of the shelf.

"What are you going to do about that?" Lexie asked, pointing to it.

"Drop it off tomorrow morning in the Murray Cemetery at eight a.m. Supposed to leave it inside one of the trees."

"What about the money?" Cliff asked.

"There's money? This is like a real business, huh?" Lexie exclaimed.

Frank ignored her. "I didn't get there. Mr. Suthers showed up and I had to hang up and improvise. Maybe it'll be in the tree."

"Great," Donnie sighed.

"You know which tree?" Cliff asked.

"I think so. I'm almost certain it's the forked one down at the end of the north side. I'm just glad to get the thing out of here. There's already enough ghosts in this house to worry about without Corey hanging here."

"And that's my cue," Lexie said. "You mind if I leave my car here until tomorrow? I was gonna call a cab."

"I can give you a ride home," Donnie said.

"You had more than I did," Lexie replied.

"True. Probably not a good idea."

"Especially if that cop thinks you all are a bunch of grave robbers. Wouldn't want to add a DUI to your rap sheet," Lexie said.

"You want me to wait outside with you?"

"Oh, you don't get a choice for that one. I'm not waiting out there by myself."

FRIDAY
36

The cicadas were loud enough for Frank to hear inside his car when he cut the engine. Damp humidity flooded the cool interior as soon as the door opened. He peered around the open land of the cemetery—not a person or car in view.

He parked next to the tree he'd been instructed to find—one that stood out from all the rest. That was an accurate description. There were maybe ten trees in Murray Cemetery, each one the same: a single trunk leading into a full crown of green shrubbery, providing shade for whatever sat underneath. This tree, about halfway up, diverged into two trunks, producing separate crowns that blended into one another. Frank knew it as the *fork tree*.

As the person said, there was a large hole at the tree's base. Frank put the large Ziploc bag containing the book inside the empty space, pushing it far as he could against the side, out of view. He looked around once more for anyone who might be watching; no one was in sight.

He got back into his truck and switched on the engine, pumping the AC to full blast. "Whoa!" he yelled when he looked back up. There was a man standing beside the passenger window. He remained still when Frank yelled, continuing to stare. "Can I help you?" Frank called through the window. The man didn't reply. Frank then inched down the window. "You scared me. How long have you been standing there?" Once again, no reply. The man looked as if he was half asleep, his eyelids were relaxed to the point of being nearly closed, and his mouth hung slightly agape. The dark circles gave Frank the impression that the man's eyes were abnormally sunken into his skull. Several small lines branched out from the side, appearing to feed into the man's long, thinning hair. He couldn't be younger than seventy. "Can I help you?"

The man lifted his hand and fluidly slid something through the cracked open window. By the time Frank's mind registered that it was an envelope, the man had begun to hobble away toward the other end of the cemetery. Frank called after him, but there was no response.

Frank picked up the envelope and looked inside: the money. All of it.

☠

At a little after nine that morning, Frank pulled into an empty parking space at the small church where Addy preached. Despite being a weekday there were a ton of cars in the lot. Frank didn't consider himself a regular church-goer, but he liked to occasionally visit on Sunday mornings in support of one of his closest friends. Addy joked that it was because the church was a hotbed for future clients—there was no one under the age of sixty. Being one of the youngest people there, Frank was like a celebrity. Whenever he made an appearance, several invitations to lunch afterward always followed.

Frank stepped inside to see a handful of women and men doing what looked to be a renovation in the main auditorium. He noticed the colorful picture of a giant whale and a VBS banner hanging from the front wall. When one of the women noticed him, she dropped what she was doing and shouted, "Well, my word!" for everyone to hear.

Frank had been talking with a group for nearly ten minutes and declined two offers to go to lunch before Addy walked into the building. "Hey man, you here to help out?" he called.

"You know it," Frank smiled. "Actually, just came by to ask you a question. You got a second?"

"Couldn't call?" Addy asked.

"I was close by, felt like coming over and seeing if anyone was here." He gave Mrs. Peggy Sykes a smile and a wink. "We'll do lunch soon, I promise. Next time I'm here Sunday morning. Hold me to it."

Peggy came and gave Frank a hug and a kiss on the cheek. "We don't have to wait until Sunday. Herb and I are usually here in the mornings. You swing by anytime you want, and lunch is on us."

"You got it. We'll do it soon," Frank said.

She leaned back out of his embrace. "Don't forget I know where you live," Peggy said.

"Miss Peggy, I thought we agreed that you wouldn't tell your husband you were coming out to see me," Frank said with a grin.

Peggy laughed and her husband, Herb, extended his hand to say goodbye. "You take her any time you want her." He paused and held his grip. "I'm serious." They both smiled.

Addy asked if Frank minded talking outside; he needed fresh air. The two walked onto the main porch and then around to the back where there were benches and a well-kept courtyard with a rock labyrinth.

"Whoa, is that new?"

"Yeah. Got put in this spring after one of the members passed back in February. The upside is that it's incredibly calming to walk. The downside is that everyone here feels the same way and it's tough to get a moment's peace. Have to work at home if I want to get anything done. What's up? Everything alright?"

"Yeah. Things are fine, just had a question. I need your help locating someone, if you wouldn't mind."

"Who? Do they attend here?"

"No, but you're Mr. Murray High. And I figured you could use your band of merry ministers to help locate him."

"Oh. So, I know them?"

"You should. Do you remember Winston Rose?"

A sly grin crept across Addy's face. "Oh yeah. I remember him. Couldn't stand him," Addy replied.

"Seems to be the running opinion of him," Frank said.

"I had him as a teacher, but he was the reason my girlfriend stopped playing basketball. That guy was a dick."

"Why?"

"Well, he called me queer on a pretty consistent basis," Addy said. "Not the most inspiring thing to tell your student in my opinion."

"No, I mean about your girlfriend. Everybody called you queer." Frank smiled.

"Thanks," Addy sighed back. He took a seat on the two-seater swing hanging underneath one of the trees and patted the empty spot next to him. "You remember Mindy, right?"

"Yeah. Mindy Manning. Still see her sometimes up at Vitello's." Frank sat down.

"Yeah. It was her. Sophomore year, she probably told me five or six times how rude—and borderline creepy—the guy could be. I remember she told me once, after they lost a game, he came into the locker room while they were changing and went off on one of the girls. I don't know what she did—I think missed a bunch of free throws or something—but he went over to her locker and pulled out her underwear, which happened to be a thong. He held it up in front of the whole team and started yelling about how if she would stop whoring herself out, she could actually take some time to work on her game."

"Are you serious," Frank said, disgusted.

"I mean, I don't know how much of that was exaggerated but I wouldn't be surprised if it wasn't. The guy was crazy."

"Did she ever say anything? Like, report him?"

"Are you kidding? No way! The girls' basketball team was incredible. I told Mindy to say something, but I think she said the girl didn't want to mess up the team."

"Damn," Frank said.

"Yeah, and it wasn't just her—or me—that had complaints. Some of the teachers I still talk to have shared horror stories about that guy."

"Really? Man, I had him as a teacher—and he *was* a dick—but I guess I never got on his bad side. I don't remember much of anything about him other than what others told me, which wasn't much."

"He never pulled your thong out of your backpack and showed it to the class?"

"Not that I can recall."

Addy leaned back, stretching his arms over the swing's back. "Yeah, there were so many stories about him," he said softly. "We had this middle eastern kid in our history class—Rod. It was spelled different, like R-A-E-D, I think. Mr. Rose *always* called him Osama Bin *Raedin*. Then he'd laugh every time as if he'd just thought it up. Luckily, Raed didn't take offense to it—least he didn't act like he did. He would laugh. I mean, we all laughed—it was funny at the time—but, looking back on it, I definitely feel bad for not saying something." Addy paused. He patted his pockets and let out a disgusted breath. "Hey, I think I left my phone in my car this morning when I came in. I need to grab it, come on." They both stood up and Addy continued talking as they made their way to the parking lot. "I don't know why the school kept him around. I told myself before I came back here that if he were still teaching, I would spend my first six months trying to get him fired. Racist, perverted, belligerent prick." Addy paused in front of his car. "What are we doin'? You wanna go to lunch?" He opened his car door. "Why you asking about Rose?"

"You have any idea where he is now?"

"None. He's been gone since I moved back. One of the high school students here goes to Murray High—didn't recognize Winston Rose when I asked."

"Well, I know he's not teaching—hasn't been for a while. And I didn't see any death notices. You think you could ask around? Maybe ask some of the other ministers in the area. See if he's going to church anywhere, or if anyone knows what happened to him?"

"Why are you trying to find him?" Addy asked.

"I know this is going to sound stupid and completely impossible. And you're not gonna believe me. But you can't tell anyone I told you this, okay?"

"What is it?"

"You promise? Pinky swear?" Frank licked his pinky and held it out for Addy to latch onto.

Addy swiped his hand away. "Ew. What the hell are you doing? What are you, ten?" Frank laughed. "And why would you lick it first?"

"To validate your commitment." Frank attempted to hold back a smile through his grave expression.

"Yeah, fine, won't tell a soul. What's goin' on?"

"I think Mr. Rose may have killed someone." He waited for a moment to see Addy's reaction.

Addy's head came forward as his eyebrows arched, signaling that he was either surprised or hadn't clearly heard Frank. "He what?"

"Cliff seems to think it's possible that he killed several people."

Addy stood motionless for a moment, perhaps waiting for Frank to announce that this was a joke. Addy finally chuckled. "Who did he kill?"

"Maybe a lot of people," Frank replied. "We think he may have had something to do with Brian Pennington. You remember him, right?"

Addy's next words came out slow, attempting to confirm what he was hearing, "Brian Pennington. Tall, two hundred fortyish pounds, meathead Brian Pennington? You think Mr. Rose—old, skin and bones Mr. Rose, *killed* Brian Pennington?"

Frank hesitated in his answer. He swayed his head back and forth, and made a high pitched "ehhhh . . ."

"Frank, Brian's parents sent him away for drugs, man."

"You sure about that? You seen him since?" Frank asked.

"I mean, pretty sure. We went our separate ways after he started doing coke, but that's the story we all got."

"From his parents?"

"Not directly. But, everybody knew it. Brian came home from school one day, parents had his bags packed, and two guys took him away."

"You ever hear of the Murray High curse?"

Addy's eyes tightened. "That stuff about kids disappearing?"

"Yup," Frank reassured.

"I heard people mention it back in the day, but I don't remember any details about it. That was almost twenty years ago."

"Alright, well, that's what Cliff thinks he's digging into. Thinks Mr. Rose may have had something to do with it. I don't know if I buy it. You know anyone named Corey Grassman? Went to Calloway. Died back in ninety-seven?"

"Corey Grassman," Addy repeated. "Yeah. Monty Suthers—he's a cop now, but he used to teach at Murray—"

"Yeah, I know him," Frank said.

"He called me the other day asking about Corey. Apparently, his grave got robbed."

Frank bit his lip as his stomach turned. He cursed in his mind. "Yeah, that's him," Frank replied.

"You think Rose killed him too?"

"I'm still working on that," Frank replied.

"So, to make sure I have this right, you think Brian and this Corey kid were both murdered by our racist, manipulative, seventy-something-year-old teacher?"

"It's an idea."

"I'm intrigued," Addy said.

"There's something else," Frank said. "You remember we talked about Bethel Cemetery the other night?" Addy nodded. "Well . . . I may have found it. I mean, I don't know for sure. But I was in LBL the other day and I ended up in a place that matches its description."

Addy's face was expressionless.

"I also sorta stumbled on something."

"What?"

Frank hesitated to the point of discomfort and finally said in a soft voice, "I think I found a body."

Addy's eyebrow lifted slightly, and then as suddenly as it appeared, the expression vanished into dread. "Wait, wait, wait." Addy was holding up his hand like a traffic cop. His eyes shifted to the grass and then back to Frank. "Tell me you're not the grave robber I've been hearing about."

Frank shrugged. "Because we're at a church, I'm not going to confirm or deny anything—"

"Oh, gimme a break! Come on Frank! Are you nuts!?"

"I didn't say I did anything," Frank replied.

"You've gotta be kidding me," Addy said, shaking his head and walking away from his car. "That's what Donnie was talking about the other day. You doin' weird shit!"

"Whoa, whoa, whoa! When were you talkin' to Donnie—"

"Are you out of your freaking mind?" Addy said, irritated. "Dammit, Frank!"

"Isn't it sort of wrong to curse on church property?" Frank asked. Addy glared back at him, tightening his lips. "Again, I don't know if you missed the part about me saying I wasn't going to confirm anything. Let's just pretend like you didn't ask me."

Addy paced through the parking lot, with his hands in his pockets. After a few moments of silence, he yelled over, "What did you find?"

Frank told him. He walked over to him and showed the picture of the bone and explained about the pager and the seashells. Addy didn't understand how that led them to a connection between Winston Rose and Brian, but Frank insisted that Addy would be better off not knowing that much about the situation and that he should trust him. "Even Cliff thinks there's something to it."

"What about Donnie?"

"He's on the fence."

"Yeah. That's what I thought."

"He's got one leg over," Frank continued, "it's just that his pants are caught at the top—"

"Look, don't drag me into something illegal, Frank."

"I'm not dragging you into this," Frank said.

"I can't afford to have something else happen, okay?" Frank said he understood. "I'm serious."

"Alright. I gotchu." Frank stood quiet for a moment. "So . . ." Frank's lips pursed as he stood looking around the landscape. "You think you can ask around about Rose?"

Addy sighed. "Yeah. I'll see what I can do. Nothing else though. I've already got a cop watching me over some stuff earlier this week. I don't need my name tied to this too."

"What happened earlier?" Frank asked. "Ahh, better not. Kinda got my name in the mud too. Let's just leave it here." Frank patted the side of Addy's shoulder and started walking back over to his car.

"You really think you found that cemetery, huh?" Addy asked.

"I found something."

"Can I see it?" Addy asked.

"Like, right now?"

"I'm not getting any work done with everyone here." He checked his watch. "And if I go back in there, I'll be forced to go to lunch again."

"That's a free lunch, though."

"I've been twice this week. I'm good," Addy replied.

The two of them picked up a bite to eat and then ran back by the house to try and talk Cliff into coming along.

"I got appointments all afternoon," Cliff said. He was loading weights onto the bench press for a client. "But even if I was just chillin' here watching Anime, I still wouldn't go out there with you."

"That scary, huh?" Addy asked.

"I don't mess around with that stuff," Cliff replied. "Ask Donnie to go."

"Has he seen it yet?" Addy asked.

"No, but he won't go. Unless . . ." He stopped. A look of strange intrigue shined across his face. He turned to Addy. "You mind doing me a favor?"

"Sure."

"Call Donnie and tell him that you need his help moving something," Frank said.

"He's with Lexie right now," Cliff said.

"I thought she left last night," Frank said.

"Nah, she got here about an hour ago."

"Even better. Go ahead," Frank said, handing Addy his phone.

"Hey, it's Addy . . . I'm calling you on Frank's phone . . . yeah I'm outside, you busy? . . . Well, I'm trying to move a couple of pieces of furniture at the church. Was gonna have Cliff and Frank help but Cliff's got a client. Figured if you're free then I can knock this thing out in less than thirty minutes . . . yeah . . . no, that's okay, bring her." Frank nodded happily, grabbing Addy's shoulders, and giving him a light shake of excitement.

37

Addy drove Frank, Donnie, and Lexie along the main road through town while Donnie described a conversation with an elderly man who called earlier that morning requesting to have his wife posed.

"Posed," Addy said. "Like, not in a coffin?"

"Not exactly. He calls and says his wife will pass away in the next couple of days and she told him that for her funeral she wants to be sitting in her rocking chair as if she's there to greet her guests. Says she wanted people to remember her how she was in life and apparently that was sitting outside on her porch."

"Wait, he wanted to have her sitting in the parlor or sitting out front?" Addy asked.

"Out front," Donnie answered.

"No way," Addy said.

"Nah, dude, this is a thing in other countries," Frank cut in. "I had a mom call about it for her son last year. He got a bad case of the flu and ended up dying. She wanted him sitting in a bean bag playing his Xbox during the memorial."

"Which game?" Addy asked.

Donnie turned and gave Addy a confused look. Lexie chuckled. The awkward conversation was proving to be enough to distract Donnie from noticing that they were not driving toward the church where Addy worked.

Frank tried to keep the conversation going, "What'd you tell him?"

"I told him no," Donnie said, surprised at the question.

"Why?"

"You're joking. You would have considered it?" Donnie asked.

"I would have *booked* it," Frank exclaimed. "If he's willing to pay money, I'll stand his wife up at the pool table and put a cue in her hand."

"That would actually be a cool idea," Addy added, eyeing Donnie in the rearview mirror.

"I'm not putting a three-hundred-pound woman on a rocking chair and sitting her out front. It's tacky."

"Who says tacky anymore?" Frank asked.

Donnie sighed. "Whatever. I'm not doing that. What if the chair breaks? What if she leaks? What if someone tries to sit on her? What if some kid mistakes her for a real person and tries to talk to her? And you know everyone's gonna want to take selfies with her."

"Of course they will! That's what you want! Dig out Dad's Polaroid camera and we make a photo booth out of it, charge two bucks a pop," Frank added enthusiastically.

"Yeah, I'm kind of with Donnie on this one," Addy said. "As fascinating—and bizarre—as all this is, I'd be kind of creeped out if I had to do a funeral for someone who was sitting in a rocker right next to me. I'd keep thinking they were gonna get up, or talk, or something."

"Weirdness aside, we need the money. Especially now!" Frank turned around in his seat to look at Donnie. "I'll remind you of our old motto, 'For the right kind of dough, get the right kind of show.'"

Donnie's brow furrowed, and he turned to Lexie. "I can promise you, no one has ever said that."

Frank turned back toward the front, "All I'm sayin' is, we're a *funeral* home. If the guy wanted a *funeral* with his wife in a rocking chair for family and friends to remember her, then that's what we gi—"

"Wait, where are we going?" Donnie asked, looking behind him. They were almost at the Highway 80 intersection on 641. "I thought we were going to the church."

The car got quiet. "Guys, what are we doing?" Donnie asked again, catching Addy's eye in the mirror.

"Don't look at me man, I'm just the driver. Talk to your brother," Addy replied.

Frank didn't say anything. "Frank. What are we doing? I told Mom I'd be gone for half an hour."

"Did you have an appointment this afternoon?" Frank asked.

"No."

"You may want to call her and say that you'll be running a bit late."

Donnie looked at Lexie whose facial expression had given way to confusion. "What's going on?" he asked her.

"I don't know," she replied.

"Dammit, Frank, where are we going?" Addy made the turn onto Highway 80. "Oh, you've gotta be kidding me. Tell me we are not going to LBL."

"We just have to make a quick stop," Frank replied. "Shouldn't take more than a couple of hours."

"A couple of hours!? Somebody needs to be at the house."

"Dude," Frank turned back around to Donnie. "Mom's got it. You said you had no appointments, we're fine. Just tell her that the move is taking longer th—"

"I'm not calling Mom. You do it." Donnie cut him off.

Frank blew out a breath and turned back, facing forward. "Fine, I'll call her. She's not gonna—"

"God! You are such a *freakin'* ball sack sometimes!" Donnie hit the back of the seat with his hand hard enough to jolt Frank forward. "I cannot believe you dragged me out here to do this. We're going to that cemetery, aren't we?"

"Lexie, I apologize for dragging you into this," Frank offered.

"Oh, it's fine! I kind of wanted to see it." She put her hand on Donnie's. He was looking out the window, obviously annoyed. She gently squeezed it. "Maybe it'll be fun," she whispered.

Frank called Ginny and told her that he and Donnie were helping Addy move and that it was going to take a lot longer than expected. She said that it was no trouble and to stay as long as needed.

"Oh! I meant to tell you," Ginny started. "I found that person you were looking for—Edward Hubbs."

"Oh yeah?" Frank asked. "Does he live in Murray? He's not dead, is he?"

"No, he's not dead. But I don't know what sort of condition he's in," Ginny replied. "I talked to Wanda this morning and I was right. Edward Hubbs is related to Shirley Hubbs. They're siblings."

"Would I know these people?"

"I doubt it. I knew Shirley. She died years ago. Wanda said the last she heard, Ed was living in Spring Hill Nursing Home. Said up until a few months ago, she would chat with him on occasion when she would go and visit her own sister. But she hasn't seen him at any of the meals in a while. She suspects he's not doing too well."

"Hmm. So, he's alive, she just doesn't know if he's sick or something?"

"Correct."

"Okay. I may go up there tomorrow. See if I can see him," Frank said. "Thanks, Mom."

"You still don't want to tell me what this is about?"

"I told you. I have a couple of questions about some spots in LBL. Someone said he would be the best person to talk with," Frank said.

"I take it the person who referred you to him didn't know Edward that well. It may be a little hard to have a conversation with him. Edward Hubbs can't talk."

Frank wasn't sure if he heard her clearly. "What?" Frank asked.

"Apparently, he doesn't have a tongue."

38

"Ew," Frank mumbled after he hung up.

"Everything alright?" Addy asked.

"Yeah, all good." Frank turned his head toward the back. "Mom found that guy I was looking for—Edward Hubbs. He's in the nursing home."

"Cool," Donnie mumbled. He was resting his head in his palm, leaning against the door, and looking out.

"Apparently he doesn't have a tongue. Not sure how I'm gonna—"

"Hey, here's a fun fact," Donnie blurted out. "I don't care." And then went back to staring out the window.

Addy parked at the trail's entrance, as far over from the road as he could and left a note on his window to indicate they were hiking. Frank walked to the back of the car to get his backpack and began tucking his pant legs into his socks. He pulled out a couple of cans of bug spray and told everyone to use it.

"What's in the bag?" Donnie asked.

"Water. Protein bars. And these," Frank replied. He gave Lexie and Addy a box of crackers and told them to make a trail as they went. They began walking down the initial path, and then followed Frank's lead into the woods. Donnie noticed the broken, bright orange crackers from Frank's first trip.

"Are we seriously laying out cheese crackers?" Donnie asked. "How far away is this place?"

"No idea," Frank said. "But with no path, cracker crumbs seem like the best way to keep us from getting lost. It worked well last time."

Frank led the way, following the cracker trail for much of the trip. He would occasionally pull out a hand-drawn map he'd created earlier with notes from the first visit. It incorporated some of the landmarks that Frank remembered, and any distinguishing details along the way to better guide him.

The group walked in silence for much of the trip, save an occasional complaint about heat, bugs, or holes in the trail. Addy and Frank reminisced over memories from high school and speculated details about the ill-reputed cemetery.

"Frank!" Donnie yelled. He and Lexie were several steps back. "Dude, it's been almost an hour! Do you have any idea where you're going?"

"Yeah! I'm following the trail."

"Are we close? Definitely getting Blair Witch vibes," Donnie said. "Thought you said this wouldn't take long."

"Bitch, bitch, bitch," Frank mumbled to himself.

"Didn't happen to bring any allergy spray, did you?" Donnie asked.

"Nah. Allergies acting up?" Frank asked.

"Yeah, man. My head is throbbing," Donnie replied.

"Yeah, my eyes keep watering," Lexie added.

"Sorry everybody, we're almost there. Should just be up here."

When Donnie finally noticed what Frank was holding, he asked to look at the drawing. "This is the only map you have?"

"Had to make my own, it's not on any other map."

"So, if it's not on a map, how did you find it?" Addy asked.

"Visitor Center," Frank said. "Above the exit, there's a big old map of LBL. It has a cemetery marker where no other one has it."

"So, just to make sure I have this right, this haunted cemetery that no one seems to be able to find is actually on a map for all to see in the Visitor Center?"

"Pretty much. But it's high up, and there's no copies of it. Honestly, who would ever notice it? It's a tiny speck in the middle of nowhere."

"How'd you see it then?" Addy asked.

"Bit of a long story. Cliff is actually the one who found it. I'd taken a picture of the map and we both just happened to be looking in the right spot."

"Did you ask anybody there about it?" Addy asked.

"Nope. Didn't want anyone knowing I was back here."

"You think it's really haunted?" Lexie asked.

"Definitely not," Frank replied.

Addy slapped his shin. "Man, I am itching like crazy! Freakin' bugs!"

"You want some spray?" Frank asked.

"I've used it twice!" Addy answered.

"I should have told you to put on pants. My bad, man," Frank said. "I promise, we're almost there. Maybe once we get up there use some of the water to wash off your legs. I brought a couple of cold packs too. That should help the itching."

"You know," Donnie yelled. He had fallen behind again, looking at the map. "It's twenty seventeen. If there was some haunted, secret cemetery out here, do you really think it would stay hidden? This whole park is a geocaching goldmine. There are hikers going through this place all the time. Plus, all this is government property. They searched this place inside and out to clear away anyone living out here. I promise you, we're not uncovering anything new."

"Maybe, but then again we're not talking about a popular place. Hardly anyone outside Kentucky knows Murray State, let alone Murray, and definitely not Land Between the Lakes," Frank said. "Besides, maybe people don't want us to find it. What if it's intentionally being hidden?" Frank reasoned.

"So, it's a conspiracy?" Donnie asked.

"Maybe," Frank replied.

"Yeah . . ." Donnie muttered. "Anyone ever search for Bethel Cemetery on the internet? Or looked up 'hidden cemeteries in LBL'? I'm sure you'll find pictures of this place."

"You won't," Lexie said. "I tried last night. Several times. Nothing."

"Same," Frank agreed. "There's articles about Bethel, but no *real* pictures." Frank motioned for them to stop so he could fish out a water bottle from his backpack. He took a sip and passed it around.

"Actually, Frank could be right," Addy said. "Maybe it's not so much *undiscovered* as it is protected. Look at the Chinese Cemetery—people have protected that thing for so long that no one even knows it exists. Frank, you know about that place, right?" Addy had unknowingly taken the lead, following the cracker path. He turned to Frank but realized he wasn't near him. "Frank?"

"Yeah?" Frank called. He was way back down the path, doubled over, resting his hands on his knees."

"You alright?" Donnie asked, turning around.

"Yeah, sorry," Frank replied, standing back up, holding his stomach. "Allergies back here are pretty bad. Just got nauseated all of a sudden." Frank took a deep breath and blew it out slowly. "It happened last time I came up here."

"You sure you're okay?" Lexie asked.

"Yeah," Frank answered. "My allergies give me this reaction sometimes; it comes and goes."

"Wanna go back?" Donnie asked.

"I'm fine." Another breath. "Alright. Let's do it. Faster we get there, faster we can get back." He quickened his pace and moved up to Addy.

"One of you mind explaining what a Chinese Cemetery is?" Donnie asked. "It's in LBL?"

They began walking again, continuing to eat and drop handfuls of crackers.

"It's an old cemetery in LBL. Not on any maps," Addy said. "Used to have an LBL reenactment actor at the church I work at. He told me that the Visitor Center acts like it's not there to keep people from going to it."

"You've seen it?" Donnie asked.

"Yeah, a couple of times. It's near the ranger station, just around back. It stays hidden because there's no reason to go back there. There's no trail to it."

"I asked about it recently," Frank said. "The guy told me where it was but asked that I not go out there. And if I didn't listen to him, then to at least respect the area and not post pictures of it online. He said they didn't want a lot of people showing up asking about it."

"So, what is it?" Donnie asked.

"No idea," Addy said. "There's a sign that says, 'Chinese Cemetery' with several unmarked graves. They think mid to late eighteen hundreds. No clue who they were, where they came from, or why there was a settlement of Chinese people living in this part of Kentucky and Tennessee."

"We actually saw it on a field trip back in elementary school. I always thought it was pretty mind blowing that there was a burial spot for Chinese people here. From two hundred years ago," Lexie added.

"Maybe that's what's going on here: they keep it off the map for a reason. Haunted or not, maybe locals just don't want people going around it."

"Speaking of blown minds," Frank called from the back, "tell your brains to get ready because I'm about to blow all of you."

"Please never say that again," Lexie replied.

They all turned to look at him. "There it is." He pointed ahead and crossed in front of them. He put the water bottle into his backpack and led the way through the brush into the open field.

39

The clearing seemed more ominous this time. Perhaps it was because Frank knew what to expect, or perhaps it was the waves of sickness in his stomach and the acid rising in his throat. He shook off the discomfort, watching everyone unknowingly step over the seashell barrier before pointing them out.

"How far do they go?" Donnie asked, massaging the temples of his head.

"I don't know. I guess all the way around?" Frank replied.

Addy and Frank made their way toward the gravestones while Lexie walked along the seashell trail and Donnie joined her. Everything was exactly as Frank had left it. The dirt over the grave hiding Frank's bag of bones was still in a fresh heap.

"Are you sure this is Bethel?" Addy asked, scratching his arm.

"Pretty sure," Frank said.

"Not as frightening of a place as I expected." Addy looked around, moving some of the overgrowth with his foot to peek at the blank gravestones. "Any significance behind these being blank?"

"No clue," Frank answered.

"You sure you're good, man? You look . . . green."

Frank swallowed again. "Speak for yourself. Look at your arms. It's like your sunburned."

"I always itch when I'm outside," Addy replied. "Which one is hers?"

"Hey!" Donnie yelled. "Come here."

"What'd you find?" Frank yelled back. Donnie was standing at the far edge of the clearing several feet away from where they entered.

"Just come here."

Addy and Frank marched over the tall grass to Donnie who was standing behind a tree, staring at something. "I told you guys this wasn't Bethel." He laughed.

"What is it?" Frank asked.

"Look," Donnie said, pointing at the tree beside where he was standing. Nailed to the bark of the tree was a wooden sign, etched with letters that were barely visible to form the words *Markgraf Cemetery*. "Nice try, though."

"Aw, no way," Frank muttered, sagging with disappointment. He stared at the sign for a long moment before finally clicking his tongue and whispering, "Are you kidding me?"

"Well," Addy sighed, "this was several hours well spent."

"How?" Frank looked around. "That doesn't make any sense. She researched all this. She had it written on the picture: Bethel Cemetery." Frank looked back toward the graves. "Maybe Markgraf is another cemetery. You guys see any other stones?" Frank started to walk around the overbrush, clutching at the side of his stomach.

"I don't mean to be a buzzkill," Lexie said, "but my eyes are *really* burning. I think I got some of the bug spray in them. Can I borrow the water?" She was holding the bottom of her shirt up over her face, pressing it into her eyes.

Frank tossed her one of the bottles from his bag and walked back over to the site of the fourteen graves. Donnie started to say something to him, but Lexie nudged him with her elbow.

"It's fine. I'm sure he's disappointed. I'm okay, just give him a second."

"I *hope* he's disappointed; dragging us all out here. My head is pounding," Donnie added. "I need to get out of here."

The group followed behind Frank back toward where they entered the clearing. He was squatting near the fresh mound of dirt and going through his backpack. Donnie asked what he was doing.

"Bethel or not, something isn't right down there, and I want to see what it is."

"Whoa, whoa. I'm not digging up a grave, man," Addy replied.

"Yeah. Plus, we don't have much time and you don't have a shovel. Can we go?" Donnie asked.

Four spades fell out onto the ground from Frank's backpack and clanged together.

"Of course, he would have shovels," Donnie sighed.

"Frank, I'm not kiddin'. I can't get caught digging up a grave," Addy protested.

"You guys don't have to dig—turn around and act like I'm not here. But I want to see if there's anything else. If not, we can go. Shouldn't take me long, it's only a couple feet down."

"I'll help," Lexie said. Donnie shot her a look.

"What?" A curious grin peeked across her mouth. "What if it *is* something?"

"I'll just hang with you, then," Donnie said to Addy. Each checked their phones—no service.

Lexie and Frank dug into the earth for the next several minutes until Frank finally uncovered the pager. He picked it up out of the dirt and brushed it off before setting it on his backpack. Addy leaned down and stared at it. "Is that a pager?" He asked.

"Yeah," Donnie replied. "This is why he thinks someone else is buried down there."

"Why would a pager be in someone's grave?" Addy asked. "Who does he think is buried down there?"

"Not sure," Frank said, flinging dirt to the side. "But I don't think they're supposed to be in here."

"I still think someone was hiking up here and dropped—" Donnie started to say when Frank leaned back and pointed at the ground.

"See?" He said. Donnie and Addy stepped over toward him to get a better look and knelt down to see a large bone. "How do you explain this? That's a bone."

"Yeah, this guy's bone," Donnie said, tapping the unengraved headstone with his foot. "Or girl."

"Two feet down?!" Frank exclaimed. "Then where's the coffin?"

"Uh, guys," Lexie called. She was digging a few feet over. Frank stood and looked toward hers. The others followed and stopped when they saw what she was holding up: a black, tattered, and torn jersey. *Murray Tigers* was across the front in block letters.

"Tell me you didn't find that in there," Addy said.

"This is a girl's basketball jersey," Lexie replied softly.

"Wasn't there something about a girl and basketball practice?" Frank asked.

"Yeah. Pam Climber," Lexie said. "Went to practice and never came back."

"Wait, wait. who's Pam Climber?" Addy asked.

"She went missing in the eighties," Lexie answered slowly, practically in a daze. "And we just found her jersey."

"We don't know it's her jersey," Donnie cut in.

"Then it's a pretty big coincidence," Frank replied.

"Yeah, okay, I'm definitely not comfortable being out here," Addy replied.

Frank picked up Lexie's spade and began digging where she left off.

"What are you doing?" Addy asked.

"Seeing if she's actually down here."

"What, you think she was just walking by on the nature trail and dropped her jersey in an open grave? Of course, she's down there." He slapped an itch on his leg and rubbed it with his hand. "We need to let the cops take this. And I need to get out of this grass!"

"No way. There's reward money if we find her." Frank replied, beginning to dig more. "Get the cold pack out of the lunchbox in my bag. It'll help with your itch."

Addy threw up his hands and cursed at him as Frank continued digging all around the hole in a frenzy, searching for anything that would indicate a body. And then he found it! Long white bones began to show through the dirt. He peered up at Addy, whose eyes were the size of ping pong balls. Addy knelt closer. "No way," he whispered, helping Frank uncover more of it.

No one said a word as the two of them uncovered a human body under just three feet of dirt. Only a portion of the mostly decomposed corpse was visible in the ground. It was wrapped in an orange windbreaker. "Okay. That jacket is definitely not that old. That's eighties or nineties, at best."

Frank peered at Addy and then Lexie. "Whoever that is, is definitely not *that* person," Frank said pointing to the headstone.

"How do you know?" Lexie asked.

"Come on. Really? Where's the coffin? Those stones are ancient. Look at what this person's wearing."

"Yeah, you couldn't get a modern hearse back here—there's no way," Addy said, a nervous tone in his voice.

Frank snapped a picture with his phone of the body and an up-close shot of the jacket and jersey.

Lexie looked behind her to ask Donnie to take a look but didn't see him. "Donnie," Lexie called.

"Yeah?"

"Where are you?" Lexie looked around.

"Right here," he replied. He was down in the weeds, digging.

Frank quickly got to his feet. "What are you doing?"

Donnie stood up, still staring at the ground where he was just kneeling. He dropped the spade.

"You okay?" Lexie asked.

"Look," he said back. Beneath him, what looked to be the sleeve of a blue jean jacket was uncovered from the earth. Donnie stooped down beside the fabric and pulled. The dirt beneath him began to crack and pop as it released its grip on the coat, finally giving in to Donnie's strength when he yanked it out with both hands. Something *thunked* onto the ground when it surfaced. "Oh shit," he whispered.

"That's a wallet," Lexie said in a hushed voice. "Looks like a woman's wallet. Is there anything inside?"

Donnie unzipped the rectangular pouch and opened it. Inside were a handful of cards, two single bills, and several coins.

"Any idea who's it is?"

Donnie raised one of the cards up to eye level. "I can't read it. It's faded. Here, take a look." He passed the ID to Lexie.

"G. E. GE," Lexie muttered. "I can't make out the last name."

"Check it out," Donnie said. He was pointing to the small, narrow object nearby. He poked it with his finger, then lifted it off the ground into his hand. "It's a pocketknife."

"Okay, we gotta call the cops," Addy said.

"Why is all this up here?" Lexie asked.

"Seriously, guys, I'm ready to go," Addy interjected. When Donnie picked up his spade from off the ground, Addy became impatient, "Hey, look, I'm leaving now. Do not start digging another hole."

"I'm not digging, I'm just hiding it from him," Donnie replied, pointing to Frank. "I wanna get out of here."

Frank got on his knees next to the pile of earth Lexie had just dug up. "Does no one want to see what's down there?"

"No!" they all exclaimed.

"Frank, this is not for us to dig up, man. Leave it alone! Let's just call the cops," Addy exclaimed.

"But then they'll—"

Then Addy lost it. "Holy shit, man! I'm not arguing with you on this! We're done! If you wanna come back up here and dig all this up, fine! But *I'm* leaving. I'm not cool with being up here." Addy began walking away, toward the entrance they came in.

"Guys, come on! These are the missing kids!" Frank yelled.

"He's right, man. This is for the cops," Donnie replied. "Plus, you look like you're about to pass out and Lexie's eyes won't stop running. And our ride is leaving. Get your stuff." Frank put the spades back in his bag and threw it on his back as Lexie and Donnie started to walk after Addy. Frank pulled out his phone and snapped a picture of the items that had come up from Donnie's efforts: the knife, the coat, and the faded license. He quickly glanced around the scene to make sure he hadn't left anything and suddenly remembered the bones from Tom Middleton he'd buried, wrapped inside Sarah Piddleton's sweater. He cursed, figuring it would be best to remove them in case the cops did come up here. He hurried back over to uncover them and place them in his bag.

"Frank! Come on, man!" Donnie yelled.

"I'm coming!" As he was stuffing the bones into his bag, he noticed something in the distance.

"Hey," he said, though not to anyone particular. He stayed still, staring out into the clearing. "What is that?" Lexie and Donnie continued walking. "Guys!" Frank whipped around and called in a louder voice. "Donnie, hold up! Look." They stopped walking and turned toward Frank. He was staring back at the far end of the clearing. A lone decaying tree loomed in the distance.

After an awkward moment of quiet, Donnie said, "What?"

Frank glanced around. "I don't...dude...I swear...I just saw someone walk by over there."

"That's not funny," Lexie said, patting the sides of her eyes with her shirt.

"I'm not trying to be funny. Right over by that tree," Frank said. Addy stopped walking and yelled "Let's go!" but they all continued to stare in the direction of Frank's finger. No one moved, unsure if something might actually be out there.

Donnie started to talk but Lexie cut him off, "Wait," she whispered, taking several hard blinks to clear her eyes. When they finally came into focus, "What is that?"

"You see it too, right?" Frank asked.

Donnie took a few steps in the direction of the tree. "I don't see—"

Lexie let out a shrill scream, startling the two brothers.

"What? What!" Donnie asked.

"There's someone over there!" Lexie was frantically waving her finger at the tree until she suddenly burst into a sprint after Addy. The fright on her face was enough to tell Frank and Donnie that it was not a joke, and they should follow fast behind.

40

The group cut from a run to a brisk walk when they were a good distance away from the field. The crackers highlighted the path, greatly shortening the amount of time it took them to get back to the car. When Donnie opened the passenger door, Frank called him out for not first offering it to Lexie. Donnie stood back away from the door and asked Lexie if she wanted to sit up front, but Frank yelled shotgun and slipped into the seat, quickly closing the door.

"So gullible, bro," Frank said, putting the window down.

Donnie nodded and took a drink from his bottle, then before Frank could get out another word, Donnie blew a torrent of water onto his face like a geyser. Both Addy and Lexie turned to look, startled.

"Ugh. Yeah, real mature," Frank said, wiping the water from his eyes. "Thank you." Everyone else laughed.

On the drive out, Addy tried to understand what Lexie saw but she had no description, only that it looked to be someone standing on the other side of the clearing. Frank verified that it was similar to what he'd seen—someone moving around near the trees.

"You see anything?" Addy asked Donnie.

"No. I ran when she screamed. Probably an animal."

"Yeah, an animal that walks upright on two legs," Frank quipped. "That makes sense." He leaned his chair back.

"You feelin' any better?" Addy asked Frank. "Better not have the flu."

"Little bit. Comes and goes. This happened last time I went out there. I'm good."

"How's your head?" Addy nodded back to Donnie, eyeing him through the rearview mirror.

"Better. She had some Ibuprofen in her purse. And some Zyrtec. It wasn't too bad as we were coming out, thank God. You still itchin'?"

"Little bit, but not that bad," Addy replied.

"You got bug bites or just allergic to grass?" Frank asked. His arm was draped across his eyes.

"No clue. I didn't see any bites. May have just been the grass. To be fair, I never spend that much time outside in the woods so who knows."

The group sat in silence for much of the ride home. Addy put the music on a low volume, trying his hardest to stay awake. The surrounding calm didn't help. Donnie was asleep with his head on Lexie's shoulder and Frank was snoring in the passenger seat with his mouth wide open. Addy kept himself awake by tickling Frank's face and mouth with an old rabbit's foot he had connected to his key ring. It took Frank slapping his face four times before he woke up to see Addy chuckling to himself. About the same time, Donnie startled awake with an audible gasp.

"Whoa, there." Lexie laughed. "You alright?"

Donnie looked around, taking a second to adjust his mind. He stared forward, wide-eyed, and then at Lexie. "Yeah." He shook his head. "Man. Nightmare. Felt like we were back in those woods and something was coming after us."

"Like what? An animal?" she asked.

"No. I don't know."

"Great," Addy grunted. "My house is creepy enough without having to think about some insidious presence stalking me."

⚫

They arrived back at the funeral home in the early evening. Addy said bye to everyone through the window and then called Frank back. Frank slid into the passenger seat and Addy asked what he was going to do about what they found.

Frank paused for a moment. "I don't know. It's gonna sound selfish but there are a couple of families offering reward money for missing persons. If that body we found today *is* Pam Climber, then it's possible there could be others up there. If I can find the others . . ." Frank stopped. "You're not gonna call the cops, are you?"

"Nope," Addy replied. "I don't want any part of this. But I will say, if the cops catch you up there, or holding out on evidence, or hiding something like this, you're screwed."

"Yeah, I know," Frank replied, holding his hands up in defense. "I know. I just need a couple of days. I'll go back up there and try to get it sorted out by sometime early next week."

Addy shook his head. Frank was going to speak up, but Addy cut in, "Look, this is your deal. But this is some serious stuff you're messing around with. I know you're thinking about the home, and your mom and dad." Addy paused and looked out at the house. "And gettin' that roof taken care of. But you're gonna lose a lot more than that if this doesn't work out how you want."

Frank looked over at him. Addy nodded over toward Donnie standing on the porch with Lexie, talking. "What do you mean?"

"I mean, if I were you, given what I've heard about some of the recent tension you guys have had, I wouldn't make him choose between protecting himself and protecting you. I don't know what you're planning on doing—don't want to know. Just sayin', friend to friend, and as someone who knows Donnie, weigh the cost of what you're doing. The *real* cost."

Frank sat in silence and then, "I know. I just—*we* just—we need that money, ya know? The damage from that storm, and the Kochs, it's getting to be too much."

"You don't have to justify this to me," Addy said. "I'm only telling you to be careful."

Frank stared out at Donnie. "The real pisser is that he wants out." Frank took a pause. "He should, it's not his thing. But I don't want him to leave. And I feel like the only way I can get him to stay is if this place is doing well—not being a burden on him."

"You can't really think he'll stay here. Right?"

"I find it's best not to think about serious stuff," Frank said. He and Addy laughed. "I'm hopeful I can convince him to open a restaurant on that open lot next door." He stared out ahead of him, noticing Addy's quizzical look in his peripheral vision. He sighed. "Yeah, I know. Who am I kidding, right? I know he won't stay in Murray. But, maybe Paducah; they've got a great restaurant scene. That way he'd get to see us more than once a year." He paused. "I don't want to be anywhere but *here*." Frank eyed the home. "He wants to be anywhere *but* here. So, at this point, whatever gets him to stay home, I'll take it."

"Even if it lands you in jail? Ruins his name? And your relationship?"

"Like I said, I choose not to think about that part." Frank winked.

Addy laughed. "I'll call you this week if I hear anything about Rose."

"Thanks man. I'll catch ya later."

SATURDAY
41

Frank arrived at Spring Hill Nursing Home a little before eight a.m. He walked up the ramp and said hello to a group of elderly men sitting quietly in chairs beside the door. They each waved acknowledgement, and all went back to staring out at the courtyard. Frank opened the door expecting to be hit with a cocktail aroma of Pine-Sol, urine, and stale diapers. He was wrong.

The main entrance, previously a nurse's station and long hallway with single rooms, had been renovated into a large foyer and check-in station with an upscale café, boutique library, and coffee bar. More important, the smell had been replaced with a unique mixture of fresh coffee grounds and something reminiscent of an ocean breeze scented candle. Frank whistled to himself a note of astonishment. "Not bad."

"Good morning! Welcome to Spring Hill. How can I help you?" A cheery receptionist stood up from her computer desk.

"Hey. Good morning," Frank replied. "I'm here to see Mr. Edward Hubbs."

"Wonderful. Are you family?"

"No, ma'am. My mother is a friend of Mr. Hubbs. I had some historical questions about the area. She said he'd be someone to talk to. If he was up to it," Frank replied.

She began typing on her keyboard. "I'm sure he'd love the company. I do know that Mr. Ed was not feeling well earlier this week. I'll walk you back to the dining hall first, then I'll see if he's up for visitors. Is that okay?" Frank nodded. The nurse reached underneath the counter and pulled out two small white boards. "Have you met with Mr. Hubbs before?"

"No, ma'am."

"Okay then. These are for you," she said, sliding two dry erase markers over the counter. "Mr. Hubbs lost the ability to speak decades ago, but he's more than comfortable using these. Just talk like you would to anyone else and he'll either answer you with a head shake or write the answer on these. If he doesn't have his ears in—his hearin' aids—you may wanna just write the question on one of these and let him respond on the other."

"Sounds good," Frank said. He grabbed the boards and slipped the markers into his pocket.

"He's a sweetheart."

"Can't wait to meet him. How did he lose his voice? Do you know?"

"I've never asked. Seems it happened a long time ago. He got sick when he was little—at least that's what I've heard."

Edward Hubbs looked like he'd blow over if the ceiling fan was on too high. The outline of his legs underneath the faded, wrinkled khaki pants could have easily been two long sticks, extending down into his black, Velcro orthopedic shoes. He shuffled his feet at a slow pace as he entered the dining hall, one hand carrying a cane and the other through the nurse's arm. There were only a handful of other residents in the dining area, preoccupied with conversations or puzzles. Frank sat alone at a table for four in the middle of the room and stood when Edward got closer. The nurse gently walked him over to the table and made an introduction for the two of them. She asked if he'd like her to scoot his chair in and he shook his head, patting her on the hand before unhooking his arm from hers. He continued standing as she walked away, even after she left the room, and even still after he placed his cane on the back of a chair beside him.

He glanced around the room and then down at Frank. He grabbed hold of the chair and pulled it out from under the table, lowering himself onto it with ease. He instantly began writing on the board. **Canes make them hold your hand.** He winked at Frank and extended his hand to shake. There was a slight tremor in the limb as he reached forward, but Frank could feel a surprising amount of strength in the grip.

"Mr. Hubbs, it's nice to meet you," Frank said.

Same, he wrote.

"Are you okay if I talk or would you like me to write?"

Edward gave a thumbs up.

"Thumbs up to the talking or to the writing?" Frank grinned.

Edward put the other thumb up and then, **Call me Ed.**

Frank nodded his head. "Sounds good. My name is Frank Burgers. I run the Burgers Brothers' Family Funeral Home."

Dave and Ginny? Ed wrote.

"Yeah. That's us."

Good people. Sisters funeral.

"Sisters funeral? Oh! We did your *sister's* funeral."

Ed held up a finger. **And my Mom. Dad. Good donuts.**

Frank smiled. "Best in Kentucky. My mom says hi."

Ed gave another thumbs up, and then waved to someone behind Frank, giving them a thumbs up as well. Frank continued talking, "I'm doing some historical research—about the area—and someone said I should talk to you. You mind if I ask you some questions?"

Gets me out of crafts. ☺

"Perfect," Frank said. "I wanted to ask you about something in LBL." The pleasantness that was in Edward's eyes faded into an expression that Frank interpreted as offense. "Is that okay?"

Ed hesitated for a moment then gave a cautious nod.

"Did you grow up in LBL?"

He nodded, more confidently.

"Good memories?"

A slight delay followed by a grave, slow shake of his head back and forth.

"Oh," Frank said. "Were you there long?"

Left in 49. Dad in 73. Mom in 80.

"Wow. Your mom stayed that long? I thought federal government forced everyone out of there."

Not her.

"Did they finally just come in and take possession of the house? How did they get her to leave?"

Ed wavered in his response, holding the marker in his hand, and tapping out a collection of black dots on the board.

"Never mind. I'm sure that's too long of an answer. It's okay," Frank said.

Edward began to write. **Gov didn't.**

"Gov didn't," Frank read aloud. "The *government* didn't make her leave?"

Ed nodded and began writing again. **Died at home. Sick.**

"Oh. I'm sorry to hear that," Frank said. Ed tilted his head down to acknowledge Frank's sentiment. He began tracing away the letters with his finger. "This is going to sound a little weird to ask—I'm sure you've heard about it—but, in high school, our principal always told us these stories about a woman who lived in LBL." Ed's finger stopped tracing. "I've heard probably four versions of this story but supposedly she was a schoolteacher who murdered a bunch of kids . . . ? The story's not too consistent with that part. But in all the versions, *something* happened to kids and the townspeople ended up burning her alive in her home." Ed was still sitting, staring at the board. Frank had noticed the abrupt stop in movement but thought maybe he was just being attentive to the story. "Did you ever hear anything like this, or stories about a woman named Avilla Bethel?" At her name, Ed's eyes raised to meet Frank's. The look on his face this time was one of revulsion. "I take that as a yes?"

Ed began to write. **No talk.**

"You don't want to talk about her?"

Ed shook his head.

"What about a woman named Mary Ellen Rhodes? Do you remember her?" Ed then appeared to be searching his memory, but his face looked to come up blank. Frank reached into his pocket and pulled out a folded piece of paper, a printout of the photo he'd taken of Mary Ellen's Bethel illustration. "She wrote a book about LBL—the cemeteries there." Ed reached into the large, hanging front pocket of his white button-up shirt and pulled out a cylinder. His reading glasses weren't on long before he thrust the paper away from him, toward Frank, and then onto the floor. A strained noise in his throat escaped in the eruption of movement and he shook his head furiously, pointing back to the board, **No talk.**

"Sorry. I'm sorry," Frank said, holding up his arms. "I wasn't trying to upset you—I'm sorry." He paused and took a breath. "I just . . . I didn't know what to make of any of this. Mary Ellen's daughter came to see me the other day. I actually stumbled on this cemetery by accident." Frank picked up the paper slowly. "I called Mrs. Rhodes to ask about it and her daughter talked to me. She told me about your letters to her mom, about how you didn't want her writing about that place."

Ed Hubbs was breathing heavier, his eyes had not moved from the table since pushing the picture to the floor. Frank shoved it into his pocket and started to speak again but Ed's hand shot out for the marker, startling Frank and cutting him off. He watched him write the words in big letters, **STAY OUT.**

"Stay out of . . . this place?" Frank asked, patting the picture in his pocket. "What's out there?"

The expression on Ed's face was empty. His head slumped slightly to one side, and his gaze seemed to be fixed somewhere just beyond Frank shoulder.

Frank turned to look behind him and then studied Ed for a moment. "Are you okay?" Frank asked.

Ed's eyes found Frank's, and then shifted slowly to the second board. He moved it over to him, a jagged edge scratching against the table's surface. He began writing on it. **Killed my mother.**

"What killed your mom? *She* killed your mom?" Ed glanced around the room, signaling to Frank that maybe he'd said that a little loud. He lowered his voice. "Avilla Bethel killed your mom?"

Ed looked back at Frank and then down at his board. He underlined the phrase and jabbed his index finger into the other whiteboard: **STAY OUT**.

"How did she kill your mom?" Frank asked. "I don't understand. You said your mom was alive in 1980. How—"

Ed let out another breath before he began scribbling, **Makes you sick. Please go.**

"Wait. Those stories about Avilla Bethel; they're real?" Ed wouldn't look up. "Is she actually buried in this cemetery?" Frank pulled the paper out once more. Ed shook his head, still fixated on the table's surface. "So, what happens if we go here?" Frank pushed the sheet closer to him, but Ed recoiled at its presence, straightening up, almost backing away. Frank paused and pulled it back. "What does that mean, she makes you sick? Like mentally? A cough? What?"

Ed wrote another line; **Please go.** Frank wasn't trying to come off as insensitive, but he could sense that was how it was sounding. One of the nurses entered and said hello to Mr. Hubbs on his way out. Ed glanced over and practically struggled to turn his mouth upward into a smile. It faded almost instantaneously when the nurse was out of sight.

The conversation had not gone as Frank anticipated. He sat in a nervous state of silence for a long moment and finally scooted his chair back. "I didn't mean to—I didn't know this was so difficult for you. I'm sorry. I'm sorry about your mom." Ed nodded that he understood. He looked up at Frank and offered a sincere hand to shake.

Frank helped him to stand and suggested he walk with him back to his room; Ed accepted. It was a short walk. He initially felt that Ed was having trouble moving. He hadn't noticed his limp before but walking with him he felt a shift of weight each time Ed stepped down with his left leg. When they got to the room, Ed's roommate was asleep with a baseball game on the TV on what had to be the highest volume. Ed hit the mute button on the remote and dropped it onto the bedside table. The roommate stirred and went back to sleep. Ed eased himself onto his bed, sitting on its edge, still holding the whiteboards. He placed his cane on the hook nearby and lifted one of whiteboards, tapping it again with his finger: **STAY OUT.**

Frank acknowledged his request with a head nod. "I will. You got my attention."

Ed held up an unsteady thumb; this time without the smile. He wrote another message, this one a little longer, **She didnt murder kids.**

Frank read it out loud while he wrote another message on the second board. Ed handed it to Frank, then erased and began writing on the other one.

AB taught kids. Sunday school. Well liked. He'd circled the word *taught*. When Frank saw it, Ed gave him the other board. **Later became sick—invalid. Church/town neglected her.**

"Neglected? What does that mean?"

Ed threw up his hands and rolled his eyes at Frank as if to say, *What do you think it means?*

"Like, didn't take care of her?"

Ed shook his head then lifted two shaky index fingers in the shape of an X and began making a face of disgust to Frank.

"They shunned her."

Head nod. Ed handed back the other board. **Folks in town start getting sick—dying.** He took the next one from Ed's hand. **Blamed her. Killed. Burned house.** Frank looked up. Ed wasn't writing anymore. "Jeez. That's messed up. So, why do people say she murdered kids—or ate them?"

Ed began writing, **Cruel jokes of kids—parents.** He erased. **People like to make monsters.**

"What did she have?" Frank asked.

Ed shrugged and wrote more. **Buried in woods to rid disease.** Then, on the next board. **Later, people getting sick again.**

"How? Same disease as her?" Frank asked.

Ed shook his head slowly. **Different kinds.**

Frank read the board and looked to Ed. "You think that was her?"

Ed looked to ponder this question for a bit and then began writing, **Said enough. Nice meeting you.**

Frank read it aloud and then watched as Ed lifted his legs onto the bed and direct his attention toward the baseball game. "It was nice to meet you, Ed. And thanks for talking to me. Sorry again for . . . you know... bringing up all this." Ed held up a hand to say it was fine. "Can I just ask..." Ed turned his head toward Frank. "Have you ever seen her?"

He held Frank's gaze for several seconds. Frank almost thought he didn't hear him until Ed lifted his pant leg to reveal an artificial limb underneath his tall white sock and then he pointed to his throat. Ed began scribbling and then turned the board around, tapping each word with his index finger. **STAY. OUT.**

42

Cliff Samson walked up the stone steps of Pogue Special Collections Library. Cliff knew the building well as it was one of the best hideaways on Murray State's campus. Nestled away from many of the main academic buildings, its occupants were mostly doctoral candidates doing research of Tennessee or Kentucky history, or those looking for a cool, quiet place to nap between classes.

The brisk air inside made Cliff smile when he walked in. Despite the dark, crypt-like entry hall, sunlight poured into the main research room to the right. The hanging lights above it weren't even needed. Long tables and large, cushioned chairs were spaced out evenly over the grand room to encourage comfortable reading and study, or in the case of the gentleman on the couch at the other end of the room, solitude for sleep.

"May I help you?" someone asked.

Cliff stepped to the information desk and peered over the counter at an elderly woman. She was stamping books. "Hey, good morning. I'm doing research on some incidents that happened at Murray High School. I was wondering if you had yearbooks that went back to the sixties and seventies."

The woman, hunched and wearing a thin white sweater over her shoulder, stared up at Cliff for a brief moment. "Seventies, huh? That was back in my time." She clicked her mouse and began typing. "If I'm not mistaken, I do believe we have *every* yearbook from Murray High School."

"Awesome," Cliff said. "You went there in the seventies?"

The woman beamed. "Aren't you sweet? No, I was the librarian there for a handful of years. Though it was ages before your time." She glanced up at him. "You don't remember me, do you?"

Cliff studied her for a moment.

"It's okay. It's been a while. Mrs. Buchanan. Murray Elementary?"

"Oh my gosh! Mrs. Buchanan! I didn't recognize you. It's so dark over here. How are you!"

She smiled. "I'm doing very well. And you look like you're doing well too. My goodness, you've grown—in every direction."

Cliff laughed. "Well, you look wonderful after all these years. Are you still at Murray Elementary?"

"No, just here. I retired this last year. This place gets me out of the house," she replied. "Let me come around and I'll show you where the yearbooks are. We've got a ton of them." She got up and came around the desk. "What do you want with old Murray High yearbooks?"

"Eh," Cliff said. "It's a long story. I heard about some kids who left—or disappeared from Murray a long time ago. I was gonna see if I could find pictures of them or see when they disappeared."

"Goodness gracious! How big are those arms?" She asked when she came out and saw him. Despite the age in her hands and eyes, her appearance was the same as Cliff remembered from childhood: a short, stocky woman, with a sweater tied around her shoulders and a hairstyle you could easily mistake for Darth Vader's helmet. Cliff have her a hug. "You could swallow me alive!" When she collected herself, the two of them began walking up the main staircase to the next floor.

"How long were you at Murray High?"

"Six years. From sixty-eight to seventy-three."

"This is gonna sound weird, but did you ever hear of something called the Murray High curse while you were there?"

She continued on, walking over to a tall shelf along the wall. "Murray High curse. No, can't say I did. Why?"

"Oh. No reason. Just wondering."

She stopped and pointed out two shelves, lined with yearbooks. "And there are some in those boxes just on top. Should have all the years, last I checked." She scanned the shelf again. "No, never heard of a Murray High curse. I *did* have a curse of my own while I was there—that was the reason I left." She chuckled to herself. "Maybe you could call *him* a Murray High curse." She caught herself and apologized. "That wasn't very nice."

Cliff stood motionless. "Wait. What does that mean?"

"Well, we had an issue with someone while I was there." She reached for a yearbook—1972—and began flipping through the pages. "I wasn't nearly as affected by him as a lot of others but what little interaction I did have was enough to convince me that I could get along quite well without high school drama."

Frank walked wearily up the front steps; he was wiped. His phone notified him that he had an appointment in an hour. "Ugh!" He opened the door to the house and made his way into the kitchen where Donnie was sautéing some chicken for a salad. "You make enough for me, by chance?"

"There's plenty, yeah. Lexie gave me a recipe for this dressing she has at her spot. It's killer!"

"She go back home?" Frank asked.

"Yeah, she left this morning," Donnie replied. The two of them ate together in near silence. "You alright?" Donnie asked.

"Yeah," Frank replied, downing a cup of water. "Just tired." After finishing his salad, he said, "I'm gonna grab a nap. Can you just make sure I'm up by twelve twenty-five? That lady's coming at twelve thirty."

"No problem," Donnie said. Frank sauntered into the living room and collapsed onto the couch.

In Frank's mind he'd only just closed his eyes when his brother began smacking him repeatedly on the side of the face, telling him to wake up. It took Frank a moment to realize where he was, what day it was, and why Donnie was waking him up.

"Your client's here," Donnie said.

Frank checked his watch. "It's twelve forty-five!" He sat up abruptly.

"Yeah. They called earlier, said they were running late. Figured I'd let you sleep. Then I forgot about ya. They're in your office now," Donnie said, whacking his brother one more time on the cheek and jumping backward as Frank went to hit him back. Frank hopped off the couch and stepped into the bathroom to splash water on his face, grabbed some coffee from the kitchen, and joined two women in his office, forgetting his phone on the coffee table near where he slept.

●

In the home's most recent remodel, Frank made *his* office practically soundproof when the door was closed. This allowed for more privacy during both funerals and client meetings. Donnie's office on the other hand was no match for outside distractions. On the fourth play through of Frank's ringtone—a man yelling "Mortal Kombat" followed by a thumping techno beat—Donnie curled his fingers and cursed at his laptop screen. He flung open the door and stomped out of his office. "How does he not hear that?" Donnie picked up the phone; several missed calls and texts—all from Cliff! "Seriously," he muttered, scrolling through the text messages:

12:41PM CLIFF: Answer your phone!
12:49PM CLIFF: Dude! Are you in a meeting? Step out and call me. Emeeerrrggggency!!!
12:51PM CLIFF: Yo you really not gonna answer the double call?
12:53PM CLIFF: Call me!
1:00PM CLIFF: Damn dude, are you dead?! I know you're reading these!

The phone rang again, and this time Donnie answered it.
"Cliff."
"Yo! Where've you been?" Cliff asked.
"It's Donnie. Frank's in a meeting. He left his phone on the table."
"He couldn't hear it going off?"
"Apparently not. What's up?"

"I sort of found something—a lot of somethings. Can you come over to Pogue Library?"

"That old library on campus?"

"Yeah," Cliff replied.

"For what?"

"Too much to explain. I've hit a gold mine of crazy stuff!"

"I think Frank'll be done in like half an hour, you want me to just tell him—" Donnie was cut off by Cliff talking to someone else on his end. He heard Cliff say, "It's Donnie," and "No, he's in a meeting," and then, "That's what I told him."

"Donnie," a female voice said into the phone, "hey, come out here."

"Lexie? What's going on?"

"A lot of stuff. Just drive over here. The old library, not the new one."

"I thought you left," Donnie exclaimed.

"I did. But I texted Cliff this morning to tell him we'd have to reschedule our chess game and he told me what he was up to. I sorta got sucked in."

43

When Donnie walked into Pogue Library's main study, his eyes were instantly drawn to the handful of tables that Cliff and Lexie had commandeered. Each one was covered with open books, maps, and printouts. He picked up a yellow legal pad lying on the table beside him and flipped through the top pages, each filled with what looked to be random scribbles and lines drawn every which direction. "What is all this?" Donnie asked. "Have you been here all morning?"

Cliff nodded, looking a little surprised himself. "Since seven a.m. Long day."

"Is this about the cemetery?" Donnie asked.

"Dude, this is about everything," Cliff said, handing the pad of paper in his hand to Donnie. The page was two columns of names and dates with several notes, arrows, and shapes scattered around the edges. "You remember the other night when we were going through all those names? Those four or five kids who disappeared?"

Donnie didn't answer. He was caught off guard by the first name on the list.

"Turns out there're a lot more," Cliff said.

Brian Pennington – 2000 (spring - Donnie's Sophomore year)
Corey Grassman – 1997
Genevieve Pfannerstill (1996)???
Ben Markham – 1993
Marcus Taylor – 1990
Pam Climber – 1988*
Paul Gardner – 1985*
Roy Dale – 1978
Jermaine Warren – 1976*

Billy Ricardo – 1973*
Nina Etheridge and Bruce Winfree – 1966
Henry Carr – 1960*

"Jeez. These were all missing students?" Donnie asked.

"For the most part." Cliff pointed to Genevieve Pfannerstill. "This one, I'm not too sure about. I think she's the one whose license you all found."

Lexie picked up an open yearbook from the table. "Remember the last name had F A N N E, and the first name began with G E." She turned the book around for Donnie to see. It was a full-page spread, welcoming Murray High's new science teacher. Lexie's finger tapped along the bold letters of the woman's name, underneath the black-and-white photo of her in a long white coat, smiling from behind a half-full beaker of liquid. "Genevieve Pfannerstill. She came in ninety-three. But, in ninety-six, she left Murray—vanished just after the start of the year. There wasn't much in the *Ledger* about it. So, *maybe* she relocated, but if that's her ID up there, then I think we can assume the worst."

Donnie repeated the name to himself, out loud. "I know that last name. I've seen it somewhere."

"Cliff ran some social media searches and came up with nothing," Lexie said.

"She doesn't fit the mold for missing students, but we figured it was worth writing down just in case," Cliff said. "Other than her, everyone else is a student from Murray High."

"Her and Corey," Lexie added.

Donnie looked back at the list of names. "How do you know all those kids are dead?" He asked. "And that they all went to Murray? I mean, you just said that the Pfannerstill lady may not be connected. She may not even be dead. So, how did you come up with all the other names?"

Cliff thumbed back to the front entrance. "It was a lot of looking for ad memoriams in the back of yearbooks, but the lady at the front desk helped me out a ton. Turns out she taught at Murray high for like five years. Taught one of these kids personally. And guess what, all these people coincide with Mr. Rose being at Murray."

"Tell him what she said about Mr. Rose."

"Dude, you gotta hear this story. Hang on." Cliff walked over to the entrance.

Donnie looked down at one of the tables. Resting on top of a yearbook was a printout of a *Ledger* article from 1982, "Tips for a Safe Summer". The words "Billy Ricardo", "1973", and "fled from home" were circled in red. He looked at the list of names in his hand. There was Billy Ricardo with 1973 beside it.

"Why are some of the names starred?" Donnie asked.

"He says they still have rewards pending," Lexie replied.

Donnie's eyebrows stretched up as his head came forward. "Reward? Like, money reward? This one is from nineteen sixty," Donnie said, pointing to Henry's name.

"Apparently it's still being offered by his brother. I don't think it's a lot. Probably like a thousand for information," Lexie replied. "Check this out." She held another open book displaying black-and-white photos of Murray High School faculty. She pointed to a picture of a young man, clean shaven and dressed in suspenders; his hair shined, slicked over to the side, and wearing thick, black rimmed glasses. "Mr. Rose in nineteen fifty-eight. Right before all this started."

"Jeez. Was there ever a time when he *didn't* look pissed off?"

Cliff reentered, with someone following close behind him. "Guys, this is Carol Buchanan—"

"Mr. Samson," Carol cut in with a harsh whisper. "Please do try to quell your voice."

"Sorry. She used to be a librarian at Murray High. Mrs. Buchanan, this is Donnie Burgers. Good friend of mine." Donnie recognized her and they shook hands. She remembered both Donnie and his brother fondly. "Would you mind telling him what you told me about Billy?" Cliff asked.

She turned to Cliff and sagged her shoulders. "You told me this was an emergency."

"I know, but you tell it so well."

"Oh, pish-posh." She swatted at him. When Cliff said *please*, she let out a frustrated sigh and checked her watch. "I have to meet someone in ten minutes so you're gonna get the abridged version."

"That's fine," Cliff said.

Carol removed her glasses and let them fall, hanging now around her neck. "Billy Ricardo, as I've already told Mr. Samson here, was a student at Murray, and to make a long story short, he had a very destructive nature. I don't like to think ill of students but to say he was disturbing would be an understatement."

"What did he do?" Donnie asked.

"Vandalism, mostly." She eyed her watch again. "One afternoon, I gave him after-school detention for writing a filthy word on one of the library tables with a protractor—don't ask what the word was, I don't remember." She waved her hands. "I went to the principal at the time—"

"Mr. Atlas," Donnie said.

"That's right. I went to Eugene and explained the situation and he said that if Billy was the only student, that it wouldn't be appropriate for me to be alone with him. It would be better for a *man* to watch him. I took offense to that, of course. You may not believe it now, but I almost went to the Olympics for shotput when I was younger. I'd grown up with four brothers and had quite a bit of strength in those days. In my mind I was not one to easily be intimidated, not by Billy or by Eugene.

"He informed me that he would stay in the building and to alert him should anything come up. Now, Billy's behavior was not unknown to the faculty. One teacher in particular had already recommended he be expelled. He'd been a topic of concern since his arrival the year before. But, as I said, I was not one to be intimidated. And so, I kept Billy alone after school. Shortly after we begin, he tells me he's going home. I stand in front of the door and politely tell him that he may go home after he serves his time. Without a moment's hesitation, Billy gets up, takes his book, and wishes me luck on stopping him. I stand my ground firmly and inform him that should he choose to leave, he will have to walk past Mr. Atlas's office, who was keenly aware of the situation and would no doubt be happy to *stop* him. I looked at him and I said, 'The only way out of here is to serve your time.'

"And right then, Billy turned to go back to the table. I thought I'd succeeded. Until, in the blink of an eye, I saw him pick up my brand-new carousel projector that I'd brought from home and chuck it as hard as he could at the large window, shattering it. He kicked out some of the glass and climbed out the window as nonchalantly as if he'd gone through the door."

"Holy crap," Donnie said.

"You betcha. Billy was my fifth and last year of at Murray High."

"Wait, so what happened? He just up and left? Did you go after him or do anything?"

"Goodness, I was too in shock. One of the other teachers heard the commotion and came in; he went after him. I learned later that it was a good thing I stayed back. That teacher, bless his heart, got struck by a rock *and* got the windshield of his car smashed in."

Donnie couldn't hide the O shape his mouth was now making in surprise.

"Needless to say, Billy was expelled shortly after that incident. There was a motion from his parents to let back in after a couple of months, but he disappeared before anything came of it." She lightened her voice. "And God forgive me for saying it, but it was a relief that he did because from what I was hearing, they were going to let him back in." She hastily checked her watch again. "Alright, that's enough out of me. I need to run. If you all need anything else, Darlene is in her office." She motioned toward the tables. "And please do try to put all this back in the proper places." Carol made her way back to the front.

"Messed up, right?" Cliff asked.

"Yeah. So, wait. What does that have to do with Mr. Rose?

"Oh. You didn't guess?" Lexie asked. "He's the one who Billy hit with the rock."

44

"Does she think Winston was involved in what happened to Billy?"

"I didn't ask about that. She said she didn't know him that well. Apparently, Mr. Rose wasn't close with many of the teachers while she was there."

Donnie nodded and glanced to the tables covered with books and maps. "So, what's all that, then?"

"*That* is the other reason I came here this morning. Frank told me what you all found yesterday." Cliff walked over to a large map lying across a table. His face was bright with anticipation as if waiting for Donnie to say something, and then, "I think you guys actually *were* in Bethel Cemetery."

Donnie rolled his eyes and Lexie offered an encouragement to hear Cliff out.

"If Frank's hunch is accurate—if those are the missing kids—then why would they all be buried up there?"

"Hold up, how do you even make that jump? We don't know it's them." Donnie said. "What did we find last night?" He looked to Lexie. "A license that may or may not belong to this Genevieve Pfannerstill person? A pager?"

"The jersey!" Lexie said excitedly.

"Okay. A basketball jersey and a license," Donnie continued. "I'm not trying to be a kill joy here, but kids are up in LBL all the time. Is it possible that Pam ran away, went through LBL, and lost her jersey?"

"Maybe," Cliff said. "But how would you explain this?" Cliff pulled out his phone. "Frank sent me the picture last night of the pocketknife you all found. I noticed something on it when I was looking at it closer—Lexie says you guys didn't see it." He handed Donnie his phone. "You notice anything about it?"

Donnie zoomed into the picture. "No. I mean, there's something written on it." He pulled the phone closer to his eyes. "What does that say? R... ROALE?"

"How about R. Dale?" Cliff said. He held up the list of names. "For Roy Dale? Murray High. Ran away in the sixties. Never came back." Donnie studied the photo. "You still think it's a coincidence?" Cliff asked.

Donnie handed the phone back to Cliff and leaned onto one of the tables, resting his butt against the edge and folding his arms. "Okay. I'll give it to you, that's a little weird."

"Right?" Cliff said. "So, if the missing kids really are up there, then why would they be in *Bethel* cemetery?" Cliff excitedly began shifting books around on the table.

"Cliff. It wasn't Bethel, man. We saw the sign. Markgraf Cemetery."

Cliff picked up a book and turned around. "You're right. *That was* Markgraf Cemetery. And Frank noticed it first on a map in the LBL Visitor Center. *That map* is not anywhere in this library. But," Cliff held open the book for Donnie, "I found *this* map." The page illustrated a detailed, hand-drawn map of the southern-most section of the Land Between the Lakes peninsula. Donnie looked at the book's spine for the title: *Stewart County, Tennessee History*.

"What is Stewart County?"

"Land Between the Lakes is made up of three counties in two states. Lyon and Trigg county in Kentucky, and Stewart County in Tennessee. The place where *you* were was in Stewart County."

Donnie nodded. Okay..."

"This map was done in nineteen-seventy." Cliff leaned in and pointed with his pen at a small, lone cross nestled in the middle of a wooded area, represented by dark shading and tiny tree sketches. "See that cross? That's Markgraf Cemetery, where you all were." Before Donnie could answer, Cliff unfolded a brochure depicting a colorful, detailed map. "This is one Frank bought last week." He traced his pen to the corresponding spot. "*Markgraf* isn't on here."

"Okay. So what?"

"Check this out—come here." Cliff set the colorful map down and walked over to a large fold out chart lying across one of the tables. The heading read Stewart County. "This is from nineteen *seventy-six*." He pointed to the same tree filled area. "See. It's not here either."

Donnie studied the area. It was blank; just a large area shaded green.

Cliff continued, "I found over a dozen maps of Stewart County and *that* cross—the cemetery Frank drug you guys to—doesn't show up on hardly any of them." Cliff opened another book, the spine cracking. He handed it to Donnie and gave him a moment to process the image. "What do you notice about this?"

The picture Donnie was staring at looked as if it had been done in pencil by a ten-year-old for a class project. It was a more focused illustration of the area Cliff kept referring to.

"This is nineteen fifty-five," Cliff said. "One of the oldest I've found." There were two horizontal lines: one at the bottom of the page and one at the top. The top line had THARP RD written above it. The area underneath Tharp Road was shaded lightly with several minuscule pine tree sketches drawn in. The mysterious cross marker appeared in this drawing, as well as something scribbled underneath it. "Does that say Markgraf?"

"Yup. You see anything else?" Cliff asked. Donnie's eyes appeared to be searching the page. "Look a little north."

Its presence was easy to miss, but Donnie finally spotted it. Blending in with the nearby tree markings was the faint shape of another cross. "There's a mark there. Is that a cemetery?" Donnie asked.

"Seems to be," Cliff replied.

"How do you know? Maybe it's just an ink mark."

"Thought you'd never ask," Cliff replied. "First off, there's tons of these little, localized maps for spots in LBL. And a ton of these books for cemetery records." Donnie looked at the spine of the book he was holding: *Stewart County Burial Records*. "They all use either a cross or a box symbol to mark cemeteries."

"Let me guess, you think *this* is Bethel?"

"I think there's something in this area people are trying to hide," Cliff replied. "But in all honesty, yes, I think this is Bethel." He turned back toward the table. "Dude, maps aside, we've gone through burial records dating through the sixties, fifties, even forties." He motioned at the stacks of books beside him. "Hardly any of them mention Markgraf Cemetery. But check this." Cliff moved over to a thin, weathered cardboard box. He carefully pulled back the flaps and removed a small stack of papers. A damp musk was noticeable immediately. He displayed the collection of yellowed papers on the table and turned them for Donnie to see, who was hiding his nose in his shirt. The top page had *Stewart County Burial Records* in light pencil, scribbled across the top. Several other scripts were evident, though their legibility had faded long ago. Cliff continued, "These were compiled in nineteen thirty-one." He flipped back through the pages carefully until finally, "Look right here." The page displayed a crooked, typewritten list of numbers from one to fourteen. The first two numbers were accompanied with names: Daniel Owen and Clifton Stone. The others were left blank; all under the heading *Markgraf Cemetery*.

Donnie's eyes scanned over the empty spaces beside the numbers. "Why are there only two names? Where are the rest?"

"Don't know," Cliff replied. He took a step back and sat down in a nearby chair.

"This doesn't make any sense," Donnie mumbled. "Why would there be twelve graves with no names?"

"Right?" Cliff commented. "I've turned this place upside down and this is the most on Markgraf Cemetery I can find." Cliff scooted up and pointed at the bottom of the page. "But here's the best part." Just below the number fourteen was a horizontal stream of dashes, likely a new section. It was followed underneath by the number 1, and a single name: *Avilla M. Bethel*.

"Hoe. Lee. Shit," Donnie whispered.

"Right?" Cliff said. He motioned toward the other papers. "She's not in Markgraf cemetery. She's in her own. And I think it's nearby where you guys were. Creepy, huh?" Cliff paused a moment. "If her names on that list, there has to be something identifying her up there."

"Why just have a single grave all by itself?" Lexie asked. "Why not just bury them all together?"

"Cemeteries are typically organized by family," Donnie said. "If that really is her grave, and the story about her is true, whoever owned Markgraf wouldn't want her anywhere near those plots. Or if she died first, Markgraf wouldn't want the family near *her*."

"Which brings me back to where we started," Cliff said. "Why would those kids be buried there of all places?"

"Because LBL has been haunted by stories of that woman for decades," Lexie replied. "Most people—if they think Bethel Cemetery exists—are too afraid to go near it. And those that don't, likely won't find it. What better spot to hide a body? In a grave that's already been dug, inside a place that no one will go."

"Bingo," Cliff said, snapping his fingers.

Donnie felt a chill over his body. "That actually isn't a bad theory. You just think of that?"

"I mean, Cliff said it to me earlier when I got here. I just added some flair to the wording." She smirked.

"Yeah, that was good," Cliff said. "Even scared me a little." His phone buzzed on the table, startling him. He cursed in surprise. "Shoot. I gotta head back to the studio. You mind giving me a hand to get this stuff picked back up?"

"You're not gonna show this to Frank?" Donnie asked.

"I can't. I have an appointment in thirty minutes. We'll have to walk him through it later. At least now you guys won't think I'm losing my mind."

Donnie looked to Lexie. "You gonna head back home?"

Lexie bit her lip. "I kinda want to go back up there and see her grave."

"Bunk. That!" Cliff called out. There was a wispy "shhh" from somewhere in the hall.

"Yeah, I'm sorta with Cliff on that," Donnie said, stacking up books. "I'm not sure I want to go back up there. It could legit be a crime scene."

"Come on, are you worried that someone will find us up there, or are you just scared?" Lexie replied.

"To be fair, I wasn't the one who ran away screaming that they thought they saw someone," Donnie said, looking back at her as he followed Cliff.

"Hey now! I did see someone! You ran away without seeing *anyone*," Lexie called out in a whisper. She followed them, carrying a stack. "Come on, all this doesn't make you a little curious? What if I did see something."

"Y'all stupid," Cliff said, shelving the books.

"Don't you have to work?" Donnie asked. But the more he tried to reason out of going back up there, the more excited Lexie became—and the more pushy.

45

Frank woke up when he heard the front door slam. He lifted his head just in time to see Donnie and Lexie walking into the office, "Are you asleep again?" Donnie asked.

"Man, I am wiped. I don't know what the deal is." Lexie entered behind Donnie. "What is she doing here?"

"Wow," Lexie replied.

"No, sorry. I mean, he said you left," Frank replied in a yawn. He looked at his watch, opening his eyes real big to try and manually adjust them. "How long have I been out?" Cliff walked in after Lexie and said hey on his way to the kitchen. "Jeez, did I miss a party? Where'd you guys go?"

"I left you a note," Donnie said, noticing the sticky note on the floor that had fallen off the door. "Which you obviously didn't get."

"Oh! Shit!" Frank exclaimed, sitting up. "Is Mom here? Was anyone listening for the door?"

"I think so—her car's here. But being how you run the place I'm sure she thought you were listening," Donnie replied. "Hopefully, nobody came by."

"What have y'all been doing?" Frank asked, easing himself out of the recliner and stretching.

"We were in Pogue," Donnie said.

Frank looked at him for a moment and then spread a mischievous grin over his mouth. "Is that code for something?" He began bumping his two index fingers together and raised his eyebrows.

Donnie stared at Frank, expressionless, and then said, "Not too sure what's goin on with your fingers there, but no. Pogue Library. Over on campus. Cliff tried calling you, but your phone was in the living room during your appointment—on the highest possible volume." He ran Frank through a summarized version of what Cliff had walked him through: the additional missing students, the money, the maps, the graves with no names, and finally, Avilla's grave.

"Man! Why didn't you come get me?!" Frank exclaimed.

"I didn't know that's what he was going to show me," Donnie replied.

"Did he check out any of the books?"

"No, everything he found is in special collections. He took some pictures, though," Donnie said.

"You should have called me to come up there."

"He did—like ten times. And sent a bunch of texts. You were in a meeting," Donnie said. Frank patted his pockets and started looking around for his phone. "I finally answered it and went down there."

"Man. This is wild," he said, looking back to Donnie. "What if we *really* found those missing kids? How much money? Did Cliff say?"

"Empathy award of the year," Lexie said, smiling. "I'm kidding." Frank waved her off as if shooing away a fly. "I wanna go back up there tomorrow," Lexie said. "Can we do it?"

"Hell yeah, we can," Frank said, clapping his hands together.

"Calm down, Lara Croft. She's not talking about going to dig. She wants to see the Bethel grave," Donnie added.

"What? We're gonna walk all that way just to look?" Frank asked.

"*We* are gonna walk all that way just to look. You can do whatever you want," Donnie replied.

"You don't want to know who's buried out there?" Frank asked.

"I think we all have a solid idea who's buried out there. Which is why I think you should call the police. You're gonna have to call them eventually. How will you explain all the holes and digging?"

"I can explain it by saying I found a bone sticking out of the ground and I started digging—I don't know!"

Donnie was looking down at Frank's large desk calendar. "Minor problem, chief: you have a three-thirty tomorrow and a seven-thirty in the morning," Donnie said.

Frank walked over to the calendar. "Seven thirty? I thought I just had the . . ." He trailed off as Donnie clapped him on the back and walked back over to the door toward Lexie. "Come on dude, this is bullshit."

"What's wrong?" Lexie asked.

"Frank offered to take my early morning appointment tomorrow. And he forgot about it."

"I didn't offer, I got conned," Frank replied.

"Either way, you have two appointments tomorrow. Just give us your map and we'll go check it out."

"Hang on. Lemme think for a second," Frank said. He walked back over to the door, appearing to reason this out in his mind. "Okay. Okay. We can be back by three thirty. As long as we leave early enough." He rested down on the arm of his recliner. "Ms. Betsy will take me at least an hour."

"Better plan for an hour and a half," Donnie added, then turned to Lexie. "She's had two funerals here in the last year—husband and daughter."

"That's awful," Lexie said.

"She's nearly ninety-five—keeps outliving everyone," Frank said. "Love her to death but the woman is a talker."

"Frank doesn't have the heart to hurry the meeting up, so he'll be in there for two hours." Donnie laughed.

"Come on, man. You're better at keeping things on track than I am. You'll be done in like thirty minutes—she doesn't like talking to you."

"What's that supposed to mean?" Donnie asked.

"Eh. She says you're a bit of a chauvinist," Frank replied, holding up his hands, with a shrug.

"What?" Donnie called out. Lexie burst out laughing.

"Please! I'll take the next one—she has two more sons after this one."

"Aw, that's terrible," Lexie exclaimed.

"No way, man. I beat you fair and square," Donnie said.

"No, you didn't. You chose Rainbow Road. That's not even fair."

Donnie spread his hands out. "You're the one who chose to settle it with *Mario Kart*. And you *let* me pick the course." He smiled. "She's all yours."

"How about if I go and get donuts tomorrow morning. Before your meeting. Will you take her? Then you can wrap up by eight-fifteen or so, and we'll be out of here and back in time for the three-thirty."

"What kind of deal is that for me?" Donnie asked.

"Donnie if he's the only one who knows how to get there, we sort of need him to go. It was a long walk. I don't think you or I are familiar enough with that trail to make it, especially since I wasn't even paying attention. Leaving at ten thirty—even ten—may be too late with it taking so long to get out there and back," Lexie commented.

"Oh! There! Good point! You *need* me to go with you and help find the place," Frank exclaimed.

"Or you can give us your map and *you* can keep the appointments you made," Donnie said. He looked at Lexie who still looked hesitant over the idea of going out into the woods without someone who knew where to go.

"Or," Frank said, "you take the meeting tomorrow morning and I won't tell her about that game you and I would play with our stuffed animals back in the day."

Donnie's eyes grew noticeably larger.

"Are you serious right now?" Donnie shot back. "Why would you even bring that up?"

Lexie laughed. "Oh, now I'm intrigued."

"When we were kids, and our parents would go out—"

"Don't even think about it," Donnie cut in.

"Up to you, bro." A boyish grin slowly spread across Frank's face. "Donuts?"

"Ugh. Fine," Donnie sighed.

"YES!" Frank shouted, throwing his arms up like a field goal signal.

"Can I go with you?" Lexie asked. "I'll buy."

"Yeah, sure. Thanks," Frank said. He said to her quietly, "I'll tell you about it in the car—"

"Dude... don't you dare."

46

Frank walked out into the foyer and hollered back at his brother, "Where'd you put my phone?"

"On the side table next to where you were sleeping," Donnie replied.

"Got it." There was a string of missed calls and unanswered texts from Addy.

> 1:50PM ADDY: Tried calling. Holla back when free.
> 1:59PM ADDY: Going in a meeting. Don't call.
> 2:14PM ADDY: Meeting sucks. Call me now.
> 2:34PM ADDY: Good talk.

Frank called.

"There you are," Addy answered.

"Sorry, man, long day. I was passed out when you called. What's goin' on?"

"Not too much, just wanted to let you know what I found, though it's probably not too helpful. This guy's hard to track down. Talked with some of our boys from school and came up with nothing. Then I called some preachers in the area last night. They knew who I was talkin' about, but same story, no one has seen him. It's like he fell of the face of the earth. Lo and behold, that's what happened."

"What do you mean?" Frank asked.

"I mean ... that's what happened," Addy replied. "Turns out Mr. Rose disappeared like eight or nine years ago."

"No way." Frank walked into the kitchen. "Where'd you hear that?"

"You remember Ed Carpenter?"

"Yeah. He's writing for the *Tennessean* now, isn't he?"

"That's what I thought," Addy replied. "Apparently, he's back in Paducah working for the *Sun*. Called and left a message last night about what I was looking for. He calls me at six this morning with the news. I just forwarded you an email. There was a small article in the *Ledger* and the *Sun* about a week after it happened. Seems the guy literally just . . . up and vanished."

"How did I miss that?" Frank asked, more to himself than Addy.

"That's what I asked. Apparently, he didn't have any family in the area, and I don't think he had kids either, so there's a good chance the whole thing was just forgotten about."

"Damn." Frank sighed. "You think he's still alive?"

"I don't know, he was pretty old when he taught us," Addy said. "He's gotta be in his late eighties now if he's alive—at least. But he *was* in decent shape back in the day so, it's possible."

"Anybody else you can think of to ask who might know him?"

"Actually, yeah. I found two people. A friend of mine—he preaches over in Mayfield, older guy—told me that Mr. Rose used to visit out there with a friend of his. Friend's name was Rob Valentine. The minister still had visitor information for Winston from back in the early two thousands. He went several times, and listed Rob as a friend. Unfortunately, this guy doesn't know what happened to Rob. Says the last he heard, Rob moved out to Benton. But, better news, if you want information on Mr. Rose, our old principal is the guy to go to."

"Mr. Atlas?"

"Yup," Addy replied. "Atlas was quoted in the article about Mr. Rose and he knew him pretty well. Maybe he can tell you something about what happened. I haven't seen that guy in forever."

"He's still around. I still see him at Mom's donut shop. I'll call him."

"Word," Addy said.

"Thanks man," Frank said. "I'll let you know what I find out."

"I'll be honest, I really don't have any interest in h—"

Frank hung up the phone before Addy could finish talking. He wrote down the names on a piece of paper and told Lexie and Donnie about Addy's news. Frank dug out a phone book from a junk drawer and looked up both names.

"They still make those things?" Donnie asked.

"Are you serious? Yeah man. Everyone's in here." Frank continued flipping the pages. "Plus, I did a funeral for a woman's sister a couple years back. She gives me a really sweet deal for a full-page ad."

"We're paying for a *phone book* ad?"

"Hell yeah. Check it!" Frank turned the page over for Donnie and Lexie to see. It was a black-and-white image of Frank standing with his arm wrapped around Donnie's neck, both smiling at the camera. Donnie recognized the photo; it had been filtered into a hand-drawn image. It was a good photo of the two of them, but the words above and below were what caught Donnie's attention. *The Burgers Brothers* was typed in large bold letters along the top. At the bottom: *Serving Murray For Over a Hundred Years. Let Our Family Serve Yours.* Donnie laid the book flat on the table. The page beside it showcased a collection of business ads inside bold, black-lined boxes. Donnie pointed at the heading.

"This is the restaurant section," Donnie said.

The grin on Frank's face looked like it was going to spread off his face. It seemed as if he could barely contain his excitement. "I know!" he said, nodding. "Bad ass, right?"

"Wha—why are you advertising in the restaurant section?" He scanned the ad again. "There's nothing even on here that says we're a funeral home."

"Yeah there is. Right here," Frank said. He pointed to barely visible type underneath the ad. It read, *The Burgers Brothers' Family Funeral Home.*

Lexie let out a snort of laughter. Donnie sighed and shook his head. "What the hell is wrong with you? How long have you had this?"

"Two years."

"Two years!" Donnie exclaimed. "Mom knows about this?"

"Yeah," Frank said, shrugging. "Maybe. I don't know."

"Frank! You're spending money on an ad that's incorrect!"

Frank took the book and flipped over toward the back. "We're not paying for this. I get it for free. This is our real ad." He dropped the book on the table. It was much sleeker, with a photo of the home and the four of them standing out front on the porch, smiling. The photo had been taken when Donnie and Frank were in high school, but it was still the one of the most complimentary and professional photos of the whole family.

"Initially, we had a quarter page ad but with phone books going out of style I called to get it taken out. Lady offered that if I would take out a full-page ad, she would give me two. It honestly wasn't much more than I was already paying, and surprisingly, people still use this."

Donnie watched Frank for an awkwardly long moment, not saying a word. Finally, "This is the stupidest thing I've ever seen," Donnie said dryly. Something then seemed to spark behind his eyes. "Wait a second—that couple that never showed up the other day. The one that called. They asked if they could make reservations."

"Yeah," Frank said back, as if it was obvious. "I get at least two of those a month. I'll usually tell them it's been misprinted but to keep us in mind for any funeral services they need. It keeps our name in front of people."

"I can't even . . ." Donnie threw up his hands and stood up. Frank wasn't sure but it looked like his brother was holding back a laugh. He walked over to the refrigerator.

"I like it," Lexie said, examining the ads again. "Definitely a little underhanded, but if I called a funeral home thinking it was a restaurant, chances are it'd be the first place I'd call back when someone died."

"That's the hottest thing you've ever said," Frank said back to her.

"I try," Lexie replied.

Frank picked up the phone book once again and began scanning, muttering names to himself.

"Are you calling Mr. Atlas?" Donnie asked, pulling a can of seltzer water out of the refrigerator.

"Yeah. I just want to ask if he knows anything about what happened to Mr. Rose." Frank dialed the number and held the phone to his ear. "He's at Mom's almost every morning. Maybe I can meet up with him for a few minutes tomorrow and ask some quest—hey! Mr. Atlas? Hey, this is Frank Burgers. Yessir, how are you?"

The conversation was brief. Eugene Atlas visited Virginia Jan's every morning at around seven o'clock and was more than happy to meet. Frank left it at just having a couple of questions about a former teacher; he didn't offer any specifics.

"Okay," Frank said, looking to Donnie, "so, you're gonna take my seven thirty. I'll go and meet with Mr. Atlas, grab some donuts, and we can leave when you're done. Hopefully by eight thirty?"

"I'll do my best," Donnie said.

Frank then turned to Lexie. "You wanna meet me here at seven and we'll go up there? You never met Mr. Atlas, did you? You moved before high school, right?"

Lexie was looking at her phone when she answered. "Actually, I can't tomorrow morning. I totally forgot I told a friend I would meet her for breakfast around the same time. Sorry. She's been trying to meet up for a couple of days."

"Oh," Frank said, sounding disappointed.

"But I can definitely meet you afterward. We won't be long. Just call when you guys are about to leave, and I'll head out from there. Will that work?"

Frank was in the process of saying it *would* work but Donnie cut in, "Who are you having breakfast with?" Donnie asked. Lexie didn't answer immediately; just looked up from her phone, appearing lost in thought. "Do I know them?" he asked.

"No. I don't think so. Just, a friend . . . she went to a different school. We played softball together."

"Oh. Okay," Donnie said. "I'll call you once I finish with Ms. Betsy, and we'll leave as soon as we can."

SUNDAY
47

Frank was awake before his alarm sounded. He walked softly downstairs into the kitchen to make himself some breakfast. His dad was finishing up a piece of toast and reading over the paper. "What are you doin' up?" Frank asked.

Dave checked his watch. "It's seven a.m., you're just now getting up?" He smiled. "It'll be time for lunch here soon."

Frank poured himself a cup of coffee and turned on a burner to make eggs.

"You have an appointment this morning?" Dave asked, getting up and putting his trash into the can.

"No, meeting someone up at Mom's. Just grabbin' a quick bite."

"Hey," Dave said, folding his newspaper back up. "Not trying to get in your business, but I saw this note with Rob Valentine's name, and Eugene Atlas." He peeled the sticky note off the table. "Interesting duo."

"Yeah, it's for some research I'm doing. Actually, I'm meeting with Mr. Atlas this morning. Tried calling the Valentine guy last night but I only got his answering machine."

"Hmm," Dave muttered, nodding his head. "Interesting. I'm surprised you got anything considering he's been dead for nearly ten years."

"Aww," Frank said, before making a sigh of disgust. "Guess that would explain why the machine had a different name. That's a bummer. Did you know him?"

"No, but we did the funeral for him. I recognize the name because his son is a writer. I've got one of his books around here somewhere."

"You met him?"

"Yeah. I had his book before that, so I knew who he was."

"Oh! So, he's a well-known writer?"

"He's not Greg Iles or Dennis Lehane, but he's up there."

"I wonder if I met him," Frank said back. "What's his name?"

"Jackson Valentine. Jake. Goes by Jake on his books. Can I ask what you're researching?"

"It's stupid." Frank shrugged and swatted at the air. "Cliff and I were looking into that old Bethel cemetery story in LBL. Addy said those two may be good contacts for it."

"Your pap used to scare the bejeesus out of me with those stories growing up." Dave's cell phone buzzed on the table. "Gotta take this. Tell Eugene I said hey." Dave picked up the phone and went out onto the back porch as Frank flipped on the radio and began making his breakfast.

Eugene Atlas—despite being an assertive and intimidating administrator—was Frank's favorite teacher. He was not known to regularly teach courses which made Frank's junior year English class unique. Eugene was a tough man with high expectations for his students but his involvement and empathy for them left a lasting impression on Frank's mind.

Frank would see him most every weekend when he went to Ginny's bakery for donuts. Eugene always sat in the same corner table, reading a copy of the *Wall Street Journal*, the *Murray Ledger*, and the *Paducah Sun*, and occasionally chatting with the other retirees in the bakery. That morning, when Eugene waved to say hello, he struggled to get to his feet, highlighting to Frank just how frail he had become. His former military-like posture had given way to a rounded back, and a slight bend at the waist. Eugene rested one hand on the table and reached the other out to signal Frank for a hug. In the embrace, Frank heard Eugene yell something at the woman behind the register. There were no waitresses at Virginia Jan's, therefore all orders were placed and received at the counter. Eugene Atlas apparently held a high status because the woman behind the counter yelled back that she'd bring two coffees right out. Frank held up a small piece of paper and attempted to go put in his order for donuts, but Eugene insisted he allow him to pay for them. After all the free coffee Ginny had given him over the years, it was the least he could do. "Just tell

Wanda what you want when she comes over. She'll bring it out," Eugene said.

"Jeez," Frank said, "I'm gonna sit with you more often. VIP treatment."

"How's your father doing?"

"He's doing well," Frank said, sitting down across from him. "Says hi. Mostly consulting now. We had a flood at the house last week, so he's been a little stressed about that."

"Sorry to hear that," Atlas replied. "Anything I can do? Anything you need?"

"No, we're fine. If you have an extra twenty grand you're not using, we'd take that," Frank chuckled.

Wanda brought over the two coffees and said hello to Frank who got up to give her a hug. Eugene promptly passed her Frank's order list with a folded bill and asked if she wouldn't mind bringing them over. Despite the incoming crowd, she seemed more than happy to make an extra trip. Eugene gave her a wink and told her to keep the change. "So, how may I be of service this morning? You said you had some questions about a former teacher?"

"Yeah. You taught at Murray High for... what? A while, right?"

"Started teaching in fifty-six. Took over as principal in sixty-one," Eugene replied. "Nearly sixty years. Long time."

"Okay, so, you were there when Winston Rose started teaching?" Frank replied.

Eugene's lips stretched back to form a thin smile. "I had a feeling that was going to be the topic of conversation." After a pause, "Can I ask the nature of the question?"

"No reason; just curious what happened to him."

"Did someone tell you to talk to me?" Frank nodded. "That's what I thought." He sighed. "I was quoted in an article several years ago and it inevitably brought me a lot of unwanted attention. Unfortunately, I don't have much to tell you about Winston. I think people direct inquiries to me because, unlike everyone else, I was deeply hurt by his disappearance."

"What do you mean? *Unlike* everyone else?" Frank asked.

Eugene's head cocked to the side with a look of skepticism. "Come on, now. We both know that Winston was not the most well liked of our faculty. The man was on the receiving end of numerous acts of vandalism throughout his tenure at Murray. Very few students—and faculty, actually—got along with Winston. I'm sure you've heard that he was being investigated for murder?"

Frank leaned as if he didn't hear him. "Uh . . . no. I never heard he was being investigated for murder. What?" He reminded himself not to get too excited. "When did that happen?"

Eugene pursed his lips and lifted his gaze slightly toward the ceiling. "Early two thousands, I believe. It was . . ." He paused and removed his glasses. "It was a long and arduous investigation."

"What happened?"

"I'm surprised you never heard. Parents and students suspected his involvement in the disappearance of several students."

"You mean all those kids who went missing back in the sixties and seventies—all those?"

Eugene sipped his coffee. "Yes. Or, what too many alumni childishly referred to as *the Murray High curse*. I don't know how much you've heard. Sometime ago—memory's a little fuzzy on the dates—several years before Winston went missing, some students banded together and initiated a series of rumors about Winston and what they found in his home. They leveled several accusations against him, made up quite a few stories to accompany those accusations, all centering around those untimely disappearances."

"You mean students tried to say that Mr. Rose was behind all of it," Frank asked.

"Oh yes. Supposedly one of our more *well-to-do* students snuck into his home. Ended up concocting a series of baseless, yet troubling, discoveries about what they found."

"What'd they find?" Frank asked.

"Nothing. That we know of. Said they found shreds of clothing—student's clothing—and an assortment of items that they claimed were linked to students who had gone missing. Obvious things: a wallet, a folder with a name in it, a picture. Mind you, they couldn't produce any evidence for these findings."

"Jeez," Frank whispered.

"*Jeez* is right," Eugene replied. "Thankfully, Winston took it as what it was—a poorly executed prank from some rather ill-behaved students. Unfortunately, word had spread throughout the school, then to the parents, and finally the police. Faculty was questioned. I was questioned, mostly about his techniques and character. They even searched his home—found nothing, by the way. Despite all of that, he never asked to resign and I never asked him to step down. He knew he was innocent, and no one had any evidence to say otherwise. That man was the definition of thick skinned." Eugene started to say more but stopped himself when Wanda came back around with two white paper sacks and placed them on the table. Eugene thanked her and then gave Frank a long, curious look.

"What? Wait, did I not tell her thank you?" Frank asked, turning around.

"No, no," Eugene said. "I was just thinking about that case." He appeared to be struggling with what to say next and then he swatted at the air. "Oh well, I guess it's old news now. I'm sure you've already heard this. We had an undercover police officer come and teach for us at one point. Taught for multiple years, actually."

Frank could feel his eyes bugging out of his skull. "No way. Mr. Suthers?"

"You already heard about that, huh?" Mr. Atlas asked.

"No," Frank said, shaking his head. "But Mr. Suthers is the only police officer I know who has any connection to teaching. Man! That's insane. So, he wasn't a real teacher?"

"He was qualified to teach, but his presence as a teacher was not entirely traditional." Eugene replied. "Monty showed up around a year or so after a student went missing from Calloway County High. We'd lost a faculty member earlier that decade—and a student if memory serves me correctly; though I don't think the two were related. But, more than likely, with all of that, plus the accusation against Winston, it prompted the Murray Police to attempt a . . . how would you say it . . . an 'undercover operation.'" Eugene made the sign of air quotes with his fingers but seemed to only be able to move his wrists up and down rather than his fingers.

"You said a teacher went missing from Murray?"

"Ms. Jean Pfannerstill. We're still not entirely sure what happened. It was all quite unfortunate and tragic. Similar to those other cases, one day she was here, and the next day she was gone. I sort of feel that she took off on her own. She had shared with me in private some personal issues between her and her parents. I'd like to think—as crass as this may sound—that they drove her away, but that theory held less water over time. I've not heard a word from her ever since."

"Who was the student? You said you didn't think they were related?"

Eugene clicked his tongue against the roof of his mouth and sucked in a breath through his teeth. "Goodness." He pondered this and then shook his head. "I can't remember. Seems like it was the Markham family—you all had a service for Mitch last week." He leaned back in his chair and took a sip of his coffee. "Around that time, I think it was his son. And no, I'm fairly certain they weren't related incidents."

Frank started to speak but stopped himself. Then, "sorry to keep dredging all this up, I'm sure this is not the conversation you wanted to have at the beginning of your day."

Eugene held up his hand. "It's okay. I've been having trouble with memory of late. There's a good chance that by the time I get home I won't even remember having this conversation." He winked.

"There was another incident, or disappearance—whatever you wanna call it—*after* Corey from Calloway, right? Do you remember a kid named Brian Pennington? He was a couple years ahead of me; good friend of my brother and Addy Michaels. Do you remember Addy?"

"Oh yes. I remember Mr. Michaels. And Mr. Pennington." Eugene nodded, looking over Frank's head, appearing as if he was trying to conjure up something in his mind. "There was some initial speculation as to whether or not Mr. Pennington's disappearance was consistent with the others, but it was confirmed by his parents that he had in fact run away. They'd claimed that he had taken some clothes and a substantial amount of money from them."

"What? He *actually* ran away?" Frank asked. "I thought his parents shipped him off or something. I tried looking him up recently but couldn't find any trace of him. I just figured he was dead and was lumped in with all the other disappearances."

"Well, now, please don't misconstrue what I'm saying. It's possible that Mr. Pennington is in fact dead. But his *disappearance*, in my opinion, was not in line with the others."

Frank sat quiet for a moment, processing. "They ever say why he ran away?"

"Not to me. Just that they believed he had. But Frank, I'll be honest with you—and as troubling as this may be to hear from someone like me—I didn't lose a lot of sleep over Brian Pennington's disappearance."

"Why's that?"

Eugene gave a puzzled expression, closely studying Frank. "Are you being coy, or do you really not know about this?"

"Mr. Atlas I can promise you I've not heard a word about Brian Pennington since high school. I remember there being some rumors about why he left but I didn't talk with him that much—if at all. He and Donnie were friends in middle school. I barely even saw him."

"Interesting." Eugene sat quiet for a moment. "Brian Pennington was one of the students who led the accusations against Winston. He's the one who snuck into his house."

48

"What?" Frank asked.

"Oh yes. He wasn't the only one involved, but he was the ringleader who initiated the conversation that led to police searching Winston's home and dragging his name through the mud."

"Wow. No, I never heard any of that."

"I'm a little surprised to be honest—your brother being friends with him and all."

"They lost touch before all that happened," Frank said. "What was Brian's deal? Why did he go after Mr. Rose?"

Eugene leaned forward, resting his elbows on the table, and interlocking his fingers. "I presume there's no harm in telling you all this now, it's been so long. Winston called me one evening and confessed something very personal to him that I will now share with you in faith that you won't use this information maliciously." Eugene stared at Frank. The man was in his nineties, with a voice one had to lean in to hear and legs that looked like they could barely carry him. But those eyes could still command attention.

Frank assumed Eugene was waiting for validation and he finally nodded. "Of course."

"Okay then." He quickly scanned past Frank's head as if keeping an eye out for privacy and took a sip of his coffee. "Winston called me in a bit of a panic that evening, confessing that he had been spotted by one of the students at Land Between the Lakes. On one hand, Winston was rather irate over the student's behavior—as he should have been, given what was said—but he was more concerned over what the student saw him doing."

"What was he doing?"

"It wasn't *what* he was doing. It's *who* he was with."

"Okay. Who was he with?"

Eugene looked around once more. "Let's put it this way, Winston's relationships were not entirely in line with our community's standards."

Frank's eyes narrowed. It took his brain only seconds to process the news. "He was gay?"

Principal Atlas closed his eyes and looked down, shaking his head. He promptly looked back up at Frank, the smallest grin across his face. "Thank you for shouting that, Frank." He sighed. "Yes. Winston was..."

"Gay."

Another playful sigh. "I know what the word is Frank. I prefer not to use a word that many in your generation associate with stupid or bad."

"Oh. Okay. He liked dudes. He was homosexual. No biggie."

"Yes. He... liked *dudes*, as you put it. Anyways, Winston confessed this to me that night on the phone—after many years of a close friendship, I might add. He was not in a formal relationship, but he had been speaking with another gentleman for several months. The two of them would meet up on Sunday afternoons after church and hike some of the trails in LBL. Winston spent a lot of time back there. Unfortunately, Brian Pennington happened to see Winston and his partner kissing."

"Weird," Frank said. He quickly realized how his tone sounded. "Sorry. I mean, it's weird to think of Mr. Rose kissing anyone."

"No doubt Mr. Pennington shared your mature outlook," Eugene said back. "And rather than just notice and pass by, Brian leveled a series of hateful remarks toward Winston which unfortunately did not exclude the word faggots." The distaste hissed from Eugene's tongue as he held out the final S. "Winston, normally quick with the comebacks and also occasionally quite rude with his comments, was too embarrassed to say anything. Instead, he and his friend made their way calmly in the other direction."

"Oh my gosh," Frank said. "So that's why Brian snuck into his home?"

"Oh no. The reason for that occurred later. I instructed Winston to keep his head down and not to say anything to Brian or the faculty. Should anything come up from the parents or the PTA, I would handle it and instruct him on appropriate next steps. But I assured him that his job was not in jeopardy."

"I don't understand. Why would parents get involved? And how would he lose his job?" Frank asked.

"Surprisingly, our local culture at that time was a little different than it is now. Albeit, not entirely different, but enough to where Winston's sexual preference could and would cause an issue given a complaint from the right force. Brian Pennington's parents were such a force."

"Damn," Frank said. "Sorry. I mean, jeez."

"It's okay. As you know, Winston's approach to student discipline could be a little controversial at times. He had a hard time holding his tongue, it got him into trouble several times. I knew Winston well enough to know his heart. He had a deep-rooted love for instructing young students like yourself. Had that not been the case, and had he not played such a prominent role in our production of high testing scores and basketball championships, he would have lost his job several times, I hate to say."

"I've heard stories," Frank said.

"At some point, Winston called me again. He'd reacted to Brian in an unprofessional manner and was sincerely apologetic over it. At the beginning of his afternoon class, Brian Pennington walked in, and handed a bouquet of roses to one of the girls. Winston commented that Brian didn't belong in the class and needed to get to where he was scheduled to be. According to Winston, Brian offered a dismissive gesture and continued conversing with the girl. Finally, Winston walked over and said something to the effect of seeing Brian with a different girl each week."

Frank made an "ooo" sound.

"This girl didn't take that lightly considering that *she* was the one who had purportedly been with Brian for a while."

"Ouch," Frank said.

"Brian of course denied it, but the surprise of the comment coupled with the sincerity of Winston's voice did its job. The damage was done.

The young woman stood up and walked the flowers over to the trash can. She also felt it appropriate to note in front of the class the supposed length of his . . . *member*, if you know what I mean."

"Awww," Frank belted with a laugh. "Nice."

"Winston confessed to me that night that he knew he shouldn't have gotten involved but wanted to give me a heads up should something happen. Neither of us could have predicted the length Mr. Pennington would go to get his revenge. That's when he apparently snuck into Winston's home in an attempt to gather anything that might embarrass him: pictures of men, letters, even pornography. Somewhere along the way he diverted on that course and decided to concoct an intricate story centering on Winston's involvement in those disappearances we spoke of earlier."

"Wait a second. How did Mr. Rose know that's what Brian was looking for? Did he find that pictures were stolen? Or did he catch him in his house?"

"Oh no. Winston didn't catch him. And nothing was stolen. A student confessed to me he'd overheard Brian say what he was going to do; break into Winston's home and look for something to embarrass him. He implied something of a more sexual nature. Of course, by the time the student told me, Brian had already done it."

"Who was the student? Can you say?"

Eugene studied Frank for another moment, as if trying to scan the inside of Frank's head with his eyes. His lips pursed and he folded his arms, tilting his head to the side. "Good friend yours. Addison Michaels."

49

"Addy?" Frank repeated.

"I take it by your surprise, Mr. Michaels hasn't let this story slip, huh?"

"I never heard anything about it."

"He was in the class where Winston made that embarrassing remark, and says he overheard Brian discussing the idea with some friends. I knew it was true when he mentioned the derogatory names Brian used for Winston."

"Man," Frank whispered. "Nah, Addy never said a word."

Eugene's head shot up over Frank's and he waved to a patron who said his name from the line coming inside.

"Does everyone know about that?" Frank asked when Eugene looked back down at him.

"About what?"

"About all this—Brian and the sneaking into the house."

"I doubt it. I made sure to keep the investigation quiet and, most important, private to those being questioned. I instructed to Brian and his parents that I did not want word of this leaking out and bluffed a threat that if they saw fit to do otherwise it would be an issue of obstructing with the investigation."

"Smart," Frank said.

"If you never heard anything about it, then I assume I did a good job," Eugene offered.

"Yeah. Never heard a word."

"Many got wind of Winston being investigated but outside of myself, Mr. Suthers, and a probably few others, no one knew anything of Brian's involvement with the whole ordeal."

"Did Mr. Suthers ever find anything against him?"

"Not to my knowledge." Eugene took another sip of coffee. "It was tragic that Winston had no family, but—forgive me for sounding insensitive—in a way it was a relief. There was no wife or children to be embarrassed by the accusations. His death or disappearance didn't leave a woman without a husband or a child without a father. There was no one to mourn him. Only me, I guess. He and I had taught together for decades so naturally it was a little hard for me, losing a friend."

"So, never any sign of what happened?" Frank asked.

"Not a one. It was like a scene out of the *Twilight Zone*, though that may have been before your time." Frank assured him he got the reference. "He left work on a Tuesday afternoon. I called him that evening about something, but never heard back. When he failed to report to work the next morning, I assumed he was sick. Then, when I didn't hear from him *that* night, I suspected something to be wrong. I went to his home shortly after his first class the following day and found no sign of him. I thought maybe he had fallen, or perhaps even that he'd been attacked. His front door was locked, there was a car in the driveway, and no sign of forced entry. I called the police from his residence; I was with them when they entered." He stopped for a beat. "It was strange. His house was in perfect order. There were no signs of struggle, it was like he took a vacation, which Winston would *never* do. A break for him would have been spent either working in his woodshed, his yard, or hiking in LBL." Eugene gave a lighthearted chuckle. "Vacationing would have surprised me more than kidnapping or foul play."

"So, that's it then. You never heard from him again?" Frank asked.

"I *never* heard from him again. I think about him quite a bit; occasionally a student will contact me about his whereabouts. He's still officially alive—there was never a funeral. And no family to declare him deceased."

"What about his partner? The guy he was with?"

"Winston never divulged that information to me. I still have no idea who that was." Eugene leaned forward and softened his voice. "I'm almost certain Winston's lying dead in the Land Between the Lakes somewhere." Eugene took another sip of his coffee.

Frank narrowed his eyes. "Why do you think that?"

"He spent a lot of his time up there, riding his bike and hiking the trails. He was a bit of a bird watcher too. Usually on Sunday afternoons he'd drive up there and take pictures, walk around. It's very likely that he fell and was unable to signal for help. Or he was attacked."

"Did the police search up there?" Frank asked.

"Oh yes. Many of us did. Nothing ever turned up though."

"What happened to his stuff? The house? Possessions?"

"The city took it. He didn't have much. Some of it was donated months after the disappearance. He had a lot of historical documents and maps that he used for his class and writings. I think some of that was donated to Land Between the Lakes."

Frank nodded his head, trying to process everything that Principal Atlas had now told him. "Actually, speaking of LBL, I have another question—completely out of left field. Did he ever talk with you about a *Bethel* Cemetery?"

Eugene chuckled. "Well, that's a blast from the past. I used to tell stories about that place. Was that before your time?"

"Oh no, I remember. They creeped me out." Frank smiled.

"Are these two questions related?"

"No. I remember hearing a lot about that place as a kid. It came up recently between me and some friends about whether or not it was a real place. You said Mr. Rose was into hiking through LBL, and that he had some historical stuff on the area. Did he think it was real?" Frank asked.

"I wouldn't know about that. I surely don't recall him saying anything about it. But if you're interested in that place, you know who you should talk to?" Eugene asked. "Officer Suthers. He's still living in the area. I see him around town all the time."

"Wait, wait," Frank said. "How does Mr. Suthers know about Bethel Cemetery?"

"I don't remember if it was after you all left or not, but one year I had him organize the Halloween festival, and he was the MC. Now, I just told stories I heard from my father about that place, but he told stories I'd never heard. And, unlike me, he's been there."

Frank's eyebrows were up in surprise. "That was definitely after I left. I used to think all that stuff was made up." This was good news—sort of. On the one hand, someone else knew about Bethel. On the other, it was the very person Frank needed to avoid. Frank checked the time. Donnie would hopefully be finishing up his meeting with Ms. Betsy. "Principal Atlas, I'm sorry, but I have to run. I gotta meet my brother." He stood up, as did Eugene. "Thanks for buying this, and for meeting with me."

"It was no problem. I'm here every morning. Please, come have a seat whenever you're here. Catching up with old students is always a pleasure."

Frank extended his hand. "Absolutely. I'll tell my parents you said hey, and thanks again for the help."

"If there's anything else I can answer, just give me a call or drop by during my office hours," he said with a wink, knocking a frail knuckle against the tabletop.

Frank maneuvered his way past the line of people and through the exit door. He stepped into the parking lot while carrying the bags of donuts and coffee in one hand and was attempting to tap in Donnie's number on his phone with the other when a loud horn went off. He jumped, nearly dropping everything. A police cruiser was idling right next to him. Frank could see it was Monty; his hands came up from behind the wheel, inaudibly asking Frank *what the hell's the matter with you*? Frank held up his arms in apology and moved back onto the sidewalk for the cruiser to pass. Monty brought down his window, "You r-realize you w-w-walked right out into the road without looking up?"

"Sorry, sir," Frank said. "I wasn't paying attention."

"That's obvious," Monty replied. "I j-just can't get away from you, c-c-can I?"

Frank considered a smart-ass comment but quickly decided against it. He needed to get attention *off* himself. "No sir, I guess not. Sorry about that. I'll be more careful." He clicked off his phone and put it into his pocket. "Seriously. Good thing *you* weren't texting, right?" Frank laughed.

"Right," Monty replied. "Good thing."

50

Monty waited in line for nearly fifteen minutes before he arrived at the counter to put in his order. He filled his coffee cup with milk and sugar and was oblivious to the elderly man waving at him from the back corner. His eyes finally registered the movement and connected with Eugene Atlas who smiled and waved him over. Eugene pushed himself up from the chair when Monty walked over. "Montgomery Suthers, good to see you." Atlas extended his hand.

"Good m-morning, Eugene. H-h-how are you?"

"I'm hanging in there. You doing okay?" Eugene eased himself back down into his seat and motioned for Monty to do the same across from him.

"Not too bad," Monty replied.

"I was just talking about you," Eugene said.

"H-h-hopefully something good," Monty replied.

"Just a student of mine—wanted to meet this morning and talk about someone you probably remember quite well: Winston Rose."

Monty, bringing the cup of coffee to his lips, paused at the name. "You w-w-wouldn't happen to b-be talking about Frank B-Burgers, would you?"

"That's him. He was just in here for breakfast. I think he wanted to know what happened to Winston all those years back. I did tell him you were working that case."

"Eugene, you r-r-realize it's probably for the best to not broadcast that information," Monty replied. "People aren't supposed to know that."

Eugene made an audible gesture of disregard. "This is a small town, Monty. I'm sure everyone knows about that now."

"W-w-why was he asking about W-Winston?"

"Curiosity, I guess. Also seemed to have an itch about that old Bethel cemetery up in Land Between the Lakes."

Monty's face furrowed. A bell dinged at the counter. The lady behind it signaled to Monty that his order was ready by waving a white bag at him. He retrieved it and returned to the table.

"I told him you would know some interesting stories about it," Eugene replied.

"W-w-why was he interested in B-Bethel?"

"I don't know." Eugene began putting the pages of the *Wall Street Journal* back together into an organized collection. "You remember telling stories to those students that one year? You had me a little scared with some of those." Eugene chuckled.

Monty snorted. "I remember that. You had me run that whole event—I didn't know what I was doing."

"You did better than I could have. Those weren't good days for my hip."

"All due r-r-respect Eugene, I don't think your hip has ever had a g-good day," Monty smiled.

Eugene smirked and gave him a slow nod. "I'd wager that Mr. Burgers and his buddies are just looking for a little adventure."

Monty sat quiet as he took all of this in, and then abruptly flicked up his wrist to see his watch. "Eugene, I'm sorry to r-r-rush off, but I need to make a q-quick stop." Monty shook Eugene's hand and made a hasty exit to his car.

When Frank arrived back at the house, it was a quarter after eight. Lexie was already inside, sitting with Donnie whose scheduled appointment was rescheduled to nine thirty.

Frank groaned at the meeting's new time, "Now what are we gonna do?"

"It's fine. You guys go. Once Ms. Betsy leaves, I'll meet you out there. Just leave a copy of that map, and make sure I can follow that cracker trail."

Cliff's voice rang out from the kitchen followed by a door closing. "Yo, yo, yo! Anybody here?"

"In here!" Donnie yelled.

"Has he ever done that while a funeral is going on?" Lexie laughed.

"No, it's pretty obvious when we're having a funeral," Frank replied.

"What's up, y'all?" Cliff asked, sitting on the couch.

"Donnie's got a meeting here in a bit and she and I are gonna go out to Bethel. You wanna go?" Frank asked.

Cliff clicked his tongue against his teeth. "Bitch, please. I scared myself in Pogue Library. Y'all have fun."

"Come on, man. You don't want to see it?"

"I *have* seen it! My dad's pictures, remember?" Cliff replied.

"What else do you have to do? You're not working today."

"Psh. I am working today. It's my catch-up day: bills, cleaning . . . organizing . . ."

"Dude. You know that you're just gonna sit over there and watch porn and Anime all day."

Cliff considered this and then looked at Lexie. "That's an exaggeration," he said.

"I didn't say anything," Lexie said back. She smirked.

Frank began to chant, softly, "Come. On. Cliff! Come. On. Cliff!" Lexie finally joined in; the two got louder and louder while Cliff stood motionless, resting his hands on his hips.

"Okay! Alright! Fine. I'll go."

"There he is!" Frank yelled, clapping his hands together. "Big man's back!"

"Yo, I'm serious, no messin' around with me while we're there. Don't point into the woods and act like you see something or make weird voices, okay?"

"Yeah, yeah, we got it," Frank replied. He rubbed his palms together. "Let's do it."

Cliff looked back over at Lexie. "I promise I'm a lot braver in real life," he said.

Lexie threw up her hands and grinned back at him. "Again, I didn't say a word."

Frank went into his office and brought out his handmade map to Bethel. He explained where to go and wrote other instructions along the sides. "I updated this sheet from the last time I went so it should be easy to navigate." Frank took a picture with his phone and handed the map to Donnie, who assured him he would be alright.

"Just make sure you leave that cracker trail. Otherwise, I'm screwed," Donnie added.

Monty sat idling in his cruiser on the side of 641, going back and forth in his mind about what to do next. Getting to Bethel was no easy task, but he couldn't shake the feeling that it was the very place he needed to be—especially when it had to do with Frank. And now this curiosity over a missing teacher? *Winston and Bethel Cemetery. Why is he asking about those two? What's in Bethel?* Monty tapped his two index fingers against the wheel, unknowingly in sync with the click of the flashers. *Why don't you just call him? Tell him that Eugene mentioned him wanting to ask a question or two.* Monty dialed the funeral home number; Ginny Burgers finally answered.

"Hello Mrs. Burgers, this is M-M-M—"

"Mr. Suthers, yes. How are you?" Ginny cut in politely. "Your number popped up on the caller ID. How can I help you?"

"Is your son at home, by chance? Frank or Donnie?"

"Well, they should be. If either one will do, I'll go get Franklin since I believe Donald is in a meeting. Just a moment." After a long moment of quiet she came back. "Mr. Suthers? I'm sorry, but I guess I'm the only one here. I thought Donald was in a meeting, but he's not in his office. And I don't know where Franklin is at the moment. Can I leave one of them a message?"

Monty politely declined, thanked her for checking, and hung up.

What if they're going up there? Your gut's been right about this whole thing. Follow them.

Monty pulled onto the road and turned toward the direction of his house. If he was going to follow those boys up to that cemetery, he needed to change.

●

Donnie answered his cell phone in the bathroom; it was Ms. Betsy's son. She now wished to push the appointment to ten due to waiting on other family to arrive from out of town. Donnie offered to come to them with his laptop and do the meeting in their living room, but the gentleman on the other end protested saying that the group they were waiting for insisted on attending. The son said that he would call back in half an hour if the family hadn't arrived. Donnie let out a frustrated breath away from the mouthpiece and suggested scheduling an appointment for tomorrow—that way everyone would be ready and available. The man agreed and said he would call in the morning if everyone was not accounted for. Donnie stopped himself from making a comment he would regret and instead offered a thank you, and a goodbye. "Some people's children," Donnie whispered. A loud knock came on the bathroom door, followed by his mother's voice.

"Donald?"

"Yeah, Mom!"

"I thought you left." Ginny said.

"Not yet. I'm about to."

"Tell me you weren't talking to a customer while you are going to the bathroom," Ginny exclaimed.

Donnie paused. "I wasn't talking to a customer while going to the bathroom . . ." He flushed the toilet.

"That's disgusting," Ginny said.

Donnie opened the door and turned on the water to wash his hands. He could see his mother in the mirror behind him, shaking her head.

"And I've told you a thousand times not to use this one. You really want this to be the first thing people smell when they walk in?"

"I didn't have a choice—Frank used the upstairs one before he left," Donnie replied. "But I do actually have to run out for a couple hours. We don't have any scheduled meetings until three thirty. I'm gonna route the calls to my cell phone."

"Oh, don't worry about that. I'm not going anywhere," Ginny said.

Donnie walked to his office to grab his keys and a hat. "Hey Mom," he yelled.

"Yes?"

"Random question, do you remember anyone in town with the name Pfannerstill? With a PF?"

Ginny smiled. "Oh sure. Anton and Madeline. They used to live over in Canterbury near your grandparents."

"Anton and Madeline, that's the name I saw in Murray Cemetery," Donnie said.

"Anton was a good friend of your Paw-Paw. What made you think of them?"

"I came across someone with their name. Genevieve Pfannerstill. Do you know that one?"

"Mmm hmm." Ginny nodded. "She was their daughter."

"Was?" Donnie asked.

"I didn't mean it like that. She may still be alive. Something happened to her. Years ago."

"What happened?"

"I wouldn't know for sure. Your dad and I weren't too close with them. Seems to me there was a falling out between Genevieve and her parents. She moved back here and next thing we knew she was gone."

"Huh. Did Genevieve teach at Murray High?"

"I don't know," Ginny replied. "Most people around here remember Anton and Madeline, ask around. They were a delightful couple. They both passed away a few years back."

"Good to know. Thanks, Mom. I gotta run and meet Frank."

"Oh! That's what I needed to tell you. Someone called for Frank a little bit ago. I think it was that police officer, Monty Suthers. Is there something I need to know?"

Donnie considered this. "I hope not. I'll let Frank know to call him."

☠

Monty's father had taken him up to LBL on several occasions when he was a boy, and a few times had led him to Bethel Cemetery, though his father never let him see her grave. They would always stand at a distance when they reached the clearing. Monty remembered the starting point near Tharpe Road that his dad always began from, but not much after that. He hoped it would all come back to him once he started on the trail.

51

Frank, now making his third trip to the peculiar clearing in the woods, still relied heavily on his hand-drawn map to navigate the woods. Lexie, on the other hand, had an innate sense of direction and surprisingly remembered much of the way from the time prior. She ended up moving ahead and confidently leading the expedition. Frank would occasionally offer a suggestion, but she assured him "this is the right way." The second time she had to ask for directions, her excitement overtook her, and she swiftly snatched the map from Frank's hand. Cliff followed a few steps behind, dropping a new trail of golden crackers along their path, occasionally eating handfuls.

The parked black car came into view and Monty slowed his cruiser to a crawl. He was almost certain it was them, though he didn't recognize the Tennessee plates. He needed to get going. Unsure of protocol, he contemplated leaving a note with his badge number in case he was in danger of being towed but reasoned that no patrol would be coming down this road any time soon. He sprayed himself for bugs and ticks, strapped his gun to the side of his belt, and grabbed a seven-iron out of his trunk.

The black car was empty. He listened for any sign of their presence nearby but all was quiet. Monty could make out visible signs of a walking path through the brush. He used his club to sweep away the grass as he moved, noting several bright orange objects beneath the overgrowth. His mind registered them as mushrooms until one of them crunched underneath his foot. "What the hell?" he whispered to himself.

Monty knelt down over an orange cluster and instantly recognized the smiling crackers. *Really?* He moved forward, abandoning his intuition, and instead followed the trail of cheddar crackers through the dense brush. A burst of laughter echoed somewhere in front of him after several minutes. The group was not much farther ahead.

They stepped over the threshold into the clearing. Though the land was familiar, Frank felt a dreadful air of unease about their presence in it. The silence was haunting. His stomach began to turn but he reasoned that this time it was more nerves than allergies.

Cliff at once spotted the collection of half-dug graves and empty headstones. "Yup. I'm not comfortable here," he whispered.

Frank could feel bile beginning to course up his throat. He took a deep breath and willed his body to get itself together. He sensed apprehension coming from Lexie as they walked together. She was cautious in her step, scanning the field, darting her head around as if she was being watched. Then without a word, she began moving away from him, in a diagonal direction, leaving Frank alone. The decaying tree looming straight ahead caught his attention. A faint sense of déjà vu came over him as he studied the landscape. "Huh," he muttered. And then his mind sparked, "The picture," he whispered to himself. The picture that the author had taken. The one Jessica brought to him in the envelope earlier in the week. The author had written *Bethel* across the top, right above the tree. Frank had initially thought Bethel was the odd cemetery he'd discovered. *But what if it referred to something else?* "What if *that's* Bethel?" Frank muttered.

☠

Lexie's path had taken her all the way to the clearing's edge—following the path of seashells around. She eyed the others: Frank was standing, staring ahead; Cliff looked to be limping and using his bat to swat at the tall grass around him. Lexi's eyes had begun to bother her. She came prepared this time with eye drops. As she was blinking to refocus her vision, leaves began crackling in the trees beyond. "Hello?" she called. *There's no one out here except us. Except maybe Donnie.* "Donnie," she called. Nothing. "Donn—" And then she saw it. Standing next to the lone tree ahead was a figure—the one Lexie had seen before. Lexie's mind wanted her to believe it was a human form, but it looked contorted. Whatever it was

stood very still. Her eyes adjusted enough to make sense of the stringy pieces hanging at the side. It was hair—a woman's. The figure looked to be hunched over, bent sideways. The legs were turned in at the knee and long strands of hair hung from the side of her head. Lexie noticed her breathing had stopped.

"Frank!" Lexie could have sworn she yelled, but what came out was nothing more than a constricted whisper. She tried again, this time a little louder, "Frank! Frank!" Frank looked up toward her. "Look!" she yelled.

Both he and Cliff followed where Lexie was pointing but nothing was there.

"What's wrong?" Frank asked.

"There's someone over by that tree," Lexie called back. "Come here!"

"Stop playin'," Cliff yelled. He was leaning on his bat, favoring his knee.

She waved her hand rapidly toward herself. "Come here! Quick!"

"I ain't goin' over there!"

"Cliff! I'm not playing around! Please, come here!"

Cliff straightened up and appeared to curse at her. He looked to be limping as fast as he could, wincing with each step. "It was over there," she said, pointing.

"And that's why we should be over there," he said, irritated, pointing over to the entrance. "You know damn well I don't want to see whatever's over there."

She sighed, looking in every direction. "I guess you're in luck. It's gone."

☠

Frank was already moving toward the tree. Lexie called for him to stop and come over to her, but he held up a finger and pointed up ahead. "Hold up," he yelled back. In the distance, he could make out something white in the long weeds and overgrowth, just by the tree's trunk.

It was hard to recognize what he was looking at initially, but when he pushed some of the grass away, he found a ring of seashells, the size of a grave. He stood still, examining both it and the tree's entangled limbs above it.

And then he saw the carving.

52

"Guys!" he called. The others looked up. "Come here!" Lexie hurried over while Cliff hobbled at a slow pace.

"You alright, man?" Frank asked.

"Nah, my knees are killing me. I think I twisted them on the way up. What'd you find—" Cliff's gaze fell downward to the circle of shells on the ground. "Whoa! What is that?"

Lexie on the other hand followed Frank's eyes. "Oh my God," she whispered.

"Right?" Frank replied.

"Did you guys not see this?" Cliff said, walking forward into the middle of the outlined space. "Is this a grave."

Lexie glanced back to see what he was looking at but something about Cliff's appearance caught her eye. He was looking down at the shells; coming down from behind the side of his head appeared to be long, sinewy gray strands. Her mind couldn't comprehend what was going on with Cliff's head, until she looked down at his shoes; he was standing with his legs apart. Just behind them, through the gap, Lexie could make out what looked to be another pair of legs bowed together at the knee. The grayish-blue hue of the bony, twig-size limbs stood out from Cliff's dark calves. "Cliff," she whispered. Lexie slowly leaned to one side and saw the makings of a someone standing behind him: a woman, decrepit and crooked. Her face then came into view. She was staring with wilted, lifeless eyes directly back at Lexie. "Cliff, Cliff, Cliff!"

Cliff straightened up, "What? What?!"

"Move! Get out of that grave! Get out of the grave!" Lexie screamed.

Cliff flailed his arms as if being swarmed by bees and jumped out of the seashell enclosed plot. "What?! What is it?!" His spastic movement hid the woman's presence long enough for her to vanish before Cliff could see anything.

"There was someone standing behind you."

"What are you talking about?" Frank asked.

"I swear. Someone was *right there*. A woman. I could see her hair just behind Cliff and when I looked down, there were legs between his." She pointed at Cliff's knees. "They were bent in—"

"Yo, that's not funny," Cliff said, snapping his head every direction. "I told y'all not to do that shit!"

"I'm not kidding," Lexie replied.

Cliff eyed the two of them. "Is she serious—are you bein' for real? Don't say shit like that to mess with me—"

Lexie groaned. "Oh my God! There was someone behind you!" Lexie positioned her knees to mimic the woman's appearance. "Her legs looked like this. They were boney, pale colored—she was right there! Behind you!"

"Then I'm out. I'll see you guys back at the car." Cliff began walking the other way.

"Hold up! Cliff! Look at this," Frank yelled.

Cliff didn't stop walking. "Nope. Screw this place!"

"Dude! Just real quick! We found it!" Frank yelled back. "Look!"

This time Cliff stopped and let out a breath as he turned around. He faced them for a moment and then, "Found what?" He walked through the overgrowth mumbling curse filled complaints, and giving the seashell grave a cautious look as he stepped by it. He lifted his head, looking to where Frank was pointing. Carved into the tree were the words,

Bethel Cem
Avilla
d. 1889

"That's it, right?" Frank asked.

"That is definitely it," Lexie added.

Cliff looked behind him on the ground. "And that must be her."

Lexie walked over to the circle and knelt down.

"Yo, what are you doin!" Cliff warned.

"It's fine. You were standing *in* it, I'll just stay out here."

Without warning, Frank shot forward and let out a sickening guttural choke. He paused, bent over at the waist for a second before resting his hand on the tree and straightening up. About the time he started to say he was okay, the colorful contents of his stomach came pouring out onto the tree's base. He groaned.

"Whoa!" Cliff said, backing up. "You alright?"

Frank took a moment to collect himself and nodded. He held up a finger, taking several deep breaths. "I'm good. Happens every time I come up here." He wiped his mouth with his hand, and took a swig of water, swishing it around and spitting it back onto the mess below. "My bad. Sorry y'all. Sure that was gross." He stood up and readjusted his sight. "I don't know what the deal is. Must be allergies, right? For my stomach to get upset every time I come up here?"

"Yeah man, I don't know," Cliff said hesitantly, watching him suspiciously. He looked around the clearing.

"Has to be. Look at my eyes," Lexie said. She was still kneeling in the grass. "They won't stop burning and watering. Same thing as last time."

"Yo, are y'all for real? You both felt sick last time you were here? Why didn't y'all tell me this before we left?" Something snapped in the woods, Lexie shot to her feet. "The hell was that?" Cliff asked.

The three of them stood still, listening.

"Probably an animal," Frank said. "Or Donnie." He cupped his hands around his mouth and was about to yell out Donnie's name, but Lexie slapped his arm with the back of her hand. Monty Suthers emerged from the trees. He seemed to be staring at the row of seashells on the edge of the entrance. His gaze followed it around a few feet, and then turned to look out across the clearing. By that point, Lexie, Cliff, and Frank had each dropped to their stomachs on the ground, concealing themselves with the overgrowth beside Avilla's grave.

"Ugh," Cliff said. "Y'all some motherfuckers, man. Draggin' me up to this haunted-ass place in the middle of nowhere."

"Shhh!" Lexie breathed.

"Bitch better not pop out again," Cliff said, frantically checking his surroundings.

"Cliff! Hush!" Her eyes grew fiery. She turned back to Monty. "How did he get up here?" Lexie asked.

"A better question—*why* is he up here?" Cliff replied.

"Guys! Both of you, quit talking!" Frank whispered. "Quick, move behind the tree." The three of them inched back, watching Monty in the distance. Whenever Monty turned to look in their direction, each of them dropped their heads as if not looking at him would make them invisible. The tree's trunk was nearly wide enough to conceal all of them. With Frank in the middle, Cliff and Lexie huddled in close and peeked around their respective sides. "What's he doing?" Frank asked.

"Nothing," Lexie said. "I mean, he's looking around, but he's just standing there."

"You think he saw us come up here?"

"He would have walked past the car, Ace," Cliff replied.

"But it's Lexie's car. And how did he know we were coming out here?" Frank asked. He reached for his cell phone, but the pocket was empty. He cursed. "Cliff, you got your cell phone?"

"In the car," Cliff replied.

"Dammit. I need to text Donnie to not come up here. He'll drive my truck—that's a dead giveaway. Lexie, you have your cell phone?"

She didn't answer.

"Lexie." Still nothing. Frank turned to look at her. She was transfixed on something at the tree's base. "What are you doin'?" She scooted around the trunk, looking curiously at the base.

"What is she doing?" Cliff whispered. He was leaning forward to look across Frank.

"I don't know. Hey," he whispered. "What are you looking at?"

"Umm..." Lexie turned to meet Frank's eyes. "You're not gonna believe this."

53

Monty's father escorted him over the seashell barrier only once. He felt a chill when he did it for the second time. He called out Frank's name, and then Donnie's, scanning the area for any movement. His foot hooked onto one of the stones, causing him to nearly tumble to the ground. The golf club fell out of his hand as he tried to catch himself.

His eyes met the stones and the fresh dirt. And the holes. Monty called out Frank's name again—with authority—but there was no response. "I know you're up here! Would make it easier if you just came out." He seemed to have an easier time not stuttering if he raised his voice. *If only I could yell all the time.* He brought out his cell phone to take photos of the dug-up earth but then heard someone in the woods, and they were coming fast.

Donnie stepped cautiously into the clearing. He'd seen Monty's cruiser on the side of the road and reasoned there was no way he'd managed to get up here by himself. He didn't want to alert him to his—or the others'—presence in case he was nearby. He peered around the clearing, kneeling and standing on his toes to try and see if they were hiding. Then, he whispered, "Where are you gu—" Something cracked behind him; Donnie whipped around, "Whoa! What are you doing here?" he asked. Monty stood several feet from him.

"I w-w-wanted to ask you the s-same q-q-qu-question," Monty replied. "Wh-wh-where is everyone else?"

Donnie looked around, confused. "I got no clue. What's going on?" Monty scanned the clearing instead of answering. "How did you get up here so fast?" Monty started to answer but Donnie cut him off, "More than that, how did you know we were coming up here."

"I f-f-fo-followed you."

"How did you follow me? I just got here. You mean you followed Frank? Where is he?"

"W-wh-what are you d-d-doing up here, Donnie?" Monty asked.

"Where's my brother?" Donnie replied.

"I haven't s-s-seen your b-br-brother. I g-g-got up here j-just b-before you did."

Donnie called for Frank, but there was no answer.

Monty glanced over to the open graves and walked carefully over the grass and weeds toward them. He pointed his golf club to the holes. "You do this?"

"I didn't do that."

"B-b-bullshit you didn't . . ." Monty's voice and attention seemed to trail off. He had spotted something on the ground. Donnie could see something of concern suddenly wash over his face. Monty used the club to push the weeds down, and then he knelt into the grass and appeared to reach for something. "Oh my God," he said to himself.

"It's not what it looks like."

When Monty stood, he was holding the blue jean jacket they had found just days earlier. "Okay. I *can* explain what that is," Donnie said.

Monty didn't say anything. He continued examining the coat with careful attention as if it would suddenly come apart with a wrong movement. He rubbed his hands over a small patch on the breast pocket that Donnie hadn't noticed. Some sort of animal patch.

"I promise, I had nothing to do with that. I can *fully* explain—"

Monty drew his gun! The movement was slow but deliberate. He pointed the barrel at Donnie. "What did you do?"

"Whoa! Whoa! What are you doin'?" Donnie threw his hands back up.

A red haze had formed in Monty's eyes. A streak ran down his cheek where Donnie saw a single tear drop off his chin. "You b-b-better start t-talkin, son. What is this doing here?"

"I don't even know what that is! It's not ours!"

"I know it's not yours. You said y-y-you could explain it. I want to know. Where. You. Got it. From." Monty spoke words with each step toward Donnie. "I swear to God... you b-better tell me right now where you g-got this."

"I said I would tell you! Can you at least put the gun down?" Donnie said.

"Where!" Monty yelled, another tear slid down his cheek.

"Officer!" Frank screamed. "Officer, wait!" Frank was running toward him, waving his hands in the air. Behind him were Cliff and Lexie. "Don't shoot! Just wait!" Frank slowed down as he neared and put his hands up as a sign of surrender. "Officer, please, don't shoot. This is a big misunderstanding."

"Oh yeah? It's a m-m-misunderstanding?" Monty turned the gun on Frank. Frank's eyes widened, he sucked in a quick breath.

"I'm not playing games with you anymore. W-w-where did you get *this* j-jacket?" Monty asked, holding it up.

"Are you crying?" Frank asked.

"Frank!" Donnie exclaimed.

"Okay! Okay!" Frank replied. "Does this really warrant a *gun*."

Monty lowered it and pushed out an irritated breath through his nose. "Start t-t-talkin'."

"You mind moving your hand from the gun?" Donnie asked.

"Hey officer," Cliff said, catching his breath and limping as he winced with each step.

"Who are you?" Monty asked Lexie.

"Lex—" She paused and looked at Monty for a few seconds. It was an awkward break, prompting the group to turn and look at her. "I'm just a friend of Donnie's, from out of town."

"Y-y-you live in Murray?"

Cliff looked from Lexie to Monty. "She went to school with these guys—" Lexie elbowed Cliff in the side. "Ow. Jeez!" Cliff recoiled and grabbed at his side, cursing at her for hitting him.

"Someone needs to start talking. Right now! Where did this coat come from?"

"Genevieve," Donnie whispered. Monty's head shot over to Donnie. "It's her jacket." Monty's whole demeanor appeared to tense at the mention of her. "You knew her." He saw Monty gulp, and another tear fall down his face. "That's why you were at the cemetery that day—in front of her parents' grave. That's why you were talking to them that day," Donnie said quietly. "You knew her."

"Hold up. What?" Frank asked.

"Mr. Suthers. We didn't have anything to do with Genevieve. Frank found—" He paused, weighing the repercussions of what he was about to say. "We found that coat up here the day before yesterday. Along with everything else over there." Donnie pointed back toward the pile of dirt beside him. "All that stuff was buried in the ground inside these graves." Monty turned and made his way over through the brush. He knelt and examined the dirt and the items embedded within it. Then he looked back down at the blue jean jacket in his hand, and held it close to his face, touching it softly against his cheek. The cop sat frozen for a moment until, suddenly, a choked, sorrowful sound escaped his throat. The tenseness of his body relaxed as Monty sank down, beginning to cry.

After a long moment, Frank spoke quietly through the side of his mouth to Donnie, "This probably isn't the best time to ask if I can go pee real quick, huh?"

Donnie swatted his brother. "Shut up."

Monty looked up at everyone, not bothering to hide the crimson that now covered his face or the tears that streaked it. "Why are you up here?"

There was a lengthy silence before Frank stepped forward, hesitantly, with hands raised. "I can explain." Frank spoke slowly, "A few days ago I was walking up here, and I tripped on one of the stones—accidentally, obviously. But when I fell, I landed on top of a grave that had sunk in. When I put my hand down to get up, it went down into the dirt and . . . well . . . it touched something. A pager." Frank pointed at the ground beside Monty. "It should still be there. And so, out of curiosity, I started moving stuff around. And then I started digging...." Frank paused, looking at the others.

"He found a bone, Mr. Suthers. Human," Donnie came in.

Monty looked at the piled-up dirt and then he nodded at the headstone. "You found a bone? In a grave?"

"I know how it sounds. But the bone was near the surface. People are buried six feet down. *This* was right on top." He pointed to the other graves. "That's why there are so many holes. There's something in nearly every one of them." Monty glanced around again as Frank continued. "The bodies buried here should be over a hundred years old by now. They'd be dust."

"The bones he found were practically fresh—well, fresher than a hundred years," Donnie added.

"That coat," Frank said, "was buried right over there. We didn't mean to dig up so much but after I found human remains, and a pager . . . something didn't seem right. So, that's what all that is." Frank pointed to his mess. "I think you should go look for yourself. If you just move some of the dirt around, you'll b—"

"I'm not touching that," Monty interrupted.

"Do you mind?" Donnie asked, cautiously moving toward the unnamed plots. "Can I show you something?" Monty didn't move or warn him to get back. Donnie walked over and picked up the Murray High Tigers basketball jersey. "We found this too. There's no name but we think it's from Pamela Climber. She went missing from Murray years ago. After basketball practice. And that pager is something a high schooler would have had in the *nineties*." He handed Monty the jersey. "We sorta think some of those missing students from years ago ended up here." Donnie reached out a hand. In between his fingers was a small card—a faded driver's license. "Along with Genevieve."

54

Monty's shoulders sagged—his whole body seemed to sink into the ground—as he held the thin, diminished ID of Genevieve Pfannerstill.

"We also think there might be a missing student from Calloway High School up here too—Corey Grassman," Donnie said.

The name jerked Monty's head back up, glaring hard at Frank. "Corey's grave in Old Salem. Was that you?"

"No sir," Frank replied.

"D-don't lie to me," Monty threatened.

"Listen, I only came up here because I thought I found Bethel Cemetery. I brought *them* along this time because they wanted to see it."

Monty's reaction escaped no one. At the mention of Bethel Cemetery, there was a spark of alarm in Monty's face. Attention was suddenly diverted from the license in his hand toward the tree. *He knows about the tree*, Frank thought. Monty was staring dreadfully at it in the distance. "Mr. Suthers," Frank said calmly. "I promise, I came up here by accident. And I stumbled on all of this by chance. I was digging up here for a good cause."

"What c-cause is that?" Monty asked.

"The parents. If the missing kids are up here, there are still several rewards being offered for their return," Frank said.

Donnie instantly looked at him, wide-eyed, "Frank!"

"R-r-reward money?"

"It's not like that," Frank replied. "I mean, if some of the parents are still offering reward money, obviously they'd want to know what happened to them—where they are. That's all I'm saying."

"Well, that's good. Cause there ain't no r-r-reward money for vandals," Monty said, attempting to get up from the ground. He got to one leg and grasped at his right hip, grimacing as he tried to stand up.

"You okay?" Donnie asked.

"Yeah. Fell over one of those stones when I got up here. Feels like my hip is outta whack." He stood finally, twisting to each direction as if trying to put something back into place at the top of his leg. "You b-boys are in a lot of t-t-tr-trouble."

"Why are *we* in trouble?" Donnie protested.

"Look around you," Monty replied.

"But look at what we found!" Frank exclaimed.

"That's Genevieve's license! Isn't that evidence enough that there's something wrong with all this!" Donnie asked.

"How did you know Genevieve?" Frank asked.

Monty's eyes locked on Frank's, "If I f-find out this is some sort of joke f-f-from you . . ."

Frank was taken aback by the severity of Monty's words and stepped back, holding up his hands. "I can promise you this is not a joke."

"Ju-Just because you may've f-f-found missing children d-doesn't mean you d-d-didn't break the law. As of now, y-you d-dug holes in a historic cemetery."

"So, if we did find the missing kids, what happens to the reward money?" Frank asked.

"Dude!" Donnie whispered.

"That's not your concern. You all are under arrest."

"Oh, come on! Are you serious?!" Frank yelled.

"You know f-for c-certain that all those k-k-kids are buried up here?"

"No," Frank replied. "But they *might* be."

"Fine. If they are, I p-promise that you'll have the c-c-credit. But once we link you to those other graves back in town, that money ain't goin to you. Not for vandalism. B-best case scenario is that a judge will use the re-re-reward money to offset the fine."

Frank started to protest but Lexie cut him off. "Officer?" Lexie wiped her eyes with her shirt and shot a glance over to Frank. "Sorry, my eyes have been bothering me since we got here. We found something else—besides all of *that*." Lexie pointed to the open graves.

"What is it?" Monty asked.

"Before I tell you," Lexie replied, looking at each one of the boys. "I need you to promise me something. You see, I can't afford—*we* can't afford—to have our name attached to anything like that—vandalism or grave robbing. We're all business owners, and something like this would put a pretty bad vibe on my reputation back home, you know what I mean? So, we're going to need to make a deal."

Donnie looked at her perplexed. "What are you talking about?"

"We think we might have solved a pretty big mystery," Lexie replied.

"If you're t-t-talking about that woman's grave over there, I know all about it," Monty cut in.

"No. Not that. I think we can confirm that something happened up here, and maybe why those graves have more in them than we think." She cursed under her breath and pulled her shirt back up to wipe the tears out. Monty stood quiet until she started speaking again. "I'm not going to give you that information unless you promise that I, and we," Lexie waved her finger toward the others, "will not be cited as vandals, grave robbers, or anything negative. If the bodies of missing students are buried up here, Frank, Donnie, and Cliff are to be credited for making the find, with no charges against them."

Monty laughed. "Excuse me?"

"Mr. Suthers, given your motivation to work at Murray High back in the day, I think *you* especially would be interested in seeing this," Frank said.

The group looked at Frank with curiosity. Monty broke the quiet, "W-what's that supposed to mean? My m-m-motivation?"

"We're not saying anything until you promise what she wanted," Frank said.

"I'm not too sure what *he's* talking about but *she's* right. You're really going to want to see this," Cliff added.

Monty appeared to be weighing the options in his mind. "W-what could you p-p-possibly have that would make me give you all a p-p-pass on this whole thing?"

"We know what happened to Winston Rose," Lexie said. "And we think there might be something connecting him to the missing students."

Monty's eyes widened. They had his attention. "How?"

Lexie broke the quiet, "No. We need your help. We want you to promise that when you call this in, these three get credit for the find, and not in the context of grave robbing." She pointed to the others. "And there is no mention of me."

"Why in the w-w-world would I do that? And how am I supposed to explain all this? You just all of a sudden stumbled on the remains of several, decades-old murder cases?"

"Sure," Frank said.

Monty made a disgruntled face, "I know you robbed those graves. You're out of your mind to think I'm gonna let you get away—"

"Yo, all due respect, Mr. Suthers, we don't have to show you," Cliff said, stepping forward. "Finding out what happened to Winston wasn't easy. I mean, he's been missing for a while, and it's highly unlikely that anyone will be as lucky as us in putting all the pieces together."

"Plus," Frank continued, "if you arrest us, it'll be on social media in less than two hours. People won't tolerate the city putting us in jail, especially when it was us who found their missing kids."

"Sounds like you d-don't need me at all, then," Monty replied.

"No. We do," Lexie said. "Because you can control how this gets out—I don't want my name anywhere near this. And they can't handle this looking like a felony."

"W-What's your deal in all this?" Monty asked.

"I have my reasons. Will you make that promise?"

Monty put his hands on his hips and hung his head, shaking it back and forth. He cursed under his breath. "You r-realize I'm not a lawyer, right. This is not a plea deal."

"We know," Lexie said. "But you can craft the narrative of discovery."

Monty's motioned to Frank. "You tell me right now: did you rob those graves? The ones back home."

Frank held his gaze. "No sir."

"Mmm hmm," Monty snorted. "So, all of this was just coincidental?" He indicated the area around him.

"Guess so," Frank replied.

Monty sighed and after a long moment of silence, said, "Fine. I'll do what I can. No charges. No fines. And no record of *you*. All c-contingent on you proving to me that W-W-Winston was involved."

"That's not enough," Lexie replied. She pulled out her phone and switched on her camera. "Please state your name, time of day, location, and who you're here with. Then please reaffirm that the Burgers family, along with Cliff Samson, will not be charged—"

Monty cut her off, holding up his hand. "Whoa, whoa, whoa. Absolutely not. I'm not r-r-recording anything." Lexie froze. "I'm not losing my job over this. I said I'll do what I can."

"How are we supposed to know you won't say anything?" Lexie asked.

"Guess you'll have to trust me," Monty replied. He looked back over to Frank. "Kinda like I'm trusting you when you say you're innocent."

55

Monty confirmed he would get someone up in the clearing to start uncovering the bodies. "In the meantime, the four of you will have to come in and give a statement about what happened and tell me what happened to Winston."

"We can do one better," Lexie said. "We'll just show you." She turned and motioned for everyone to follow her. Monty hung back as the group moved toward the tree; Lexie beckoned him to follow.

When they got closer to it, Lexie pointed out the tree's base and Avilla's name to Donnie. He cursed in intrigue, forgetting all about the dull ache that had begun manifesting in the center of his forehead. He stretched and massaged his temples as he stared at the grave. Frank and Cliff came up slowly, each looking incredibly exhausted, Frank holding on to his stomach and Cliff limping with each step. Monty's gaze followed the lot of them as they stopped underneath the tree's decaying branches. He maintained his distance, standing several feet away. "How m-m-many times have y-you all b-been near this?" Monty asked, looking up at it.

"First time—well, second time, I guess. We found it today," Frank replied.

Monty took a couple steps forward and stopped before he spoke. "I don't w-want to sound m-morose. B-but no matter what we find up here—w-w-what you're ab-b-bout to show me—I don't think it's a g-good idea to k-keep coming b-back." He looked over at the plot surrounded by shells. "We shouldn't be here now."

"Best idea I've heard all day," Cliff muttered.

"W-w-what's this got to do with W-Winston?" Monty asked.

Lexie motioned him over to the tree's side. Monty exhaled and moved cautiously toward the spot on the tree where she was pointing. She gave him a moment. "You see it?" she asked.

There were several limbs piled and twisted together on the ground beside the base. "I see a bunch of tree branches," Monty replied.

"Yup. Now look a little closer," Lexie said, tapping one of the limbs with her foot. Monty leaned forward, resting his hands on his knees. After a beat, "Huh," he mumbled.

"You see it now?" Lexie asked.

"W-W-What is that?" Monty asked back.

"See for yourself," she replied, stepping away.

Monty reached forward and pulled away a sizeable dead limb. There were several smaller branches but the hole they were concealing had become more visible. He kicked away the brush and knelt beside the tree. Lexie gestured her head for him to look inside. The hole was a large, oblong cavity in the tree; about the size of a small child. He got to his hands and knees and crawled forward to stick his head inside but almost instantaneously recoiled with a curse, causing Lexie to yelp. There was something huddled inside, against the tree's interior wall. Monty knew instantly what it was but asked for a flashlight. Lexie handed him her phone.

"I'll be damned," Monty muttered. The remains of an upper torso, still wearing pieces of what could be a button-up shirt, was propped up against the tree's back. It was immediately clear that this person had at one point been ravaged by something. The skull was not attached; it was lying upside down against the other side. The bones of the arms and legs had become detached and were spread out in the tree's interior. What Monty thought may be the femur was resting on top of a large hunting knife. "My God," Monty muttered.

"It's like an animal got him, right?" Cliff said. "Those branches were only covering a portion of that hole. We moved 'em but only enough get a better look. We didn't touch anything in there."

Monty whipped a handkerchief out from his back pocket and reached in a hand to grab the knife from underneath the bone. Several other items were lying along the ground: strips of clothing, a shoe, broken glasses. "Y-y-you said this was W-Wi-Winston Rose. H-how do you know?"

Frank and Lexie exchanged glances. "Alright, so, maybe *I* touched something." Frank dug out his phone and shined a light inside the tree against the bottom of the torso. A black object was resting there, barely visible in the dirt. "That's his wallet."

Monty scooted inside the hole, using his handkerchief to grab the item. When he came out, he unfolded the wallet and stared at its faded contents. They were right. Just inside, behind the clear slipcover, was an aged, discolored ID of Winston Rose. Monty fell back onto his rear, twisting in discomfort over his hip. He hissed out something and readjusted his position, trying to rub the side of his leg. Finally, he exhaled and sat still, staring at the wallet's picture.

"You okay, sir?" Donnie asked, after a lengthy silence.

"She was here the whole time," Monty whispered.

"She? Mr. Rose was a woman?" Frank asked.

Donnie looked at Frank in annoyance. "You're an idiot." He knelt beside Monty. "Mr. Suthers. How did you know Genevieve? Did you work with her?"

Monty continued staring ahead into the tree's hole. "She was my fiancée."

Frank mumbled a curse of surprise and Donnie asked, "You guys were engaged?"

"Close enough," Monty replied. After a moment and a long breath, he spoke gently. "We m-met w-well before I moved out here—while I lived in Virginia. Caught her speeding. The next night, caught her again at the same spot." He turned and looked at them. "She did it again the third night—said it m-m-must be fate—and asked me out for a *decaf* coffee that night, after my shift." He smiled. "G-g-girl had some guts. She later confessed that she j-just wanted to see me again." Monty folded the wallet up and tried to maneuver himself off the ground with no success. He reached for Donnie's hand to help him up. As he dusted himself off, he continued, "She was a teacher at the high school in town where I lived. We saw each other for almost two years. About the time I was g-g-gonna p-propose, she got a call about an opening for a job teaching high school Chemistry at Murray High, where she grew up. I encouraged her to take it." Monty stood now with his hands on his hips looking down as he continued. "I um... I p-put off the proposal for a while, gave her time to get adjusted. Then after several months—going b-b-back and forth about the whole thing—I showed up in town on a weekend and p-p-p—" He stopped and drew in a breath. "Asked her to marry me." Frank could see tears beginning to slide down his face. "She um... she was hesitant. Then, told me no. Said she w-w-wanted to get m-married but it w-wasn't a good time. Something to do with her parents." He looked up at them. "I said I understood. We spent that night together and the next morning I left. Went back home and that was the last time I saw her."

"I'm so sorry," Lexie said after a moment.

"What happened?" Frank asked.

"I didn't know," Monty replied. "Like I said, I went b-back home that night. Didn't hear from her for a couple of days. Thought she may just be b-b-busy or too n-nervous to call—I don't know. Finally called her, didn't hear back. Week went by, still nothing. Called the school the next week, they said she'd been missing since the weekend, and I drove down that night. Not a trace of her anywhere. Her house was locked, car and purse were gone. Thought m-maybe she tried driving up to see me and got into an accident, but there was never a report."

"What about her parents? Didn't you talk to them? What'd they say?" Donnie asked.

"I d-didn't speak with them; d-didn't even know them," Monty confessed.

"You guys were practically engaged, how did you not know them?" Frank asked.

"Jean and her parents had a b-bad falling out several years b-b-before she moved back. Coming to Murray was her attempt to rebuild that relationship but even then, it was a slow r-r-re-rekindling. She kept distant. There was never an opportunity—or a reason, I guess—to tell them about me. Which made it a little more difficult when I showed up unannounced to explain that Jean was missing, and what my relationship to her was—why I was looking for her."

"You didn't come to Murray High for Corey," Frank whispered. Monty's eyes met his. "You moved here because you thought something happened to *her*."

"What does that mean?" Donnie asked.

"He was an undercover cop," Frank replied. "That's why he was teaching at Murray. Principal Atlas told me about it this morning. But you came to teach because you thought maybe something had happened to Genevieve."

"You were an undercover teacher?" Cliff asked.

Monty nodded. "I'll ask you boys to keep that b-between yourselves. That's not public information. But yes, that's why I came to Murray. Her p-parents and I had gotten closer after her disappearance. They were so heartbroken over the things that had happened b-between them and Jean. I often felt like my presence in their life w-was a way for them to still b-be close with her. They'd m-missed so many years, I liked to think I w-was able to give a few of them back."

"Did they ask you to come here?" Donnie asked.

"No. That was me. I r-r-remembered, early on in our relationship, Jean hearing about a news story of a student who had gone missing in her hometown. At Murray High. That was maybe two or three years before she moved back. That gentleman from the funeral last w-week? Markham. It was his son that disappeared." The group nodded their heads. They already knew about Ben. Monty continued, "Then, about a year after Jean, I'm talking to Anton on the phone and he m-m-mentions something about another boy missing in town. Not at Jean's school, but same r-r-result as her. No one had seen the boy. I r-remember Anton writing it off, saying the kid p-probably ran away—until recently, I didn't make the connection that Anton w-was talking about Corey. R-related or not, my gut told me something happened to *Jean*. So, I put in for a transfer, talked with Anton and M-Madeline about my idea to investigate Murray High, and they pulled some strings with the m-mayor and the sheriff, who b-both happened to be close friends of theirs."

"Did anyone know about you and her? You and Jean?"

"Not a soul, other than her parents. And I wanted to keep it that way." Monty lifted Winston's wallet and looked again at the ID. "I had my s-s-suspicions about him b-before I even came here. Jean used to talk about him over the phone with me—a w-wretched, despicable old man. And I w-w-wasn't the only one. Several of us had our s-suspicions about his involvement. At least about his b-behavior. I just n-n-never could p-put anything together that linked him back to Jean—or Corey. Or anyone." He paused and looked at the group who was standing motionless. "Until now." Monty laid the wallet on the ground and took a picture of it with his cell phone, and the inside of the tree as he spoke his next words, "You r-r-rotten son of a bitch." He tossed the wallet back into the tree and turned once again to face the group. "I can't b-believe you all found this."

Frank was doubled over, resting his hands on the tops of his knees. He looked up at Monty and forced a smile. "As long as you're willing to say we did, that's all that matters to me."

ONE WEEK LATER
56

Within a week, officials had secured approval for exhuming the fourteen graves in Markgraf Cemetery. Students who had been reported missing from as far back as 1960 were discovered in the unidentified burial plots. To Donnie's surprise—and Frank's joy—a handful of rewards were still available for information regarding the missing students, and every family with a current offer was more than happy to pay. Frank estimated those rewards, coupled with the two anonymous cash gifts to the Burgers Funeral Home, would total nearly sixty thousand dollars—split four ways of course. It wouldn't fully restore the home, but it was a start toward making some necessary modifications after the roof was complete. And it was legal money.

City papers across Kentucky and Tennessee—even parts of Illinois and Virginia—featured stories of the brothers and their home along with Cliff and his gym. Likes and hits on the funeral home Facebook page skyrocketed. Phone calls and emails began coming in from as far as an hour away, inquiring about prices and scheduling. The article made mention of Donnie's background and his involvement with the home's catering service which resulted in a flood of requests and premium offers for him to come and cook for family gatherings, social events, weddings, and company dinners. Donnie declined the offers initially but told a few individuals to call back in a month once everything had calmed down. Murray Signs negotiated a donation to the home—and Cliff's gym—for new outdoor signs. And per her request, there was no mention of Lexie Porter.

When Saturday came, Ginny and Dave offered to take the phones and office hours to give Frank and Donnie a break. No services were scheduled for the weekend, but the following week already had five top-tier services scheduled and it looked like more were on the way. The brothers spent much of the day lounging in the living room bingeing

Stranger Things, playing pool, and throwing wooden batons across the front yard in games of Kubb.

Donnie was getting ready to start when he asked, "Hey, what did you end up doing with that sweater? From the woman."

"Oh. Piddleton?" Frank asked. Donnie looked around, making sure no one heard Frank yell out the name, then nodded. "Put it in that coffin the other day. Underneath." Frank pantomimed the action. "After you brought her up."

"Are you serious?" Donnie replied. "Didn't think to tell me first?"

"You would have said no," Frank replied.

During their conversation, Lexie's car pulled up on the side of the road and she began walking up, out of Donnie's view. Donnie continued talking as Lexie put her index finger to her lips for Frank to stay quiet. When Donnie was getting ready to throw his baton to try and knock down one of Frank's field pieces, Lexie stood motionless behind him. Then, in a sudden burst of movement, she grabbed both sides of his waist yelling "boo!" Donnie's hand jerked upward, sending the baton nowhere near its target. He screamed and jumped back, nearly knocking her down. It took him a brief second to understand what happened. "What is wrong with you?!" he exclaimed. Frank laughed.

"I scare you?" she asked.

He let out a breath. "I think I'm seeing spots," he said.

"Hey Frank. How you been?"

"Great!" he replied, throwing the first piece over toward Donnie.

"Saw you guys in the *Tennessean*—nice little write-up. Especially liked your product placement."

"What?" Donnie asked. He turned to Frank and then Lexie.

"The picture. He was wearing one of y'all's t-shirts."

Donnie's head drew back in confusion.

"Oh. Maybe one of *his* t-shirts, then," Lexie said. "It said *The Best for the Rest of Your Lifetime* in block letters, with Burgers Brothers Funeral at the bottom."

"Are you serious?" Donnie said, irritated. "That's what you sent in?"

"What? It was a good picture," Frank replied, throwing his baton.

"Should I even ask what he sent of me?"

"Oh, don't worry, yours was boring."

"Of course, it was." Donnie sighed. He couldn't help but laugh a little as he stepped closer to her. "It's good seein' ya. Kind of thought you vanished—tried calling you like fifteen times."

"Yeah . . . it's been a busy week. Had some things to get sorted out. Plus, even though I said I wanted no press, somehow word still got out that I was involved so there's been a lot of maneuvering to make sure I stay out of the spotlight." She could see Donnie was perplexed by her decision. "I don't need my social media blowing up or people coming in wanting interviews—like to keep things normal, ya know? But you guys are doin' well, right? Holy cow! You're getting a new sign? That's awesome!"

"Yeah! Crazy, right! And free! Plus, the roof got done and we had more than enough to pay for that. We can finally put some needed updates in this place," Donnie replied.

"Like a hot tub!" Frank yelled, his baton knocking down two of Donnie's pieces.

"Yes. A hot tub. That's what I'm most excited about," Donnie said dryly.

"I don't know what sort of updates you need to do," Lexie said. "I like the homey look. It's comforting."

"It's old," Donnie replied. "They'll have the sign up next week. The mockup looks amazing, it lights up and everything—even has a space at the bottom where you can customize lettering, though I'm not sure how we're going to use that."

"Definitely going to use that," Frank called over. "Maybe do like a birthday promotion each week. Every Wednesday we wish someone a happy birthday and pay for that person to get a free donut at Mom's, or something like that. You're up."

Donnie lowered his voice to her, "As I said, we're still not sure how we're going to use that."

Lexie laughed.

"You wanna throw?" Donnie asked, handing a baton to her.

"I have no idea what you all are doing," she chuckled.

"It's Kubb!" Frank yelled.

"Yeah, still no idea," Lexie said back. She held out her hand and took the baton then looked at him. "Actually, I wanted to talk to you about something. If you have a second."

"Yeah," Donnie replied. "Wait. This isn't one of those conversations where you tell me you don't want to see me again, is it?"

"I'm fairly sure I wouldn't drive two hours to tell you that. You're not that special," she replied.

"Ouch," Donnie said. He looked at Frank. "Halftime. I'll be right back. No moving anything."

"Ugh. Fine. I'll go make a drink," Frank replied. When Lexie and his brother had gone inside, Frank surveyed Donnie's remaining field pieces. Then he carelessly knocked one of them down.

Lexie closed the door to Donnie's office. He grabbed her by the waist, turned her around, and kissed her.

"I've missed that," she said.

"What happened to you? Really. I mean, one day we're chatting on the phone and then all of a sudden, nothing. No calls back, no texts—"

"I know," Lexie replied, breaking away. She stepped back, over to Donnie's desk chair and turned to face him. "I was serious when I said I didn't want my name attached to this, or my social media blowing up. But it's not because of my job."

Donnie waited a moment, thinking she'd finish the thought. "So... what is it?"

Lexie sat quiet for a moment and then, "It's my dad." Donnie furrowed his eyebrows. "I didn't want anyone finding out about my dad . . . or who *I* was."

"I don't get it. You mean, that you came from Murray? Or that you don't want people in Murray finding out who you are? Who's your dad?"

Lexie took a deep breath and reached into her pocket. She extended her hand toward Donnie. "Here. It's probably best if I start with this."

Donnie unfolded the piece of paper. It looked to be out of a notebook—or a journal. The paper was lined, with cursive script on each side. Donnie turned the page over in his hand and looked at her. "What is this?"

"You can't guess?"

He noticed a tear along the paper's edge. Then he saw the name at top, *Corey*. "Is this from Corey's book?"

She nodded.

Donnie looked down at the note's end. It was signed *LP*. "This is you?"

She nodded again.

"When—why do you have this? We didn't read this, did we?"

She shook her head slowly, not breaking eye contact.

"Did you tear this out?" Donnie asked.

"I did." As Donnie was asking how she cut him off. "The other day in Frank's office, when we decided to read through it. I remembered exactly where it was. That's why I kept asking if we could go out to eat. Once we all got in the car, I told you I had to get my purse. I left my purse in here so I could come back and tear it out. I didn't want you all seeing what I wrote—or worse, figuring out that it was me."

By this point Donnie was already reading. Lexie stood waiting for him to reach the letter's most revealing detail.

. . . I'm sorry but I cannot keep this baby. I know in the movies the girl always keeps the baby of her dead lover so that a piece of him can stay behind—or something like that—but I don't think I can have only a piece of you. Every day seeing a part of you, knowing that all of you was gone. That

I couldn't see or talk with you anymore. Touch you anymore. I can't bear to think what it will be like having to raise this child without you...

"Wait a minute. What?!" Donnie exclaimed, gazing up at her. "You were pregnant? You and... *Corey?*"

"Yes."

His mouth hung open, looking as if a word wanted to come out yet it was frozen. "How? I thought you said you didn't know him. He died in what? Ninety-seven? You were like..."

"A lot younger. I know. I know! Everything happened so fast."

"How did you guys even meet? And..." He stopped and stared at her.

"How did I get pregnant? Yeah."

"Sorry... I don't really know what to ask—"

"No, it's a fair question. And it's why I came back. I figured with everything going on, and... you know... me and you... you had a right to know." She let out a long breath out and took a seat in his desk chair. Donnie sat on the floor, leaning his back against his bookshelf.

"Corey was a senior when I was a freshman. He and I were at the same party, right after homecoming—I'd never met him before then. It was my first party; my friend forced me to go. I was able to talk my dad into letting me stay out because I told him we were going to a movie. And I only stayed at the party because I didn't want to call my dad. My parents were already divorced by this point, my mom was in a different state."

"Must have been a popular freshman," Donnie said.

"Oh no, not at all. My friend told me it was her cousin's house. Still have no idea if that was true. She was a shitty friend—left me after twenty minutes to go hook up with some guy. I ended up sitting on a couch by myself watching a baseball game next to two couples who were making out, one of which kept trying to get me to join in, by the way." She laughed and shook her head.

"Ew, really?"

"The guy kept slipping his hand on my leg while this other girl was straddling him. I kept scooting away or brushing it off, finally I just started putting it on random objects: the couch, a book, the dog." Donnie laughed. "Eventually, I went outside to the backyard and sat on a swing. I contemplated walking home, but I couldn't get in without my dad knowing, and I had no clue where I was. So, I just sat. Waiting for my friend. Crying. And that's when he came out. He sat on the steps of the porch for a little bit talking to himself—obviously upset because he kept calling someone a bitch and cursing. Then he pulled out a cigarette and saw me on the swing."

"He say anything to you or did you talk first?"

"*He* did. He walked over to me—asked what I was doing there, and how old I was. Some random freshman at a senior party sitting outside by herself; little awkward, I'm sure. But he was super chill. He took a seat next to me and we just sorta hit it off. He asked me a bunch of questions. At first, he wouldn't say why he was so mad but eventually it all just kinda came out of him. He told me some girl had tried to hook up with him inside. She faked being sick, made him take her to the bathroom and sit with her for like twenty minutes or something crazy, and then suddenly started undoing his pants. She was acting sick so that she could get him alone. He didn't have any interest in hooking up with her and when he realized that she tricked him, he left her in the bathroom."

She continued, "After a while, when it was obvious my friend was *not* coming out, he offered to give me a ride home."

"Random dude offers you a ride home at a party and you say yes?" Donnie asked, playfully.

"I was cold, pissed off, hungry, and supremely uncomfortable sitting at someone's house I didn't know. I would have taken a ride home from Jeffrey Dahmer if he asked. He took me home and it was nearly five in the morning. My dad was just waking up. I remember seeing his bedroom light on and told Corey that I couldn't go in—he'd know that I'd gone to a party. So, we kept driving, and ended up at some church playground. We stayed up watching the sun rise, lying in one of those tubes you crawl through, just talking. And then, all of a sudden, we're kissing and then . . . well . . . yeah. Not where I expected the night to go. And once it was over, we lay inside that tube for a little while longer. When I was certain my dad had left for church, that's when he took me home. Dad never knew. He always assumed I stayed over at what's-her-name's house and came back while he was gone."

"Smart," Donnie said softly.

"After that, we continued talking on the phone and seeing each other in private—I was still a freshman. Not the most accepted of social norms, you know?"

"Did he know about the baby?"

"No." Her face was expressionless, lost almost. "I wanted to—God, so many times did I want to. I just never knew how. I didn't know how to tell anyone. I finally got the courage to ask to see him in person and that was the day he found out that he was expelled."

"He got expelled?"

"Yup. About two weeks before he disappeared. You remember us talking about that girl Connie Lancaster—the one who said Corey raped her?" Donnie nodded. "That's who he was with that night. The two of them had dated and been sort of off and on through high school. At least that's what he *told* me. When he disappeared, I thought she had something to do with it. About two weeks after that party, it started to go around that he had raped her. Then it started going around that she had to have an abortion. That lie went quick and basically ruined his last month on earth. Teachers, students— even my dad—got involved. I remember he contacted the principal over at Calloway to try and get Corey expelled when he heard the news. But he didn't rape her. I *know* he didn't. I wanted so badly to tell Corey about the baby but I didn't know how he'd react. Hearing that he really did get someone pregnant, ya know?" Lexie paused. "Or maybe I was just scared he'd push me away."

After another pause Donnie spoke: "wait, so, who was your dad then? Do I know them?" No reply. "It wasn't Mr. Rose was it?"

Lexie took another breath.

57

"Eugene Atlas," Lexie said, timidly.

Donnie's eyes widened. "What? *Principal* Atlas? How? Your last name is Porter. I knew you for years before you left, how did I never know that? More important, why are you just now telling me?"

"Porter is my mom's name. Even before they divorced, I never wanted anyone in school to know that my dad was a high school principal. That was the only thing he and I could ever agree on. I wanted to be treated like everyone else—I never wanted to be singled out because of him. And I'm telling you now because it's *you*. Hardly anyone else knows."

"So, when you left . . ." Donnie began.

"I left Murray because I was pregnant, and I was deathly afraid of what my dad would do to Corey if he found out. When Corey told me he'd been expelled, I worked up a way to go and live with my mom."

"What'd Corey say?"

"He was heartbroken. I made up some story about my mom being sick—I felt like I was suddenly lying to everyone I knew. My intention was to wait until everything with the expulsion calmed down and then tell him. But about a week after I moved, he disappeared." Lexie's shoulders shrugged, lifting her hands in an expression of helplessness.

"Did your mom know you were pregnant?"

"At first, no. I feigned emotional withdrawal from my mother, and Dad didn't want to press the issue too much, so he let me go. Once I heard about Corey's disappearance, I didn't have a choice; I had to tell her—had to tell someone. I admitted that I was considering having an abortion and instead of talking me out of it, she drove me to the clinic. It was the opposite of what I wanted. I know I wrote that I couldn't do it," she said, motioning to the paper, "but the more I thought about it, I was okay with a baby. I didn't mind the idea of having a new life and having a piece of Corey there with me. But boy oh boy, my mom. She just, she didn't want it. She thought it would be a terrible idea and . . . well . . . yeah." Lexie cleared away the tears that began falling from her eyes. "I guess she won in the end."

"And your dad still doesn't know?"

She remained silent for a long while before answering. "Until last week, I still wasn't sure about my dad's involvement with Corey's disappearance." Donnie uttered a "what?" quietly in response. "I know, everyone suspected Mr. Rose—and I did too in the beginning—but my dad, he was so indignant over what happened to Connie. When Corey was officially expelled, I remember Dad telling me about it at dinner—he didn't know I knew him. And it was almost like he was disgusted by the punishment, like Corey deserved *worse* than expulsion. Corey needed to experience real harm, apparently. And remember, this was all a rumor. Corey never touched her. But I remember Dad telling me that and then he had this grin on his face and he said, 'Principal Burton'—over at Calloway—'should have called me. I would have told him to give the boy Saturday detention. Maybe have a couple of guys there waiting on him . . . drive him somewhere. Make sure he never does anything like that ever again.'"

"Oh my gosh," Donnie replied. "Mr. Atlas—your dad—said that?!"

"I know. Weird, right? I'd never heard my dad talk like that. He could be a hard man, but I'd never heard anything that . . . *violent* come out of his mouth. And so, when it happened—when Corey disappeared—I suspected Connie or Mr. Rose because of the other accusations, but in the back of my mind I always wondered if it was Dad. From that moment on, he scared me. Even more unsettling was imagining what might happen if he found out about *me*, and that it was Corey's."

Donnie sat quietly. He couldn't believe it. This was one of the most well-liked people in the community. "That's why you didn't want to do the interviews. You didn't want anyone tracing you to your dad, or digging too much into your past," Donnie said.

"Bingo," Lexie replied, getting up out of the chair. "You're the only one who knows this outside of a few close friends I have back home. I know hardly anyone remembers me, but I'd like to keep it that way."

"Can I tell Frank?"

"If I say no are you still going to tell him?"

"No. If you don't want him to know, I won't tell him," Donnie said.

"It's okay. You can tell him. Just make sure he knows to keep it to himself."

Donnie straightened up and took her hand. "So, what now? Now that you know about Mr. Rose, are you gonna see your dad?"

"I don't know. I probably should get over myself and call him. Maybe next time I'm in town."

"When's that?"

"Depends. You gonna stick around here or head back to New York?"

"I'm here for now—promised Frank I'd be here till January. Told him I'd help get the place back on its feet—if that's possible." Donnie grabbed her hand and her closer to him. "But that may depend on if you would come visit me more here or up in New York?" They both laughed and shared a kiss.

Donnie walked Lexie out to her car. She hugged the rest of the family goodbye on her way out. Frank told her that if her and Donnie stopped seeing each other to look him up on farmersonly.com. She rolled her eyes and said she would certainly do that.

Lexie sat inside her car and pressed the ignition button to turn on the air conditioner.

"I'm sure you want this," Donnie said, holding out the torn note. She took it and placed it in her bra.

"Did they ever find out anything on Mr. Rose? How he died or why he was in the tree?"

"No. They're running tests. The theory right now is that he was attacked by something and drug into that tree, or he had a heart attack while he was up there. And was then drug into that tree. Mr. Suthers is supposed to give us an update in a week or so."

"Alright. Keep me posted. I'll call you tonight."

"See you in two weeks?" Donnie asked.

"If you're lucky," she stood up out of the car and kissed him once more.

SATURDAY
58

Early the next morning the brothers dropped off their mom at Virginia Jan's and stayed for breakfast. Everyone greeted them when they walked in; several even offered to buy their breakfast—they had become royalty overnight. Principal Eugene Atlas walked past their table toward the restroom and offered a congratulations on their discovery. Neither Frank nor Donnie could shake Lexie's story from their minds.

When he made his way back to the table, Principal Atlas stopped beside Frank's chair. "I drove out by you all yesterday and saw your sign was down. Did something happen?"

"Yeah! Murray Signs donated a new one to the home. Should be up by late next week."

"That's wonderful."

"I'm trying to work with them on some ideas, it should look pretty sharp when it's done. I'm excited." Frank smiled. "You doin' okay?"

"Oh, I'm just fine. I'm looking to have another surgery at the end of next month—trying something experimental this time around. I've been to my doctor twenty times in the last four months trying to figure out what I can do," Principal Atlas said, rubbing the side of his hip and indicating his cane.

"Twenty times?" Donnie said, surprised.

"Twenty," Atlas reiterated. "*With a TW*. I've had problems with my legs for decades, but it's been taking its toll recently. I'll tell you boys right now, a wheelchair doesn't sound half bad."

"Oh my gosh. Well, if you need something, call us," Donnie said. He wasn't sure why he said that. Judging from the look on Frank's face, neither was his brother.

"I appreciate that. But I should be okay. Getting old ain't for the weak." He forced a grin across his mouth and patted the table. "You boys have a good one, I'll see ya 'round." Eugene walked back over to his table in the far corner and sat down. Donnie wanted to ask about his daughter but figured it best to keep his mouth shut.

Factoring in all the talking and interruptions for selfies, the brothers were there for nearly forty-five minutes. They knew the fame would be short lived, but they intended to milk it for all they could. *It's good for business*, Frank would say. And Donnie believed he could use all the good press he could get to help counteract the bad he'd received in New York.

The boys said goodbye to their mom and made their way toward the door but for some reason Frank couldn't stop staring at Principal Atlas. Most of the elderly crowd had left, giving room for those who had placed their orders to sit. Eugene, facing away from them, had a copy of the *Ledger* unfolded and out in front of him. "Hey hold up, will ya?" Frank motioned to Donnie.

"What's up?" Donnie replied.

Frank stood still; his gaze fixed on his former principal. "*TW*," he whispered.

"What?"

"He said, 'twenty with a TW,'" Frank said, more to himself than Donnie.

"Who?"

"Mr. Atlas."

"What does that mean?"

"I've heard that before." Frank stood quietly, rolling thoughts around in his head. "You ever heard someone say that? Twenty with a TW?"

"No."

Frank mumbled to himself, a series of half words and sounds, occasionally shaking his head and shifting his mouth to the side. "TW . . . TW . . ." He began saying it in difference pitches. Finally, in a low, raspy, slow robotic tone he muttered, "T . . . W . . ."

"You sure you're not having a stroke?" Donnie asked.

"Holy shit," Frank whispered. He looked at Donnie, and swatted his arm with each word, "Hoe. Lee. Shit. The phone call—the guy on the phone." Frank scooted out of someone's way as they walked past to exit. "He's the guy who called me—it's him!"

"How do you know?"

"'Twenty with a TW.' The guy on the phone said the same thing to me—that exact same phrase. You think it was really him?"

"I don't know, man. Why don't you just go ask him?" Donnie said back, sarcastically. Someone bumped his elbow as they walked by and out the exit. "It's a little crowded here though, can we—"

"Good idea," Frank interrupted, making his way over to Eugene's table.

"Wait, that's no—" Donnie couldn't reply before Frank was out of earshot.

"Mr. Atlas? You got a second?" Frank asked.

"Hello Frank. Pull up a seat." Eugene said, lowering his newspaper.

"Just had a question for you. I don't really know how to ask this," Frank started. "It's a little awkward." He paused. Eugene started to speak but Frank cut him off. "Did you find what you wanted in Corey's book?" Frank asked.

59

The reaction was instantaneous. Eugene Atlas's smile slowly turned down; his eyelids fell to a thin slit over the eyes. It was all Frank needed to tell them that Principal Atlas was the mysterious caller. The warm smile on Atlas's face reappeared. He laid his newspaper on the table, never breaking eye contact. "I don't know what you're talking about."

"I think you do. TW? That's what hit me. You said that over the phone. Twenty with a TW." There was a twitch in Atlas's cheek. And then Frank asked, "Have you spoken to Lexie recently?" Donnie muttered something as he swatted Frank's arm.

The question was another blow to Eugene's armor. He methodically folded the paper back to its original state and slid it to the side. Interlocking his fingers in front of him, he leaned forward. "Was she with you?"

"She was for a little while. Sorry, I thought she would have spoken to you."

Even in his old age, his aura still had echoes of intimidation—especially in the eyes. "Where's the rest of it?" he asked.

"The rest of what? The book?" Frank asked.

"There's a page missing."

"I gave you ever—" Frank began, but Donnie cut him off.

"She tore it out," Donnie interrupted. Frank looked up at his brother. Donnie crossed his arms, feeling a little awkward to still be the only one standing. "Lexie. She has it. She found the book in his office and read through some of it before we gave it to you."

"Does she know you gave it to *me*?" Eugene asked.

"No. I didn't even know it was you until thirty seconds ago. Frank here is the one who suspected you."

"So, she *was* hiding something," Principal Atlas whispered.

"You'll have to talk to her about that," Donnie replied.

"If I could talk to her, I wouldn't have hired *him* to get that book, now would I?" Atlas said back, slowly.

"What were you wanting to know?" Frank asked.

Atlas sat quietly, gazing at them. "What I wanted to know is of no concern to either of you. And now out of my reach, thanks to her getting her hands on it. The fact that she's hiding something about the Grassman boy only confirms to me that *he* belonged up in Bethel with rest of them."

Frank was about to speak but stopped. In the last week, Frank and Donnie had given dozens of interviews, answered hundreds of questions, and even been the focus of a two-page article in the *Murray Ledger*. However, at no point was there ever any mention of Bethel or Markgraf cemetery. The location agreed upon by authorities was a large clearing in LBL to keep locals and tourists from hiking around the area. "Wait. How did you know they were in Bethel?" Frank whispered.

Atlas sat quiet for a moment then appeared to concede. He clicked his tongue and scooted back in his chair. "You boys come with me."

Frank jerked back, unsure of the elderly man's next action. "Where are we going?"

Eugene struggled to stand up. "Outside," he grunted. "I don't want to have this conversation in here." He slid the newspapers under his arm, and picked up his mug of coffee, taking it to the counter. He spoke pleasantly with the cashier for a moment while she handed him a to-go cup with fresh coffee. Eugene tipped his head to her and placed a bill in the jar beside him before limping toward the exit.

Frank and Donnie, wary of what to make of what was happening, made their way outside the restaurant where he was shaking hands and smiling to a group of patrons eating their breakfast. Eugene stopped at his car and unlocked it as the brothers stood nearby.

"How did you know about Bethel?" Frank asked.

Eugene ignored him. He hooked his cane on the car's side mirror and eased himself down to lean onto the car's hood. With his shoulders hunched forward, and his arms crossed, he took a breath and began to speak quietly, as not to be heard by anyone but Frank and Donnie. "You need to understand, first of all, those kids got what they deserved."

"I'm sorry," Donnie said, perplexed. "What?" Atlas stood coolly, his tongue moving around his teeth as if trying to pick out food. "What does that mean they got what they—"

"You boys read the *Ledger* the last few days?" Eugene asked. The brothers stood motionless. "Of course, you have. Your little group is practically the star of it now. Have you read the other articles? About the students?"

"A couple of them, yeah," Donnie replied.

"The *Ledger* has run a lengthy write-up on each of those students over the last few days. Their lives here in Murray, their endeavors, their accolades, who they were as individuals—framing each of them for us in a final, beautifully written memory. I've probably spent five hours on the phone, digging in the recesses of my brain to provide personal stories about each and every one of them. Others have too: teachers, coaches, friends who knew them. The pieces are wonderful." A cold, menacing expression came over Eugene's face. "But to some, beautifully written memories won't mask the foul nature of those kids; stuff the articles can't tell you. They can't tell you that *Nina Etheridge* played a sadistic game with several of our teachers—females included—where she would secretly plant nude Polaroids of herself in their desks, and on their persons, threatening to reveal them in public if they gave her any grade lower than an A.

"Those articles won't tell you that during a party *Ben Markham* walked in on a girl going to the bathroom and assaulted her—raped her. Then he went to go find the girl she came with, lied to her and said that the other girl needed help. He raped her too while the other one lay passed out on the floor.

"It took all that I had to not tell the papers that *Marcus Taylor*, though not a user himself, employed several students at Murray high as drug *dealers*. That he took the butt of a shotgun to the head of two students at Calloway High in the matter of a hundred dollars of missing drug money.

"I fought against the urge to tell the story of one who jumped an African American student after a basketball game, tied him to a rail and punched him repeatedly in his eyes, finally carving out the word *coon* in the flesh of his forehead with a knife. I didn't say any of this because, what's the use? What's done is done, and in the end, each of them got theirs."

Principal Atlas continued, "I don't know what Lexie told you, but *Corey Grassman*, whose book you found, was no exception. Did she tell you that he too raped a young girl? That he forced her to get an abortion." Frank shook his head no, but Donnie remained still. "And if my sources are correct, he did something similar to my daughter."

"Wait, wait, wait," Donnie cut in. "You knew what Mr. Rose was doing the whole time?"

Atlas's eyes jumped between Frank and Donnie. Finally, he whispered confidently, "Boys. Winston had nothing to do with it. *I* put those kids up there."

60

Donnie stood still, looking confusedly at Eugene. "I don't understand."

"Don't trouble yourself. You don't have to understand."

"Wait. What about Mr. Rose? That was him, right?" Frank asked.

"It was." Eugene took a sip of his coffee from the Styrofoam cup. "But I couldn't tell you how he ended up there."

"What does that mean?" Frank asked.

"The whole time," Donnie cut in, his voice soft but not without indignation. "All those accusations against Mr. Rose. The parents that came to you. Suthers investigating." Donnie paused. "It was *you* the whole time?"

Eugene sipped his coffee and replied almost sympathetically. "As I said, you don't have to understand. And whether you do or not won't change what I did or how I feel about it." Someone walked by and waved at Eugene, then the brothers. Only Eugene smiled and waved back. When they walked away, Eugene continued speaking, "Couple years ago someone sent me a video on the YouTube of a high school girl standing on her teacher's desk, trying to hit him with her coat. After standing there for far too long telling her to get down—I'm sure you can guess how effective that was—he advanced on her and pulled her off. Put her over his shoulder until she began to beat on his back, causing him to drop her. She put on a show and fell back, screaming. You know what happened to the teacher?"

"He got fired," Frank replied. "I remember reading about that."

"He. Got. Fired," Eugene said back, punching each word. He shook his head. "And the girl?" Frank and Donnie both shook their heads. "Ah, didn't hear *this* part, did you? *Nothing*. Slap on the wrist by the administration." He leaned back. "But a week later, she did it again. Thankfully *that* teacher didn't touch her. About a month later she did the same thing for a third time, and on this go-around, she slapped a teacher across his face—a good friend of mine—terrific man. He shoved her back in defense and she toppled over a desk, this time breaking her arm. He was fired immediately. The mans had nearly forty years of experience in the classroom. And he still can't find a school to hire him.

"Options for formal instruction are limited when kids won't listen to authority—or respect it. Others get hurt by their influence, and the situations escalate the longer we allow it to happen. It's a different world for teachers, now. A student gets in a fight, you can't break it up because you may touch them." Atlas rolled his eyes. "I read about schools that can't keep order: they can't fail their students, they can't assign homework, they can't take phones. They can't instruct. And the student's behavior and disruption only becomes more severe. Schools have lost the ability to protect the other students, and most important, to protect the teachers."

"All due respect, what's your point?" Donnie asked.

"My point is, why do you think our school had so few of these incidents occurring on a regular basis? Think back to times when you heard about incidents of gangs, bullying, students mouthing off in class or disrespecting our teachers—while you were there. Instances of sexual misconduct." He paused to let the brothers consider the memory. "I guarantee you could count them on one hand. I always encouraged teachers to be smart and hold control of their classroom *their* way but in difficult cases, such a student only had to visit my office once before he got the message."

"Because you threatened to kill them?" Donnie muttered.

"Oh no. There were never any threats," Eugene replied matter-of-factly.

Donnie scowled at his former principal, "Who the hell do you think you are? You're a fucking teacher! They're kids. They grow up."

Atlas's eyes became piercing. "You might be right. But how many lives are you willing to let them ruin before they do?"

Donnie turned and began walking.

"Where are you going?" Eugene asked. Donnie didn't answer. "Mr. Burgers!" Donnie turned to face him. "What exactly are you going to do?" Eugene straightened up and reached for his cane off the mirror.

He walked carefully over to Donnie, keeping his voice between them. "You're going to go to the police?" Donnie didn't respond. "They found their killer, remember? What could you possibly say? Old Principal Atlas is the real killer?" There was a pause as Donnie considered this. Atlas continued, "The knife they found in that tree will show traces of Brian Pennington's DNA. And Winston's. It was his knife."

"What happened to Genevieve?" Donnie asked abruptly.

"Who?" Eugene asked, confused.

"Genevieve Pfannerstill. She taught at Murray High. She was up there—"

"Jean," Eugene cut in, softly. "Jean was an accident." There was a sudden, sorrowful expression on Principal Atlas's face. "I reacted prematurely, and she got herself in the wrong place, at the wrong time."

"You killed her?" Donnie asked.

"Not intentionally. But yes. I've regretted it every day since."

"Oh, I'm glad there's *something* you regret—that makes it better." Donnie exclaimed. "Give me the keys, Frank."

Eugene winced at his hip and shifted his balance. He turned sharply and began moving back toward the car, addressing Donnie from over his shoulder. "I was at the school late. Alone. Funny, I can't even remember why. And I recall that I was walking from the restroom back to my office when I began to hear voices. Loud. There seemed to be an argument between two boys coming from outside. And then I heard a *gunshot*, clear as day. I ran to the south door, just past the cafeteria and exited into the courtyard. There was a boy on the ground clutching his stomach."

"Who was it?" Frank asked.

"Don't remember. Young white student. I knelt beside the boy; he couldn't speak more than telling me he'd been shot. I asked where the other one ran off to and he pointed around the side of the building. I told him I was going to go call 911, and ran off to do so, but first wanted to get a glimpse around the side to see if I could see anyone. Foolish mistake," Eugene confessed. He eased himself back onto the hood of the car and picked up his coffee cup. "I should have immediately called the police." He took a drawn-out breath and continued, "At the time, I was carrying a large pocketknife. I flicked it out as I ran to the opposite side of the building in pursuit, getting ready to turn down the back pathway when all of a sudden someone in a hood turned the corner and ran into me." His gaze had shifted down to the ground. "There were no lights on that side of the building. It was so dark I wouldn't have recognized my own mother had she been standing there. I panicked and shoved the blade of my knife straight into the hood, right in their neck. It all happened so quickly. I reacted poorly—out of fear, thinking whoever it was may still have that gun and be able to use it."

"It was her," Frank said.

Eugene nodded, still staring at the ground. "She died instantly. Fell into my arms. For several seconds, I thought I'd gotten the son of a bitch who shot that boy. I laid her down and pulled back her coat's hood. My eyes told me what I was seeing but my brain kept trying to counter it, make me believe that the darkness was playing tricks on me. I didn't want to believe it." There was a lengthy pause. Eugene looked up toward the restaurant and then back down at the ground. He shook his head. "I assume she was picking up something from her classroom. Probably heard the gunshot and came out to investigate. She was a magnificent teacher—"

"And instead of going to the police, you buried her in the woods?" Donnie asked, horrified.

Eugene glanced up as if looking at a plane. "At the time, I was scared. I knew what I'd done—both to her and to others. Her death would raise too many questions. I didn't need the police looking into me or my history."

"But what about the boy—he saw you, right? And the police didn't suspect something when they realized a teacher was missing around the same time someone got shot on school property?"

"The police didn't suspect anything because there *was* no boy," Eugene replied. "When I looked back around the corner, he was gone. No one had seen a thing. Boy likely mustered all the strength he had left and hightailed it out of there when I mentioned I would be calling the police. I pulled my car around to the back of the building, placed Jean in the trunk, and cleaned the blood off the grass in the courtyard. I was there nearly all night."

"What about her car?" Frank asked.

"It sat in my garage under a tarp until I could drive it up to the lake."

"You piece of shit," Donnie whispered. "You *fucking* piece of shit."

Eugene slightly raised his free hand and shoulder, making a face that said, *it is what it is.*

"Fuck you," Donnie said. "You killed Mr. Rose, too?"

"I didn't touch Winston," Eugene shot back. "I *found* Winston. In that tree. I can only speculate as to why he was in there."

"The knife," Frank said. "Why did he have it?"

"Winston had loaned me that knife at one point. Figured it was in my best interest to return it." He looked at Frank. "Everything I told you about Winston was true. One day he was here, the next day he was gone. I went to his house, called the police, couldn't find any sign of him. About a week later I was up in that cemetery and found his jacket on the ground. And his keys, his wallet, glasses, shoes—all scattered as if he'd been attacked. I found a shoe over near the tree and when I walked around to the other side—where the hole was—there *he* was. Huddled up against the inside like he'd seen a ghost."

"So, what we saw in there, that's how you found him?" Frank asked. "It looked like he'd been ravaged by an animal."

Eugene seemed troubled at that remark. "Oh. No. He wasn't like that." He folded his arms and nodded. "I guess it is reasonable that animals would be a factor. All I did was put the items inside—carefully of course."

"Why didn't you just bury him?" Donnie asked.

Eugene gave a sly grin. "Insurance. For a time like now when someone would go up there and screw around. I needed a scapegoat. Someone to take the pressure off me. The knife sealed the deal."

"What do you think happened?" Frank asked.

"I think *she* got him," Atlas replied. Donnie cursed at Eugene again. "I know how it sounds, but that area has a history for a reason."

"Come on Frank, let's go."

"Wait a second. Hang on," Frank said. "When we were up there, your daughter swore she saw someone—a woman," Frank said.

"I'm sure she did. And if the two of you wouldn't mind, I'd prefer if you kept my daughter away from that place," Atlas replied. "Lot of folks—myself included—have paid the price for meddling around up there, and according to its history, lots of folks have died. The people who buried her eventually considered that spot of her burial to be cursed, and so they put a ... a kind of fence around the area to warn people. Keep them out."

"The shells," Frank said.

His head bobbed. "My father and mother lived in LBL—where I grew up—and though he'd never speak of that woman, my father did take me up there once. He wouldn't cross that barrier, but he let me look out over the clearing and at that tree. He warned me to *never* go in. Said she made things happen, bad things. It's why I buried those kids where I did. No one who knows about that spot actually goes to visit. To them, it's a place best forgotten. So, when I did go in, I never stayed longer than I had to. I never walked past her grave, and I kept my head down the whole time."

"I heard she makes you sick," Frank said, softly.

Eugene looked at Frank and then down at his legs. He rubbed them. "That's one way to think about it," Eugene replied flatly. "Don't think I got off scot free. She's taken her toll on my body in more ways than one."

Donnie groaned. "You're going to jail. I don't know how, but I'm not letting this go."

"You can take me to court if you want but I'll tell you right now, there isn't a person in this town who will believe you." Eugene scanned the area as if looking for bystanders. "Winston painted himself into a corner—he's the one everybody suspected, and *he's* the one they found. As far as the city is concerned, they got their killer. You two did me a favor by being up there."

"Yeah. We'll see," Donnie said, then looking to Frank. "I'll be in the car." He turned and left.

61

Frank called after his brother, but Donnie opened his car door and sat down inside. He turned back to Eugene and said, "Can I ask you something?"

"If you must," he replied.

"When did it start? I mean, how did you ever..." Frank trailed off.

There wasn't much empty air before Eugene obliged and began to speak, "When I first started teaching, a student robbed my home. I let the incident go, though I was almost certain who did it—a fellow by the name of Henry Carr. Henry had no interest in discipline for his life. I knew his parents well; they were fine people. While it's certainly possible they secretly abused him, I've since concluded that some students are just dreadful human beings—no reason for it.

"One afternoon, a student came to me in my office. He's the one who'd been tied to a rail and got the word *coon* written across his head. Told me that Henry carried that knife around school. Said he'd made repeated threats to him—and others—with it and said that Henry always kept it in his front right sock. So, when I confronted Henry about it, and asked him to take his shoes and socks off, I confiscated it. Even informed his parents about it that night. And then, the next night, my house gets broken into. No damage and nothing missing."

"You know it was him?" Frank asked.

"Not that time I didn't," Eugene replied. "On the last day of school before summer he asked me for the knife back and I told him no. His response was that he'd get it back one way or another. I knew exactly what that meant. I should have gone to his parents—should have gone to the police—but wasn't sure what he'd do, and there was no way to prove anything. So, I waited for him. I became paranoid. I started to park my car away from the house to give the illusion I wasn't home so I could catch him—teach him a lesson. It consumed my summer evenings when finally, at the end, just before school, he came.

"I had gone for a late-night walk with my dog and when I returned and came inside, he jumped me in the kitchen. He attacked me with a knife. Not the one I'd taken—I'd disposed of that one. I struck him across the face with my fist and knocked him to the ground. I tried to get him to calm down, but he wouldn't stop—said he was gonna kill me." Atlas paused and connected eyes with Frank. "Henry was standing, by this point, near my laundry room where my arthritic dog was barking with every bit of energy he had left. And suddenly, without any hesitation, Henry turned and plunged his knife into its back. Over. And over."

"Jeez," Frank whispered.

"So, with about as much hesitation as he showed my dog, I grabbed a signed baseball bat on the wall just inside my living room, and...well..." Eugene stopped. He shook his head and lifted his hands up, perhaps in an apology. "I can't explain the amount of guilt and regret I felt for what I did to that boy. Was going to turn myself in before school started but on that first day I overheard a teacher comment that she was relieved when Henry had been reported missing. I'll never forget what she said, remember it clear as can be. She said, 'I was tired of having to show up to class afraid.' She felt bad for making that comment but she was right. With Henry gone, kids weren't being threatened with violence, teachers weren't worrying about their students. A weight lifted for me. I still didn't like what I did, but...it seemed to make things better.

"I can't even tell you how I got Henry to that cemetery—memory's a little fuzzy on that one. I do remember being up there. It took me all night to find that place. I must have tripped a dozen times on my way up, bruised my hip to pieces. I remember digging that hole in indescribable agony. Felt like my hip was just gonna slip out and leave me paralyzed up there." Atlas laughed to himself. "Needless to say, I got that body under enough dirt to cover him and hobbled as quickly as I could out of there. Never went back." He paused again. "Until Ms. Nina Etheridge nearly six years later."

"My parents used to tell me about her when I was a kid—her disappearing in LBL."

Eugene clicked his tongue. "Tragic what happened to her. Not the accident, just, how she became what she did. A bright student. I was visiting my mother in Cadiz and making my way back to the high school for the homecoming dance—trying to get there for the end of the event. On the way, I see this stalled car and a young girl in a dress waving me down. Turns out her friend had lost control of the vehicle and crashed, knocking him unconscious. She wanted to know if I could give her a ride to the hospital and call an ambulance."

"She recognized you?"

"Of course, she did. I told her to get in and I quickly ran over and checked on the fellow she was with. He was breathing, seemed a little banged up, but he looked fine. The car, however, was covered in glass shards and reeked of alcohol. Plus, his pants were undone and slightly lowered. I had already been approached by several faculty members about Nina's behavior, and one in particular about her promiscuity.

"This was before cell phones and being stranded in LBL late at night is most certainly not safe. I told her to get in and then I attempted to move the boy into my car, but she insisted I leave him. She claimed she was worried he'd broken his neck or his back in the accident. So, I said I'd first drive to the nearest phone, and call an ambulance. I would need to return and wait until they arrived, then I could take her home. She agreed, but on the way, she asked if I could drop her off at a friend's house and notify the police myself—without including her. I declined and said we needed to get an ambulance and get back to her friend." Atlas stopped talking. Something like disgust came over his face. "She began rubbing my leg. And then she started moving her hand . . ." He paused. "I told her to back away, but she continued, telling me how I couldn't notify her parents, and how it would make her look if word got out that she was drinking. I shoved her hand away from me and thought she was done but I heard something start to rip. I look over and she's tearing her gown at the top, and up her leg. She tells me that if I don't take her home, she's going to tell everyone I attempted to take advantage of her on the way to the hospital."

"What?" Frank said.

"I lost focus on the road until a look of horror came across her face and she began screaming that there was a deer. I swerved, clipped the side railing on the road, and ended up slamming into a tree. The impact threw her into my windshield, broke her neck, and she was gone."

"It was an accident," Frank said.

"It was. And I did the only thing I knew I could, I hid the body. I couldn't very well call the police. My mind reasoned that they would discover what happened to Henry, or think that I had done something to Nina with alcohol on her breath and her clothes in tatters. I'd be ruined."

"What happened to the guy? Bruce, right? Bruce Winfree?"

"No one ever found him. I put Nina's body in my trunk and drove back toward Murray. To my surprise, the stalled car was gone."

"Wait a minute. He's still out there?" Frank asked.

"It is a possibility. But I'm not sure how easy it would be to find him. The name Bruce Winfree came from one of her friends who claimed to have met them both before the dance at dinner. I tried to track him down several weeks after. That name wasn't linked with anyone in Murray. I assumed that when Mr. Winfree discovered that Nina had gone missing, he never looked back."

"Unbelievable," Frank muttered. "So, you have no idea what happened to him?"

"None. I was able to get my car home, with Nina in the trunk. Put it in the garage and took my old jalopy to the dance to make an appearance. Buried her the next day when it was light. It was unsettling to walk back to that clearing, and painful. More painful the second time." Eugene straightened up again and grimaced. He opened his car door and slid uneasily into the driver's seat. "I kept telling myself I wouldn't do it again. But it just kept happening."

"All the stuff about Brian and Mr. Rose; was that true?" Frank asked.

Eugene nodded. "After I heard about what Brian had done to Winston, I forged a note from Brian's band teacher. The morning they were to leave for Florida for their annual competition, I had Brian show up an hour early to help load the buses." Frank was speechless, his mouth agape. Eugene took a sip of his coffee. "It was five in the morning—wasn't a soul at that building. And the buses were loaded the night before. When he came into the band room, I was there to meet him."

Frank could feel his heart rate beginning to pick up. For some reason, of all the things that had just been revealed, this one terrified him the most. Brian's death hadn't been an accident. Brian's death was calculated, manipulative, and outright terrifying. He swallowed. "You think Mr. Rose followed you up there?" Frank asked.

"No. I think Winston stumbled upon the place by accident. He did a lot of hiking up there when he got older. We'd talked about the lore of Bethel cemetery before, but I never mentioned being up there or what I'd seen and then one day he says to me that he may have found it. I always assumed Winston got curious, made the hike, and got too close."

Frank stood silent again, unsure of how to respond—*if* he should respond. He had just watched local hero Eugene Atlas struggle to get to his car, nearly putting him out of breath. It was hard to believe this same man, in fifty years, had gruesomely murdered so many. The man who wrote his college recommendation letters—before he decided not to go. Who encouraged him and taught him. To Frank, this was the real George Feeney. But now... "You're a fuckin' monster," Frank whispered.

It was there and gone in a flash, but Frank swore he saw anguish on Atlas' face when he uttered those words. Eugene dropped his head for a moment, and then Frank noticed him fishing around his pocket. He pulled out a small MP3 recorder. Without speaking he attached a pair of earbuds to it and handed them to Frank. "Take a listen to this, will ya?" he said.

Frank asked what it was, but Eugene only pointed to his ears as he turned to face forward and start the car. Frank put the buds in his ears and listened. He recognized the voice immediately; it was the mysterious caller. And then it was his own.

"*What kind of job?*"

"*You did some specific work for Tom recently, correct?*"

Frank sighed. "*Fine, yes, I did. And it's done.*"

"*What did you do?*"

"*Who is this?*" Frank asked.

"*Did you dig up Tom's wife?*" the voice asked.

Frank paused. "*Yes.*"

"*Were you paid?*" the voice asked.

"*That's none of your business.*"

"*How much?*"

"*I'm not telling you that.*" A pause. Frank's voice continued. "*You can give me the silent treatment all you want but I'm not te—*" A click.

"Dumb ass," Frank whispered to himself.

Principal Atlas stopped the recording. "I have the entire exchange." He gently pulled the buds from Frank's hand, wrapping them around the device. "You or your brother mention me to the police, this goes straight to them." He paused and connected eyes with Frank. "There's not a shred of evidence tying me to those bodies, Frank. You and I both know no one will buy that. And if this gets out, I think it's safe to say your business with this town is done."

Frank felt himself starting to sweat underneath his arms. He was dumbfounded, and there was nothing to say. He broke eye contact from Atlas. "Okay, so, now what?" Frank asked.

Atlas held out his hand to shake. "Now, we go about our lives. Why ruin a good thing?" Atlas lowered his hand after Frank ignored it. "You can't bring those kids back to life, but you *did* bring them home. Everyone's happy. I got what I wanted: cleared name, along with information about my daughter, and you got what you wanted—money. And your funeral home has statewide fame. I keep your secrets, and you keep mine."

Frank glanced over at Donnie in the car and then back to Atlas as the car engine came alive. "Tom Middleton. They said he died unexpectedly." Frank paused. "It was you wasn't it."

Eugene laughed softly. He stared ahead, drumming his fingers on the wheel and then, "Just how would I do that?" He turned to meet eyes. "I'm in my nineties, Frank. I can't even walk over to your mother's restaurant without getting out of breath." He closed the door to his car and rested his elbow on the now open window. "Word of advice: I'd keep out of that cemetery up there if I were you." And with that Principal Atlas moved the shifter into reverse and backed out of the parking space. He rapped his hand on the car's side twice and said, "See ya'round."

Donnie had been sitting in the car for nearly ten minutes before Frank collapsed into the seat and slammed the door. "You good?" Donnie asked.

Frank sat quiet, staring ahead toward the restaurant.

"We gonna go or just sit—?" Donnie began.

"All those kids," Frank whispered. "He killed 'em . . ."

Donnie sighed. "Yeah."

"What are we gonna do?" Frank asked.

"I don't know, man. I've been sittin' here trying to figure that out."

"We gotta tell somebody—call up Suthers, or something."

"Whoa, whoa, whoa—" Donnie tried to interject.

"Or whoever did the article on us in the *Ledger*, maybe they can write up something about Mr. Atlas and how he—"

"Frank," Donnie cut in, "that's not gonna work." Frank turned to his brother with a look of agitation. "Think about it: what are you gonna tell them?"

"What do you mean what am I gonna tell them? Did you not hear that shit?"

"I did but did you record any of it?"

"No, I didn't record it. We got two witnesses—me and you!"

"Frank, it doesn't work that way."

"Well then how does it work, Donnie? Guy confesses to killing kids and we're just supposed to sit on that?"

"Would you stop?" Donnie exclaimed. "I'm not saying that. I'm saying it's probably not a good idea to just go to Suthers now and tell him; you're gonna need something on him."

"We have something on him!" Frank yelled back. "He literally just told us!"

"Okay, fine. You go to Suthers and say that Principal Atlas is the real killer. You think they're just gonna bring him in? No questions asked? What do you think Atlas is gonna say? 'Oh, I guess you got me. Darn,'" Donnie mimicked. "At this point, all you have is our word against his, and I can guarantee you, on something like this, our word is pretty useless."

Frank began softly tapping his fist against the door. "He recorded our phone conversation—about Corey's book. Asked me a ton of questions about my involvement with Tom," he said. Donnie cursed. "Says he'll turn it over to the police if we come after him."

"He showed it to you?"

"Listened to it, yeah." Frank sat quiet for another moment and then, "I don't care though, man. If it means putting that fucker down, I'll give up the house. If I have to go to jail or pay a fine . . ."

Donnie spoke softly, "But you won't put him down, that's what I'm trying to say. You go against him, you're not only gonna lose money, you're gonna lose the home. You're gonna embarrass yourself, Mom and Dad, Cliff—me. And in the end, for what? Because I can almost guarantee you, at the end of it all, we'll be the ones who've lost everything."

Frank sat with his hand resting on the window, rubbing his forehead. "So, what then? What do we do? Wait for evidence to pop up randomly?"

"No," Donnie said coldly. "We're not sitting on this. But we're gonna play it smart; keep our heads down and start trying to use what we know to piece together evidence. Anything to help build a case against him."

"That's gonna take a while," Frank said. "And we're gonna need some help."

Donnie looked to his brother. "You mean Suthers?"

Frank shrugged. "I think if we can convince him, we're off to a good start."

FOUR MONTHS LATER
62

Frank hung up his cell phone with Addy a split-second before it began ringing again. A Virginia number Frank didn't recognize. "Burgers Funeral, this is Frank."

"Hi. Frank Burgers?"

"This is him."

"Hello Frank. This is Jake Valentine. I'm sure you don't remember me, but you left a message on my voicemail about four or five months ago—"

"Oh! Mr. Valentine! Of course, I remember. Thanks for calling back. I thought I had the wrong number."

"No, no. Right number, just wrong house." He laughed. "That house belonged to my dad years ago. Keep it as a rental property, but no one seems to see the appeal of it. Again, my apologies for the long delay. I've been out of the country for nearly six months and just got back into town last week. My assistant told me you called, and I remembered the name—Burgers."

"Glad you remembered us," Frank said.

"Well, you're hard to forget. I bought a travel mug from somebody over there back in twenty ten. Had 'We Rule' across the bottom and a picture of a skeleton with his arms up, holding a banana—"

Frank's eyes lit up. "And a name tag that said O'Doyle!"

Jake laughed. "Man, I thought that was the funniest thing."

"That was me! Yeah, I do a yearly mug for the home. That was my first one."

"Use it all the time," Jake said happily. "Anyways, I'm sure by now you've probably figured out that my dad passed away. Was there something I can help you with?"

"Well, depends on how close you were with your dad. I was looking for some information on a good friend of his. Winston Rose. That name ring a bell?"

Jake repeated it a couple of times. "No, I can't say it does. But that shouldn't say anything about their friendship. Dad may have talked about him—I mean, I may have even met him—I just don't remember. Been too long."

"That's okay. It was a long shot. The school here is wanting to put together an article about Winston and I heard he and your dad were pretty close. Thought he could share some stories of their time together," Frank lied.

"You know, come to think of it, I may have something. Any idea when he and dad may have known each other? Were they long-time friends? Do you know?"

Frank's heart skipped. "I don't know," he replied, running through his memory. "I know they were friends in the early two thousands. What do you have?"

"Well, I may still have dad's journals. They're either here with me or over in storage . . ." He continued talking, mostly to himself. Then, "Tell ya what, I gotta be up there in about a few weeks. Let me do some digging. If I've still got 'em, I'll get my assistant to scan through them for the fellow you're talking about. What was the name again?"

"Winston Rose."

"Okay. Can't promise anything. Dad's journals weren't too exciting— mostly dry entries with a summary of the week's activities. But I'll take a look."

"Mr. Valentine, this is awesome! Thank you so much."

"You still got more of those mugs?"

"Of course. Plenty of twenty seventeens, and a handful from last year."

Jake laughed. "I love it. May drop by when I'm in town and pick one up."

"It would be my pleasure," Frank beamed.

Monty Suthers rapped his knuckles against the open door. "Hey preacher," he said, stepping into the hospital room. Addy turned his head, attempting to sit up but quickly stopped himself and cringed in pain. Monty laughed. "N-no n-need to get up." He stepped inside, looking around the hospital room. "How ya holdin' up?"

"Not bad," Addy replied, lying back down, and motioning a hand to the TV. "Just watching the game."

"Ah, don't tell me the score. I got it recordin' at home," Monty said. He held up a hand to shield the screen. He pulled up a chair next to the bed and sat.

Addy switched off the TV. "Thanks for coming by. It's good to see ya."

"Likewise," Monty said. "How long they keepin' ya here?"

"Hopefully just a couple more hours," Addy replied, looking at the clock on the wall. "Couple complications but gallbladder's out—should be good now."

"I remember getting mine out; I was there for days. Miserable," Monty said. "Anything I can get ya? You got a ride home?"

"Yeah, Frank's coming to get me. And I think I'm good. My parents are coming in this afternoon; they're helpin' me out." He surveyed Monty and said, "I guess it's my duty as a minister to ask: how you holdin' up now? What's the word?"

"W-w-what do you mean?"

Addy rolled his eyes. "Mr. Suthers. I've got more connections in this town than a mob boss. You think I don't know? I got a phone call that night from someone in Sally's who saw it."

Monty tapped his thumbs on the arm rests and then finally he shrugged. "What'd you hear?"

"That you dropped him faster than anyone there could snap their fingers." Addy relished every word.

Monty smirked as his head began to nod. "Yeah, it was p-pretty quick.

Can't say I condone w-what I did, though." He let out a long breath and rested his head back against the chair, staring at the ceiling. "Of course, I can't say I wouldn't do it again."

Addy smiled. "So, what happened?"

"Eh," Monty waved a hand at the question and got up. "Stupid." He shook his head and walked over to window. "He and some friends came in Sally's late—drunk—being loud, obnoxious. I d-didn't say anything, just let him do his thing—n-nobody was in there anyways. Till he got r-ready to leave and then he started tellin' Sophia that she needed to take him home. Her shift wasn't done so she couldn't, b-but he just kept on. Finally, she came and sat across from me and s-said she was g-gonna cash out; I offered to take him home if she n-needed to stay. N-Nick, however, saw her sitting across from me and I guess he got p-paranoid. Started m-m-mouthin' off at her, callin' her names and p-p-pullin' at her to get up. I told him to stop." Monty paused, and then he started to chuckle to himself. "L-long story short, he strung together a b-bunch of d-derogatory words I can't r-remember and then finally said that if I w-wasn't in uniform, he'd w-whip my ass." Monty turned to Addy and raised his hands as if to say *very well*. "Pretty sure it was at that point I l-lost touch with r-rationality. I w-went out to my car, pulled off my shirt and badge; threw on a pair of shorts and a t-shirt. W-walked over to the glass and knocked." Monty tapped on the counter's edge with his knuckle. "Stood there in my t-shirt and shorts; he got the message."

Addy sat in silence for a second and then, "I think you're my new hero."

"Don't know about that. P-probation ain't all that fun." Monty checked his watch. "That sound about like what you heard?"

"I mean, in the version I heard you ripped your police uniform off Superman style and knocked seven guys unconscious."

Monty laughed. "I l-like that one m-more." He turned to Addy and patted his leg. "Listen, I won't keep ya. I need to grab a b-bite before a m-meeting."

They shook hands and Addy asked, "It's hard to hold back on a bully." He paused. "Isn't it?"

"You'd know, wouldn't ya?" Monty grinned.

"I would," Addy said softly, letting go of Monty's hand. "The last church I was at; one of the leaders there . . ." Addy stopped and appeared to be weighing his thoughts. "He was a . . . a pretty twisted guy. Mean, ya know? Anyways, he and his wife had two daughters and at some point they adopted a son." Monty started back toward the bed, intrigued. "I didn't have any evidence for it, but I got the feelin' he was beating on the *boy*. One day after service, I remember walking outside and hearing yelling—crying—coming from behind the building. I thought I was the last to leave so I walked back there and saw this guy's car parked in the back alley. I went slowly at first because I didn't want to be seen. I got to the window, and I stood there, watching. It was just him and this boy, Chad—that was his name." Monty nodded.

"The guy was in a rage; shouting, pounding his fist into the dashboard. Chad finally made eye contact with me, and the dad stopped; turned back and saw me standing there. He smiled, as if nothing was wrong, and asked if I was heading home.

"I told him I'd heard screaming and asked if everything was alright. Tells me he was just having a conversation with his son, but I cut him off and said I wasn't talking to him. I looked past him and asked if Chad was okay." Addy chuckled. "He didn't like that all. As soon as I said it, he didn't miss a beat. Did the whole 'excuse me' thing and opened his car door. I stepped back to let him out of the car, but I didn't move any more than I had to. He got right in my face and I stood there, staring him down. Told me it would be best if I minded my own business; that his son had acted up in church and he needed to be disciplined.

"Then he made some snide comment that I wouldn't know anything about that—no kids and all—and I remarked that I *would* know about him needing to get his attitude under control. That *really* pissed him off. He steps right in my face and starts raising his voice at me. And so, I inch closer, which catches him off guard and quiets him. By this point we're practically touching noses and after a moment I move my head over to look at Chad and then back to him. And I said, soft enough where Chad couldn't hear, 'Unless you really want to embarrass yourself in front of your son, I'd get back in your car and go home.' He nodded and smiled for a second. And then, you know what he did? That piece of shit laughed at me. *Laughed.* Then he patted my shoulder. Got in his car. And left."

Monty let Addy's words settle into his mind. "Let me guess, he set the others in motion to fire you?"

"Oh, no. The firing came about two weeks later when Chad called my cell and told me that he got in trouble at school. Said he was scared his dad was gonna hurt him. So, I drove out to his place and told him to get in my car and wait. He said his dad was out back in his woodshed. I go around to the shed and there he was, standing over a piece of machinery, sanding down a paddle to beat his kid with. Like a fraternity paddle." Addy sized it out with his hands. "I stood there and watched him, and I kid you not, he was whistling. He kept holding it up, rubbing it, and admiring it as if making a Christmas gift. He put it down and walked over to get something and that's when I stepped inside. When he saw me, he tried to be cordial. But then he saw me eye the paddle, and his whole demeanor switched. Started cursing at me—not yelling or anything. Talking as calmly as I am now. But then the threats started to come out. And that's when I picked up the paddle. I didn't say a word, just picked it up and stared back at him. Finally, he did the same shit again—he *laughed.* He laughed and he picked up a hammer lying on the work bench nearby." Addy sighed. "Few minutes later, I put that bastard in the hospital with his own paddle.

"Jesus."

"Chad lied to the police and said his dad was about to attack him when I arrived. It was all self-defense. Guy got out of the hospital and the church fired me immediately."

"They f-fired you? W-w-what about him?"

"Oh, they made him step down, but it doesn't look good to have a preacher who gets arrested for putting someone in the hospital."

Monty nodded. "I can see that. Especially when said p-preacher tends to m-make a big deal over a God who got unjustly arrested and beaten and didn't do a thing to fight back."

"Yeah, I get it." Addy sighed. "Like I said, though." He eyed Monty with a half-smile. "I really make a big deal about that, huh?"

A grin cut across Monty's empathetic expression. "Thanks for t-tellin' me."

"Figured it was okay now that you've joined the club." Addy shot him a thumbs up. "Just, keep it between you and me, huh."

"N-no problem," Monty said. "You need anything, you call me, okay?" He turned to leave.

"Did you really come to see me, or did you come to see him?"

Monty stopped and looked back. "Who?"

Addy motioned with his eyes out to the hallway. "Mr. Atlas," Addy replied.

Monty glanced behind him as if someone might be listening. "He's here?"

"Down the hall."

"Hunh," Monty grunted. "Why would I be here to see him?"

Addy shrugged. "Don't know. Just asking."

Monty's eyes narrowed at Addy. "What do you know?"

Addy let the question hang in the air for a moment, and then said, "enough."

"Frank tell you?" Monty asked quietly.

"Who else," Addy replied.

"I d-didn't know he w-was here," Monty said.

"Yup," Addy said, turning the game back on and making sure to hit the mute button. He stared at the screen for a bit, looking as if in a trance. Then he spoke. "Good friend of mine disappeared in high school. Always thought he got sent away. Come to find out he got killed. Thrown out into the middle of nowhere and buried like he was nothin.'"

"Yeah. We're workin' on it."

"You remember when you came by my house? Told me I should take my own advice? Pray to get myself under control?" Addy asked. Monty nodded. "Let's just say when I found out what *really* happened to Brian, I started praying."

63

Monty stood outside Eugene Atlas's open door for a long moment wondering if it was a wise decision to go in. Nearly four months ago, Donnie and Frank Burgers explained to him that Eugene Atlas—not Winston Rose—was behind the disappearance of the missing teenagers. Monty was not so quick to believe the theory—especially when Donnie explained that they couldn't openly pursue an investigation. Everything had to be done in private. Monty had almost written off the tip until Frank explained how Eugene not only buried Genevieve in Markgraf Cemetery but had been the one to take her life. It was Frank's sincerity—a behavior Monty was not used to seeing—that convinced him. He couldn't remember ever crying that hard.

For almost four months he'd been working with Frank and Donnie to try and put together a case, but in that time the three of them still had next to nothing to stand on. Someone suddenly bumped into Monty. "Oh, my goodness, I am so sorry," a nurse said, looking up from her clipboard. "Are you okay? Pardon me. Wasn't even looking where I was going."

"It's okay," Monty replied with a smile. The nurse maneuvered past him into Eugene's room speaking cheerily as she went. Monty could hear Eugene's deep voice; a little weak but still full of life and charm. He could hear him asking about what happened in the hall, then the nurse explaining she bumped into a policeman. "Stocky fellow, black hair. Good smile." She laughed.

"A stocky policeman?" Eugene said. "Is that Monty Suthers out there?"

Monty stepped in with a light knock on the door. "Hey Eugene."

"Well, I'll be. Monty Suthers. What are you doing here? Come in, come in. Eliza, this is Monty Suthers. He used to teach for us over at Murray High."

Eliza waved and began talking again to Eugene.

"I didn't r-realize you were here," Monty said softly. "I'll l-let you get back to it."

"Oh, no, no," Eugene began. "She's just checking in." He turned to Eliza and the two of them spoke briefly before she patted his hand and exited the room. Eugene continued to Monty, "How ya been? I feel as if I haven't seen you in ages."

"Had a lot goin' on," Monty replied, stepping in. "What happened to you?"

"Nothing new. Fell and shattered a part of my hip. I'll be okay though. Doc says it's gonna be tough haul getting my mobility up again, but I'm used to it. Come in, sit down."

"No, I can't. I've gotta r-run to a m-meeting. I w-was just here visiting someone else and saw you were here."

"Oh? Who? I could use someone to talk to." Eugene gave a soft laugh.

Monty hesitated. "Addy Michaels."

A brief look of concern flashed over Eugene's face. "He okay?"

"Gallbladder. He's fine. Leaving today." Eugene nodded and suddenly let out a hard cough. And then another, each more intense. He tried to talk but appeared to have trouble sucking in air. Monty asked if he was okay, Eugene nodded, holding up a finger, and taking a sip of water from his large thermos. A crackly, slurping sound signaled the last drops of water. Eugene cleared his throat and gave Monty a thumbs up.

Monty eyed the clock wall. "Listen, I b-b-better get goin." He extended his hand, fighting the urge to reach out and strangle him.

Eugene lifted a feeble hand and clasped Monty's. The strength in those fingers given his current condition was unnerving. "Thanks for dropping in. It was good to see ya. And I was terribly sorry to hear about Jean."

A dull, dreadful sensation spread through Monty's stomach into his limbs. He tried to speak but stuttered over himself before he got it out. "Excuse me?"

"I knew you two were friends when she was teaching. She used to talk about you," Eugene said, letting out another cough and reaching for his water. "I kept meaning—after I heard about the discovery—to express my condolences to you in a more formal way. Sorry it's taken me this long to say something." He brought the straw to his mouth, obviously forgetting it was empty, and tried to suck, but it was only air. Eugene made a frustrated noise and attempted to clear his throat, which in turn sent him into a sudden and harsh coughing fit. He held up his thermos to Monty as he attempted to cover his mouth with the other arm. He appeared to be signaling for more water.

Monty stepped forward. "Sure. One second." He walked over to the sink and turned on the tap. He reminded himself to breathe. The thermos was shaking in his hands, and his heart was beating so hard he could feel it pounding in his eyes. The water began overflowing and Monty cut the water. *This whole time.* He twisted on the top as he turned toward Eugene. A coughing fit was robbing the man from getting a breath. Eugene was entangled in his sheets, trying desperately to turn on to his side, sounding with each violent cough as if he were going to suddenly vomit.

Sorry about Jean.

Monty set the thermos next to the sink, out of Eugene's reach. He walked out of the room without saying a word and closed the door behind him.

THE FOLLOWING SUMMER
EPILOGUE

It was the one-year anniversary of the brothers' discovery in Bethel. The two of them were about to open their newest addition on the Burgers property; a small, sit-down restaurant. It was a compromise to Frank's bed and breakfast idea—for now. The idea came to Frank after they received more reviews on Yelp for Donnie's food. Frank wisely approached Lexie and encouraged her to plant the bug in his brother's head. Donnie came to Frank two weeks later and pitched the idea Frank had been dreaming of.

Frank was happy to use *special* funds to invest, and Donnie had no problem securing backing from former colleagues who were confident in his work. It would be a traditional American-style eatery and bar—perfect for the area—offering a stage for live entertainment. *Comfort food,* as Frank liked to emphasize. The restaurant's name was the most complicated piece. Donnie wanted something familial, while Frank was stuck on *Burgers and Cries*. Suddenly, an idea hit Donnie and within seconds of saying it aloud, both of them were sold. *Genevieve's.*

Though the new Burgers' business was still several days from opening, Frank and Donnie planned a Sunday evening get-together for a few close friends to help celebrate the addition.

It was nearly 6 p.m. when Frank returned home from picking up Ginny and Dave from the airport. Given all the excitement over the home and the discovery, Ginny and Dave decided it was time to travel for the first time since Frank was born. They had spent the last week in Colorado. Frank pulled into the driveway and popped the trunk. He collected their bags and noticed a pouch of bright colored gummies inside his mother's purse.

"Gummies, huh?" Frank asked, nodding excitedly.

"Stay out of there," Ginny said, swiping her bag back.

Frank laughed and teased with the idea of seeing a new side of his mother. She kissed him on the cheek and walked into the house. It was the first time Frank had seen his mother use the middle finger.

Virginia Jan's had received record high sales over the last year. The weekend popularity had become enough to get her to *finally* stay open longer than the early afternoon. Guests were coming from as far away as Louisville to experience her donuts, and make a day of exploring Land Between the Lakes. There was talk that she would open another restaurant, but when the topic came up around her, she was quick to change the subject.

Dave Burgers continued consulting and helping out at Jan's. Most mornings, he would be found at the kitchen table or on the porch typing away on his laptop. He told everyone he was working on his autobiography but after a couple of sneak peeks, Frank got the impression it was fiction, and centered on a funeral director who solves crimes.

☠

Lexie and Donnie came out to greet them as Ginny and Dave walked up the porch stairs. They were as close to an item as one could get without putting a title on it. Twice a month she came in to visit Donnie and even accompanied him on a couple of trips to New York. Regarding her father, Lexie continued to avoid contact with him. Like Frank, her initial reaction was to go to the police, but with no hard evidence, simply being the man's daughter with a handful of unsettling memories, wasn't enough to start a war.

☠

The five of them weren't on the porch for more than five minutes before Monty's car pulled up. Both he and Sophia stepped out of the car and began walking up the driveway. Sophia filed for divorce shortly after Monty's altercation with Nick. After the incident, Nick forced her to leave Sally's, and cease any communication with Monty. Several weeks later, she showed up on Monty's doorstep in tears. That morning, during winter break at the university, Nick had been scheduled to do electrical work inside the campus' newest dorm. Unfortunately, a gas leak resulted in a massive explosion on the unoccupied dorm's lowest level. Sophia spent all morning trying to get a hold of her husband, only to discover—when he came home for lunch unaware of the incident—that he had been in Mayfield, sleeping with a co-worker. Sophia moved in with her parents and scheduled a time to collect her belongings from the house when Nick would not be there. Monty went in her stead, and Nick was—not to Monty's surprise—waiting on the porch. Short of appearing in court, and an apology email, Sophia never heard from Nick again. A couple of times Sophia asked Monty if Nick was there that night when he collected her things, but each time Monty pursed his lips and said, "N-n-nope. Just me." He'd smirk at her, and she'd smirk back, offering the tiniest shake of her head.

Frank came down the steps, and gave Sophia a hug. "Thanks for coming."

"Are you kidding? I wouldn't miss this! Getting *him* to come, though, that's another story," Sophia said, casting a thumb behind her.

"Hey now," Monty cut in, shaking Frank's hand. "I was up front with my intention to w-watch the Cards and the Cubs today. Should say a lot that I'm choosing to be here."

Frank eyed the bag in Monty's hand. "This is for you," Monty said. It was a bottle of wine and a small bag of coffee inscribed with the words *Kopi Luwak*. "Friend of mine got that at a wedding. Turned around and gave it to me."

Frank's eyes lit up. "Is this cat poop coffee? Are you serious?"

"I figured if anyone w-was gonna drink something like that, it'd be you."

Addy's car pulled in and he walked up, shaking Monty's hand. "Missed ya at church this morning."

"You're supposed to be on vacation," Monty replied.

"I am. Still go to church, though."

"Yeah, well, quit letting the youth minister preach when you're gone, maybe I'll stay longer than communion."

Sophia swatted his arm. "Monty!" She chuckled.

"Last sermon I heard from him was based around a vegetable cartoon," Monty quipped, and then turned to Addy, "let me know when you're back from vacation."

"No gift from you?" Frank asked.

"You know preachers don't make any money," Addy replied.

Ginny waved from the porch. "Hello Monty! Oh, is that Sophia?"

"It is!" Sophia replied, walking toward the house. She and Donnie hugged and chatted briefly as they passed, and she continued up the steps engaged in conversation with Ginny.

"What's up big buy?" Cliff said, appearing from behind Monty. "Look'a dem sexy biceps!" Cliff rubbed Monty's arm.

"They're getting there, thanks to you," Monty replied.

Cliff waved off the compliment. "I'm just there to make sure you don't hurt yourself or die. You doin' all the work." Cliff's popularity had grown so much since the discovery that he was forced to purchase a second space—in walking distance from Murray State's campus. The extra business—along with a cut from Bones to Bishops—allowed him to purchase more items and hire some employees. Before the spring semester, he'd been propositioned to be an adjunct professor for anatomy and kinesiology courses at the university, which he happily accepted. He had also spent the better part of the last year working through a degree in massage therapy, and was scheduled to complete it next fall. Frank was especially excited that he could now offer funeral home patrons a massage coupon for choosing them over the Kochs. Cliff was still on the fence with that one.

☠

The group of them chatted in the driveway until Donnie nodded at Frank. "Hey, you show him the thing?"

Everyone got quiet. "What thing?" Addy asked.

Frank looked around to make sure he was in the clear and pulled a compact black notebook from his back pocket. He held it in his hand and looked at Monty and the others. "Guys. I think we have our start."

"What is that?" Monty asked.

Frank opened it up and began flipping through the pages. "This is from someone whose dad knew Mr. Rose really well. Like, really well, if you know what I mean." There was a pause and Frank looked up at them. "Like, *really* well—"

"I think they get it," Donnie cut in.

"Anyway, guy called me up months ago and told me that his dad kept all these journals. I gave him some dates to look at and asked if his dad had written anything about Mr. Rose. Now, there's nothing in here that will link it to Atlas but . . ." Frank found the page he wanted, with several lines highlighted, and turned the book over to Monty. "It does give dated records of where Winston was on two specific nights. The nights Jean and Brian disappeared."

Monty took the book and scanned through the pages.

Frank continued, "Mr. Rose and this guy were together on both occasions. I have another book inside that says they were out of town when Corey disappeared. Some bed and breakfast in Indiana. Even has a receipt taped inside."

"I'll be damned," Monty said with a short laugh. "How long were they together?"

"No clue. There're at least three other books with Winston in them. Apparently these two were friends for a while. Not like friends, but *friends* if you know—"

"Frank," Donnie cut in again.

"Sorry. Yeah. Three others," Frank replied. "I don't wanna jump the gun here but, I think we may have enough to open this case up. At least to prove it wasn't Mr. Rose."

Monty closed the book. "This is more than enough," he said. The front door of the house closed; Ginny, Dave, and Sophia began coming down the stairs. "Let's talk this week," Monty said, handing the book back to Frank. "You did good."

"It's about time," Addy said, motioning to Frank for the book. "That guy is at every funeral recently. It's everything in me to not say something to him, or trip him, bash his head into the casket." He looked at Lexie and apologized.

"Believe me," Lexie replied. "No apology necessary."

"You're so violent," Frank said, pocketing the book.

"Hey. I hold it together, alright? I'm cordial. I shake his hand, make the small talk. Might squeeze the hand a little hard sometimes but I'm under control," Addy replied, winking at Monty.

Dave appeared nearby. "Donnie, Alberto called. They're ready for us."

●

Donnie gave the group a tour while the sous chef, Alberto, and his team prepared a meal and set a table. They all sat together as the dishes made their way out. Hardly any time passed before the accolades came. Everyone—especially Cliff and Addy—were overjoyed with the selections and flavors. Monty added, "And, I think you all know I love the name." Sophia put her hand over Monty's; he turned it over and squeezed hers back.

"Whatever this cabbage dish is, I love it," Lexie said.

"Everything is great, man," Addy said. "You guys are gonna kill it here."

"Don't say that too loud; Frank will use it as a tag line," Dave said.

Frank, who had disappeared to the house after he ate, reentered holding his laptop. "Okay guys, one final thing to show!" He sat down at the table and placed the laptop in the middle. "Check it, this is the new website." Some audible noises were made to indicate approval over the home page.

"Who took the pictures of the food?" Cliff asked. "Those are great!"

"I did," Frank said. "Well, I hired the guy." He clicked on the menu to show several professionally shot photos.

Not even Donnie had seen the page yet. "Dude. This looks awesome. Who did this?"

"Mostly me, but I had a friend of mine work with me. The basic ideas were mine."

"Wow! Frank, this is incredible. The pictures . . . the layout . . ." He turned and looked at his brother. "Thanks, man."

They hugged for a moment and then Frank broke away, leaning back down toward the laptop, "Alright, now, the best part!" He clicked back to the home page. "I had this idea that when you click on one of the fries in the background, it takes you to a hidden page." He clicked on it. "Taa-daa!" he exclaimed.

The screen displayed a skeleton holding a platter of food beside a grill. The words, *You found a killer deal!*, were stenciled above in the smoke.

"What do you think? Now we can do a combined thing where we offer *coupons* for both the funeral home and the restaura—"

He was cut off by an overwhelming response from the table, *"No!"*

AUTHOR'S NOTE II

Writing a book, like most anything in life, goes a lot smoother when there are people to help.

In no particular order:

To my wife, Gina, this wouldn't have been possible without you. Thank you for letting me constantly talk about where to take this story next, and for always being willing to read through it.

To Rachel Kuldell, thanks for your honesty and suggestions, even though you hated the best title for this book.

Chris Rhatigan, thank you for your ideas, your feedback, and for always insisting I cut—even when I didn't want to.

Thank you, Jaye Manus, for putting all of this together and making it look professional.

Stephanie Woods, wow! Thank you so much for not only wanting to illustrate this book but for taking the time to do it. I apologize about that tree, but couldn't be happier with what you did for it.

Lynn Andreozzi, your work is outstanding! Thank you for not only taking an interest in this project, but also for guiding me through the process, and for creating something magnificent.

Matt Markgraf, thanks for helping me bring these guys to life (pun intended) over several nights in 911-A and Huddle House. So many hashbrowns.

Finally, to you reader, thanks for picking up the book, and making it this far. I hope you had fun!

Those who live in or have spent time in Murray, KY will likely recognize many of the landmarks and possibly some events mentioned in the story. It's a great little city and I treasure the time I spent there. If you've never been to Land Between the Lakes, it is an interesting, and enjoyable place to visit. *To my knowledge*, there are no hidden cemeteries or stories of witches and ghosts in LBL. Having said that, it's hard for one's mind not to conjure that stuff up when you're exploring the area alone.

Clayton Tune is the author of *The Burgers Brothers' Family Funeral Home*. He is a licensed massage therapist, a sports enthusiast, and a '90s nerd. Currently he resides outside Washington DC with his wife Gina, their two children, and a dog named Sausage Ball. He also makes a decent Old Fashioned.

Made in the USA
Middletown, DE
26 September 2024